D1006334

Every Kind
of Wicked

Books by Lisa Black

Every Kind of Wicked

LISA BLACK

KENSINGTON BOOKS
www.kensingtonbooks.com

KENSINGTON BOOKS are published by

Kensington Publishing Corp.
119 West 40th Street
New York, NY 10018

All Kensington titles, imprints, and distributed lines are available at special quantity discounts for bulk purchases for sales promotion, premiums, fund-raising, educational, or institutional use. Special book excerpts or customized printings can also be created to fit specific needs. For details, write or phone the office of the Kensington Special Sales Manager: Attn. Special Sales Department. Kensington Publishing Corp, 119 West 40th Street, New York, NY 10018. Phone: 1-800-221-2647.

Library of Congress Card Catalogue Number: 2020935637

Kensington and the K logo Reg. U.S. Pat. & TM Off.

ISBN-13: 978-1-4967-2238-6
ISBN-10: 1-4967-2238-8
First Kensington Hardcover Edition: September 2020

ISBN-13: 978-1-4967-2240-9 (ebook)
ISBN-10: 1-4967-2240-X (ebook)

10 9 8 7 6 5 4 3 2 1

Printed in the United States of America

For my brothers, John and Michael
Everything big brothers should be.

"They have become filled with every kind of wickedness, evil, greed and depravity. They are full of envy, murder, strife, deceit and malice."
— *Romans 1:29*

Chapter 1

"Well, that's less than helpful," Maggie said of the snow.

The white flakes drifted lazily downward, landing on the frozen grass, the bare limbs of the large trees, the bloodstains sprinkled across the worn stones and the very stiff body of a young man who had not dressed well for the weather. Yet exposure hadn't killed him—he had been dead long before his body froze.

From the deep red stain blossoming from the center of his chest, Maggie Gardiner assumed a gunshot—or shots—had been the likely cause of death. Something had penetrated his internal systems to leak his lifeblood out across his white shirt and over the stones beneath him, which marked, coincidentally, a grave. But Maggie didn't say so; declaring cause of death was a pathologist's job and she worked as a forensic specialist. Her job would be to find the evidence around said death in order to help her colleagues at the police department determine who had walked away from this boy's last encounter.

Which would be more difficult to do with each passing

moment as the snow slowly covered up the body, the blood, and all her evidence.

She had arrived at the scene immediately before the assigned detectives, and now felt them standing on either side of her, Jack Renner to her right and Thomas Riley to her left. Renner, tall, only a bit dark and not so handsome, and his partner, distinctly shorter but lighter in both coloring and personality. And her, an inch shorter than Riley and nearly half his body weight, pale with deep brown hair falling past her shoulders, no gun, no badge, a civilian employee in a department of sworn officers. A uniformed patrol officer hovered somewhere among the graves as well. They made a somber and all too familiar tableau. A frigid breeze lifted her hair, chilled her neck, and moved on.

"A dead guy in a cemetery," Riley said. "That's—what's the word?"

"Weird?" Maggie suggested.

"I was going to say redundant." He took a step closer to the body and she spread out both arms like a railroad crossing, stopping both detectives. It wouldn't hold them for long, she knew.

She crouched, looking not at the body but the ground around it, finally poking the ground with a latex-gloved finger.

"Shoe prints?" Jack asked.

She answered with disappointment. The canopy of trees in the cemetery kept the grass sparse, and if the man had been killed during a thaw there might be nice prints in the Ohio clay-mud. But the ground had been frozen much too solid for the killer's feet to create prints. At least she didn't have to pour casts, always a chore in any kind of weather, but especially in snow where the reaction as the cast hardened created warmth and melted the print. A forensic Catch-22.

The cops took this as an all-clear and moved closer to the body. So did she. The patrolman stayed where he was. He had already strung yellow crime scene tape across the now-opened gates at either end of the cemetery and the high stone walls protected the rest. Crowd control at an inner-city cemetery on a snowy weekday didn't present much of a problem. Outside those walls, office buildings towered over the scene, only half a mile from the Public Square. Cars hummed along the surrounding streets, calm now that the morning rush hour had ended. She could work in relative, if chilly, peace.

Maggie observed their young victim. He lay facing the sky, eyes unable to shut against the precipitation. He wore jeans, a T-shirt, and a satin jacket that would have been at home inside a disco circa 1985, with thin padding unlikely to be much protection against Cleveland weather in mid-December. Maggie put his age at about twenty-five. He had brown hair, brown eyes, and a deeper hue to his skin even with the pallor of death over it, possibly mixed-race. His hair was cut short, no apparent piercings or tattoos that she could see.

"Any ID?" Riley asked. "Wallet? Phone?"

She patted his pockets—empty—and they couldn't turn him over to examine any rear pockets until the Medical Examiner's investigator arrived.

But under the open jacket he wore a white badge pinned to his shirt. It had rounded edges and red letters which said only "Evan." A streak of red dots crossed right over the *v* and continued along the shirt. Maggie noted some round stains on his chest and abdomen, and an irregular blotch over his collarbone.

Riley said, "So somebody shot him—"

"I'm not so sure. See those drops? Round spots imply blood fell on him when he was already laid out. I don't know why a gun would be that bloody when it wasn't close enough to leave a jagged hole or the powdery soot of fouling. Unlikely that enough tissue would get on the barrel to drip off later."

Jack had followed her reasoning. "So you think it's a stab wound?"

"That is my guess, but I can't be positive either way. Autopsy will tell. But a stab wound would make more sense, if the killer stood here for a second while blood dripped off the weapon and caused those spots. They didn't come from the victim's hands—they're clean."

"So the killer waited," Jack said. "Making sure he was dead."

He ought to know, Maggie thought.

She said, "No injury to our victim's hands. Either he can't throw much of a punch, or he was swinging a weapon himself and the killer took it away with him, or this was a blitz attack. He didn't even have time to put a hand up and feel his own wounds."

Jack looked around. "So the guy walked out of here with a bloody weapon."

"Or not," Riley said. "We'll have to check those cans at the exits."

The patrolman had been checking his social media but listening as well, because he immediately put the phone away. "Me?"

"Lift the lid off, but don't touch anything inside." As the young man walked off, Riley said, "If it's not there we'll have to search the whole grounds. Lucky for us it's not a big cemetery."

Maggie continued her usual crime scene examination. She took close-up photos of the victim's hands, without moving them. His right lay palm up, his left palm down. As she had noted, no torn nails, no bruising, no bloodstains. They seemed in fairly good shape, the skin smooth—whatever the guy did for a living probably didn't involve heavy manual labor. They were bare, something she never understood since she pulled her gloves out of the closet as soon as the temperature dipped below sixty, and wished she could get them out of her pocket now—even two layers of her thin latex gloves didn't begin to insulate against the chill.

Riley said, as if thinking out loud, "We should check the entire cemetery anyway. This guy was probably walking home from work or from the bar, and somebody saw a target. There could be homeless camping in here—handy stone walls to hide behind, nice and dark at night, not a place that cops or pedestrians would be scoping out on a regular basis."

Maggie said, "In winter? I'd think they'd want to be near a steam grate, or up against the window of an occupied building. I can't imagine anything colder than a cemetery in winter."

"Yeah, the only people around have zero body warmth." Riley chuckled at his own joke. "But break into one of those little mausoleums and you could probably start a small fire without anyone noticing. Or maybe your standard mugger saw this guy taking a nice, isolated shortcut . . . it would have had to be before this place closed, though, or our victim couldn't have gotten in. Unless they both jumped the fence."

Maggie took in the victim's pants and shoes, free of scrapes. But then the cemetery had the high stone wall only on its two long sides. The east and west walls consisted of a shorter iron fence. The young man looked agile enough, especially if he found something to climb on first to allow him to clear the spiky finial at the top of each picket.

Jack walked around the large headstone behind where the victim lay and alerted her to the slim wallet lying up against the back of the stone, protruding from the gathering snow. After Maggie photographed it in place, Jack gloved up and opened it. Riley, knees creaking, crouched to scatter the snow with one hand to look for any other clues that might be steadily disappearing from view.

The wallet stayed slim because it contained almost nothing. "No DL, no credit cards, and certainly no money," Jack grumbled, checking all its compartments. Something fell as he did so, and Maggie caught it before it hit the ground. A dark green plastic key card, the magnetic strip clearly visible.

"Credit card?" Jack asked.

She turned it over, showing him that it was blank on both sides. No numbers, no name, only the ghost image, in lighter green, of a scowling face wearing a horned hat.

"A Viking?" Jack asked.

"Cleveland State," Maggie said.

"Their football team?"

"Basketball. They don't have a football team."

"Are you sure? About the school?"

She didn't take offense at the query. He knew her well enough to know she wasn't exactly the biggest sports fan in the world. If that were the only thing he knew about her, things would be so much less complicated.

"I went there. Green is their color, too. This must be some sort of student ID card."

Riley straightened up and looked around at the whitening landscape. "I don't see anything else. I'd feel a lot better if we could have a sudden, miraculous thaw right about now. Who knows what else is out here?"

Jack dug a few scraps of paper with unlabeled phone numbers and the business card for two area tech stores out of the wallet, then dropped the whole bundle into a paper bag Maggie held out. They would have to follow up those leads later, unless they were lucky and the guy had an ID card in his back pocket.

Maggie could see a mugger taking the cash and credit cards but, assuming the guy had one, why the driver's license? "Maybe the mugger resembles the dead boy enough to keep the DL in case he needed it to use the credit card, or cards?"

Jack said, "Risky. We could check surveillance videos wherever the cards have been used in the past, say, twelve hours . . . of course that's *if* we knew the guy's name."

"Maybe that's why he took the driver's license."

Riley said, "Your average mugger isn't that smart. Trust me on that."

She did. "So our killer is either really smart or really dumb."

"Or this guy didn't carry any identification," Jack said.

Maggie shivered. She couldn't stop thinking about her last visit to the Erie Street Cemetery. She had first entered Jack Renner's orbit that day, eight months and a lifetime ago. The gravesites had been dampened with spring grass and the body of a young girl. Trafficked, abused, murdered, and disposed of.

Jack hadn't killed the girl, of course. But a day later he killed the man who'd killed her. Maggie had discovered that and done nothing about it. Then Maggie had made her own violent decision and her life had not been the same since.

No one—besides Jack, of course—knew that. But not even he knew that she still woke up every morning wondering how long she could carry this burden before she broke under the weight, told someone—anyone—the truth, and created an opening for both her and Jack at the nearest jail. She had not spoken to anyone about this perfect storm of threat and guilt. Not her friends, not her only sibling, not the assigned department-ordered psychologist. Not even Jack.

Not yet, anyway.

She studied his face, wondering if any of these thoughts churned in his head, whether he made the connection between their first case together and this one. Wondering if they had come full circle, wondering if her period of crazy had ended, if she might be ready to go back to being the person she'd been before.

The uniformed patrol officer interrupted her thoughts. He hadn't seen anything of any interest in either garbage can, at least not on the surface. "What's on top don't look fresh, either . . . I doubt this place gets a lot of traffic in the winter. I mean, you can check, but if you ask me, your weapon isn't buried in there."

"Duly noted," Jack said. "Thank you."

"No problem. At least I'm not in the middle of a cluster in some apartment building with psycho moms threatening to beat my ass, like, say, my shift yesterday. Much rather be out here with my nose going numb and—hey, you know who this is?"

The two cops and Maggie gave the young cop their full attention. Riley said, "What? You know our victim?"

"No, not him. Whose grave he's lying on."

Disappointed, Maggie tried to read the large stone looming up from the snow, but the elements of too many years had worn down the surface. Then she noticed, for the first time, that the slab the victim sprawled across had broken and slightly separated, with grass springing up in the cracks as if they were flagstones. "Somebody famous?" she asked, to be polite, since the two detectives showed no interest.

"Chief Joc-O-sot."

She squinted. Indeed, the raised letters of the broken slab spelled that out in a line above the victim's head.

"He was an Indian chief in the Black Hawk War."

Now Riley did show some interest. "What the hell was the Black Hawk War?"

"I have no idea, but it sounds cool, don't it? He wasn't actually from Cleveland. He came here with some friend of his and became sort of a media darling. Queen Victoria had his portrait painted when he visited her in England." Now that all three of his companions stared at him, he explained, "My kid had to do a history report on this cemetery."

"Ah," Maggie said.

He spoke more quickly, recognizing short attention spans when he found them. "Supposedly he haunts this area. The trip to England aggravated an old wound, and he was trying to get to his old home to be buried with his tribe, but only made it back to Cleveland before dying. So his spirit doesn't really want to be here. Supposedly."

"I doubt a ghost gutted this guy," Riley said.

"Doesn't have to be the Indian," the cop mused aloud. "This cemetery used to be a lot bigger, but when downtown real estate needed to expand, they moved a bunch of graves. Might have ticked off a lot of spirits. Like in *Poltergeist*."

Riley argued, "No, in the movie they built over the graves. Here, as long as they actually moved them it should be cool."

"Tell that to the ghosts."

"If you guys are finished discussing the supernatural," Jack said, "I see the ME is here."

The Medical Examiner's Office investigator, a middle-aged man with very dark skin and zero body fat, prodded the body but discovered no new insights. Maggie helped him turn the now-stiff corpse over, but the back pockets were as empty as the front. No phone, no further items, no ID. The jacket similarly held nothing of interest.

"The body snatchers are going to be a while," he told them. "They're stuck at a four-car pileup at Dead Man's Curve."

"Bunch of fatalities?" Riley asked.

"No, but traffic's backed up for two miles and they're looking for an exit."

Riley groaned as if this inefficiency were a personal affront and turned to Jack. "Why don't you see if CSU can tell us anything about that swipe card? I'll stand here and freeze my toes to Popsicles and hear more about Chief Jackspit."

"Joc-O-sot," the patrol officer corrected.

"I'll go with you," Maggie said.

Both cops stared at her.

She said, "Cleveland State's a sprawling campus. It takes a half hour of wandering around to find anything if you're not familiar with it. It's only two blocks away." They didn't seem convinced, but she added firmly, "Let's go," and began to walk.

After fifteen or twenty feet, Jack glanced back to make sure they were out of earshot, "What was all that about?"

Maggie said, "We need to talk."

Chapter 2

They exited the cemetery at the west end, across from the baseball stadium, now as frigid and vacated as the gravesites, and did a U-turn onto the short, brick-paved Erie Court. Conscious of their coworkers on the other side of the stone wall, they kept their voices low.

"What's up?" Jack asked. He didn't worry that Riley would find their tête-à-tête suspicious; he and Maggie had let everyone believe they were sleeping together. They weren't, of course, but it provided a handy explanation for these occasional conferences. And Maggie had thought it might discourage the interest of her ex-husband, another homicide detective named—

"Rick."

"He hassling you?" Rick Gardiner wasn't the most even-tempered guy.

"No, but I think he's planning to hassle *you*."

They emerged onto East 14th. She turned left and he followed.

"He stopped by to see me this morning, supposedly to pick up a fingerprint report on a case of his, which of course he didn't need because we always send copies over to your unit as soon as they're ready. Then he told me a funny story about one of those phone scammers calling and pretending to be his grandson needing money for bail—"

"He has a grandson?"

"Of course not. Even if we'd had children, their kids wouldn't be old enough to get arrested, so that insulted him more than the loss of his credit card information would have. But then he started asking about you. Where you grew up, where you became a cop."

"And what did you tell him?"

"The truth: I have no idea. You're not exactly chatty."

Strictly true. And even if he were, no chance arose for a heart-to-heart chat about his past since they weren't really dating. Even if they *were* dating, Jack thought, Maggie already knew more of his prior activities than she wanted to. *Way* more.

"He's going to Chicago."

Jack stepped off the curb, nearly into the path of a tractor-trailer so large, it seemed to brush the lowest prisms of the chandelier demarking Playhouse Square. Maggie grabbed his arm, saving him from death by Peterbilt.

"He said there were similar vigilante-type murders of scumbags there." Similar to the men he had killed in Cleveland, she meant. She hadn't let go of his arm, maintained one steady pull until he faced her. "Were there?"

He hesitated, but lying to her would not help anything, and nodded.

This couldn't be news to her, but still her shoulders slumped in worry.

The light changed and they stepped into the crosswalk, and she tried to rally. "He *did* add that it's hard to conclude anything from that, given the number of murders in Chicago. However—he said he might go on to Minneapolis."

Theater marquees provided spotty shelter from the still-falling snow as they passed beneath. "The vigilante case was reassigned to me." That should have kept Rick Gardiner away from Jack's handiwork.

"This trip isn't official. It's all on his own. I don't think I need to describe how rare it is that Rick does anything on his own."

Jack agreed. Maggie's ex would never be known as a go-getter. Not for the first time, he wondered what had ever attracted her to the man in the first place, but stopped himself—not the issue here. What Rick Gardiner might uncover from Jack's old stomping grounds, *that* was the issue.

His reluctant, erstwhile, accidental partner in crime could no longer contain her anxiety. "What are you going to do? What's he going to find, Jack?"

"Calm down," he said—two words one should *never* say to a woman. He regretted them immediately.

"I am perfectly calm!" Except she wasn't, and several other people also waiting for the light at East 18th didn't think so either as they turned at her sharp tone, their glances then sliding away to give them as much privacy as could be afforded on a busy city street.

Jack, wisely and promptly, backpedaled. "Yes, okay. Let him go. He won't find anything."

"You're sure? He asked if I had a photo of you. Not in so many words, I mean. As he pretended to be chatting, he asked why we didn't have any selfies on Facebook or something. Since I haven't posted on Facebook since my niece's birthday last year, that seemed like a stupid comment . . . until I figured out what he was after." The light changed. The people around them moved and Maggie continued to talk as if she couldn't help herself, a measure of her agitation. Jack knew that. Maggie represented a walking time bomb, one that could detonate the cover life he'd built for himself in this city. If one more straw of guilt broke the back of her conscience . . . yes, he *might* wind up in jail, but more likely he'd simply move on. Maggie would at least give him a heads-up before confessing. Wouldn't she?

She might figure he had already overstayed his welcome. The person he had followed to Cleveland in order to destroy had been destroyed. He and Maggie had agreed that waiting six months should allow him to leave without causing suspicion. But it had been eight months, and here he remained.

She was saying, "Obviously he's trying to come up with a picture of you to take with him. He got called away to an overdose, but that's what he was angling around to. Rick was always a lousy actor. I figured out he was cheating on me, like, two days after he started—"

"He did?" Why the hell—

She waved that away with a gloved hand and no hitch in her stride. "Long story. What can he do if he visits those police departments?"

Cue the knee-jerk reaction. "Nothing. It will be fine."

"Are you sure?"

Somewhat sure. Chicago had a huge force, and he had used a different name there. First Rick would have to weasel Jack's ID photo out of Cleveland's human resources unit, then happen to show his picture to the very few guys in Chicago who might actually remember him. On top of that, cops don't care for people outside their agency asking about their guys, even if those people were also cops. And Chicago had been slammed in the news for several years, so they would be doubly reticent to speak ill of anyone who might have once worn their uniform. Yes, he doubted Rick would find anything to connect Jack to the city at all.

"Positive," he told Maggie, more calmly.

She appeared no more reassured than he felt. "What about Minneapolis?"

A slightly smaller force, and Rick had the name of a lieutenant there. If he got to that man with a photo of Jack or even a thorough description, the man would know it didn't match the Officer Jack Renner he'd supervised. That would lead them both to ask why the Jack Renner now in Cleveland had been working in Minneapolis under a different name. "No problem."

"You're *sure*?"

He stopped, turned to face her. "Maggie. Don't worry."

"Oh, I'm worried."

He should have known a simple platitude would hardly dissuade the logical, thorough, and sometimes frighteningly sharp Maggie Gardiner. She had much more to lose than he did. He had designed a fake life in Cleveland, but she had a real one. She had friends, family, career, history. Guilt didn't often trouble him, but it did now. "Rick isn't going to find anything to make him more suspicious of me. Let him go, let him investigate his heart out. When he comes up with nothing it will convince him to give it up once and for all and I'll be clear for good. We'll both be clear, for good."

She studied his face, and he watched as she debated whether to accept this. The vigilante murders had stopped—or so the city, and Maggie, believed—and the case assigned to him, the one man guaranteed not to solve them. Rick remained the only cloud on their horizon, but even Riley believed that simple jealousy motivated Rick, the common annoyance of seeing his ex-wife with another man. Jack knew what trails he had left in other cities, and if he wasn't grabbing his go-bag and heading for the city limits . . . the understandable desire to believe that all would be well won her over.

"Okay," she said at last.

"Okay," he agreed, and looked up at the towering center building of Cleveland State University. "Where are we going?"

"Registrar's office, I guess."

Maggie hadn't exaggerated the time he might spend wandering around before he found answers. The campus sprawled, signs and directionals of limited help in the network of buildings and walkways, all pulsing with forced air heat and vivacious students. The Registrar's office sent them to Security, who said the card appeared to be for student housing, and they trouped through several buildings to reach *that* main desk. It was much quieter there than the chaotic Registrar's, with the quarter close to ending and final tests and grading scheduled. Only one slouching boy waited ahead of them.

Once at the counter, the bright young lady recognized the card immediately.

"Oh yes, that's a unit key. That's why we don't put the address on it, or even the unit number—so if someone found it, they'd have to try it in every door in every building to break in or burgle the place or whatever. Thank you so much for turning it in. I'll be sure to find who it belongs to and see that they get it back. They'll probably be coming in here looking for a replacement anyway."

"No, he won't." Jack pulled out his badge and explained that the former holder of the key card had died. The girl's face plummeted into a look of such sympathy that he hoped she wouldn't burst into sobs.

"That's *awful*! What happened? Car accident?"

Jack made his voice sympathetic but ignored her question. "We need to know the name and address associated with this card."

"But I can't tell you that—I mean, the cards are usually made up at each individual facility. They, um, they would know who lives there . . . but I might, should, be able to tell you the building."

"That would be really helpful," Jack said, perhaps too sweetly. Maggie gave him an odd look; the girl gulped and swiped the card though a reader tucked behind the desk.

Then she told him that that card belonged to the Domain at Cleveland, two blocks away.

"Thank you," Jack said.

"It's a neat old building," she sniffed, handing the card back. "It used to be a YMCA."

"Very interesting," he offered.

"Built in, like, eighteen hundred something."

"Thank you," Maggie told her.

"Have a nice day," the girl said, inconsolable, and went to hunt up a tissue. Jack and Maggie plunged back into the frigid winter air.

"I think we ruined that poor girl's day," Jack commented. Anything to keep the conversation away from Maggie's ex-husband and his potential damage.

"Might not be a bad thing," she said, which surprised him. At his look she added, "Everyone can use the occasional reminder that life is short."

He hoped this meditation on mortality did not stem from a lack of confidence in their future, but figured it was merely Maggie being sensible. People who work around death a great deal tend to lose the sentimentality and increase the respect. She pointed to the building they sought, looming through the falling snow at East 22nd and Prospect.

The girl at the desk had known her stuff. Built in 1889, the structure had once been the city's YMCA, those letters still engraved in the stone frontispiece. More interesting to Jack, it stood only one block from the Erie Street Cemetery. It could explain why the victim hadn't been dressed for a longer trek through the cold. He might have been making a beer run or returning from a meal out . . . though the name tag indicated a part-time job.

A clean, tailored lobby included a door labeled OFFICE, and their luck held. The tiny space held one occupant, a wisp of a young woman with pink tips on her brown hair and too many piercings to count. She didn't bat an eye when Jack produced his badge and handed her the key card. Without a word she swiped it through another reader, then stared at the minuscule screen for so long, he thought it had malfunctioned.

"Does the card belong here?" he finally prompted.

"Yeah."

"Great. Whose room is it?"

She switched her gaze to him. "I think that's confidential."

"I think you're wrong. Your resident is dead, and we need to identify him."

She said nothing, still trying mightily to reconcile her responsibility to protect a fellow student from The Man with any legal ramifications said Man might lower on her, first, and her facility second. It took Jack painting a picture of this poor dead boy ending up in an unmarked grave, plus two phone calls to a supervisor, but she finally consented to give Jack a name: Evan Harding. Also his unit number, the better to fill in a search warrant with because there was no way she was going to let him enter the apartment without one. Whether the stipulation came from her or her supervisor didn't matter. Jack had figured he would need to get a warrant, so he may as well drop off Maggie and pick up his partner first.

They returned to the Erie Street Cemetery, moving fast to stay warm. The body snatchers—officially the "ambulance crew" although everyone they picked up would be well past the point where medical attention could help—had finally been freed from the traffic snarl and were loading the white body bag onto a gurney.

"Have a nice walk?" Riley smirked. He, along with the rest of the department, believed the official story that Jack and Maggie were dating. He even tried to help Jack along where he could, with subtle prompts meant to steer him into proper boyfriend behavior, because Riley was a kindly man and a loyal partner. So much so that Jack felt much more guilty about deceiving him than Jack could ever feel about dispatching violent criminals into the next life.

"Yes," Jack said to him now. "Thanks."

Chapter 3

On the other side of the Cuyahoga River, perhaps three miles from where Jack and Maggie stood, Rick Gardiner turned up his collar against the wind off the lake and sniffed the air. They stood outside in the alley between the market and the river, but odors seemed to escape even through the market's brick walls. A rime of gusting snow covered everything in a thin, unbroken layer, including the corpse. "What is that smell?"

"Dead body?" his partner suggested.

"No. I think it's sauerkraut. I could go for a hot dog with kraut. And a little mustard." In the winter months the West Side Market worked as a skeleton of its summer persona, but the few stalls open did manage a brisk business during lunchtime. The place always made Rick think of the 1920s scenes from *The Godfather*; shopping in old-world streets full of carts and vendors and fresh fruits and sausages.

Will Dembrowski, tall and wiry, pointed out that they had eaten breakfast only an hour before.

"Don't matter. Hot dogs are like popcorn. You smell it, you gotta have it."

"You want a tube of mystery meat in your stomach, no problem. But what about this guy?"

Rick looked down past his own slight paunch at the body of the dead man. Straggly dirty-blond beard, straggly dirty-blond hair, skin and features that appeared to be a mix of several different racial categories, clothes that hadn't been laundered in a month covered with a worn puffy parka. "What about him? The needle still in his arm pretty much says it all."

Will could not deny that the needle pretty much *did* say it all. There were no obvious injuries, no disturbance to the ensemble other than the rolled-up sleeve. The man had apparently been sitting on an overturned plastic milk crate, maybe leaning up against a surprisingly solid tower of empty wooden boxes that had once held vegetables. A weathered label on the side showed some sort of beet or turnip or whatever—Rick had never been particularly interested in vegetables unless they were deep fried in tempura. And usually not even then.

Under an overhang and between the boxes and the brick wall, the spot felt surprisingly cozy despite the December weather. None of the boxes seemed out of place, the milk crate squarely flush, two sheets of plywood still propped on their short ends against the brick. If a fight to the death had occurred there, it had been expertly cleaned up. Most likely this was exactly what it looked like: a victim who took one gram too many of an illegal drug and died a lonely death.

The Medical Examiner's investigator had declined to respond, reserving their limited manpower for less open-and-shut situations. Because of that, the two cops were free to check the pockets and move the body.

Rick put on latex gloves for this. He didn't like touching dead people, or dead people's stuff, and especially dead homeless people's stuff. His nose wrinkled just to flip the coat open. "Bet he didn't smell too good when he was alive . . . certainly not now."

Will said, "That's one helpful thing about the cold. Everything about this would be worse in August. Not only him but old food, rotten meat. Bugs."

Rick pulled the pockets open, gingerly searching the insides, wary of open syringes or needles. "You're one of those friggin' optimistic people, aren't you?"

"Guess so."

"I hate that."

The victim had something in every pocket, usually crumpled pieces of paper, their edges wearing away, flyers, halves of cigarettes, the occasional coin. Nothing of any significance, no more drugs, no cell phone. Rick grunted and stood halfway up, grasping the right arm. Will understood the shorthand and grabbed the right ankle. They flipped the guy onto his stomach.

Will pulled the parka up, then gave a shout as a large cockroach scuttled out and headed for the warm brick building.

Rick was too surprised to step on it and didn't want bug guts on the bottom of his shoe anyway. "Sheesh, that thing's as big as a mouse! And it's winter! Shouldn't they be dead?"

"It's warm inside. They find a spot to hang out and survive." Still, Will patted the man's back pants pockets with extra caution. No more insects emerged, but he found a wallet.

It contained two dollars, two quarters, business cards to five different bars—none bearing any sort of notation, like the phone number of his dealer or that of a friendly barmaid—and a faded photograph of a young girl, maybe ten or eleven years of age. Of more interest to Rick, a driver's license and Medicare card in the name of Marlon Toner. He held it toward his partner.

"Address?"

"West Twenty-Ninth. If he's got an address, why does he smell as if he hasn't washed his clothes in six months?"

"The Maytag is on the fritz?"

"Or it's an old address. I don't see his bags, so he must have his stuff stashed somewhere."

"Only one way to find out."

"DOB. . . ." Rick looked from the card to the victim, to the card, to the victim. "This guy looks a lot older than twenty-six."

"It's not the years, it's the mileage. No phone?"

Rick pulled one out of the other pocket and tossed it to him. "Ask and ye shall receive."

Will pushed the phone's home button. Nothing. He pushed more buttons. Nothing. "It's dead."

"These guys usually have those pay-as-you-go burners. You can't pay, it burns."

"Either way, useless to us."

Rick called Dispatch and got the guy's criminal history, which consisted of a minor drug charge and a speeding ticket, both from twelve months prior. Then they waited for the body snatchers. Rick rocked back and forth on his feet to keep the blood moving and thought more about hot dogs.

"Where are you going next week?" Will suddenly asked, startling him out of his reverie of condiments. "You told me but I forgot."

"Um . . . Chicago."

"That's right. What for?"

Rick, usually voluble about any plan, thought or desire of his own making, hesitated until Will prompted, "Visiting family? Vacation with that—what was her name again?"

"Maura," Rick said, referring to a woman he'd dated a few times in the past month. "No, it's, um—my nephew's graduation."

"In December?"

"Yeah."

"Oh. You'll be back by next weekend?"

"Yeah." That was all his partner needed to know. Will certainly didn't need to know that Rick intended to visit the Chicago PD to ask if Jack Renner had ever worked there and in what capacity.

Rick didn't expect full and prompt cooperation from the city. The huge force had taken a lot of PR flack the past few years. They'd be super hesitant to kick over any rocks, to admit that the guy had worked for them, to admit that the guy *hadn't* worked for them, to admit that they'd had a bunch of scumbags killed without figuring out it had all been done by one vigilante and they never figured it out. Rick being a fellow officer as well probably wouldn't open any doors, not with the siege that city had become, and they'd probably want to call CPD and check his credentials first. That would lead to questions from his nominal supervisor, the HR department, and Will.

But he was willing to take that chance.

If he had a working theory, it was this: Jack Renner was obsessed. He had followed this vigilante killer's trail across the country, doing anything to stay on his trail—using another cop's name, discrediting guys like Rick to get assigned to the case, cozying up to the hot forensics chick to get the inside scoop on what was found at the scenes and maybe some help with manipulating the evidence. Like a malevolent version of the grifter in *The Music Man*. That's the analogy he should use with Maggie. She liked that movie. And if he could convince her that she'd been used, her fury would make Genghis Khan look like Strawberry Shortcake.

Plus, if he could prove that Jack Renner had used different names and different backstories to infiltrate other police departments, the CPD would have to face up to that and get rid of the guy. Get him out of Cleveland and out of Maggie's life. She would see that Rick had been right all along.

It wasn't jealousy that motivated him, Rick told himself for the umpteenth time. It was concern.

But Will, or Maggie, or the homicide unit powers that be

would never believe that. Better to get the evidence first than to waste time arguing with them. Then there would be nothing Renner could do. What did they call that? A *fait accompli*? Besides, road trips were supposed to be good for the soul.

Will flagged down the body snatchers, startling Rick out of his thoughts, and he moved out of the way. Keeping a watch for any more of those rodent-sized cockroaches, he didn't offer to help. Picking up stiffs was not his job.

And they did so, but only after an in-depth discussion of which butchers made the best beef jerky. "They all make their own," body snatcher number one said. "I like Czuchraj's."

Number two said, "Sebastian's Meats."

One gave a grunt that was neither agreement nor disagreement, more of the result of exertion as they hefted the body bag onto the gurney.

Will voted: "Dohar's. When will the post be?"

Two said, "Maybe later today. They're not too busy so far. Want them to call you?"

"Yes," Will said.

"No," Rick told them, and said to his partner, "Open and shut. And we've got a notification to do." He had a bag to pack, car to gas up, GPS to program, and he didn't need some druggie's autopsy wasting his time. He waved the envelope holding Marlon Toner's driver's license.

Will conceded. "Yeah, okay. Let's go see who lives on West Twenty-Ninth. You gonna forget about the dog with kraut?"

"Hell no," Rick said. "We can do that first."

Chapter 4

The girl with the piercings and the pink tips to her hair studied the search warrant; Jack watched her eyes follow each line as she read, and wondered if she might be studying law, or had a bad history with police departments, or simply believed that any job worth doing was worth doing very, very well. But she found it satisfactory, because she retrieved the master key from inside two different locked cabinets and led them to the elevator without a word.

Equally soundless, she traveled up to a fourth-floor hallway to a door second from the end and knocked. Jack had asked before if Evan Harding lived with a roommate, but there had been nothing in the building's records and indeed no one answered his door. That the dead guy's name had been the only one on the lease helped them get the search warrant in record time, since no one else's privacy could be violated.

The girl pulled out her master key card but Jack used the one found on the body. He wanted to be sure they were in the right place. He heard the mechanism slide around so he could open the door.

The unit had been painted white, and with the light gray sky and the snow outside it blinded at first. Jack and Riley established the emptiness of the unit with only a few steps. Easy enough, the only interior door led to the small bathroom and the outer room consisted of a minimal kitchen area, a double bed, and a desk. Nothing hung on the walls, but a multicolored paisley print bedspread lent a splash of color.

Jack's gaze fell on a framed photo sitting on the second shelf of one of the built-ins. A happy couple in front of the Rock & Roll Hall of Fame—the victim, with a slight young woman whose jet-black hair fell slightly past her shoulders. He had one arm around her; she had both of hers around him.

They were in the right place. Jack picked up the photo and held it toward the building manager woman. "This is him. Do you know him?"

She said no. "I mean, I've seen him coming and going, but I don't know him personally. I don't think I ever had a conversation with him."

"What about her?"

She peered. "I've seen her around, too."

"Does she live in this room? Or another unit?"

"I see them walking through the lobby. I don't have any idea where they go."

Jack went to the doorless closet. Flannel shirts, hoodies, but also two tops with sequins and plunging necklines, a sweater with flowers appliquéd on its sleeves, and a leather jacket with fringes, too small for even the victim to have worn. Add to that a bra strewn across the unmade bed, and Jack would bet that the girl in the picture lived in this unit whether she was on the lease or not.

"Thanks," he told the pink-tipped woman. "We'll take it from here."

She looked around, uncertain.

"We will most likely be here for hours," Riley told her,

and she backed out with great reluctance, clearly not trusting them, yet also not able to spend her whole workday on the fourth floor.

Once she'd left, Jack and Riley could get down to work. Jack started at the wall with the bed and Riley moved into the bathroom, quickly and methodically moving, examining, replacing every item present. Who was Evan Harding, where had he come from, what was he doing/studying/active in, and who might have had a motive to kill him—all on the very outside chance that it had not been a random mugger?

Jack focused on these questions, more comfortable than the question of Rick Gardiner's goals or what he might find.

The bed didn't tell him anything except that the occupants felt making one was a waste of time and that they didn't get too concerned about mixing dirty laundry with clean. The floor underneath it held some old magazines, boxes of supplies such as shampoo and macaroni, and more lost laundry. Jack pulled out a decorative wooden box and opened it to poke through an assortment of trinkets, a Chinese coin, a matchbook from a bar he'd never heard of, two plain gold bands, three bracelets made of round colored beads, a luggage tag from Carnival Cruise Lines, and a ticket stub from Playhouse Square. Jack couldn't guess if the box belonged to the victim or his girlfriend.

But no weapons, no drugs, nothing that would make the guy a target. He moved on to the closet, finding only more clothes, clean ones hung up or stacked on the built-in shelves, with dirty items on the floor. A decently heavy parka made Jack wonder why the guy hadn't been wearing it. Riley had finished in the bathroom and now moved into the kitchen. Jack took the desk, the only spot in the room still unexplored.

Cosmetics—both male and female varieties—magazines, charging cords for at least two different electronic items, and a bowl with the dregs of that morning's cereal littered the surface. Two pens, one pencil, and one small spiral-bound notebook in the shallow drawer—the desk didn't seem to be used for a lot of writing, or study.

"I'm thinking girlfriend lives here," Jack said aloud.

"If she wanted her privacy secured, she should have put her name on the lease. I doubt it would make any difference to the price. Or she doesn't live here but stays over a lot."

In the desk drawer Jack found a worn envelope with money in it—Jack counted twenty-three dollars, some kind of petty cash fund.

Behind him, Riley opened and closed cabinets. "They're not rich, but they're not living on ramen. Fresh vegetables in the fridge, no alcohol, no TV dinners, organic chicken breasts in the freezer. Health nuts. So many kids are these days."

"Either of your girls go vegan yet?" Jack asked. Riley had two daughters, somewhere in their middle school years. Jack could never remember their ages.

"Not yet, but I'm waiting. I'm sure Natalie will come up with all sorts of woo-woo things. Hannah, forget it. Hannah lives for bacon cheeseburgers and chicken wings." He paused. "I hope she never changes."

He sounded so wistful that Jack hoped so, too.

"No drugs, either," Riley went on. "Not even prescription. You got anything?"

Jack said, "Nada. Not even what should be here—like textbooks, notebooks, homework. I'm wondering if they're really students."

"I would think they'd have to be to live here."

"I would think so, too."

"Kids do a lot online now. Assignments, projects, required supplies, it's all posted on the school's site by the teachers. And they're going to e-books to avoid the weight and expense of textbooks—not that they cost any less. Could be these two carry an entire course around in their phone."

"Could be."

Riley said, "It also could be that they faked being students to get the low rent. Though that's a notebook," he added, pointing to the one in Jack's hand.

"No subject I ever got a grade in." He handed it over, watched as Riley paged through the columns of dates and numbers. No other information, not even a name on the front cover, only entries of numbers for an ever-increasing tally.

"Money?" Riley guessed.

"Or a video game score."

"If it's money, he—or she—has now accumulated close to, let's see, nine hundred bucks. Hardly seems worth killing over. I know life is cheap in the big city, but I hope it's not that cheap."

Jack shrugged. "It would make me think he's dealing, except there's not a single baggie or pill or white dust or crumb of pot to be found."

"If girlfriend knew he was dead, she might have cleaned up."

"Then she did one hell of a job."

"I found these in a drawer with the spoons." Riley held out two slips of paper. They seemed to be perforated ends torn off some larger form, with a preprinted number across the top and sections below to be filled in. No section had, save one: *Amount—$750.00.* The second slip was similarly blank, with a different preprinted number at the top and amount of $525.00. But along the edge, in narrow, stylized script, a logo read *A to Z Check Cashing.*

Riley said, "So he's got a job that requires a name tag, maybe makes a habit of cashing his paycheck at a check cashing place before walking home. A perfect target."

"Maybe," Jack said, giving the small apartment a frustrated, sweeping glance. "Why not a bank account? Or at least a credit card statement? Who has such a small amount of . . . *stuff?*"

Other than him, of course. His tiny rented bungalow

could give the Spartan student's apartment a run for its money in the no-strings department. But he knew why he kept his life bare—the lack of evidence hid a host of activity. What did this kid have to hide?

"Maybe they just moved here. Students bring only what they need—at least they *should*." He sighed, no doubt worried about moving a tractor-trailer full of possessions when the time came for his girls, or worried about paying for college courses, dorms, and books, or worried about that inevitable day when he realized they were no longer girls but young women.

Jack didn't envy him any of that.

They heard the lock mechanism cycle a split second before it opened, and the girl in the photo spilled into the apartment. Unlike her boyfriend, she had dressed for the cold in a black padded all-weather coat, knit gloves, and puffy nylon boots. When she saw the men, her skin seemed pale from more than the chill. Dark eyes and jet-black hair gave her an Asian cast, and for one long breath Jack thought she would bolt. He watched her debate with herself and said, "Police. Do you live here?"

More debating.

Riley asked, "Do you know Evan Harding?"

The girl let out the breath she'd been holding, and the eternal energy her youth bestowed seemed to leak out as well. She knew exactly what they were going to say, and it would not come as a surprise. Shock, yes. Surprise, no.

She shut the door and came into the room to pull off the gloves and toss the coat over the back of the desk chair. Then she faced them, visibly bracing herself. "What happened?"

"Do you know Evan Harding?" Riley repeated.

"Yes."

"Do you live here with him?"

"Yes."

"What's your name?"

Only a slight wait this time. "Shanaya Thomas."

"What's your relationship to Evan Harding?"

"I'm his girlfriend. What's happened to him?" She spoke slowly. Most people would have ended each answer with this demand, but she seemed to know the news was going to be bad and didn't mind procrastinating.

"I'm afraid he's been killed," Riley said, his voice gentle. There was no good way tell someone that.

The girl's eyes instantly swam with unshed tears and she put a hand to her mouth. "I knew it. I knew something was wrong when he didn't come home last night."

"When did you last speak to him?"

"About four, I think."

"A.m. or p.m.?" Jack asked.

"P.m. He called, just to—just to say hi. Sometimes he'd get bored at work, call me."

"Where does he work?"

Her gaze fell on the shelves behind him and she pushed between them, trancelike, to reach the framed photo Jack had examined before. She ran a finger over the dead boy's face, then collapsed onto the bed as if her knees could no longer hold her, cradling the photo to her breasts. "He, um, he started a new job a few weeks ago. At the movie theater, the one at Tower City."

"Okay," Riley said. From Tower City to the Erie Street Cemetery to where they now sat formed a straight line, a logical path home after work. "How long have you known him?"

"A year, year and a half."

"You're not students here, are you?" Jack asked, trying to keep all accusation out of his voice.

After a second she shook her head, staring at the floor. "We were—but then we were working all the time and couldn't keep up with the coursework. We didn't tell the building . . . we need the low rent. Will you have to tell them?"

"Not unless they ask," Riley said.

She looked at Jack. He knew his face never appeared too reassuring under the best of circumstances, but he couldn't help that. She said, "It doesn't matter. I couldn't afford even the student rate by myself anyway."

"Do you have a job?"

"Yes, in customer service, but it doesn't pay much. It's my one day off, today. That's why I went out for some breakfast." She sniffed, then reached over to snatch a tissue from a small box on the desk.

"What is this?" Jack asked, holding out the notebook. She glanced at it without interest and said she didn't know.

Riley took her through where she and Evan were from—she, Youngstown, him, Pittsburgh—and his family and significant others. She only knew of a mother, somewhere in Indiana. "He never said anything about his father and didn't have any brothers or sisters. His mom's number should be in his phone," she added.

"We didn't find a phone."

"But . . . it has to be there. Did you look in his coat pocket? Even if a car smashed it you can still—"

"This wasn't an accident," Riley said, and told her that her boyfriend had been murdered, possibly shot by person or persons unknown. She didn't cry so much as gasp, cringe, and moan; that she'd never seen her boyfriend again had been bad enough, but knowing that someone had purposely done that to them made it too horrific to take in. Riley did his typically good work, drawing every last detail he could from her while probing for a support system—did she have family, friends that he and Jack could call? Would she like to hear from a victim advocate who could walk her through what would be done with Evan's body? Was there anyone else who might have a name and number for this mother in Indiana?

No, no, and no—but she would be fine. When she could

think straight again she'd try to message some friends to see if they had any ideas about next of kin. Riley said they would also check out Evan's workplace to see if Evan had written anything on his employment application that might be a lead to his family, and Shanaya shot him a look of grim gratitude.

Jack asked about the cell phone service. She told them it was Sprint and gave them the phone number. She checked her own phone to see if there had been any further messages or e-mails from Evan she had missed, said there were not since that call at 3:48 p.m. the previous day. She had tried him four times during the evening, but they had all gone straight to voice mail. She figured he was busy and hadn't worried about it.

With nothing else to do, they stated their condolences once again and left the young woman sitting on the rumpled bed, holding the photograph of her dead boyfriend and staring at nothing.

They rode the elevator down in silence.

Riley buttoned his coat as they passed out into the snow, the air so cold relative to inside that it made Jack's nostrils stick together when he breathed in. That was the way to tell *cold* from *really cold*.

"Partner," Riley said, his tone much less light than his words, "let's go to the movies."

"Yeah. There's something about this I don't like, either."

Shanaya made herself count to thirty. That should be enough time for the cops to get into the elevator and out of her hallway, unlikely to bang on the door with one last question.

It took some self-discipline to wait. She'd always been good at both those things, but hearing that Evani had been murdered knocked some of her abilities for a loop. She hadn't been lying about knowing that something had to be wrong.

Evani always came home. He might go out for a drink, he might hit the slots at the casino despite her threats to stab him in the groin if he lost more than two of their dollars on gambling. If he lost five she would gut him and stuff the entrails in his mouth as he died, she had said more than once, but who knew what he got up to when she wasn't there to watch him? He might even have gotten drunk and gone home with another woman—unlikely, since they'd always been quite compatible in that respect. More than compatible.

But getting himself freakin' *murdered*—that was way out there.

Maybe she should leave. Throw what little she had into a bag and keep herself safe.

But if whoever killed him knew about this apartment or wanted to get into it, he would have taken Evani's key card and shown up last night. The guy, or guys, hadn't been interested in the card. That *should* mean she was good.

She got to thirty. Surely the cops had to be on their way out of the building. She flipped the photo frame over and ripped the cardboard stand out of its slot. It had to be there. It *had* to.

Under the photo was a plain sheet of paper, and between that and the cardboard backing had been stuffed two sheets of folded paper. But what she sought wasn't there.

Of course it wasn't. Evani never did what she told him, the damn paranoid idiot.

Chapter 5

The glass-topped, gleaming white expanse of Tower City Mall seemed relatively sedate in the middle of a weekday. Three floors, plus a basement where the Rapid Transit trains came and went, it had fountains, a food court, both pricey and not-too-ridiculously-pricey shops, and an eleven-screen movie theater.

Where, it turned out, they had never heard of Evan Harding. The manager on duty, a friendly, competent, and skinny black kid who didn't look old enough to see some of their current attractions scoured his computer and even called the corporate offices to confirm: no one named Evan Harding worked there. Not now, not previously. Jack showed him the cell-phone photo he had taken of the picture of the victim with Shanaya. The only other photo he had was one he'd taken at the crime scene, with the reddened shirt and the open, staring eyes—show that to a witness and they wouldn't see past the blood. But the manager didn't recognize Evan Harding, and neither did any other employee currently on duty.

Their name tags, Jack noted, didn't look anything like the plain white plate the victim had pinned to his shirt.

Back out in the atrium, Jack said, "The girlfriend lied."

"Or he lied to the girlfriend," Riley said, crunching popcorn from a bag he'd bought at the concession stand.

"I don't know. How often does the live-in girlfriend know so little about a guy? Girlfriends are usually kind of nosy, aren't they?"

Riley gave him a look—that *what does she see in you?* look—and Jack backpedaled before his partner could ask the question aloud. The only thing more difficult than maintaining a real romantic relationship was maintaining a fictional one. "I'm saying I'm suspicious of her inability to tell us anything useful. The dead guy had no family, no friends—there's no sign in that room that either of them were *ever* students. Maybe it's shock and a minimalistic approach to possessions, or maybe he was into something shady and she's covering for him."

Riley crumpled up the paper bag. "Possibly. But when did you last see a drug dealer wearing a name tag?"

Jack considered this as Riley pitched his balled-up bag into a rounded garbage can for a perfect nothing-but-net score. "Shady jobs don't issue name tags. But if it wasn't shady, why not tell the girlfriend about it?"

"Do staff at strip joints wear tags? There's a job he wouldn't want to tell her about, how he's surrounded by the scantily clad all day."

"I don't know. About the tags."

"We could stop in at a few and check it out," Riley said, currently between girlfriends and only half joking. Then a toddler somewhere behind them burst into a screeching peal, which echoed and grew as it bounced off the marble and the glass, piercing eardrums with the ease born of practice. "Either way, let's get out of here."

As they exited onto Public Square, Jack noted aloud that

they would have to get a search warrant for the victim's phone. He had already called the homicide unit's administrative assistant to see if Sprint could get the phone located on the chance the mugger had kept it. Technology could only triangulate to an area and not a pinpoint on the map, but anything would help when they had so little to work with.

Snow kept falling, a few desultory flakes at a time. The tall buildings occasionally sheltered them from the wind and other times turned the street into a tunnel that funneled and concentrated it to a biting, shoving force of frigidity. "We have a car, you know," Riley grumbled. "We don't actually have to walk everywhere."

"It's only two blocks." Jack didn't like the cold but liked moving in and out, from cold air to overly warm buildings or cars and back again even less. And he hated driving in the stuff, the sickening lurch of the frame as the tires fought for traction. He hadn't been raised in a cold climate and couldn't figure out why, though he had a decent furnace, his house always felt chilly to him. He should get an electric blanket. If he planned to stay.

Riley continued to grouse. "Two blocks in June is one thing. Two blocks in December is another."

"Didn't your doctor recommend exercise?"

"No," Riley said. "No, I have never discussed my doctor visits with you. You're like a whole freakin' two years younger than me so don't—you're going to get killed like that, you know. Speaking of health."

Jack had been tapping on his smart phone with one thumb, nearly stepping into the path of a passing car. "I figure we got one other clue."

"A to Z Check Cashing?" Riley guessed.

Jack covered his surprise. He really shouldn't make the mistake of thinking Riley wasn't that sharp just because Jack had managed, so far, to keep his extracurricular activities off Riley's radar. Overconfidence would take Jack out much more easily than a speeding automobile. "Uh—yeah. It's on the next street from our crime scene. Might as well check it out. That's near where the car's parked anyway," he added as an incentive.

"That's more than two blocks," Riley grunted, and Jack let him have the last word on the subject.

A to Z Check Cashing did, indeed, exist in a storefront in the triangular building where Bolivar met Prospect Road, one street over from where the victim had been found. A loud set of bells jangled from the pneumatic arm of the door when they entered, giving an old-school alert to the cashier that a customer had arrived. Not that there was much storefront to keep an eye on—the customer area consisted of an empty, ten by fifteen square of dingy linoleum facing a solid, chest-high counter area. Perhaps five inches of space existed between this counter and an upper wall of clear but not clean plexiglass. There were cameras in each corner of the customer area, more visible in the ceiling behind the plexiglass. Employees must have to enter via the rear—no door or opening existed to get a human being to move from in front of the counter to behind it, which must go a long way toward discouraging robbers.

The air smelled a bit like a greenhouse tinged with both mildew and despair, but was blissfully warm. Riley let out an audible sigh. Compared to the city streets, they had walked into a sauna.

A paunchy, middle-aged man with thick black-framed glasses emerged from the back and took them in with one sweeping glance before his face stilled into a look of utter neutrality, having pegged them as cops. Cops who would probably be annoying him with questions about his less than upstanding customers. Cops who might scare those customers away if they hung around long enough. Before the man even opened his mouth, Jack knew he would sound brisk, businesslike, and ostensibly cooperative, and all with one motive: to get them out of there as quickly as possible.

The man said, with the barest trace of an accent Jack couldn't identify, "How can I help you?"

Jack waited for Riley, always better at putting potential witnesses at ease, but his partner said nothing, staring instead at the man's name tag, crookedly pinned to a red polo shirt. A plain white badge with rounded edges and red letters spelled "Ralph."

Jack said, "We're here about Evan Harding."

The man's eyes widened in surprise and something like fear. "Well. I see." He straightened a bit; his chin came up, and he spoke more firmly. "I'd like to know where he is, too. He's forty-five minutes late."

Jack hid a smile. Finally, they might be getting somewhere. "He works here?"

"For me, yeah."

"How long?"

The guy shrugged as if relaxing slightly. Something they'd said had reassured him, and Jack couldn't guess what that had been. "Four, five months. Real reliable."

In response to further questions he told them that he, Ralph, had owned the business for over ten years, he had five employees, that Evan had been a cashier working the front desk, and nothing else. He'd never had a problem with the kid's work, no money missing, no customer complaints, forms always filled out properly. He didn't know anything else about Evan Harding, not family, friends savory or un-, hobbies, vices. He didn't come out and say that he didn't care, but strongly implied it. He had last seen Evan about six p.m. the previous evening when he, Ralph, had left. Evan would be closing up that night.

"Did he often close?" Riley asked.

"Yeah, plenty times."

Jack said, "You have cameras."

The boss hesitated as if he might deny it, then realized the futility. "This is a cash business. Yeah, I got cameras up the wazoo."

"Good. We'll need to see those. And his employment application."

Another hesitation while he calculated the futility. "Okay."

He instructed them to walk around the building to the other side and find the entry door, which he would open for them. This time when Jack plunged back into the cold, it felt like a relief. "I see why the guy didn't wear a heavier coat."

"Yeah, but he didn't go straight home from here," Riley observed, and Jack stopped to orient himself. Across the street sat a medieval building and on the other side of that, the Erie Street cemetery. The student housing building could be found a few blocks directly east. From his workplace, Evan should have turned left on Prospect, away from the cemetery.

"He could have picked up some groceries or something, which the mugger helped himself to along with his money and phone. Or he grabbed a beer with a buddy. Could be anything." But Jack kept staring at the building as if he could see through it to the cemetery on the other side. A large, squat fortification of red brick and sandstone, it would have looked at home in Morocco or Prague. "What *is* that?"

"Huh? Oh. Grays Armory."

"An armory?"

"Yeah . . . the Grays were a civilian defense militia, kept their weapons there, but they were also a social organization like a Moose Lodge or Elks Hall or whatever."

"When was this?"

"Like a hundred years ago, one-twenty, one-thirty. It's a museum now but you can still rent the place out—I went to a wedding there once." He kept walking, the stored warmth from the storefront having quickly worn off.

Jack caught up. "Looks pretty—solid."

"Iron bars with spikes on the windows, and that gate in the entryway comes all the way down. If there's ever a zombie apocalypse, that's the place you're gonna want to hole up."

"I'll keep that in mind." They reached the tip of the triangular building, stepped from Bolivar onto Prospect, and found the unlabeled employee's entrance to A to Z Check Cashing. Jack knocked, half expecting a tiny door to open and Ralph's olive face to peer out and demand a password. But these were modern times and yet another camera gazed at them as they heard the locks being thrown.

"This might be my second choice," Riley said, "when the zombies come."

Ralph hustled them inside. The rear of the store wasn't a whole lot bigger than the front, but held two safes with both electronic and keyed locking mechanisms, shelves full of forms, and a messy, dusty desk with mysterious gaps in its surface, as if some items had been hastily placed out of sight while they walked around the corner. There was nothing wrong with a check cashing service, Jack knew. A healthy percentage of U.S. citizens did not possess a bank account and without one, of course, direct deposit was not possible. This made cashing their paycheck or reimbursement check more difficult. The service cost, fees were deducted, but as ATM fees, shipping and handling charges, and turnpike tolls proved, Americans were willing to pay for convenience.

But Ralph didn't have it easy. A sign proclaimed the store open from six a.m. until midnight, six days a week. Obviously robbery remained a realistic and constant threat, not only from the baseline criminals assumed to exist around an inner-city location, but from his own customers. Many people might use check cashing services because they were in a hurry, didn't trust banks, didn't feel a need for banks, or were in transition from one town to another. But many others didn't have a bank account because they couldn't stay mentally or physically stable long enough to get one. And yet others were trying to cash checks that weren't quite kosher—those for faked medical conditions, the social security payments of deceased parents, or ones stolen out of other people's mailboxes. Those customers could become desperate and unpredictable.

Nor was foul behavior restricted to the public side of the counter. Check cashing fees might veer from reasonable to usurious—and any business that saw large exchanges of cash could be easily tweaked to include fraud and money laundering.

Either way, Jack could guess a number of reasons why Ralph would be less than enthusiastic to see cops on his doorstep. At the same time he had a vested interest in finding out what had happened to his employee, just in case it related to his job.

"Is there any money missing?" Jack asked the A to Z boss.

A gruff *no*. Ralph checked exactly that every morning, and all seemed to be as it should. Evan had closed up, leaving the paperwork tidy, all locks turned, overhead lights out. The man stood as he spoke, awkwardly using a mouse on the back of a clipboard to flick through screens displayed on a forty-inch flat screen mounted on the wall above the desk. Apparently he didn't feel comfortable sitting with his back to the two detectives. "I used to keep all the lights on all night, hoping it would discourage burglars. But the drunks, they see the lights and they think we're still open, so one, two in the morning they'd be banging on the door. Once people were leaving a party across the street and called the cops. Another time one of them broke the door, so I started turning the lights out. Same reason there's no chairs in the lobby. I put chairs out there, the homeless guys hang out here all day just to stay warm."

"It *is* toasty in here," Riley agreed. He had already shaken out of his parka.

"Yeah." Ralph grinned at the TV screen, the first smile they'd seen on him. "My one indulgence. I don't care if it snows outside, I'm not going to shiver all day to save a few bucks on the gas bill. Here. That's Evan."

The display screen split into fourteen equal-sized boxes. Four each showed the public area, the counter area, and the office, and one each hung above the outside of the front and rear doors. The time stamp read 18:15—six-fifteen p.m.—the previous evening. The victim, very much alive, worked the front counter, processing customers' checks and forms and dispensing cash from a drawer built into the counter. As they watched in fast-forward mode, he restocked the drawer during slow times, taking cash from a small safe in the office.

"I stock that little one before I leave for the day. No one can get in the big ones except me," Ralph explained.

In between customers, Evan disappeared into the tiny restroom, snacked out of a bag he kept in the office mini-fridge, surfed the apps on his phone, and used the cashier computer to check what appeared to be his social media pages and online shopping sites.

"They're not supposed to do that," Ralph growled. "Damn Facebook." However, he seemed cheered that his employee had not been up to anything untoward, and asked how much the officers wanted to see. The time stamp now read 20:05.

"Let it run," Jack said.

He didn't expect to learn much. Evan Harding had left the business in its usual condition, and therefore hadn't been robbed or abducted. But they were there and the tape was queued, so they might as well watch all of it rather than risk missing something that might explain how Evan Harding had come to be dead in the snow, one street over.

Customers came and went. Most turned over their form, endorsed their check or showed a receipt on their phone, took their cash and left. Some, as the owner predicted, seemed to enjoy the warmth or simply having something to do and hung around chatting. Evan Harding would lean against the counter, arms crossed—polite but not encouraging.

When no customers were present, Evan spent time on his phone—hardly unusual in today's world. He also used downtime to tap at the keyboard. "What's he doing?" Jack asked, when Ralph did not seem interested in this activity.

"Online transfers."

"What does that mean?"

"We have a website. Just like Western Union. You can go on the site and transfer money to another person's bank account, as long as you have their name and account numbers. Or to your own account, of course. We receive the request, make sure everything is filled out and that the account the money come from is legit, and put the transfer through."

"So you have access to people's bank account numbers?"

"No, no. The site encrypts that part. It's like when you put your password in to get your e-mail—all you see is row of dots? Same thing here. So we can't see bank account numbers."

"Then how do you know they're legit?"

"Because funds go through."

During another quiet period on the recording as Evan Harding typed some more, double-checked his work on the screen, and then opened the cash drawer and counted out a stack of bills. These, he put in his own pocket.

Again, his boss did not seem concerned. When Jack asked, he shrugged. "Probably cashing his own money. I let my guys do that, cash their checks, welfare, reimbursement. Why would I want some other boss getting my percentage?"

"But he didn't have a check."

"Online, then." His head swiveled as he took in both cops' expressions, sighed, and said, "I can look it up."

"Yes," Riley said. "Please look it up."

He sat at his desk and used another mouse to search the

previous day's transactions, narrowing things down by the time stamp on the video. "Credit card."

"What?" Riley asked.

"He took a cash advance on a credit card. Five hundred dollars." He checked again. "Visa."

"Do your employees do that a lot?"

One hand gave a short wave. "Sometimes. They need money and I don't give advances."

"Did he have money problems? In need of cash for some reason?"

"I don't know. They're my employees, not my friends. We don't chat about personal things. I do that, they get comfortable. Start asking for more hours, less hours, more raises, bonus, that sort of thing."

Plainly, Ralph didn't care what his employees did—so long as the books balanced at the end of the day.

Jack had been keeping an eye on the video as they spoke. With the video running at two times normal speed, he saw Evan Harding once again take cash from the drawer after a computer entry. This prompted another check of the ledger, Ralph now more pensive. This cash withdrawal had been paid for by another credit card, a Discover. Four hundred dollars.

They didn't bother asking Ralph what his employee needed all the cash for.

"So our victim left the store with nine hundred dollars cash in his pockets," Riley said. "He might as well send a smoke signal to the Murphy's Law gods saying, *Now would be a great time for me to get mugged.*"

On the surveillance tape the time stamp now read 21:48, nine forty-eight p.m. Evan Harding had been learning on the counter, chin on one hand, staring at nothing in particular, when the door opened and a young woman entered. Black skin, light-colored coat, a knit beret posed to keep her ears both warm and stylishly attired. She immediately crossed to the counter and began to speak. Forcefully, to judge from her unwavering gaze, the taut knuckles of each hand gripping the counter, the way she leaned so close to the plexiglass that her breath occasionally caused a faint sheen to appear on its surface. She had a purpose, and right then it focused on Evan Harding.

From the cameras behind the counter, Jack watched Evan straighten, take one step back, eventually raise both hands in weak protest. He responded to the woman, though whatever he said neither appeased nor much slowed her torrent of words.

Riley had been watching, as well. "Unhappy customer? Or psycho ex-girlfriend?"

"Without words, it's hard to tell."

She didn't produce any paperwork to bolster a claim of funds gone awry, but Jack couldn't quite see her as an ex, either. Evan hadn't raised an eyebrow when she first walked in, hadn't lifted his chin off his hand until she reached the counter. Jack had seen enough domestic disputes to know they usually involved a great deal of gesturing, with hands to the heart, head, stomach, sweeping angry swishes of the arms, back to the heart—all the places in which wounds were felt most deeply. This woman didn't gesture much at all, though she was clearly very, very angry. So much so that, safe behind his plexiglass wall, Evan Harding took another step back.

But no inching toward a phone or panic button and the woman had no weapon, so not robbery. Something personal.

Finally Evan began to speak up. From his breathing and the tension in his neck he didn't shout like the woman had, only spoke fast, pouring out words.

Whatever the confrontation had been about, it had not been resolved. The woman kept shouting, Evan kept up his weak defense, and it ended when she marched to the exit, tossed one last thought over her shoulder, and threw the door open so that it bounced against the adjacent window and rebounded with such force it would have hit her had she not been moving so fast.

Evan watched her go with a worried, wide-eyed expression, arms hugging himself.

But he did nothing, didn't call the police, didn't—apparently—leave a note or an e-mail to inform his boss of the incident. Just watched her go. It took some time before his posture relaxed again.

There were only two more customers after the woman, two men an hour apart, cashing routine checks. The first came and promptly went, the second wandered the lobby a bit, chatting, perhaps enjoying the last warmth he would feel that night, until it got too much even for him and he took his leave. About eleven forty-five Evan Harding began what must have been his closing routine, straightening stacks of forms, counting the cash in the drawer and locking same, exiting the building to go around and lock the outer door, and reentering the back to shut down the counter computer and turn out the lights.

Then he left.

The rear outside camera showed him stepping out onto the sidewalk, giving the knob one last shake to ensure the security of the door, and walking off to the west, the opposite direction of his apartment. The camera's bubble eye caught only the portion of the sidewalk directly outside the door, but it appeared to be as deserted as one would expect at midnight on a very cold weekday.

The cameras continued to record their dark, empty rooms.

"Huh," Riley said. "Where the hell was he going at midnight?"

"And who was the woman lambasting him up one side and down the other?" Jack asked, then said to the boss, "Can we download a copy of that video? From the woman's visit on?"

Ralph had been typing on his computer, intently enough that Jack had to repeat himself to get the man's attention. When he glanced over the boss's shoulder the screen showed columns of numbers . . . he had been double-checking his stores, making absolutely certain that no money had gone missing, that Evan's cash advances had been legitimate. The man turned with a satisfied sigh and said, "Sure. Only to USB, though. I don't have a DVD burner in it."

"Okay. Do you have a spare USB drive?"

Ralph scowled as if Jack had asked to date his teenage daughter. "No."

"Can you e-mail the video?"

"No-oo. I tried that once, and it was too big."

"Can you break it into smaller videos?"

"I look like Bill Gates? Or that Zuckerberg kid? I don't know how to do that." Ralph was losing patience, and Jack couldn't entirely blame him. Evan Harding's death didn't appear, so far, to have anything to do with his work at A to Z. It wasn't Ralph's job to investigate, and no crime had been committed against the check cashing store. On top of that he now needed to hire a new employee, and finding someone he could trust around stores of cash would not be easy.

"Okay," Jack said. "I'll call Maggie."

Chapter 6

She greeted them with: "Aren't you going to the autopsy? I was heading over there to pick up the tapings."

"Why?" Jack asked. In murders with close physical contact, such as a bludgeoning or a stabbing, transparent tape was pressed to the surface of the victim's outer clothes to pick up hairs, fibers, and other trace evidence possibly deposited by the killer. But when a gun was used. . . .

"Because your guy wasn't shot. He was stabbed. No exit, no projectile on the X-ray."

"So, not shot," Riley said.

"Not shot."

Jack said, "Either way, this might be important."

Maggie's gaze swept the area, taking in the large flat-screen, the cluttered desk, the mouse. She pulled a USB drive out of her pocket. "Where's the unit?" she asked Ralph.

The owner of A to Z Check Cashing had forgotten his impatience and need to get on with his workday as soon as he had opened the door to the Cleveland Police forensic specialist. He now ushered her to his swivel chair with the holes in its upholstery, hovered over her to click through the video system menu, and went so far as to offer her a cup of coffee. "Are you sure? It's of very good beans. I order them special from Ecuador. The best coffee is in Ecuador."

Jack could tell from the way she scooted as far to the side of her seat as she could that the A to Z boss invaded her personal space. He moved closer, hoping his looming presence would discourage the man. He knew he tended to intimidate people, usually when he didn't mean to. Right now he meant to.

And right now it didn't work. Ralph, apparently, didn't notice.

"That would be great," Maggie said. "I love fresh coffee."

The man presented the mouse to her as if it were a crumpet on a doily and hustled off to a worn drip coffeemaker with a dingy glass pot. Maggie immediately began to flick through the menu on the screen, twice as quickly as Ralph had, and with her usual efficiency she had the video playing back the confrontation of the unknown woman before Ralph got the filter in the pot.

Through the first viewing Jack had been watching for a physical confrontation or some sort of action to erupt. Upon re-watching, he was struck by the impossibility of it. Evan Harding had been completely safe behind the barriers formed by the plexiglass and the counter. Yet—

"She's threatening him," Maggie said.

"With what?"

"Don't know. But he *looks* threatened."

He did indeed. Evan Harding didn't argue back, not very forcefully at least, as he might if they were talking about some romantic conflict. He didn't seem impatient or defensive, as an employee might with a disgruntled customer. He looked worried. *Very* worried.

Ralph returned with a Styrofoam cup of liquid the color of pitch. He tried to wedge himself in next to Maggie but couldn't penetrate the cops flanking her; Jack plucked the cup from his fingers and placed it next to the keyboard. "Do you know that woman?"

Unhappy, the boss glanced up at the screen. "Nope."

"She hasn't been in here?"

The man took another look, seemed sincere when he answered, "Not that I know of."

"Any idea what she might have been complaining about?"

"Who knows? Everyone complains. People say they will send money and they don't and say they did. Or they send money and people say they didn't get it, you gotta send more. People think they sent money and they didn't because their brains are no good. Always, somebody's complaining. These people . . ." His voice trailed off, and his shrug seemed to sum up what a world of difficulties existed for those on the fringes of society, people without a home in nice suburbs, two cars in the drive, and a steady income.

Maggie set the backup program to copy the video clip to her external drive. A long white box with an inner line through it appeared, a spot of green at the left end. After several seconds, it grew another millimeter in a desultory way. Maggie politely took a sip of the coffee, though Jack knew she didn't drink hers black.

"How long is this going to take?" Jack asked.

"As long as it takes. They're all different."

Riley said, "We could go on to the autopsy. There's nothing else we need to do here—"

"No," Jack said. They could learn more from the victim's last hours than from the track the knife had taken through his body. This decision had nothing to do with the A to Z boss practically salivating over Maggie's shoulder.

She had meanwhile returned to the confrontation scene and zoomed in to one frame. "There's a logo on her bag."

The woman carried a tote bag hitched over one shoulder. Jack had thought the white on dark pattern might be a decoration, but now he saw it formed stylized letters led by some sort of half-circle blob of an icon. "I can't make that out."

The three men watched the cursor move as Maggie sorted through a few menu and preference options, then clicked on a tiny camera symbol. A still .jpg of the frame appeared on the screen. Then she went searching for a photo enhancement program, discovering a basic form of Photoshop.

Even Ralph tore his gaze away from Maggie's hair. "How did you do that? I didn't know you could do that."

She rattled off some directions, her voice fading as she tried to sharpen the picture. The icon became an amorphous shape under a thin half-moon arch, and there seemed to be three separate words. Jack still couldn't make them out.

"I could be wrong," Maggie began, which Jack knew meant she probably wasn't, "but I think that's the Cleveland Public Library."

"Huh," Jack said.

"Really?" Riley asked.

"Pretty sure. It's, like, an open book with the pages fanning and then the name. I know I've seen it there."

"Cool. Maybe she works there."

Maggie tempered this optimism. "They have a gift shop. Her being a library patron doesn't narrow your suspect pool much."

Riley said. "Sure it does. I haven't had a library card in thirty years."

"That, young man," Maggie told him, "is nothing to be proud of."

"Maybe so. Can you print me her picture?"

"No color," the boss of A to Z said. His fascination with Forensic Specialist Gardiner didn't mean he would be providing ink and paper to anyone who asked. He was a businessman, after all.

Maggie clicked the Print button, then selected a few other stills of the woman and the victim to save to the USB drive.

The green bar eventually reached its apex and, after another polite pretend sip of the coffee, she retracted the USB drive and thanked the boss of A to Z with a smile that made him forgive her the theft of a piece of copy paper. He bid her adieu with deep and obvious regret.

Riley asked his standard ending question: Was there anything else Ralph could possibly tell them about Evan Harding? Had he seemed worried? Stressed?

"No, and no. He was my easy employee. The guy I have on days—well, you can see he still isn't here. Every day it's a different excuse; the bus broke down, his stepson sick, the dog ran away. Sheesh. But Evan, a model. Customers like him, I like him, his girlfriend not have kids that get sick. No problems."

"What girlfriend?" Jack asked, hoping the comment had not been rhetorical.

"Skinny little thing, cute enough. Almost as pretty as that girl that was here. What was her name?"

The cops waited, then realized that he wasn't asking himself what Evan's girlfriend's name was, he was asking them what Maggie's name was. Jack's tone sharpened by a few strokes of the whetstone. "You've seen Evan Harding's girlfriend?"

"Yeah. She comes in here sometimes, stops by to say hi to him. They say sweet nothings through the plexiglass. I don't let people in the back unless I'm paying them to be here. I don't let my guys screw around on the clock, no holding customers up, but she was okay, never stayed long. Hi, how's it going, and she's back outside."

"What does she look like?"

Ralph grew solemn under their intense stares. "Black hair, maybe to here, straight. About so high. Maybe a hundred pounds, hundred-twenty. White skin. Not much breasts."

After that they could think of nothing else to do but thank him for his time and leave.

Outside on the sidewalk, again, the frosty air felt good for the first few minutes after the near-sauna of the A to Z offices, a sop to Jack's blossoming irritation. "Girlfriend lied to us from start to finish. She sent us to the movie theater purely to screw us over."

Riley agreed, not even complaining about the short hike back to their car. "If we hadn't noticed the name on those stubs, hadn't grasped at that straw, our victim would have stayed a ghost. Why? What's she hiding?"

"I suggest we go and ask her." Jack snapped open the car door with a bit more force than necessary. They drove the three city blocks, and promptly realized it would have been faster to walk by the time they located the entrance to the parking facility, got their ticket, and found a space. But this let them enter the building from the side and avoid the too-watchful girl at the building office. Jack had gotten away with retaining the victim's key card, and used it after a series of knocks went unanswered. Perhaps bursting in on Shanaya Thomas could be considered an unauthorized entry, but Jack had the strong feeling it wasn't going to matter.

They entered the room.

No, it wasn't going to matter.

Because Shanaya Thomas wasn't there. Neither were her clothes, her makeup, the photo of herself and Evan Harding.

"She bolted," Riley said in amazement, as if no other suspect or witness had ever done that to him before. "*Why?*"

"We find that out, we'll probably find out why Evan Harding is dead."

Chapter 7

With a sauerkraut dog happily swirling in his stomach, Rick Gardiner approached a trim two-story building on West 29th. The victim's apartment sat over a tea shop, and scents of jasmine and muffins wafted out to the street. Three bundled-up workers moved along the flat roof. One dropped a sheet of tar paper or melded shingles, Rick couldn't tell, off the end of the building to a dumpster on the ground below. It appeared to land smack in the center, the noise of impact increased by the vibration of the dumpster's walls.

"Who the hell gets a new roof in the winter?" Rick mused aloud.

"Someone whose ceiling leaks melted snow?"

"Those guys have got to be colder than a witch's tit."

Will opened the front entry door. It led them through a narrow hallway between the tea shop and a hair salon. "Just think, next time we have to cuff a guy with breath like a garbage can or chat up some punk or respond to a decomp, you can think, *Damn glad I'm not a roofer.*"

Rick had no intention of conceding toughest job status. "Don't know. They probably make more money."

A stairwell took them to the second floor. His partner, Will, had long been one of those health nuts, the kind that always wants to take the stairs instead of the elevator, even up to five or six flights. He often abandoned Rick in lobbies, and more annoyingly, still beat him to whatever floor they sought. But Rick didn't argue in dinky places with what might be questionable maintenance. The last thing he wanted to do was get stuck in an elevator until he was starving or dying of thirst or needing to pee, waiting on some pretty boy fireman dying to try out his ax for rescue.

They found the relevant door and knocked. The victim hadn't had any keys on him, and they wanted to try the simple approach before hunting up a building super and convincing him or her to open the door for them.

It paid off. The bright spot of the peephole darkened, and a woman's voice called out, "What is it?"

Rick and Will held up their badges and asked if they could speak with her.

"What about?"

"About Marlon Toner."

They heard the locks sliding open, and the woman opened the door. "What's he done now?"

After another check of their badges, she let them in to a small but tidy living/dining area with classic wooden moldings and thick area rugs over the hardwood floor. She gave her name as Jennifer Toner, then waved them to her sofa but didn't sit herself, standing in the middle of the room with her arms crossed. About thirty years of age, she had black skin, wavy hair to the middle of her neck, a medium build, and wore a thick sweater over dark blue jeans. She fixed them with a look that wavered between angry and hopeless. When Will suggested she sit down, she refused. She didn't offer them any coffee, which Rick could have used after that sauerkraut dog, but that was just as well. No need to drag this process out. He'd had family members spend twenty minutes puttering in the kitchen, grasping at any activity to put off the moment when they were told the very bad news.

No, this wasn't a social call.

Will asked if she were the wife of Marlon Toner.

"Sister."

Rick said nothing, and neither did Will for a moment. Jennifer Toner was definitely African-American, and the dead Marlon had been pale long before dying in the cold. But sometimes kids took wholly after one parent or the other, or perhaps they were stepsiblings. Whatever.

Will, always more—what do they call it, Rick thought, inclusionary?—went on. That's why they made a good team, Rick believed. Will handled all the touchy-feely crap, with Rick there to take down the bad guys when necessary. "Does he live here?"

"No."

Will said, "He has this address on his driver's license."

She flexed an eyebrow, a tiny reaction that told Rick she hadn't known that, but it also didn't surprise her.

She asked, "Has he been arrested?"

"You knew he had a drug problem?"

She didn't seem to notice the use of the past tense. "Yes—he didn't always. He was clean his whole life. Even in high school he wasn't part of that mess, no gangs, no dealing. Football kept him busy and that was all he cared about. Got a job, everything going good. It was that doctor." She sat down after all, absently sinking into an armchair.

"What doctor?" Rick asked.

Jennifer Toner settled back in her chair and rubbed one temple with long fingers. "It started five, six months ago. He stopped by—we're close, you know? There's only the two of us since my parents passed. Talkin' and catching up, but I could tell something wasn't right. He said he had a summer cold, but finally I asked him if he was high. He said no, then left. Couple weeks, he stops by work, looks the same . . . I know the signs. Called me all dragging because his girlfriend had left him but all perky by the time he showed up and it wasn't because I cheered him up, 'cause *I* told him he was an idiot, she had been great for him and he should get her back. Three months ago, he loses his job. Like I said, the signs."

Will bobbed his head sympathetically.

Yeah, yeah, yeah, Rick thought. Same old story. If he had five bucks for every time a family member said *but he was turning his life around . . .*

"The next time I saw him, I asked where he was living since he broke up with Taya and he wouldn't quite answer me. I told him flat-out he was a junkie and needed help, that I wasn't going to watch him die like practically everyone else we grew up with."

"Do you know what he was on?"

"Pills. That's why he kept trying to tell me he wasn't an addict, it was medicine; a doctor said he should take them. He had a real prescription from a real doctor, got the stuff from a real pharmacy, nothing illegal about it. I said he sure as hell looked exactly like the guys who live in the stairwells around St. Malachi's so I don't see what difference a prescription makes. We—" Her gaze fell to her lap, and she finished in what was surely an understatement, "We had a fight."

"We found him with a syringe," Will said, gentle but straightforward—she seemed like a chick who appreciated straight talk—but left out how it had still been in his arm. "So he had graduated from pills, or started shooting them."

Again, the flick of an eyebrow. Not surprising. The rise and fall of a drug addict's life had been witnessed so many times by people stuck in a certain milieu that small children could probably sketch it out for show-and-tell.

Jennifer Toner straightened, clearly deciding that enough of her family's dirty laundry had been sufficiently aired for one day. "Where is he now? Can I bail him out? Or is he at St. Vincent?"

The two cops exchanged a glance instead of answering, and grief invaded with the speed of lightning. "Oh no. No, no, no, no—"

"Ms. Toner, I'm sorry to have to tell you—"

"No, no, *NO!*"

This went on for a while. Will murmured soothing comments, made her some tea, offered to call in a Victim's Advocate to help make funeral arrangements and contact family members.

Rick spent the time surreptitiously checking his phone. He half expected Maggie to call or text, to try in some subtle way to find out more about his trip west. Surely she had clued the new boyfriend in, told him that Rick planned to check out Chicago and Minneapolis and follow the trail of that woman's nightmarish nursing homes and, with luck, pick up the trail of the vigilante who might have been stalking and finally killed her. Then behind *him* the trail of the guy who followed him from city to city, appropriating other cops' names in order to hide his obsession. That would be quite the coup for Rick—catch the vigilante, and expose Jack Renner as a lying, phony psycho.

He realized he was smiling and stopped before the grieving sister could catch him at it.

"What doctor?" he heard his partner ask.

She sniffled into a paper towel Will had fetched for her. "He showed me a pill bottle last week, trying to convince me that he wasn't taking *drugs*, it was *medicine*. Percodan. The doctor's name was Phillip Castleman. I Googled, looking for an address. I planned to go to his office and read him the riot act about being a pill pusher. Except he don't exist, at least not in Cleveland."

"Huh," Will said. "Unfortunately fake scripts can be gotten from all sorts of outlets, even mail order."

"No, the pharmacy had an address on East Fifty-fifth. I can't remember the name, something-something-pharmacy—

I know that doesn't help—but I remember Fifty-fifth. He'd get Medicare checks to pay for them. He told me all that, trying to convince me it was all legit, because I kept expecting him to ask me for money—that's how it always goes, right? But he never did. But he also wasn't old enough for Medicare, so I have no idea what that was all about."

"Not Medicaid?" Will asked.

"He said Medicare."

Rick found this less than fascinating. He and Will could tell the guys in Vice about it and be done. It was their job, not the homicide unit's.

Perhaps Will thought so too, because he finally got back on track, nailing down the standard details to include in the report. "When was the last time you saw your brother?"

"Two, two and a half weeks ago. That's when we argued—well, every time I see him now we argue—about the pills and where he was getting them."

"Okay. Had you spoken to him since then?"

"Yeah, couple times."

"When was the last?"

"About an hour ago." Her voice cracked. "I knew something was really wrong this time. He was talking crazy, like totally out of his head—"

"An *hour* ago?" Rick asked.

"Hour, hour and a half," she said, then noticed the cops' expressions. "What? What is it?"

Rick gulped.

Because the dead man behind the West Side Market had probably been dead since the evening before.

He got to his feet, took the victim's driver's license from an envelope in his pocket, and crossed the four feet of space in a blur of uncharacteristic speed. "Ms. Toner, is this your brother?"

She stared at the rectangle of laminated plastic. She turned it over as if an explanation may have been printed on the back. Then she turned it to the front, stared again.

The tears dried up as if under a heat lamp. Hope brightened her face and she nearly smiled. "I congratulate you two on your lack of stereotyping," she said, holding the card out to him, "but my brother Marlon is *black*."

"Then who's this?" Rick asked.

"Gentlemen, I have not the slightest idea."

Friday, 1:15 p.m.

The Medical Examiner's office staff had only begun the autopsy on Evan Harding when Maggie arrived. They had been delayed due to a contamination threat, a possible case of spinal meningitis, which had turned out to be a false alarm. Still Maggie entered the autopsy anteroom with light steps, her body automatically assuming that if she stayed very quiet perhaps the germs would not notice her.

The staff, however, did. They greeted her as a familiar face and asked where the detectives were.

"They should be right behind me."

"We're not waiting," one warned absently. Autopsies waited for no man, woman, or detective and the cops knew it.

Maggie knew it too and doubted the examination would present any information they couldn't already guess from the deep stains over the victim's chest. Maggie wanted to tape the clothes, so she watched as the autopsy assistants—called dieners—removed the victim's lightweight jacket and hung it on a disposable hanger. It would be damp from the now-melted snowflakes and the few trails of blood that never had a chance to dry in the cold, but there was nothing she could do about that. The tape would still work even on slightly damp material. The T-shirt, hung next, would not be as cooperative. Any loose hairs or fibers might now be glued to its surface by the sticky blood. But she'd try for whatever she could get. Even with all the advances of technology over the years, forensic science still required a large amount of luck.

"What did this guy get stabbed with?" one asked Maggie.

"I don't know. It wasn't left at the scene."

"Not a knife?" suggested the second diener.

The first disagreed, poking at the bloody chest to get a better look at something in that mass of red. "It's so small. And not linear."

Maggie moved closer. As the diener wiped the chest off with a sponge and a squirt bottle of dish detergent, she could see what he meant. The wounds—two of them—were small and round, the size of a cigarette burn.

"An ice pick?" the second diener tried.

"In the library with Professor Plum?" the first chortled. The second joined in. Evidently they had a standing joke of relating crimes to the *Clue* game. He checked the pants pockets—carefully, the risk of syringes or other sharp objects ever-present—and found an empty white envelope with nothing written on it and a tube of mint ChapStick in one, an open pack of gum and a toothpick in the other. These items were spread out on a tray to be photographed and stored under personal property, to be released to the family if they weren't wanted as evidence. The clothing would be retained until a trial or plea occurred.

Then they removed his shoes, socks, and pants, working quickly and efficiently. They had stripped nude so many dead that it seemed no different than putting more paper in the copier, yet there was always that unspoken twinge of empathy, that unavoidable pathos in seeing a fellow human so helplessly vulnerable. They could only get it over with as briskly as possible. A bit of distraction never hurt, either; today the two men discussed the current incarnation of a popular video game, and whether it would be an appropriate Christmas gift for their respective children.

"I don't think so," one said as he unzipped Evan Harding's jeans. "Those aliens, man. My girl would be okay, but my boy's too little. He'll have nightmares. When he has nightmares, then he's in bed with my wife and me."

"It's a trade-off," the other agreed, helping him pull the pants off with a sharp downward yank. "Bug you in the middle of the night, maybe, but you got peace all evening while they're glued to the TV."

"I'm not going to say anything about your parenting—what the hell is this?"

Maggie moved forward and craned her neck to see around the two large men. Evan Harding had something on his ankle. For a second she thought it might be a tattoo, but then the shape defined itself.

A key. The victim had a small, flat key taped to his ankle with a piece of clear packaging tape.

"Don't see that too often," the first diener said.

"You've seen it ever?" Maggie asked.

"You'd be amazed at the things people wear under their clothes," he intoned, and waited for the photographer to get a picture of it before peeling the tape, with the key adhered to it, away from the skin. Maggie thought of fingerprints and best preservation techniques, but didn't worry overmuch. The dead man appeared healthy, other than the damage to his chest. No injuries, no major scars, no bruises, nothing to suggest that he'd been abused, coerced, or trafficked, so she had no reason to think he hadn't taped the key to his ankle himself. She held out a sheet of the clear acetate, to which she placed tapes from clothing, and the diener spread it on the sheet, adhesive side down.

Mosler had been engraved on the body of the key. Maggie assumed it to be the name of the manufacturer. She doubted anyone else would put a decorative engraving on such a utilitarian object.

"What kind of key is that?" she asked.

"Hell if I know. Padlock? Safe deposit box? Locker?"

"Maybe it opens his diary. His little black book of secrets." the other joked.

Maggie held the transparent sheet with the key up to the light. "Maybe it does."

Chapter 8

Jack and Riley searched the small efficiency once again, more quickly this time since it now held a slightly smaller amount of stuff. Shanaya had clearly restricted herself to what she could carry, makeup, the photo (minus the frame, now scattered on the bed), some clean clothes and, Riley swore, a few packs of granola bars. He said, "If I were inclined to extend the benefit of the doubt, maybe she figured she'd better skedaddle before the management figured out she'd been living here without their knowledge. She said she can't afford the rent on one income anyway so maybe she decided to avoid this month's payment. Maybe. Except I'm not feeling inclined to extend much in the way of benefits after she lied to us about the victim's job."

Jack said, "And she took the notebook. Even though she had no idea what it was."

"Fabulous. Because *we* still have no idea what it was."

"But she sure as hell does. And I'll bet she knows who killed her boyfriend, too. Question is, is she running from us or from them?"

Riley examined the bathroom, opening and shutting

drawers. "And is she out there renting another apartment, or asking a friend to flop on their couch, or heading back to wherever home is?"

"Girlfriend travels pretty light," Jack said, observing again the lack of significant clutter over the entire room. "She could have left the city entirely."

Riley had finished and leaned in the doorway. "If she has a home, I'll bet it's not close. Kids who go home on weekends pick up more stuff, bring it back. My parents drove me to college in my dad's Mustang. They had to use my brother's van to bring me home at the end of the year. Though these two weren't really students, so all bets may be off."

"Wait," Jack said, "you went to college?"

His partner scowled. "Oh, ha ha. For a while, yes. And my now-honed brain says we should canvas the other kids on this floor, see if they know anything about Mr. and Ms. Check Cashing."

Jack didn't relish the idea. "They won't talk to us."

"They might if we tell them Shanaya may be in danger. Besides"—he glanced around the room, so hastily abandoned—"that's probably even true."

Friday, 10:15 a.m.

Jennifer Toner adjusted to the shock of learning her brother was *not* dead much more quickly than the shock of learning that he *was*. Ignoring the detectives' questions, she had simply called the man, and when a voice sounded on the other end of her palm-sized phone, pure joy suffused her face and her lungs sucked in the first full breath she'd taken in a half hour.

But cresting on this wave of soul ointment bobbed the fly of how she had just told two police officers that brother was a raging drug addict and, for extra splash, who his supplier might be. She blurted to her brother that a dead addict had been found using his name and her address and that cops were with her now, then abruptly rang off without letting said cops speak to him. She did reluctantly give them her brother's phone number, warning that he often didn't charge it or didn't pay the bill. Rick took that to mean that Marlon Toner would not be answering any calls from numbers he didn't recognize, effectively immediately.

"It must have been some guy with the same name," she said, almost happily.

"But his license had this address."

That *was* puzzling. "Then he must have stolen Marlon's identity."

"Has your brother reported getting bills that weren't his? Charges on his credit card?"

"I'm pretty sure he's outdoors, Detective. I don't think he gets bills at all."

Rick asked if she knew anything more about this doctor, the location of his office, what kind of medicine he practiced.

No hesitation on this topic. "Phillip Castleman. I remember thinking it sounded like a character in a made-for-TV movie. I did a web search for his name, but the address listed there is now an accounting firm. I haven't had a chance to look any more than that. I hope you can find him—if the doctor has to stop giving my brother the pills, maybe he'll have a chance to break off from the stuff. You'll track him down, right? See if he's a real doctor? Report him to the licensing board or whoever?"

Rick said, before Will could start making promises, "We'll give all this information to our Vice unit. They handle drug offenses."

She didn't argue, too busy spilling everything she could about Dr. Castleman to get annoyed at this passing of the responsibility buck. "I never got exactly straight what he treated Marlon for. Marlon said an old football injury acted up, but he never had an injury. Not once. He broke, like, a record about it. They called him Untouchable. So I know that wasn't it."

Will asked again about the pharmacy on East Fifty-fifth, which didn't garner them any new information, but Rick figured his partner wanted to go the extra mile, keep Jennifer Toner from suing the police department for scaring the ever-living crap out of her. So far she seemed too busy feeling relieved to get angry.

Which made it a good time to exit stage left. Rick stood, Will took the hint, they expressed more apologies and regrets and best wishes, sidled out the door, and reached the stairs without speaking. But then a roofer tossed a section of old shingles down to the dumpster and it clanged with such a heart-punching boom that Rick let out a very short scream. The echo of the noise covered it, to his everlasting luck. Will would have ragged him for the next four months.

Back in the car, he tried to sum up. "Okay, so we've got a drug addict getting fake scripts, which isn't our problem, and a dead guy who's using the first guy's name, which is. What now?"

"We go old-school," Will said, putting the car into drive and sliding a bit on the slush as he pulled away from the curb. "Fingerprints. DNA. They're probably doing his autopsy right now, unless he needs to thaw a bit first."

"Aw, hell," Rick said.

Friday, 1:55 p.m.

"Have you eaten yet?" Carol asked as Maggie entered the police Forensics Unit.

"Uh . . . no."

"Records had their Christmas party and, as usual, had too much food so they sent a plate of sandwiches over."

"Isn't it kind of early for Christmas parties?"

"Holiday party, to be more accurate. And you know Records—it's never too early to eat. They sent cookies, too."

"Say no more," Maggie said, and veered into the tiny space that held a sink, a mini-fridge, and the coffeemaker. It had been a long morning; she needed sustenance and especially a hot beverage. The city car she'd driven to the Medical Examiner's and back had no heat.

She made sure a fresh pot brewed and then dumped the tapings on the desk. Carol typed at her desk, the only sound in the place. "Where is everyone?"

"Denny's at court on that baby death case." Denny was their supervisor, a tall, too-slender black man with three children, including a newborn, at home. Maggie would check in with him when he returned, in case he wanted to talk about having to talk about a very small, very dead child. She guessed he probably wouldn't. "Josh is lecturing to the police academy group and Amy is somewhere collecting a toothbrush in a missing person case. How was your dead guy?"

"Too young to be dead. Other than that, probable mugging."

Carol stopped typing. "We don't have muggings in Cleveland. I mean, not fatal ones."

"I know." Maggie filled her mug with steaming coffee, added cream, and sank heavily into her desk chair. She sat perhaps fifteen feet from Carol but they could easily hear each other, with no fume hoods, thermocyclers, or chromatographs currently running. "But his wallet's been emptied, he hadn't been in a fight, and he had a key taped to his ankle."

This got Carol's attention. "A key?"

Maggie described the plain, small key affixed with tape.

"What's it go to?"

"I don't know," Maggie said, "and we couldn't exactly ask Evan Harding."

"Let me see it."

"I don't have it. It's at the ME's with the rest of his personal property. I doubt it has anything to do with anything . . . if the killer had known about it and thought it worth killing for, you'd think he would have tried harder to find it." She nibbled a cookie.

"You eat a sandwich too, young lady," Carol said. "You can't live on sweets."

"Holiday calories don't count."

"The calories you could use, but I'd prefer that you throw a little nutrition in there as well. What are you getting Jack for Christmas?"

Maggie choked on colored sprinkles, recovered, and said, "I'm not sure yet." Largely because she wasn't, of course, planning to do any such thing. People locked in uneasy and illegal conspiracies, she assumed, didn't usually exchange gifts on holidays. Except that she and Jack had used dating as a cover story, and dating people usually did.

"What's he getting you?"

"I don't know! Aren't gifts supposed to be a surprise?"

"Sometimes," Carol conceded. "It depends on the gift."

Maggie didn't know what the older woman might be getting at, but felt pretty certain she didn't want to know, so she helped herself to a placating wedge of turkey on whole wheat. Then the arrival of their boss rescued her from further speculation on appropriate gifts within newly-together, not-so-secret workplace romances.

"How did it go?" she asked Denny.

"Continued."

She and Carol groaned in unison. The only thing worse than testifying in court—always inconvenient, uncomfortable, annoying at best and gut-wrenching/grueling at worst—was getting psychologically prepared to be thrust into that vortex of uncertainty only to be told never mind, we'll try again tomorrow. When a case pled or was dismissed, that was different; one had bothered to change clothes and review the notes and done the deep breathing, but a plea meant it had ended. That induced a put-down-your-pencils-the-test-is-over, leaving-the-dentist's-office feeling of elated relief. But a continuance simply prolonged the agony, since not only did you conduct all the requisite psyching-up for nothing, you had to go through it all over again tomorrow or next week or next month. Maggie spoke with feeling. "That sucks."

"We have sandwiches," Carol added.

"Here." Denny shifted his briefcase to another hand and gave Maggie a large white envelope. "I passed Rick in the hallway. He said to tell you he has to know who this guy is."

She took the envelope as if it might spark and catch on fire. Was this some trick of Rick's? Some piece of evidence that might bolster his case against Jack? "Guy—?"

"OD victim found at the West Side Market this morning. I guess he had a fake ID on him."

She said okay, trying not to sound suspiciously relieved, and bit into one of Records' hand-me-down sandwiches.

Friday, 1:15 p.m.

Jack and Riley drove through streets padded with snow back to the station. The students they'd been able to find on Evan Harding's floor uniformly reported that "the guy and that Sherry girl" were polite but not particularly outgoing. They were only passed in the hall or laundromat; they didn't hang out and talk, didn't attend movies or games or social events in the common areas, and were never seen in the computer lab or fitness center. From there he and Riley had gone to the Medical Examiner's office, to be told that the autopsy had been completed without their presence—no surprise, the place couldn't afford to get backed up—and that their victim had died of two stab wounds with a sharply pointed, sticklike object—also no surprise. Aside from the aforementioned wound, the victim had been completely healthy, no signs of mistreatment, illness, malnutrition, or drug abuse.

Since he had died of homicide, they collected his personal property, consisting of the largely empty wallet, a plain silver ring, an inexpensive watch, the name tag, and the small key still affixed to its piece of tape. Jack thought to ask if anyone had called to pick up the body or ask about the property, but the deskmen said no one had.

"Girlfriend doesn't care?" Riley speculated as he steered the car up Carnegie. "Or she's still too discombobulated?"

"I don't even have a guess. Maybe she's skipping out on the rent and is on her way back to her family or his family. Maybe she can't afford a funeral so she's not acknowledging the body. Maybe she has a pretty good idea who killed him for reasons anything but random, and she's making herself scarce."

Riley frowned. "For all we know, she may have been the target all along. The guy killed the cashier to get to her."

Jack reasoned aloud. "But this wasn't any drawn-out confrontation. Evan Harding wasn't tortured to get him to give up the girl's location. And if he caved immediately, the killer didn't go get the girl."

"Maybe he couldn't get in. The building had security, pretty solid doors. There probably wouldn't have been students to follow in, not after midnight in the freezing cold."

"Or maybe the murder was quick and simple because they meant to kill Evan and only Evan."

"The question is did he pick the wrong girlfriend, or did she pick the wrong boyfriend? Right now we have no way to know."

"Nope," Jack agreed. "Let's go see Maggie."

"Any reason other than the obvious?"

"I want to see what she thinks of this key."

She didn't think much of the key. "Yeah, I saw that. He had it taped to his ankle."

"What does it go to?"

"I don't know."

The two detectives stared at her blankly. She stared back, equally blank. "What do you think, I have a database of keys?"

"Yes," Riley said around a mouthful of corned beef. He had snagged the last of Records' leftovers. "Don't you?"

She gave him a look, part pity, part annoyance, and slid a sheet of paper across her desk toward them, trading for the key inside its clear plastic Property bag. "Here. I cropped the clearest photo I could grab from the video, cleaned it up as best I could—meaning I played with the contrast a bit. The video analysis unit might be able to do a little more, but probably not. Out here in the real world, video quality is what it is."

Jack picked up the photo of the woman from the check cashing store. She had short hair and wide eyes, appeared to be of average height and build, though height could be difficult to estimate with the camera angled down from the ceiling.

The second photo showed both the woman and Evan Harding. When Jack had watched the video it seemed that Evan had been nearly cowering, looking right and left for escape, but now that this one frame had caught his expression . . . he seemed more concerned than scared. He seemed to be looking for something, scanning the rear of the counter for some item that would satisfy the woman.

Maggie had been typing while he looked, and Riley ate. "It probably goes to a safe or a safe deposit box."

Riley coughed up a rye seed. "I thought you said you didn't have a database of keys!"

"I guess I do. It's called Google. The Mosler Safe Company started in Cincinnati and lasted over a hundred years. Filed Chapter 11 in 2001, but part of it merged with a Canadian company and Diebold bought the rest." She picked up the clear Evidence bag again, gazing at the small, flat key, its head rounded on either side like a cherub's cheeks. The teeth were squared off, not shaped with jagged angles like most house or car keys. "I don't find a way to distinguish a safe key from a safe deposit box key. It could even open a smaller box inside a safe."

"So we're looking for a safe made or a bank built prior to 2001," Jack summed up.

"Most likely."

"That's—" Riley said.

"Not very helpful, I know. We could try contacting Diebold."

A knock sounded, and Carol opened the door to admit Rick and Will. Will, Carol, Riley, and Josh, now back at his desk checking his Facebook posts, immediately looked uncomfortable. Rick scowled. Jack frowned. Maggie sighed.

The detectives signed in and approached, Riley and Will, at least, exchanging hellos. Rick pointedly ignored Jack and spoke to Maggie. "Did you ID those prints?"

"Maybe." She stood and moved to the computer terminal with the fingerprint program. A few taps and her voice brightened by a few photons. "Yes, actually. I only scanned his right thumb to begin with and the pattern lights up like a Christmas tree . . . pardon the topical reference. Raymond Winchester, date of birth 4-27-83. I'll print you a copy."

Rick and Will exchanged a glance. "So why is he using Marlon Toner's name and address?"

"Stolen ID?" Riley suggested.

"It's got something to do with fake scripts," Will said. "Don't know what yet. Maybe the doctor can give us a hint. What's up with your guy in the cemetery?"

"Might be supersimple, might be superweird. All I'm sure of so far is that it's not going to be something in between."

Rick had pulled out his phone, fiddling with some of its icons. Maggie figured this provided a way to avoid eye contact with anyone, especially Jack, seated at Maggie's side, but then he suddenly raised its rear surface to the two of them and said, "Say *cheese*."

The digital *click* sounded before her jaw could drop.

"What are you doing?" Her tone sounded disproportionally sharp, a bit panicked, and guilty as hell.

"Getting a picture of the happy couple." He stared at Jack with equal parts challenge and triumph. There was nothing Jack could do; with both Riley and Will standing there, he could hardly protest or demand the photo be deleted. He had to play it as cool as ever, as if he had nothing to hide, no reason for concern. He sat as if made of stone.

Maggie tried to copy him, but her heart pounded and she knew her face could not conceal this turmoil. She must look stricken. She tried to breathe in, tried to distance herself. This was Jack's problem, and Jack would have to deal with it.

Except if Jack's true past were revealed, it would become her problem. Very much indeed her problem.

"Let's go," Rick said to Will, almost giddily. Maggie handed him the copy of Raymond Winchester's fingerprint card. When he glanced down to take it, however, the giddiness evanesced as if it had never been. "What the hell?"

Then Will saw it, too. He picked up one of the pictures that Maggie had printed. "What are you doing with a picture of Toner's sister?"

Chapter 9

Friday, 2:30 p.m.

All four detectives went together to speak to Jennifer Toner, a joint effort that appealed to exactly no one. But their investigations had dovetailed, and they needed answers. Now that Jennifer had her brother back, she didn't need to be forthcoming with them and instead had the incentive not to be—especially if she'd somehow been involved in Evan Harding's death.

So now all four of them smelled the jasmine tea and climbed up the worn steps. Roofers were hard at work and Jack felt a prick of amusement when the boom of falling shingles falling echoed up and down the stairwell, making Rick start. He wondered if he shouldn't be so petty. Rick might be lazy, but nothing worse could be said about him. Then he remembered that the guy had cheated on Maggie, and that made it not petty at all.

Besides, he could handle Rick Gardiner.

To everyone's relief, Jennifer Toner had remained at home and answered the door, albeit with an unenthusiastic expression. "You brought reinforcements?"

No coffee would be offered this trip, either. She sat in an

armchair and let the men form a semicircle around the other side of the room. Will and Rick sat on the sofa, Riley pulled over a kitchen chair, and Jack leaned against a windowsill, caught between chill coming off the glass and heat spilling from the radiator.

As they had agreed before driving over, Rick and Will went first, asking if she knew a man named Raymond Winchester (no), if they could speak to her brother, who was not in any trouble (she'd ask him to call them, but professed no knowledge of where he might be, where he slept nights, or who he might hang out with), or where he found this doctor who didn't have an address listed on the Internet (she didn't know).

It took about twenty minutes to exhaust their reexamination, and then Will sat back into the overstuffed sofa and turned it over to Jack and Riley.

Riley said, "Do you ever use check cashing services?"

Her expression seemed so baffled at this change in topics that Jack thought perhaps they had all been mistaken, that Jennifer Toner only bore a resemblance to the woman at A to Z. "No. Why?"

"Not even one on Bolivar?"

No, Jack thought, they weren't mistaken. Jennifer Toner went still from scalp to toes.

They waited.

"What's this about?" she asked, her voice low and tightly controlled.

Riley spoke with equal calmness. "Were you at A to Z Check Cashing last night?"

Jack saw her calculating chances, weighing possible scenarios in her mind. Then a deep breath and maybe the realization that she hadn't done anything wrong—at least on camera—prompted her to tell what sounded like the truth. "Yes."

"Why?"

"That's where he cashes the checks."

"Marlon?"

"Yes. That's why he doesn't ask me for money—he's getting checks from Medicare to pay for these medications. Big checks. He told me so to prove to me that the prescriptions are real, it's a real doctor giving him real meds, and so that's why I shouldn't worry about him."

Riley took his time to formulate a question. "So he's getting checks you think are for a fraudulent claim."

"I don't think. I know. Marlon turns into an addict and then he winds up with a boatload of cash as well? There's something way shady going on here, more than a doc selling pills on the side."

"Yes, I see. But what does—what did you say to Evan Harding?"

"Who?"

"The cashier. The guy behind the counter."

"The *cashier*? Why, he complain? I didn't yell at him. I didn't use any bad language . . . well, not *really* bad. I mean, seriously—"

"What *did* you say to him?"

"I asked how they could cash thirty thousand dollars in checks from a drug addict! They had to know they were fake. Did they get a cut or what?"

"Thirty thousand?"

"That's what the receipt showed—he came 'round here waving bills, acting big. He knew I suspected he was dealing so he showed me the receipt, that it was for medical reimbursement. Nothing to worry about. I said he should take that money and pay for the best rehab facility we could find. He walked out and wouldn't pick up the phone for a couple days. It made me so mad, I went down there—last night." Something occurred to her. "How'd you guys know?"

"You were on video."

She had enough other things on her mind to put off asking why they'd reviewed the A to Z security tapes in the first place. "How'd you get from a video to—did that guy complain about me? Remember my brother's name?"

"You told him about your brother?" Rick asked.

She glanced at the detective as if he might be a bit slow. "Yes. That's why I was there. I wanted to know why they kept cashing checks for a Marlon Toner that they had to know were not right. Mostly I wanted to know who issued the checks." She rubbed her forehead. "I wanted to work backward to Marlon's source of the pills. I also thought maybe he had to give an address to cash the checks, and that would tell me where he's staying. But he, the cashier, didn't tell me anything."

"So you didn't know Evan Harding previously?" Riley asked.

Clearly all four of them were a bit slow. "The cashier guy? No, of course not."

"Had you ever been to A to Z before?"

"No," she said, then added, "I have direct deposit."

"Where do you work?"

"The library. Downtown branch." Their emphasis on the check cashing store instead of her brother confused her, and they kept up the questions to keep her from pondering the connections. If she had killed Evan Harding, this would be the best way to trip her up. If she hadn't, she'd stay perplexed.

"What did Ev—the cashier say?" Riley asked.

"He played dumb. Didn't know who I was talking about, they cash checks, they wouldn't cash the check if it wasn't good because they all know what government checks look like and they have lists of what the address should be and the numbers that are supposed to be in the routing, blah, blah, blah. No matter what I asked—what I really wanted was this Dr. Castleman's phone or address or anything—he kept saying he didn't know, didn't have any information about where the checks come from, they won't know anything about the claims that prompt the payments, he just works there, more blah. I wanted him to find the check so I could see if it had the doctor's address, or an account number or patient number or *anything*, but he insisted he couldn't do that. First, he said it would be impossible to find it in all the checks that had come in, especially if I didn't know the exact date and time cashed, and even then the memo information would be confidential, and so on and so on. I finally gave up. I didn't hit him or anything," she added. "No matter what he says. Well, if you've got the cameras, you know."

"He looked awfully worried. Are you sure that's all you said?"

She straightened her spine. "I didn't threaten him."

But her face didn't seem as certain.

"Are you sure?" Will pressed, his voice gentle but implacable. Jack saw how Will was clearly the people person in that partnership, as Riley took that role in theirs. The idea that he, Jack, might have something in common with Rick messed with his world a little bit.

"I said I would call the police. That could hardly be considered a *threat*."

"Was that all to the conversation?"

She considered this. "Yes. Obviously he wasn't going to tell me anything, so I left."

"You gave up?"

"I'd never give up on my brother," she declared with grave dignity. "I thought I would contact the medical license board, the A.M.A., whoever might be able to give me contact information on this Dr. Castleman. I was going to start on that today, but—then you guys showed up."

A pause. Jack felt pretty certain that this woman had nothing to do with Evan Harding's impalement in the Erie Street Cemetery, but he couldn't be 100 percent certain. He had been fooled by an innocent expression before . . . albeit not often.

Will said, "Evan Harding was murdered last night."

The slightest hesitation while she recalled his name once more. "The cashier guy?"

"Yes."

"Oh, how awful." Instantly her face lost its angry cast and turned to deep sympathy. "Somebody shoot him? Rob the place?"

"No."

That caught her up short. The vulnerabilities of a cash store open during the late night were easy to picture. "Then what happened?"

"It's an open investigation," Riley answered without answering. He asked if she had seen anyone or anything suspicious during her visit, not necessarily in the store but on the street, if Evan had said anything to indicate he expected either company or trouble, how long she had been in the area afterward. A chorus of nos; she had left the street immediately.

Jack moved away from the radiator, now scorching his thigh. A bizarre coincidence that two deaths in one night seemed to be vaguely connected by one Jennifer Toner, but that had to be all it was. A coincidence. They did occur, even in police work.

Just not often.

Chapter 10

Maggie, fortified by sandwiches and the calm that had descended on the unit once all the detectives left, wrote up her identification of the West Side Market victim as Raymond Winchester and set it aside for either Josh or Amy, both also trained in latent print analysis, to verify her conclusion. Now she had time to look at the tapings from Evan Harding's clothing.

Tapings were akin to opening a book, an introduction to the person's life and current situation, their backstory written in fur from their pets and paint crumbles from the worn walls of their apartment and a long, wavy hair with colored tips from their last date. But without those corresponding facts in hand, the lines she drew from the tiny trace evidence went nowhere, so tapings were more like an ancient tablet crammed with cuneiform: interesting to look at, but impossible to read.

She tried to make out what she could.

She quickly screened the tapings with a stereomicroscope. Its large lens functioned as a magnifying glass, lights aimed onto the surface from adjustable side bulbs. But the focus could waver with the not-perfectly-applied piece of tape, so to really get a good look at something she had to use xylene to dissolve the tape adhesive and transfer the hair or fiber or fragment item, very carefully, to a glass slide. There she could drop it into a tiny pool of mounting media and trap it forever between the slide and a cover slip, made of an incredibly thin slice of glass. Then the item could be viewed with transmitted light, and the hardened liquid media and the glass substrates worked with the optics of the microscopes instead of against it.

Evan Harding's girlfriend, Maggie guessed, had longer hair than his, hence the single, undulating strand of jet black on the sheet from his jacket. He didn't have a cat or a dog. He had the general conglomeration of random fibers that everyone had on their clothes—cottons, synthetics that glowed under fluorescent light, larger, thicker ones from a carpet or some other heavy-duty upholstery. Flat, brown fragments with desiccated veins running through them—dead winter leaves, no doubt from lying in the cemetery with its collection of graceful magnolias. There were many smaller ones, flakes of old leaves. Perhaps the groundskeepers had mulched them at some point. There were a *lot* of those, as if he'd been rolling around on the ground . . . while keeping his clothing remarkably clean at the same time, plus leaving the blood in one place at the scene.

After mounting some of these brittle items on a slide, she rotated the oculars until she could see the surface of the leaf fragment with as much magnification as possible. The lab lacked a scanning electron microscope, but that seemed a silly thought because even with one she still wouldn't know what she was looking at. Aside from marijuana with its distinctive hairs and sticky surface, she could identify vegetation as vegetation and no more than that. There would be no determining a silver maple from a New Zealand Kauri, certainly not from a dead, barely two-millimeter square flake.

These flakes had hairs, she noticed, but they didn't taper to an end like marijuana. They seemed to end in a stump or a ball-like shape.

Also among the flakes and the fibers she saw a number of frilly sticks, thin slivers with even thinner slivers branching on each side in a uniform pattern. More leaves, with the lamina overlay decomposed away, leaving only the ribs and veins? But veins in vegetation were randomly spaced. She rotated the oculars, increasing the magnification from 10x to 20x.

If this came from a leaf, it was the most obsessively uniform plant structure she'd ever seen. The main center rib had side ribs coming off it, each at a perfect forty-five-degree angle, each equidistant from the next like slats in Venetian blinds. At the higher magnification she could see a second set of ribs emitting from the entire length of the side ribs, also at forty-five-degree angles and also equidistant. This second set branched again, structures so tiny she could only see a suggestion of texture rather than the actual construction.

There were a great many of these fragments as well, but not all chopped to similar sizes like the leaves.

Maggie sat back, her neck beginning to ache from bending over the eyepiece, and considered. She knew what they were. But what were they doing all over Evan Harding?

Jack appeared at the door shortly afterward. "You texted?"

"I did." She let him in, after he dutifully signed the entry log. He said nothing until sinking heavily into a spare swivel chair near her desk. Then he glanced around to see might be in earshot.

"Rick didn't say anything to me about his field trip," he began. "But as I said before, if you try to convince him not to go, it will only make him more suspicious. I don't care what he does, but even if there's a worst-case scenario and I have to bail, then I have to bail. Nothing he would find could damage you anyway so . . ." His voice trailed off as he noticed her slightly perplexed expression. "That's not what you texted about?"

She couldn't help but smile. "Nope."

"Okay . . . what, then?"

"This is going to sound a little crazy."

He rubbed one temple. "The whole day so far has been a little crazy."

"Did Evan Harding have any pets?"

He blinked, but it didn't hold up his answer. "No."

"Or his girlfriend?"

"It was a one-room apartment, and pretty bare. We would have found a puppy hiding under the bed."

"What about a bird?"

He blinked again.

She told him about the tapings, the leaf fragments and the other type of fragments. "They're feathers. The soft, downy feathers that keep birds warm and cushioned. And there are a lot of them. We've been to his workplace and Ralph didn't have a cockatiel in the office or anything like that, so if he didn't have a bird in his apartment, where are all these feathers coming from?"

"Pigeons?"

"If he'd been sleeping in a coop, or even on the street near a statue, maybe. But his clothes were clean. Of course he might have a mother who keeps parakeets and she does his laundry twice a week . . . that would explain it."

Jack said, "It's going to be difficult to find family with the girlfriend in the wind—and according to her he didn't have any. So far, 'Evan Harding' doesn't really exist. No credit history, no record, no social media, no phone records, no prior addresses have turned up. Social Security said the number he listed on his employment application isn't fake, but they're running it down now."

So a bunch of feathers on the victim's coat and pants

seemed unimportant . . . but with such a lack of available information, every little bit might help. Besides, Maggie loved coming up with theories, answers to the puzzle. It was why she had become a forensic specialist in the first place. "Then there's the leaves, or flakes of leaves. I think they're tobacco. I can't be a hundred percent sure because there are a number of leaves that have sort of spiky stalks on their surface—"

Jack seemed even less impressed by leaves than he did by feathers. She spoke more hastily. "But the victim wasn't a smoker, I didn't get a whiff off his clothes. Did the girlfriend—?"

"No."

"And Ralph's workplace, bless his heart, smelled of curry and week-old coffee but not smoke. So I started to think, I've got feathers and maybe tobacco, leaf tobacco, not the tinier, twistier cured tobacco that's in cigarettes. So I called up my friend Quesha at the Historical Society—"

"The what?"

"The Cleveland Historical Society," she explained, not patiently. She had told him many months ago that she was on the board . . . but at that moment they'd been caught between a murderer and her dying victims so perhaps he could be forgiven if her choice of extracurricular activity had slipped his mind. "Quesha looked up past and current cigar manufacturers. Cigars are usually rolled from the whole leaf. Tobacco used in cigarettes is minced up before its rolled . . . though of course this debris could be from precut leaves. . . ." She paused, feeling how absurd this theory must be, but unwilling to forget it now that she'd put the work in.

"Go on," he told her. "Evan Harding had tobacco and feathers on his clothing."

"Exactly. Two things that don't normally go together. After she found a long list of defunct cigar manufacturers, I asked her to check if any of those buildings had also housed down factories."

"Down—"

"Down pillows, cushions, etc."

"Feathers."

"Exactly," she said again.

Jack's expression shifted to one of more interest. "I'm assuming you found one, or you wouldn't have brought this up."

"You assume correctly." If she hadn't been successful, she never would have breathed such a crazy idea to him. "I found two."

"*Two?*"

"One we're not so sure of. It was a cigar factory in the mid-1800s and a mattress company in the early 1900s."

"That was a long time ago."

"I think so, too. But the other is a bit more promising. It's actually an interesting story—"

"Maggie—"

"I'll talk fast. A twenty-year-old Hungarian immigrant named Julius Caeser Newman started a cigar-making operation in 1895 with one employee—himself. Everything goes great until the advent of cigarettes, until there's only him and one other cigar maker in town, Grover Mendelsohn. They merge to form M & N Cigar Manufacturers, expand to a building across from what's now Jacobs Field. He eventually bought out Grover."

"You mean Progressive Field," Jack said, trusting there to be a payoff from this history lesson.

"Whatever. Times stayed tight for cigars, though, and all the premium makers had moved to Florida. So in 1954 he moved the whole operation to Tampa, where they still operate today. J.C. Newman is actually the oldest cigar manufacturer in the country."

"And you think the tobacco on Evan Harding's clothes has been hanging around for nearly seventy years?"

"It sounds a bit far-fetched when you put it that way. But yes, it's there on his clothes, and there's no feathers or cigars at A to Z Check Cashing or, according to you, his apartment. The building stayed empty for many years during one of Cleveland's downturns. Then the Ohio Feather Company—yes, that's the real name—expanded into the old cigar factory. They left it for Cincinnati to specialize in custom-made down products for luxury stores and hotels."

"And they moved out in—?"

"2005. Right before the financial crash melted down the mortgage and rental market for both homeowners and businesses. Not to mention that business startup and expansion ground to a halt, so the building stayed empty for a long time."

"With abandoned feathers still inside."

"Theoretically. I know this is a long shot, but—"

"I'll take it."

She didn't hide her surprise. "Really? It's—this theory assumes that large factory buildings aren't scrubbed and vacuumed like an office suite or a house would be, which, yeah, they're not graded on looks, but still that's a lot of debris hanging around for a really long time."

"Doesn't matter. I've got nothing else, and I'm not ready to write Evan Harding off as a random robbery-homicide until I can clear up at least a few of these details." He paused as if mentally flipping through his thin pile of facts. "You said that building is across from Progressive Field?"

"East Ninth and Bolivar." Literally up the street from A to Z and on the next corner from the Erie Street Cemetery. That was why she had shared her crazy theory. The building's location was one more coincidence in a growing pile of coincidences. "That could be where he went after work last night, why he turned left instead of right after leaving Ralph's, why he wound up in the cemetery instead of on a direct route home."

Jack rubbed his eyes with the long fingers of one hand. "Time for a field trip. Thanks—that's . . . good work."

"The beauty of trace evidence. It may be tiny, but it's real."

He leaned forward, preparing to leave, and his gaze intensified. "And about Rick," he began, then faltered.

"I'm not worried," she said, making her voice sound firm and calm and truthful. Lies, in other words, because she felt very worried indeed.

"Nothing can come back to you," he said.

As if that were her only concern.

Chapter 11

Friday, 3 p.m.

The woman on the phone wept. Her words came between the tightly controlled sobs. "But I got a refund! How did they send me a refund if I owe?"

"You made an error on your return. It was caught during a routine audit," Shanaya said, trying to sound sympathetic. She had been trained to stay firm, keep up the pressure, but she preferred to sound like a kindly government employee just doing her job. It added realism. It also took less energy, and she often lacked energy. Shifts at the center lasted twelve, sixteen, and sometimes eighteen hours when a worker didn't show up and their phone had to be covered. And workers often didn't show up—they moved on, got a different job, went on a bender or developed empathy for real.

Then when she finally got into her bed, Evani would come in from the check cashing store and wake her again. Shanaya couldn't remember the last time she'd had an uninterrupted night of sleep. But it would all be worth it if they stuck to their plan.

Problem was, Evani hadn't stuck to the plan.

Now she said into her headset, "Don't worry too much.

This can still be fixed if you take care of it immediately. You might not have to go to jail if you can make up the funds right away."

A shuddering breath. The woman—what was her name again?—tried to get herself under control before entering the bank. "Okay. I've got it. Four thousand dollars, right?"

"Yes," Shanaya said, then added, since this had been going so well, "you might want to get four thousand five hundred, in case there are extra charges for paying by phone." She heard a car door slam and an increased wind, other engines and background noise as her victim now stood outside in her bank's parking lot.

The victim didn't ask why Shanaya, in charge of taking the payment by phone, wouldn't already know if there were charges for paying by phone. But then, she hadn't asked why the Internal Revenue Service wanted her to pay back taxes using iTunes gift cards. She hadn't asked why the IRS made first contact by phone instead of a registered letter. She hadn't asked why she should immediately get in the car and drive to her bank to get four thousand dollars in cash, then afterward take that cash to a Walgreens or CVS and use it to purchase gift cards, the numbers of which she would relay over the phone to a complete stranger. All the woman thought about, obviously, was staving off that knock at the door where U.S. Marshals would take her into custody, seize all her assets, and drag her off to the federal penitentiary.

Which suited Shanaya fine. Especially since she didn't have particularly good answers to any of those questions and didn't even know where the nearest federal penitentiary might be located. She hadn't heard of any in the Cleveland area, but she'd only been there about three years.

Through her headset she heard a chime in the background of the woman's world, perhaps from the bank's door as she entered. "Remember, don't tell the people at the bank why you want the money. Just withdraw it." She had told Mrs. Whoever that before, but who knew how much the frazzled woman heard or retained?

"Why not?"

"They will freeze your accounts if they learn you are under indictment by the IRS. Then you won't get the money to fix this situation and we will have no choice but to arrest you."

"Oh my God."

"Don't worry." It wouldn't do Shanaya any good for the woman to have a heart attack on the marble floor of Fifth Third. "I will help you fix this today, and you won't have to be scared anymore."

"Oh, thank you."

No, Shanaya thought, thank *you* for making it an easy day for me. A decent haul would get her pit boss off her back. The guy was relentless, patrolling the aisles like a junkyard dog, ready to bite anybody who hung up without immediately connecting the next call in the queue, who spent too much time on a bathroom break, who took four or five seconds to check their personal phone, who sounded as if they were going soft on a customer. The big boss's pit *bull*, trained to attack.

"If they weren't guilty of something, they wouldn't give in so quickly," he told his staff over and over. "If they didn't have money to spare, they wouldn't hand it over because of a phone call. They are the haves. We are the have-nots."

So even when, for instance, the last Mr. Whoever insisted that he had only four hundred dollars in the bank and had already fallen a month behind in his rent, Shanaya didn't falter. "Would you rather deal with your landlord or the U.S. Marshal service?" Yes, she told him, it seemed awful that one child languished in jail and the other had died of leukemia, and he had no siblings or even friends that might give him a place to sleep, but that did not change the fact that this money had to be repaid to the government or the criminal charges would stand. And he had, after what seemed like two solid hours of wheedling—on his part, not hers—given her the four hundred dollars via an Apple Pay card.

They are the haves. Because surely, if losing the funds would cripple them so much, they wouldn't do it. Right?

"I'm waiting in line," Mrs. Whoever said, as if Shanaya might be getting impatient.

"I understand," she said, with a clear undertone of *as long as you understand in turn that the U.S. government doesn't have all day.* The trips to the bank or the Western Union or the CVS or the ATM were the most nerve-wracking part of this. Not only was it pure downtime without any money coming in, it gave the person a chance to think without Shanaya barking in their ear. For that reason Shanaya preferred women with children. Children provided enough distraction to bamboozle a brain surgeon. They whined, cried, argued, or simply talked nonstop. Plus they formed the greatest combination stick/carrot in the universe. "What will happen to your children if you go to jail?" The very image broke the most savvy target.

So glad she didn't have any.

Aside from those annoyances and the grueling schedule, her job had a few perks. Free parking or discounted bus/rapid transit passes. A day-care center on site for those who had small children (though anyone who left their desks to check on those kids for more than five minutes each hour would be fired—and bathroom and meal breaks came out of that same pool of break time). Quality headsets attached to the phones. Best of all were the meals—breakfast served during a ten-minute window each morning, forcing her to get to work on time, and then a fifteen-minute lunch. These perks worked to the management's advantage, keeping employees from having any excuse to arrive late, go home early, or leave the building at all, but still free food was free food. They had comfortable chairs, at least, and personal things like photos could be taped to the cubicle walls to personalize the place a bit, which Shanaya never did. A tiny sticker depicting a pair of cherries on the stem fixed to the edge of her monitor represented the only piece of whimsy in her workspace and she hadn't even put it there. Comfortable didn't mean homey, but she didn't need it to. And the pay was good. Very good, especially the way Shanaya did it.

A rustling sound, and Mrs. Whoever's voice became muffled. She had dropped her phone into a pocket or purse or might be holding it against her shoulder while she carried on a conversation with the bank teller. It seemed to go on longer than a simple "I wish to make a withdrawal" should.

Shanaya exhaled in a sharp, frustrated breath. "What's she saying? What are you doing?" she demanded of the pocket, or purse, or shoulder.

A pause, and then as if she had heard her, Mrs. Whoever came back on the line. "The teller says she has to check something."

"Check what? Don't you have enough money in the account?"

"I *should*."

"I'm very sorry, but that may not be good enough to dismiss the warrant. You will still be subject to arrest if the amount is not paid in full." The pit bull hovered behind her, Shanaya knew. Like a bell on a cat, his aftershave announced his presence. She kept her voice calm but insistent, her computer screen open to what they called the code reception page, the blank boxes ready for the gift card, credit card, wire transfer numbers as soon as she could pry them out of this deadbeat.

"No, I have it. I know I have it. Unless—"

"Unless *what*?" Shanaya asked without wanting to know. She had already had to listen to the sad tale of the woman's dead daughter, whom she had raised single-handedly after her husband went off to make a career in the military and got killed by an IED. (Mrs. Whoever described that as an IUD.

Shanaya didn't correct her.) And to have that daughter murdered by her own no-good husband twenty years to the day after her daddy had bought it. Yes, Shanaya had agreed, very sad, figuring that now she didn't need that much money, with only herself to look after. Right?

"Unless . . . wait." Muffling again, the phone stashed out of sight, the woman doing her level best to keep her fugitive status a secret from the bank personnel.

More low tones. Try as she might—and it wasn't easy because the chubby guy in the next cubicle who always seemed to eat things with cabbage in them kept shouting as if unaware that the headset mouthpiece rested only one inch from his lips—Shanaya couldn't make out any of the words of the conversation.

Mrs. Whoever returned. "She's getting a manager."

No, no, *no!* "Why?"

"She says she has to clear it with him."

"Clear what?"

"She says this could be a scam. That this happens a lot."

"This is not a scam." Shanaya spoke in a level tone. It wasn't anything she hadn't already said like a million and three times. She could speak that lie as smoothly as she could say her own name.

"She says there's been a lot of people in here saying the IRS is after them and I've done my banking here for almost ten years and she wouldn't want to see anything bad happen to me."

"That's what we're trying to do here. Keep anything bad from happening to you."

"She says—"

"I'm sure she knows her job as a bank teller"—Shanaya pronounced *teller* with the tone often reserved for used car salesmen—"but I know my job as a federal agent. So who would know more about tax arrears and arrest warrants?"

"I know. *I* get it, but—"

"I'm afraid I may have let sympathy hold me back from doing my job for too long a time. I must tell my boss that the funds are not forthcoming and the warrant will be enforced."

"No! Wait! I'm sure I can make them see—okay, a man is coming over here." She stashed the phone before Shanaya could protest. More muffled conversation ensued. The words weren't discernible, but clearly the bank manager didn't feel the need for diplomacy as the teller had.

Over Mrs. Whoever's protests, the muting vanished as if the manager had pulled the phone from the woman's hand.

"Who is this?"

Shanaya made her voice as stern as his, knowing that she would probably lose this one. Once the element of doubt crept in, it required a miracle to keep the thing on track. She rattled off the name she used at the shop, along with the random number she quoted as her federal agent identification number. She had stared down suspicious daughters-in-law and neighbors and bank tellers before. She wouldn't give up until absolutely no hope remained. Especially not with the pit bull at her shoulder.

The bank manager barely let her finish before sneering, "Oh really? And you're telling this woman that she's under arrest for—what, exactly?"

"I can't violate the citizen's privacy by discussing her case with you. Please put her back on the phone."

"You have this sweet old lady scared out of her wits, all so you can steal her money. As if the IRS wants payments made by Apple Pay cards? You seriously expect anyone to believe that?"

You'd be amazed, she thought, then recited the line about that form of payment was "allowed" in order to be "more convenient for the citizen."

The man laughed. She pictured a skinny guy in a three-piece suit in his stupid little local branch with Formica counters and weak coffee in the lobby. This might be the most exciting thing he did all week, berating an unseen girl long distance. "You're a damn scam artist, is what you are. How do you sleep at night?"

Not that great, she wanted to say, but not because of you or the Mrs. Whoevers of the world. "I am a federal agent—"

"Where's your office? Who's your supervisor?"

She read an address in Washington, D.C., and name, both printed on a card taped to the metal cubicle wall, and debated whether she should hang up and keep from wasting any more of the day's time. Shanaya had engineered some stunning reversals, but not many. Once third parties got involved—

"You should be ashamed of yourself! Taking advantage of innocent, vulnerable people—"

The best defense is a good offense. "You're the one interfering with this woman's right to her own bank account. She is going to suffer because of your"—her mind went temporarily blank—"busybodyness!"

A peal of genuine laughter came over the phone's tinny receiver, and Shanaya could hear Mrs. Whoever in the background, laughing as well. Then the "bank manager" said, "Oh my God, you bitch, can't you figure it out? You're blown. We know you're full of shit. We're going to trace this call and have the cops at *your* door—"

Shanaya's heart sank, but not because there could be any chance of Joe Stupid Citizen tracing the number that had been spoofed and routed through a second server so that it appeared to be coming from D.C. And even if she'd accidentally connected to NORAD or some other super-sophisticated security agency, the phone didn't belong to her. Not the phone, the desk, the cheap cubicle walls, or the proceeds of illegally obtained gift card numbers. That all belonged to the big boss, and surely he hid behind a wall of fake names and transferred accounts.

No, her heart slumped because this case had been lost and there would not be any last-minute windfalls. Hang up now, don't waste another second on losers that could be spent on a payoff—

The guy was talking, oh so proud of getting her hopes up and wasting nearly forty minutes of her time. "We stuck the phone out the window to sound like outdoors and thumped a table to sound like a car door. How do you like it, you bitch? You like someone playing you?"

Shanaya knew she shouldn't take it personally. It was only business, and like any business you had good days and bad days. But she couldn't stop the wave of white-hot rage that washed over her, making her hand grip the headset and a string of expletives to well up in her mouth. "You have that cash now? Do you?"

The abrupt non sequitur confused the man. "No, of course not—"

She continued as if he hadn't spoken. "Then what I want you to do is roll it all up in a tight little stick, got it? Roll it tight. Then bend over and shove it up your—"

"Shanaya," the pit bull said at her elbow.

She disconnected the phone.

"Don't waste time," he barked, but without his usual heat.

She pulled the headset off. "What is *wrong* with these people that they'll waste over a half hour of their lives just to screw with someone?" she couldn't stop herself from asking aloud. A tear pricked her eyeball in uncharacteristic self-pity. "That's just so—*mean*."

"Don't worry about it. Take a break." He put a hand on her shoulder and she instinctively flinched. He might be acting nice because Shanaya regularly appeared in the top ten most productive in the room and he didn't want her to burn out, or he might figure that a soft answer turneth into some job perks of his own that she sure as hell didn't care to provide. She managed to stand up and move past him with any two parts of their relative anatomies actually touching, mumbled some thanks, and trotted toward the ladies' room. The pit bull had been right about one thing. She needed a break.

She passed the day care room, where a harried young woman carried an infant in her arms while two toddlers pulled at her shirt, one crying while the other tried to show her a toy. Of three other kids in the room, one used crayons in a tattered book, one played with a toy truck, and the third simply dashed from one end of the small room to the other, touching the wall at either end. Shanaya saw only very small children; school-age kids would be in class somewhere. On the weekends, the day care room got completely crazy.

After using the toilet she stood at the sink, letting cold water wash over her wrists, something her mother had always told her to do when she got "sweated up" running around with her cousins. According to ancient family wisdom, drinking cold water in such a state would make you sick. But running it over the skin where blood vessels congregated would accomplish the same goal more gently.

Even as a child she had scoffed at this, but now the coolness comforted her.

Perhaps she had abandoned the apartment too hastily. It saved her this month's rent, and a girlfriend had taken her in, but the friend's boyfriend hadn't seemed too friendly and Shanaya didn't think it would last. If Evani's killers had wanted to track him to his source, they had had all night and the next morning to do so. They had time to make her suffer the same fate as Evani, and yet no one had taken his key card and paid her a midnight visit. No one was after her.

A good thing, and it bought her some time. Without her partner to plan with, she did not feel sure of what her next step should be. They'd been so close to their goal.

She dried her hands, took a breath, and went back out into the foray.

She worked on the second floor, but it had a staircase and a section open to the first above the entrance and what could be called a lobby. This didn't separate the noise between the nearly fifty people working phones, only multiplied it. Avoiding eye contact with her coworkers—never a good idea to get close to unnecessary people—she glanced over the railing, down through the hole in the floor to what would be a reception desk if there were ever a receptionist manning it.

And her breath gasped out of her.

Chapter 12

"Feathers," Riley said, turning a corner. A bit sharply, and the rear wheels scooted to the side a few inches more than they should.

"Cheer up. We can have lunch at that Thai place."

"I wasn't complaining. It's better than tracking down dealers and fake scripts like Gardiner's going to have to."

"Might not be so bad. Nothing like chasing the group on the corner as they scatter down the alleys to warm you up."

"Plus they can't even run that fast because fourteen layers of clothes weigh them down. How else can you deal out of doors for hours in the winter without layering?"

The car had barely warmed up before it was time to get out of it again. They left it at the curb in one of the few spaces allowed for that sort of thing and then paused to assess their target. A brick structure with evenly spaced windows over the heavy block sills, solid and plain, and Jack could easily believe that it had been there for a hundred years or whatever. He had searched the address and found only a real estate company that didn't employ someone to answer the phone. Now, no sign arched over the entrance on

East Ninth. The grimy glass squares of the windows had been coated with something reflective, and the doors were bare of titles or hours of operations. Jack felt oddly glad they had come armed.

Jack put his hand on the pull latch of the bare door and tugged. It opened to an air lock, but when he pulled on the second set of doors, nothing happened. Their surface had been coated on the inside with a dark brown matte paint, so from the street it looked like an empty interior.

Jack could detect a low murmur, a collective rustling, something felt rather than heard that told him the building was anything but empty.

No directory, no lettering. The foyer had no more information than the outer door, but it did have a small black plastic grill attached to the wall. A circle in the grill might be a button. With no other options presented, Jack pushed it.

Nothing.

He pushed again.

This time it crackled and an annoyed voice said only, "What?"

"Police," Jack snapped back. If the person didn't have time to equivocate, neither did he.

A pause to reassess, and then the voice said, "I'll be right with you."

"He'll be right with us," Jack muttered to his partner.

Riley's hand rested on his hip, one inch from his holstered gun. "Please tell me we're not walking into a meth lab."

"We'd smell it if it were meth. It could be cocaine."

Riley slid the bottom of his sweater up and put his hand on the butt of the gun, still buckled into its holster. "Or fentanyl," he breathed.

Fentanyl seemed to terrify Riley. A white powder, it could function like a magic spell or a superpoison from a bad spy film—one whiff, an errant touch with an ungloved hand, and a strong grown man could drop to the floor. All officers carried the antidote Narcan in the car, but that required one of them to get to the kit and back in time to save their partner. If both of them went down, they were as good as in the coffins. There was nothing magical about that.

He heard the *snick* of a dead bolt and the door flew open, revealing a thirtyish man in a suit, too well-dressed to be a drug lord. Every dark hair in place, teeth gleaming, he thrust out a hand armed with nothing more than a wide gold band around one finger. "Gentlemen! What can I do for you?"

A wall of noise billowed out the door around him. What sounded like a room full of voices, all in different conversation—but none that seemed in distress or even particular haste. After shaking the man's damp hand Jack held up his badge and Riley did the same. Jack spoke with clunky syntax: "This building has turned up as of interest to an investigation. Are you the owner?"

"I'm the owner of the business. I rent the space. Mark Hawking." He began to offer his hand again, then realized he had already done that and let it drop. "What can I do for you?"

"What is your business?"

"We do tech support for a number of companies."

The noise continued unabated. Doors locked during work hours violated fire code, but Hawking's hand rested on a push bar on the inside of the inner door. So employees could get *out*—Mr. Hawking simply didn't want unexpected visitors. Nothing particularly wrong with that, especially as the reception desk behind him sat empty and dust-covered.

"Which companies?" Riley asked. He liked to ask people detailed questions. It made lying that much more difficult, and you never knew what such information might turn up.

"Mostly smaller ones, places you've probably never heard of." Riley's gaze compelled him to add more. "Mantra Services, Silver Thread, Kay Home Care, The Heartsaver Association."

Jack had never heard of any of them, but again, that could

hardly be considered suspicious. Conducting the entire interview in the air lock, however—"Could we come in? Maybe sit down with you, if you can spare us a few minutes?"

Mark Hawking, he felt sure, would not refuse. Mark Hawking wanted very much to seem like a good guy.

And indeed, the man hesitated only the splittest of seconds. "Of course. We can speak in my office." He stood back, held the door, and ushered them into his world.

Stepping inside, Jack immediately saw where the noise came from. Cubicles filled the room, two rows of desks facing each other with a five-foot modular walls on three sides. They were centered in the room, leaving a wide aisle between the two sets and another circling them all, leaving the large windows and the inner wall free. The room only spread perhaps forty feet by forty, brick walls and exposed concrete and pipes, not enough space or cushioning to absorb much of the sound. No wonder it assaulted the ears. Hawking led them up a staircase in front of them to another floor with its own set of noise.

Looking around, Jack could completely see trace evidence lingering there for twenty or sixty years. The carpeting appeared ancient, speckled here and there with scraps of paper and pieces of snack wrappers. The windows were opaque with grime. Nothing that could be considered décor except an ancient motivational poster of a team rowing on a river, the poster's corners curling, the lettering faded. Dust tickled his nose. The wall at the top of the stairwell had lost most of its drywall, leaving the gas pipes and a fluffy whitish insulation visible.

"Is that feathers?" he asked Hawking.

The man glanced at the gaping drywall, not pausing in his stride. "Yep. Used to be a feather factory here, and they used the discards for insulation. Why not? They had plenty of it and it works well enough for ducks."

They followed him along the inner wall. The cubicle arrangement seemed identical to the first floor.

Despite the dust and noise, no one seemed uncomfortable. Each employee sat in a padded swivel chair, wearing new-looking headsets and typing on wireless keyboards with flat-screen monitors. The cubicle barriers were thin metal, not white or bulletin boards, but some had been personalized with photos of children or pets, significant others or funny memes. The temperature felt cozy without being overly warm. They had passed two clearly labeled restrooms and even a child care room with a high window in a sturdy door at the top of the stairs. The smell of decent coffee wafted from a long table against the inner wall, where Jack could see cups, plates, condiments, and a few individually wrapped cookies. Some workers watched the visitors with sharp, interested glares, while others glanced up and away from the two cops with an utter lack of concern.

Snatches of words became clear. "I can help you with that." "What is the number?" "I am doing well, thank you for asking."

Mark Hawking entered the last room along the interior wall. He waved them inside and shut the door behind them. The noise level instantly dropped to livable.

Perhaps eight by eight, the boss's office didn't do décor any more than the work area did. One small set of mounted shelves held haphazard stacks of paper, as did the desk, along with a well-used ashtray, a coffee mug with a broken handle overflowing with pens and pencils, and not less than three cups with actual coffee, all half-full. Two narrow chairs with metal frames and molded plastic seats were provided for guests, and Jack and Riley made use of them without an invitation to do so.

"So you'd like the rental company's name?" Hawking asked, ever-helpful.

Riley settled in his chair. "How long have you been at this location?"

"Three years." The answer came quickly, easily. "How is this building of concern to your investigation? What are you investigating?"

But they weren't there to answer his questions, of course. "Do you know what company occupied this space before you?"

"No."

"Is phone support the only business you conduct at this location?"

"Yes . . . what other business would I be doing? The call center is my only business. Our clients rely on us for, um, reliable support." He tugged at his tie, seemed to realize that the nervous gesture didn't fit his image, then smoothed it down with ink- and nicotine-stained fingers.

"Do you have an employee by the name of Evan Harding?"

"No." No hesitation.

"You're sure? Don't need to check your books?"

"I only have the employees that you see here, forty or so people, fifty tops. I know all their names."

Riley smiled as if at this impressive recall. "Could he have been a past employee?"

"No."

"You're sure?"

"Yes." He spoke with such easy sincerity that Jack found himself convinced. The guy seemed hyper and cautious about his little fiefdom, but seemed utterly relaxed on the topic of a man named Evan Harding. More than that, he seemed curious. "Who is that? What does he have to do with Hawk Enterprises?"

It seemed a rather grand name for a staff of fifty, but no doubt Mark Hawking had big plans for the future. Good for him. To be thorough, however, Jack decided to persist. "We have reason to believe that he may have been in the building."

A frown. "That should not be. No one should be in here

except my workers. I don't allow family members to breeze in and out, distracting them from their jobs." The frown cleared. "We do provide day care for our staff who need it. It's possible he came to pick up his child from a spouse . . . but that very rarely happens. And he still shouldn't have been inside."

Sounded like Hawking ran the place with an iron fist in a nice suit.

Riley handed him the photo, which they'd printed after cropping out Shanaya Thomas. "This is him."

Hawking studied the sheet. "I've never seen him. He's certainly never worked here."

"Huh. Well, all right then. Thank you for your time."

"No problem at all. I'm sorry I couldn't be more help," he said graciously, but wasted no time moving to open the door to usher them out. Again they caravaned downstairs to the door. Again the workers at their headsets barely noticed.

"What sort of tech support do you do here?" Jack asked.

"Mostly computer interface issues."

A neatly ambiguous phrase. "More than one seem to be taking credit-card numbers or talking about payments."

Hawking developed a tightness in his throat, or perhaps it came from the effort of raising his voice to be heard over the cacophony. "Some clients charge the customer directly for our services. Some don't."

Jack halted. "I could swear I heard a guy say he was a federal agent."

"No, no," Hawking scoffed, one arm swinging, trying to push the air toward the exit as if it might carry the cops along with it. "He told the customer he was calling on *behalf* of a federal agency. We have a few as clients."

Riley had picked up on Jack's concern. "Really? Which ones?"

"The Office of, um, Local Land Management, and the Gambling Tax Authority Liaison Administration."

"Oh," Riley said. "Huh."

Jack listened, but the babble of voices blended together into an innocuous murmur. He couldn't think of anything else to do or ask, so he let Mark Hawking show them out with friendly words and visible relief.

The relative quiet of a snow-cushioned midday street comforted their ears, and neither spoke as they turned the corner and headed up the sidewalk to the car.

"What do you think?" Riley asked him.

"I think the only believable thing that guy said was how he had no idea who Evan Harding is. Or was."

Riley sighed, his breath expelling in a brief balloon of fog. "So you don't believe there's an Office of Local Land Management?"

"I do not."

"Me, neither. So what *are* they doing in there? And where does that leave us?"

"Hey," said a voice behind them.

Standing on the sidewalk with only a cardigan sweater for warmth, stood Shanaya Thomas.

She said, "Hi."

Chapter 13

Snow drifted down the back of Jack's collar and melted, sending tiny streams of icy water down his neck. They'd only been outside for perhaps forty-five seconds and he could already feel the cold moving up through the soles of his shoes. He stared at Shanaya Thomas, wondering only what to ask first.

She didn't give him a chance. "I saw you guys talking to Mr. Hawking. What are you doing here? Were you looking for me?"

"You work here?" Riley asked, which somewhat, and inadvertently, answered her question.

"Yes."

"Why did you leave your apartment?" Jack asked.

Her eyes widened. She couldn't have known they'd gone back. "I was afraid. I mean, after what happened to Evani—it's probably stupid, but I couldn't stay there alone. And," she admitted, "it was the final day of the rent period. I figured I'd save money if I left before midnight. About Evani—"

Except she had left before noon, and what rental period

ended midweek, in the midmonth? "Where did you go? Where are you staying?"

"With a friend of mine . . . until I can get my final paycheck and go home."

"Where's home?"

"Tennessee."

Riley said, "You left all of your boyfriend's stuff at the apartment."

She held up bare hands, telegraphing helplessness. "I could only take what I can carry. His stuff was just—stuff. Nothing sentimental, so—I have to be practical. I've learned to travel light."

Riley handed her his notepad and a pen. "Write down the address. We have to be able to get hold of you, in case we have more questions about Evan. You can't bail like that."

She took it but didn't write anything. "You have my phone number."

"You didn't answer."

"We're not allowed to take personal calls at work. Look, this"—she gestured toward the building behind her, then wrapped the sweater around herself more tightly—"is a sweatshop. A decent sweatshop, but still a sweatshop. I'm going to be docked pay for coming back five minutes late from break. But I need to ask about Evan's—"

"Did Evan work here?" Jack asked.

The question plainly surprised her. "No."

"Did he visit you here?"

"No, never."

"Why did you tell us Evan worked at the movie theater?"

Her eyelids flickered, but she didn't skip a beat. "He did."

"He worked at A to Z Check Cashing."

No hesitation. "He used to. He quit there and went to the theater."

"When?"

"About a month ago."

"No, he didn't. He still worked at A to Z."

She bounced on her toes, probably to keep the blood flowing rather than any concern at his statement. "Well, that's what he told me."

Jack ground a tooth in frustration. He couldn't challenge her on this, because they hadn't asked Ralph exactly *when* he had last seen Shanaya at A to Z. She had purposely lied to them about the movie theater, just as she absolutely lied to them now. But why did she want to steer them away from A to Z? "Are you sure Evan never worked here? We found evidence from this building on his clothing."

Bafflement that wasn't a lie, for a change. He thought he could see the wheels working in her head, the spark of interest in how they managed to trace a person to a building, then the spark ground under her heel in the need to move forward before she got docked another five minutes. "That's not possible. He's never been here. Mr. Hawking doesn't allow personal visitors."

"What is it you do here?"

"Customer service."

"Computer interface issue support?" Jack knew vague, non-answers meant to befuddle him when he heard them. He'd invented enough for himself over the years. But this girl could give him lessons.

"Yes."

The stuff had probably come off *her* clothes, and transferred to Evan's when they hugged, made love, hung their coats in the same closet. Still, Jack now distrusted nearly anything the young woman uttered, so he filed that denial away as she finished by asking a question of her own.

"Evani's stuff—the things he had with him when he died. Can I have them back?"

Jack's mind went to the key.

"He had a ring—I bought it for him when . . . well, it's silly. But I'd like to have it. I'd like to have one single thing to remember him by." Her voice broke, tears welled up and threatened to spill. It would rend hearts, her standing there shivering in the snow with her cheeks turning red, a picture of young love in all its fresh, tragic beauty.

"Of course, we can get you his ring back," Jack said. "Come to our office when you get off work. You still have my card?" No, he knew, because she'd abandoned it in her old apartment along with her boyfriend's clothing. He handed her a new one. "Call anytime, to make sure we're there. Then you can come in and we'll sign Evan's property over to you."

Except maybe for that damn key, he thought. He itched to ask her what it opened, but even if she answered he wouldn't believe what she said. *Patience.* Come into my parlor, little fly, drawn to the bright light of that winking little key.

She nodded miserably, then turned without another word and trotted back up the sidewalk, a precarious pace on the icy walkway. One foot slid too far as she turned the corner, but she recovered, incentivized by either the warmth of the call center or the hope of getting back to her cubicle before her supervisor noticed her absence.

Jack and Riley exchanged a glance but didn't waste time with conversation that could be had inside the shelter of their vehicle. It had cooled to the same temperature as the outdoors, but at least it kept more snow from sneaking down Jack's collar. As the engine warmed up, Riley said, "Okay. Now I'm *really* confused."

"Not so much. The stuff on his clothes came from her. Evan Harding's link to this building was his girlfriend, that's all."

"Which means we've spent an hour without getting a whit closer to who killed Harding."

"What is a 'whit,' anyway?"

Riley ignored this. "I'm confused about why she bolts the second we leave her apartment, but then flags us down when we had no idea she worked here."

"She didn't know we had no idea. For all she knew, we came here looking for her."

Riley said, "Preemptive strike. The most direct explanation for her fleeing their apartment is that she's afraid. She and Harding were faking status to get cheap rent, maybe the check cashing place isn't totally on the up-and-up, and who knows what the hell they're doing in *there*, but I'll bet it isn't guiding customers through warranty claims or telling middle managers how to access their e-mail. Everything about her is shady—but then she seeks us out."

Jack said, "So whoever it is she's afraid of, it's not the cops."

Friday, 7:10 p.m.

Maggie had been tying the last bow on a gift for one of her nieces when the phone rang. She wanted to get the box in the mail so that Alex and Daisy could nestle the toys and dresses under the tree for Christmas morning, or whatever sort of tree or wreath or candle sufficed as tradition in the life of a traveling musician. Her brother usually tried to fit in a visit to Cleveland around the holiday, or she would go to them. But this year he had a gig too lucrative to pass up in Idaho, where at least the landscape of snowy mountains would be picture-perfect on December twenty-fifth even if their family had to stop at only its nucleus. Maggie didn't feel able to take time off—Amy had been so looking forward to opening presents with her toddler, Carol had her granddaughters, Josh faced the first major holiday as a newlywed, and Denny's house would be a damn Norman Rockwell painting with his kick-ass wife and three gloriously vibrant kids.

Still, the idea of pristine snow—not the slush grayed by city streets—in what she imagined would be the quiet wilderness of Idaho made her wish she could fly out and meet them, take a quick vacation outside her life, not to mention reconnect with the only family member she had left. Maybe remember who she used to be. It would be good for her. She had felt unmoored after that first violent conflict, when she learned who and what Jack Renner was. That had been April. It was now December, and she got herself to sleep every night by telling her brain how she had made her peace with it. She had done what she had done and nothing remained to be said about it. They were both doing good work now, functioning firmly on the side of the angels for the protection of society.

Then she would wake up each morning and know that peace remained an illusion, a pretty picture from another world, as far away as the snow-capped mountains of Idaho.

And Alex might see that, the unease, the change in her. He knew her too well.

Best to leave well enough alone. She put the ribbon down and picked up the phone.

"Has Dispatch called you?" Jack asked, which immediately let her know he had not called for personal reasons—which would have been unusual.

She said no, not looking forward to going out to a crime scene for reasons that had nothing to do with Jack Renner and the conflicts he represented. It was freakin' cold out there. "What's up?"

"Remember that woman in the video, the one your ex had interviewed?"

"Yeah."

"We're going to need you to come to her apartment."

Chapter 14

Streetlights blocked out the stars and reflected off the ice. Maggie drove the city car to West 29th as slowly as the traffic around her would allow, and still it fishtailed slightly at two different corners. She gave herself plenty of time to brake often and carefully in order to tuck it in at the curb in front of the small plaza. The shops on the first floor were empty and dark, dim lights glowing only for security. The second floor, by contrast, had lights on in nearly every window.

Jack waited on the sidewalk, hunched into his jacket, hands stuffed in his pockets.

"Too bad the tea place isn't open," she said by way of greeting, and pulled her camera bag and her crime scene kit out of the trunk.

"Only if you like a lot of jasmine."

She had no idea what that meant but didn't bother to ask. "Lead on, MacDuff."

She followed him though the narrow hallway and up a stairwell. The second floor held all the activity the first floor lacked, with a uniformed patrol officer and Riley standing outside an open door and random neighbors either peeking or openly watching from their own doorways. One used an oversized cell phone to film the authorities' milling around. Riley greeted Maggie by waving at the open door and saying, "In there."

She set her cases down to attach the external flash to her camera. Without a word the patrolman and Riley stepped back from the doorway so they wouldn't be in the shot when she photographed the door with its numbered placard. Then she stepped into the opening.

A table lamp gave the room a cozy glow. Maggie swept the camera slowly from side to side, snapping a photo of each section of the apartment. A tidy living area, couch, end tables, framed pictures, a table with a few dishes and pieces of mail on it, an armchair, a vase on the windowsill with silk flowers, a counter framing the kitchen. Everything neat and orderly, nothing out of place, other than the dead woman in the middle of the floor, lying faceup with a patch of red staining the center of her chest.

But Maggie ignored the body until she finished her preliminaries, and continued to take photographs of the kitchenette, the bedroom, the bathroom, a smaller second bedroom that served as a combination office and repository of spare items. Nothing anywhere raised a red flag. No visible traces of blood in the kitchen sink or the bathroom with its snow-white shower curtain, towels, and tile walls. If the killer had cleaned bloody hands in that room, he had to be a complete genius at leaving no signs of it. The medicine cabinet contained nothing stronger than Midol, the wastebasket had no pile of empty bottles, the refrigerator had one half-full bottle of Moscato. No evidence of an unhealthy or self-destructive lifestyle, no illegal activities that might beckon danger in.

She returned to the body. Jack and Riley had moved back into the room, discussing what they needed to do next. Apparently neighbors had not seen anything, heard anything, noticed anything, had not seen Jennifer Toner since the day before. In many neighborhoods this would be the *de rigueur* answer, but these people seemed sincere. It made Riley propose aloud that Jennifer had been killed before her neighbors returned home from work. Maggie would see if rigor mortis bore out that theory.

But first she took more focused photos of the dead woman on the rug, being sure to take close-ups of her face and hands. The victim wore jeans and a thick-knit white sweater, the entire middle of which had turned to a dark red. Maggie assumed there must be a wound in there somewhere, but couldn't see the defect in the heavy knit yarns. Nothing on her feet but warm socks. Her face tilted toward the sofa, her skin unmarred, eyes open and an expression more of disappointment than fear or anger. Her left arm lay by her side, her right folded up with fingers resting against her right shoulder. The fingernails were clean of blood, filed and painted with a snowflake decal at the end of each one, still perfect.

Jennifer Toner had not seen it coming. Or she had, and had not put up a fight.

Maggie bet on the former.

"This was Gardiner's case," Jack observed. "I'm not complaining, but why are we here?"

Riley said, "Gardiner already started his vacation and Will took his family skiing for the weekend for his kid's birthday. He called in but I told him we'd handle it, since this victim had that weird connection to our victim." He filled Maggie in on their visit to Jennifer Toner's apartment, including a summary of Rick and Will's visit before that.

"So she's got a drug-addicted brother," Jack said.

"Who just became suspect number one," Riley pointed out. "But only because we don't know of anyone else involved in her life. Evan Harding would make a good suspect, since she got in his face. Unfortunately he was already dead."

Maggie cheated a little on the don't-touch-the-body-until-the-ME-investigator-arrives rule by tugging on the woman's jaw with firm, latexed fingers. Then she poked one of the fingers. Rigor had begun. That meant it had been, on average, between two and six hours since death. She couldn't make the guess any more specific without testing rigor in other areas of the body, and she couldn't do that without moving it more than her bend in the rule would allow.

Still crouched by the body, she said, "Sounds as if this Dr. Castleman might have a motive, too. Maybe she got in *his* face."

Riley said, "If she found him. As of this morning, she hadn't."

"Perhaps she had more success after we left," Jack wondered. "We might be able to tell if we could find her phone."

Maggie prodded the woman's hips, then the edge of the one butt cheek she could reach. "Unless it's in her left rear pocket, it's not on her."

She stood up. Nothing more could be done with the body until the ME staff arrived. She got her clipboard and made a rough sketch of the room, then examined the door. No signs of prying or breaking around the molding or the dead bolt.

"Was the door open?" she asked the detectives. "When you arrived?"

Jack said yes. "A neighbor found it ajar, poked her head in, screamed, and called us."

So Jennifer Toner had either left her door unlocked or had let her killer inside, and then he ran out without closing it all the way. Maggie used fingerprint powder on the knobs, even though the cops had already used the outer one. Nothing. She rarely, very very rarely, got a usable print from a door-knob. Or a light switch, even the wide, flat kind—annoying, because those were two items you could be *sure* someone had touched.

After that Maggie took a flashlight and examined every

surface in the room, holding the flashlight at an angle to look for dust that had been disturbed or an item that didn't seem to be where it belonged. The mail on the table matched that address and Jennifer's name. A dish held soggy Cheerios in a tablespoon of milk. Jennifer had been reading a romance novel, perched precariously on the coffee table next to a laptop which, when opened, showed a blissfully password-free home screen.

"Sweet." Riley sank into the sofa next to the Jack to look at it. Maggie had to smile at the sight of the two men so close together and so intensely focused on the same thing. They reminded her of old pictures of little boys lying on their stomachs in front of a TV set, entranced by an episode of *The Lone Ranger.*

But then Riley said, "She doesn't send e-mail to her brother. At least not recently. Girlfriends, a guy she is—she *was*—going to meet for dinner tomorrow night . . . we'll have to check him out . . . Amazon order notifications, Friends of the Library newsletter."

Maggie continued her sweep. The armchair had a few tiny stains along one armrest, too orangey to be blood, more like enchilada sauce. The credenza held an array of items between two heavy bookends—Atlas holding up globes enameled in blue and green. Maggie lifted one a millimeter or two to judge its density. Too bad Jennifer hadn't been close enough to grab one and smash it into her attacker's temple. That might have made him think twice about his next actions.

Behind her, Riley said, "There's a second e-mail account."

"Looks like work stuff," Jack said. "Library events, work schedule, shipments."

"Let's try search history."

Maggie listened absently as she continued examining the apartment, something that was technically the detectives' job but since, usually, ninety-nine percent of a person's home had nothing to do with why they'd been killed, they could always use help. Among the books and manuals and photos between the bookends there were pieces of old mail, a birthday card from someone named Jerome and a mini-calendar from the previous year, with social events and appointments written in below pictures of kittens. Maggie flipped through it very quickly, not seeing what could be learned from appointments now well over a year old. Besides, the minuscule layer of dust over the credenza had not been disturbed.

Except at the end nearest the door. There, the motes had been swept aside and something else left behind.

A swath of red-brown color ran from the side edge to the front edge, forming a sort of triangle with the corner. It had been lost against the woodgrain-patterned laminate of the credenza, until the sharp beam of the flashlight caught it.

"I have some blood over here," she said aloud.

The detectives, too engrossed in the victim's e-mails, ignored her. The presence of blood at a murder scene could hardly be considered earth-shattering.

But blood so far away from the body held out certain possibilities. Obviously the victim hadn't staggered over and put out a hand to steady herself, since her fingers were unstained and she hadn't left any drops on her pants, socks, or the floor in-between. She'd gone down and stayed down after the fatal blow.

Most likely the killer had gotten some blood on his hand and then used it to steady himself on the credenza. Then he either wiped it off or used the other hand to turn the doorknob, so it stayed clean.

Maggie looked closer, then got a magnifying loupe out of her crime scene kit.

At the end of the smear the blood formed a pattern, a rounded set of tiny lines. Each line swooped and swayed and split into two and sometimes came to a stop altogether.

A fingerprint. The killer had left his fingerprint, in blood.

His blood would be good, giving them two forms of positive identification—a latent print match *and* DNA. But hers would be better, pinning him inside that room at the time of the murder.

She swabbed up a sample from the beginning of the streak, where there were no visible ridges, so they could get a DNA profile without disturbing the pattern she needed to photograph. She'd collected swabs from the small pool at Jennifer Toner's side as well, not that anyone who viewed a photograph of the scene could have any doubt as to whom that blood belonged. But surely if she didn't, some attorney, at some point in the future, would ask why she hadn't.

Then she needed to photograph the print. Lifting it as she usually did when prints were developed with black powder would not be possible. Blood would not transfer to the tape adhesive like powder, and powder wouldn't stick well to the dried blood. Ideally she should take a jigsaw and cut a wide square around the print—the laminate surface didn't suggest a valuable antique and Jennifer would no longer care. Maggie could also take the whole credenza—something she hadn't ruled out, but she would try other methods first before stacking up random furniture in the lab, or risk disturbing the print while wrestling the large item out of the building and into a city vehicle.

Usually she dyed blood prints with Amido Black, a stain that turned even the faintest bloodstains to a deep purply black. But against the walnut-colored laminate, making the print darker would not help. A fluorescent dye like Luminol or Bluestar would increase the contrast but might also wash away part of the ridges and the glow only lasted for second. No, she'd start with basic photography, no dyes, no filters, and see how it went.

The two detectives moved on to Jennifer's browsing history, while Maggie set up her tripod and detachable flash.

"She wasn't lying," Riley said to no one in particular. "She had been hunting for this Phillip Castleman on Ohio eLicense, Healthgrades, and RateMDs. The state Attorney General's Office—I bet she checked out how to file a complaint with the medical board."

"Why?" Maggie asked as she worked. "What was she complaining about?"

Jack told her how the victim had believed the doctor had turned her brother into an addict. "Of course just because she didn't think her brother needed medication didn't mean he didn't."

Riley said, "True. Big sisters are always hot on toughening you up."

Maggie attached the flash cord to her camera and watched Jack for any reaction. Did he have a big sister? A little sister? Any siblings at all? An ex-wife somewhere? A child?

Sometimes she wondered. Most of the time didn't let herself. Curiosity might teach a harsh lesson in this case. "She said he had been cashing large checks from this doctor?"

"Yes. That's the weird part. The brother should be paying the doc, not the other way around."

"Medical fraud."

Both detectives stared at her.

"There's a million ways to do it. Usually doctors file insurance claims for procedures they didn't do or exams they didn't make. They say they did a complete physical when the patient was in and out in five minutes. They'll say a patient is diabetic or has cancer, bill for meds and equipment that was never ordered or used. Often the patient doesn't even know about it."

Jack said, "Okay. But then why is Toner cashing the checks?"

She positioned her tripod carefully, propping a piece of cardboard under the camera mount because the worn-out item couldn't keep the heavy camera from falling against the tripod pole. "Laundering money? The government's been trying to cut down on medical fraud for years. Maybe there's a red flag if a doctor gets outsize reimbursements. But if the patients are paid individually it's spread out."

"So the doctor files the forms for the patient, and the patient gives the money back to the doctor."

Riley said, "He'd have to really trust his patients."

"He's got their pills," Jack said. "A reliable, steady supply. And they want those more than they want money. Spread it among enough patients, even if one does a runner here and there, it's still lucrative and low-risk."

"It's only a guess," Maggie said, and focused on the bloody fingerprint.

Jack said, "We need to find Marlon Toner."

Riley said, "Will said she spoke to him. We could probably get a damned sight closer to him if we could find her damned *phone*. Why do our victims never have their phones?"

"Because the killer knew it might connect them to the victim. Killers," Jack amended. "*Or* because Toner and Harding were killed by an addict and a mugger respectively, and a phone can be sold on the street for a couple of bucks. To them it would be like leaving a ten-dollar bill on the floor. What are you doing?"

Maggie realized he was speaking to her. "I think I have a usable print." In the silence she heard them wondering what would be interesting about one particular fingerprint in a person's home, so she added, "In blood."

Jack left Jennifer Toner's browser history with Riley while he used Maggie's flashlight to see the tiny lines of the dried blood. She didn't have to point out that the victim couldn't have left the print; his quick turn to the body and back again meant he had figured that out.

Jack didn't exactly peer over her shoulder as she photographed the print, but he stayed close. A fingerprint hit could solve their case for them before bedtime, if she were so inclined to go back to the lab and get the print into the system that day.

She *was* so inclined, but first she had to get the photograph and the laminate did not make a good surface. Even its low gloss reflected the camera's flash. Without it the photo came out too dark, with it the bright light blanked out the print's ridges. It took a good deal of trial and error to get the angle, the lens, and the flash level working in harmony.

While she toiled, the Medical Examiner's Office investigator arrived, a different man from the lean one she'd met that morning. This one was larger and more talkative, his white cheeks rounded and flushed with cold like Jolly St. Nick—all well and good, except the credenza happened to be the item of furniture closest to the door and he managed to jostle her tripod four times before he got himself settled to examine the body. She worked fast while the detectives brought him up to speed, and from what she could see in the small screen on the back of the camera, the print appeared legible enough.

The investigator confirmed her estimate of the rigor mortis timing and thought Jennifer had been dead since midafternoon. He also didn't make any comments they hadn't already made—the victim had no defensive wounds and had died relatively quickly, without even enough time to clasp her hands to her chest. When he pulled the sweater up, they could see a deep red, gelatinous blob where a wound sat underneath her left breast.

"Gunshot?" Riley asked.

The investigator examined the sweater, then the skin. "Possible, but I don't think so. No singeing of the edges. I'd guess a knife. Probably went straight to the heart."

"Professional," Riley said.

"Or lucky. I see a lot of deaths from single stab wounds. All they have to do is see a movie where the assassin steps up close and drives a stiletto up and under the rib cage. Shred the ventricles or aorta and unless you're actually standing inside the emergency room when it happens—and probably even then—you're dead. There's no chance."

"Is that what you think it was?" Maggie asked. "A stiletto?"

The investigator paused and rethought, in light of the intensity of her question, examined the wound again. "It's very small, and . . . more circular than linear."

"Like something round and thin. Like an ice pick."

He gazed at her. "Yeah. Why?"

Jack said, "Because we had a guy this morning with the same kind of wound."

"Huh. Really."

"Is that unusual?" Maggie asked.

"Well, yes. Most stabbing are knives. Wide, thin blades with or without serrations, double-edge or single-edged. Something like this . . . yes, it's unusual. Where would you even *find* an ice pick in this day and age?"

"Maybe it's some kind of industrial tool?" Maggie asked.

"Maybe," he said doubtfully. "What's this lady got to do with your guy this morning?"

Riley said, "We haven't the slightest idea."

The investigator turned the body over, with Maggie's help. Some blood had pooled on the floor and soaked into the sweater, but not much. Jennifer Toner's heart had stopped beating too quickly.

No wounds in the back—and no cell phone either. Riley grumbled.

The body snatchers came and loaded up the earthly remains of Jennifer Toner, while Maggie decided against taking a Sawzall to the credenza. She had a series of photographs and the DNA swabs. There wouldn't be much more she could do with the credenza at the lab.

Leaving a crime scene always made her uncomfortable.

Had she done everything? Seen everything? Collected everything that needed to be collected? There could be no do-overs. Once they released the apartment, they couldn't come back without getting a warrant and, more importantly, creating serious chain-of-custody issues down the road since none of them would be able to swear to the integrity of the scene in the meantime. But on the other hand, they couldn't stay there forever, nor did Maggie want to. It had been a long day and she still had presents to wrap.

Yet on still another hand, two people who had encountered each other only the night before were now dead. Murdered. That *could* be coincidence, yes, but . . .

"What now?" she asked the two detectives.

"We need to find Marlon Toner," Jack said.

"I can't believe no one in this building has video surveillance," Riley said. "A bubble over the cash register, a nanny cam, anything."

Jack said, "He had the best motive. Sister was nagging him about his drug habit and threatening to run down his source. We can do a warrant request to get her phone history from her carrier."

Maggie said, "What about Evan Harding?"

"I think he's got an alibi," Riley said. "Ah, I crack myself up."

"I mean in his case. What's the, er, next step there?"

Jack said, "We find out what that key opens. Though since the killer didn't take it or even seem to look for it, it was probably some stash he was hiding from his girlfriend and had nothing to do with his death by random mugging. We'll wait for her to come in and ask for it, then maybe we can get some more information out of her. Only two places along Bolivar had video surveillance and they both had to call their tech guys to retrieve it, so maybe that will bear fruit tomorrow—I mean today." The clock dials had passed midnight, and now that she knew it Maggie could feel the weariness flood into her.

"Other than the girlfriend and Ralph, the guy seemed to have no enemies, no friends, no dealings or relationships at all. So," Jack summed up, "we're open to suggestions."

"I wish I had some," Maggie said.

Chapter 15

Shanaya turned over, tangling the sheet and nearly shoving the pillow out onto the dog-hair-covered carpeting. When her girlfriend from the next row of cubicles offered Shanaya a place to flop she hadn't clarified that her "couch" was actually a love seat, so that Shanaya's knees had to stay bent at a ninety-degree angle, unless she wanted to stretch her calves over the armrest until her feet fell asleep. She also hadn't mentioned that every possible surface held a thick layer of animal dander, produced by the Rottweiler now snuffling around her shoes and the at-death's-door Pomeranian now dragging itself to the water bowl with a series of grunts and wheezes too loud for such a tiny being to produce. Both of them were clearly visible since the thin curtains didn't even try to block out the streetlights outside the building. She shouldn't have left the apartment—that had been an over-reaction. No one could have found her there. The cops had only done it through Evani's key card. She hadn't needed to run to this flea-infested coop.

Still, though, better safe than sorry. That mantra had kept

her from serious pain for most of her life. People got caught because they waited too long, downplayed the signs, got too comfortable in place. At least on her friend's sofa—correction, *love seat*—Shanaya could close her eyes and take a few easy breaths. And she rather liked the Rottweiler, other than his penchant for shedding, an animal of such heft that the floorboards creaked when he walked. Anyone who came through that door would get a deep-throated growl and two rows of terrifyingly big teeth. She found the animal more reassuring than Evani had ever been.

If she really wanted to be safe, she should stop going to work at the call center, from which all her problems stemmed. But it wasn't easy to get decent-paying work when you didn't have much of an education, or experience, or even the correct personal identification. And she certainly wasn't leaving town without their savings. So she might as well keep showing up for her shift.

To get her mind off her cramping calves, she delineated her problems. There were two: getting Evani's property back from those two cops, and evading The Guy.

The Rottweiler nudged her hand, and she patted his head. His tail thumped against the wooden floor. The downstairs neighbors often called to complain that the dog made more noise than a herd of buffalo when he ran around the room, claws clicking against the planks. Shanaya had told her friend to ask them how they knew what a herd of buffalo sounded like, but her friend thought that might not be prudent.

Shanaya didn't know The Guy's name, or how he had found her, or how he kept getting the correct phone number to the call center. At first he hadn't seemed threatening at all, more curious than annoyed. Certainly not dangerous.

But that had changed over the past month. Since the scam required people to call "the IRS" back, he just kept calling until he connected to her. And she had to pick up the phone when a call routed to her. If she didn't, she'd be out on her ass before the next break. The pit bull would see to that.

She thought The Guy had been following her, as well. She would catch a movement out of the corner of her eye, a shadow lingering in a doorway fifty paces behind her, quite noticeable during these days when people hustled inside and out of the cold as quickly as possible. There would be a figure hovering outside the empty ballpark, a burnt-orange car driving slowly behind her as she walked home. She had searched for a back exit to the center, but found only one, with chains and a padlock on it. The bosses *really* didn't want workers to leave during working hours, fire safety laws be damned.

She tried to leave with a group each day, and when the other people broke off, she took a different route back to the apartment, going out of the way as much as her paranoia and the frigid temps would allow.

It could be her imagination. Big deal if some former customer who had lost money to them couldn't get over it. Shanaya had heard of that once—a friend of hers had a target get so nasty and personal occasionally that he made the mistake of calling the man back to berate him. His real phone number showed up on the person's caller ID and they kept calling. Really ruined his intake for the day with the line tied up like that.

Since he wasn't getting petted, the Rottweiler wandered away.

She had a risky occupation, she knew that. Most of the time failed calls resulted in obscenities and comments about her personal defects, but when real money had been lost, a customer's feelings could go way beyond annoyance. And it worried her that she didn't know what The Guy looked like. If those fleeting shadows were real, they only told her that he was big. Other than that he could be anyone. Even one of those two cops.

But The Guy couldn't have had anything to do with Evani getting killed, could he? Even if he found her, how could he connect her to Evani? Perhaps he had followed her home despite her efforts, but then why not attack her instead?

But if not The Guy, then who?

She heard the angry-bee sound of her cell phone on vibrate. It started her heart pounding with an instinctive, visceral terror that made no sense, and yet it did, because no one except Evani had her number.

And Evani was dead.

She had spread her coat across herself for warmth and now she reached into the pocket. It would be a wrong number, she told herself. It would be someone exactly like her, someone from some shit country who couldn't even figure out world time zones, who wanted to lower her credit card interest rates or get her a great deal on satellite TV. That would be hilarious, she decided, and maybe even a little karmic.

But the display showed Evani's number. Not his name, of course. They both used burners and kept all personal information off of them. No data plan, no selfies, no texts that would reveal anything more than what they wanted for dinner. Definitely no names, not even their nicknames. Only their numbers.

Evani was dead. This meant that whoever had made him dead had taken his phone, knew what they'd been doing and was now trying to find her.

It stopped vibrating.

Shanaya threw off the blankets and coat and padded to the kitchen. She flicked on the light and ripped open the back of the cell phone—lucky for her it was such a cheap one that she could remove the battery and the chip thing that had all the information on it. She looked around for tools, wanting to smash it with a hammer but had to content herself with a pliers. With that she snapped the chip in two. A dirty popcorn bowl sat in the sink; Shanaya filled it with water and dropped the rest of the phone inside. That should do it, right? With the battery out, the phone couldn't do anything and it didn't have a GPS or "find my phone" ability anyway. The chip looked irreparable but to be safe she could drop it in a garbage can on her next trip to work. . . . On second thought she fished it out and put it in the old and noisy microwave. The circuits sparked and made a bad smell. She stopped when a tiny flame appeared, so that the chip left only a small brown mark on its rotating plate. She inspected the few melted spots with satisfaction and dropped it into the bowl's sparse soapsuds. Then she turned out the light and bundled herself back into the couch.

Evani's killer had called her. Whoever had killed Evani was trying to find her, and not to express condolences.

What could they have gotten off the phone? The killer, of course, didn't necessarily know anything about her. The killer still could be, and most probably was, a random mugger who had taken the phone to use or resell. The person now hitting redial might have bought the phone for a few bucks and felt like amusing themselves by trying the only number in its history, the only one Evani should have been calling.

It could be the police. They might have found the killer with the phone, or they had the phone the whole time and lied to her about it . . . but then they would have called right away, and not in the middle of the night. Would that be a better scenario, or a worse one?

Either way, she needed to work fast. A countdown had begun with Evani's death, but without one of those handy LED readouts with the numbers ticking backward to let her know exactly where she stood.

The Rottweiler reappeared with a tennis ball in his mouth,

tail wagging. She took it and tossed the slimy thing to the far corner, listening with satisfaction as his paws thundered across the floorboards. If she couldn't sleep, the neighbors might as well be awake, too.

Saturday, 1:35 a.m.

Maggie retrieved a sweater from the lab's closet. The climate-controlled interior stayed at a steady temperature twenty-four/seven, but somehow it always felt chillier in the wee hours of the morning whether winter or summer outside. This must be largely psychosomatic, she thought, but didn't know what else to do about it besides put on a sweater.

She could be home in bed. Nothing in her job description obligated her to stay up all night to run the bloody fingerprint against the database. But finding the killer's print in the victim's blood, well, that was like a real estate agent hanging out a SOLD sign on the most expensive property in the city or an advertising executive landing a contract with a large auto insurance company—merely one part of a professional's day, but an enormously satisfying part that didn't come around often.

So she had transferred the best photograph of the print she had to the system, then changed the coloring to gray scale, increased the contrast, used the software's markers to denote where the friction ridges came to an end or divided into two. Then it was ready to run.

Searching the print against each of ten fingers of each person in the database could take twenty or thirty minutes. Searching it against only ten prints of one person took seconds, so Maggie first set the program to search it against Marlon Toner, and only Marlon Toner. If it matched, her work would be done and she could go home to get a few short but happy hours of sleep. She had already checked and knew his prints were there. She assumed his prior arrests had been drug related, but that information didn't come up in the fingerprint database and at that time of the night she wasn't sufficiently curious to look it up in the reporting system.

The search had, indeed, only taken seconds, but also produced only three suggestions by the system how the print might correlate to one of Marlon Toner's fingers. None appeared even reasonably close. Maggie printed out his ten-print card and examined each finger herself, glancing between the blood print enlarged on her monitor and the paper in her hand. The machine hadn't been wrong. The blood print ridges formed an incomplete but definite whorl, and all ten of Toner's prints were arches. In no known universe could he have left that print.

She'd have to look forward to even fewer hours of—she hoped—satisfied sleep, and set the system to run the blood print against all the prints in the database. She got up and made herself a cup of coffee to battle that early-morning-office chill. She made it a priority so that it jumped ahead of the automated, nighttime work, the continual comparison of previously unidentified latent prints to the standards of the new arrestees.

Then she retook her seat, sipped the hot liquid, and stared at the tiny magnifying glass symbol in the lower right corner of her monitor screen, the only visible indication that the system was searching. When the power saving option triggered and turned the screen to black, she jostled the mouse to wake it back up. She could probably get other work done while she was there, but didn't feel capable of prompting her tired brain to handle anything more than sipping coffee and watching the tiny icon.

Why didn't Jack seem more concerned about what Rick might find in Chicago? Was there truly nothing to find? Had he covered his tracks that well, or better yet, had never been to the city in his life? Or did he tell her not to worry simply to keep her from panicking? He had been doing this for years, and no doubt had an infallible exit strategy to slip out of town if there were any chance of his fellow officers showing up at his door with anything other than a barbecue invitation. She knew him at least that well, by now.

If he planned to leave, would he tell her?

Would she want him to? Best if she didn't know, best if she didn't have to fake her shock and surprise, best to keep that plausible deniability going. But the idea that he would leave without even giving her a heads-up came like a splash of cold water on a hot face. How could he just walk out and leave her to pick up the pieces of what used to be her totally normal life? If there had been one tiny inadequate comfort in bearing the terrible secret she now carried, it had been the existence of at least one other person in the world who knew, who understood what had happened and, maybe, why. That bond had been painfully forged in an unwanted fire, but it remained a bond nonetheless.

The tiny magnifying glass finally turned to an arrow, which meant the tireless automaton had finished one job and waited for the next. She clicked on the spreadsheet line with the information of her blood print. This opened a bisected display with the print on one side and the prints that the system's logarithms thought most closely matched on the other. She could click on a list at the bottom to change this view to the system's second choice, then its third, and so on. Parallel lines crossed the screen, pointing up the corresponding areas, the various colors used making the images light up like Christmas trees. It looked good, Maggie thought. At first glance she could see a pile of similarities and no differences.

Then she looked at the list at the bottom of the screen, to see to whom this print belonged.

That couldn't be right.

She gazed at the two prints again, followed each line of correspondence. This ridge ending to that ridge ending. Two ridges in between, then a fork in a ridge forming a bifurcation. Another ridge in between and slightly upward to a short ridge. And so on, and so on, until she got to the edges of the bloody print and ran out of ridges to look at.

She printed out the ten-print card and a glossy hard copy of the bloody print she had photographed, laid them side by side on her desktop and used two jeweler's loupes to examine them without the aid of the computer. She used two old-fashioned picks, skinny metal sticks with a point at one end and a wooden handle at the other, the whole instrument more narrow than the average ink pen. She used those to hold her place in one print while she examined the corresponding location in the other print. Same result.

This isn't necessary *bad*, she told herself. Confusing, yes, but it doesn't have to be bad.

But her body knew better. Her heart had begun to pound the minute she saw that name at the top of the list. This was bad, all right. It couldn't *not* be bad.

Her fingers reached for the phone and she found herself scrolling to Jack's name in her contact list before she even realized it, and made her thumb stop a millimeter from the phone icon, with only the tiniest bit of atmosphere keeping the electrical charge in her skin from activating the call.

The need to speak to him was urgent, primal. She had been pondering how he had turned her world turbulent and unpredictable and then in the next breath he became, illogically, ironically, the foundation to which she needed to cling.

She could dial. Or she could do what was *right*.

She sat frozen in that chill, dark hour of the night, in a silent office on a silent floor, trapped in her little bubble of existence, cut off from the rest of humanity.

Then her hand moved.

The cheery ringing tones seemed to last an eternity, but finally a voice sounded on the other end of the digital connection.

Maggie took a breath and used words she had probably

never spoken to him. "Denny, I'm so sorry to wake you up in the middle of the night, but I didn't know what else to do."

Her boss shrugged off the slumber that quickly, his tone firm and worried. "Maggie? What's wrong?"

"I have something here I don't know what to do with. I mean, I do, but—"

"Slow down. Start from the beginning."

She could hear rustling sounds, Denny slipping out of the bed and bedroom to avoid disturbing his wife any further, padding to the kitchen or living room as he kept his voice low to avoid waking one or all of their three children. Maggie quickly outlined the evening's murder case and crime scene. She told him that Rick and Will had questioned the woman early that day about her brother, that they had gone back with Jack and Riley about Evan Harding, and then Jack and Riley went back again in the evening after a neighbor found her dead. She explained in one sentence the location and condition of the print in blood. Denny made encouraging sounds, patiently waiting for her to get to the part that required dragging her boss out of bed on this cold December night.

"It didn't match the brother so I ran it against the whole database, of course. And it found a match. I've looked and looked, but it's really a pretty good print so I don't see how I could have gotten this wrong. Unless I've totally lost my mind—"

Even Denny's patience had a limit. "Maggie. Why did you call me? Whose print is it?"

"I don't understand this," she said. "No matter what sort of explanation I come up with, it doesn't make sense, not even a little."

"Maggie. *Whose?*"

"That's just it," she said. "It's Rick's."

Chapter 16

Okay, so Jack became her *second* call, and she let him sleep most of the night before she made it. Denny hadn't even tried to convince her to go home and get at least a little rest; instead he came in and verified the print for her. They quadruple-checked the paperwork before he disturbed the head of the homicide unit at breakfast to tell him that one of his detectives had, inexplicably, become a suspect in the murder of a woman he'd known less than a day.

"What?" Jack said. "*What?*"

She repeated herself.

"I'll be right there."

And he was, behind the chief of detectives and ahead of his partner, Riley. The chief of detectives asked Maggie and Denny seven times if they were sure, and, having received the same answer each time, went off shaking his head in bewilderment.

Riley now asked the question and got the same answer.

"Did you try calling him?" Jack asked.

She hadn't even thought of it. The implication struck her immediately and with the shock of an ice bath. Had it been

Jack, she would have called instantly, demanded an explanation, warned him that trouble brewed, thereby committing a crime by interfering in an investigation. She hadn't even considered doing so in Rick's case, but she would have protected Jack.

Her very bones seemed to tremble.

Had she fallen that far?

Take a breath. Maybe she wouldn't have—if she thought Jack had murdered an innocent woman, stabbed her to death on her own apartment floor, that would violate their unholy agreement. So after some thought, perhaps she wouldn't warn him. Even though to expose Jack would expose herself, in the end.

"Maggie?" he asked. "You okay? Do you want to sit down?"

He touched the fist she had pressed to her mouth while thinking. She unwrapped her arms from her torso, where they'd been getting a physical and mental grip and told herself this, firmly: what is different in Rick's case is that Rick, she could be certain, had not murdered anybody.

"The homicide chief did," she said in answer to Jack's question. "No answer. They tried Will but he doesn't answer either; probably has his phone turned off for family time. Since it's only a weekend trip, he didn't mention where they were going. They'll try all the resorts within driving distance; there aren't that many."

"Maggie," Riley said, "let me get some background. As crazy as this all seems, it's still our case and we have to investigate it like we would any other."

"I know that." Why would he think she *didn't* know that?

"Let me take a load off. That was a pretty short night, and I guess it wasn't a night at all for you." He pulled over one of the task chairs and made a show of planting his decently broad girth into its seat. She knew he hoped this would prompt her to sit down rather than having to sound condescending by suggesting that she might *need* to sit down in order to deal with the trauma of answering questions about her possibly murderous ex-husband.

Purely because this was Riley, she cut him some slack by sitting without an invitation. "He didn't do it, you know."

Riley glanced up from his notepad. "What?"

"I don't know what's going on, but I don't for a minute believe that Rick killed that woman. Come on, Riley, you've known him for years. Can you see Rick killing anyone?"

He said, carefully noncommittal, "He's got a pretty short fuse."

She almost laughed. "Verbally, yes. But physically? Rick was all bark, no bite. He was never, ever, *ever* violent with me, not even during our worst fights. And why would he kill some woman he barely knew? You had been there earlier—-was there any indication that they had met before?"

Riley glanced at his phone, almost certainly to avoid having to tell her that *he* was supposed to be asking the questions. "No. Nothing about her or her apartment seemed familiar to you?"

"Me? No. Not in the slightest."

Riley asked his questions without relish, and without expecting Jack to help—which he didn't. Jack sat like an uncertain lump, his gaze never leaving her face.

"She was a pretty girl. Is there any chance he—"

"Went there to make a pass at her and went crazy when she refused? No. Rick may have been a teenage boy where women were concerned, but he wasn't a complete Neanderthal. Besides, he was basically, well, a racist."

"Sometimes that's why they think they can get away with it," Riley said, painstakingly gentle.

"Seriously?" Maggie demanded—with astonishment. She didn't even bother with anger.

He spread his hands. "No, I don't seriously think that. I'm throwing out possibilities because I don't know what else to do. Let's hope Rick can clear it up when we find him.

I just got a text—they made entry to his apartment but he isn't there."

Maggie goggled. "You broke into his *apartment*? He's going to be mad."

"That's the least of his worries right now," Jack said quietly, and with that, more than anything, the shock settled in completely. The worry that had been churning at the bottom of her stomach rose and blossomed into a panicky flower that unfurled in her chest.

"Maybe they got the building manager to let them in," Riley soothed. "We need his contact information—he doesn't have any kids, right, or any other exes? Do you know his current girlfriend? No? What about parents?"

"They live near Dayton. He's got two sisters and a brother, but they're scattered in different states, last I heard."

Riley persisted. "Do you think, if he were in trouble, he'd go to his parents?"

Absolutely, she thought. Running home to Mama is exactly what Rick would do. "Yes, but please don't bother them . . . I hate to see you . . . they're not bad people. And I don't believe Rick is in trouble, I mean that way. Obviously he's in some kind of trouble because no one can find him, but—"

Jack reached out and took her hand. She looked at him in surprise—she must sound more discombobulated than she realized. After a brief squeeze he let go and she forced her words into logical sentences. "I don't believe, at *all*, that Rick is guilty of murder. He must have gone there to follow up on something and walked in on Jennifer's killer, tried to help her, and then gave chase."

For once, Jack and Riley had the same look on both their faces.

Pity.

The poor little sweet wife, believing in her (ex) man despite all evidence to the contrary.

But she could be angry about that later. Right now she

reasoned through the scenario. "The guy must have still been there, or Rick thought he was there . . . that's the only reason he wouldn't have at least called an ambulance before pursuing. Rick could be—in real trouble. He could be hurt somewhere."

"We have a BOLO out on him and his car," Riley said.

"Look—try calling him."

"The chief said—"

"Yeah, I know, but . . . maybe if he's screening calls, he'll pick up for you."

Because if he is a murderer on the run, he might get sentimental enough to talk to the woman he still carries a torch for. She didn't hide the eye-roll but cut it short. They were only following the evidence. She pulled out her cell and found him in her contacts. If it might help, she'd try anything.

The ringing tone sounded and sounded again. Eventually Rick's digital answering app came on.

She didn't leave a message. He'd see the number—if he could.

Chapter 17

"What do you think?" Riley asked as soon as they were alone, which didn't occur for a number of hours. There had been much activity in the homicide unit, all of it stilted and awkward and seriously confused.

"I didn't like the guy." Jack pulled the car door shut, the silence of the parking garage a sharp contrast after the morning. "He resided miles past the asshole border, but I can't believe he'd kill some woman he barely knew for no apparent reason. We were there with them—he didn't know her, had no particular reaction to her at all. He's not that good of an actor."

"Agreed." The vehicle emerged onto the street, the world outside one single shade of light gray.

"As uber-convenient as it may be, Maggie's explanation might make more sense."

"He interrupted the murder? Then where is he now? Dead somewhere, or held hostage? I'm ..." Riley's voice stalled as he waited for a red light. "I don't have quite the faith in Rick Gardiner as harmless jerk that you and his ex-wife do. I have nothing to hang it on, but I've never trusted the guy. Squirrelly."

Jack considered this, still dismissed the notion. Of course he didn't know Rick like Riley and certainly Maggie did, and despite her words, Maggie seemed deeply disturbed. Maybe that was *why*—because deep down she knew what Rick Gardiner might be capable of. It had kept her up all night, working, doing anything to distract herself. She had even driven to the Medical Examiner's and taped the dead woman's clothing, examining hairs and fibers during the wee hours—to no end, she had said. No foreign hairs, no fibers or animal fur of note. No feathers or cigar leaves.

They were on their way to East Fifty-fifth Street. Jennifer Toner had looked up the three addresses on her laptop, and with both Gardiner and Marlon Toner in the wind, retracing her last steps seemed their only avenue of investigation. They had no guarantee that she had gotten any closer to the pharmacies than Googling their locations, but again, Jack didn't see a lot of choices, and hanging around the police department had given him a tension headache. "I checked out these places on the state pharmacy board website. For what it's worth, all three have a license in good standing and no disciplinary actions."

"Well, look at you, being all researchy," Riley joked without malice. "When did you have time to do that?"

"While you were in the bathroom. I didn't check with Vice to see if they had any on their radar. I couldn't find that in RMS." He meant the Report Management System.

"No, that's going to require actually talking to someone."

An activity Jack avoided whenever possible. "*But* I checked prior reports and there's been no calls for service, other than a couple robberies."

"Hardly surprising for a place that sells drugs in a sorta not-so-picturesque part of town." Riley pulled up to the curb and parked. The small storefront of Herron's Pharmacy in a beat-up plaza with inadequate parking could use a coat of paint but otherwise seemed respectable enough, tucked in between a laundromat and a convenience store. Under a bright gray sky one customer came out and another went in, cars drove by, and it all seemed as unthreatening as a bingo hall.

They entered. Brick-colored tiles covered the floor of the waiting area and a chest-high counter blocked the back half of the facility. A thick glass partition extended down from the ceiling and ended about five inches above the counter. It reminded Jack of the check-cashing store, except this place had a way to get from the front to the back: one very heavy-looking, stainless-steel door.

Two young men in white lab coats worked behind it; one tended the cash register and the other placed bulky envelopes into colored bins on the shelves. Both looked at the cops, tensed, and looked again. The one at the cash register quickly categorized them as cops, not robbers, and relaxed halfway. The one at the shelves either couldn't place them or found cops equally problematic, and remained frozen with his hand stretched toward an upper shelf until the bag in it began to slip from his fingers.

Jack and Riley waited until the elderly woman at the counter had been served. She turned around, saw them, worried for an instant but had them made even more quickly than the boy at the counter had. With a curl of her lip she strode past them and out the door without so much as a nod.

They flashed their badges, then asked the cashier if a Jennifer Toner had been in, possibly asking about a prescription for a Marlon Toner.

The cashier shook his head. About thirty, with tight black skin stretching over high cheekbones, he had worked on Friday until they closed at six p.m., didn't recall the name, and didn't give a flicker of an eyelash at the woman's photo when they showed it to him.

"She might have been upset about you filling a prescription for her brother."

"Why?"

"Because he's an addict."

The guy shook his head again, this time for a different reason. "No shortage of those these days. But we ain't shady here. We check the prescribing doctor, make sure they have a current license and a physical address. If the script's for a large amount or they want an advance on the next refill, we call and check. You see the sign." He hooked his thumb toward a posted, professionally made placard that said the management reserved the right to refuse service to anyone, without clarification of "service" or "anyone." "If someone looks like they're in a bad way, the script looks fake, they act aggressive or under the influence, we send 'em out of here. Boss don't put up with no nonsense." He seemed a bit defensive, and Jack couldn't blame him. Since the advent of pill mills and the opioid crisis, pharmacies smaller than the average CVS were viewed with suspicion.

"Okay. What about this guy?" He held up a photo of Marlon Toner. No recognition. He tried a mug shot of Raymond Winchester. Nothing.

The door gave a *bing* and a customer entered, a young woman with a baby on her hip, both bundled up with puffy coats and hats and mittens. Only the baby's eyes were visible above the zipped-up collar, liquid pools of deep brown.

"We need to know if this guy ever filled a prescription here—" Riley began, but the cashier suggested they step into the office and asked the other worker to take over the counter.

They moved to the door and listened to at least three bolts slide before it opened. The cashier ushered them into a very cramped storage room and quickly locked the door behind them. "Sorry, but we can't be too careful. We've been robbed three times in the past two years, and that's not even bad for a little place like this. The bulletproof glass and the steel door talk most guys out of it, but some be desperate enough to shove a gun under that partition. 'Course that doesn't give them a lot of room to maneuver. I was here one time, a guy tried that on me, and I grabbed it away from him. You can't get no leverage when you stick your hand through a hole."

As he chatted, he squeezed between them and shelves of boxes and flexible envelopes bulging with small bottles and led the way to an even more cramped office of sorts. Three of the walls had shelving utilized to the last inch and the desk held a computer and piles of paperwork and two energy drink cans and exactly one square foot of available work-space. A place for guests to sit was out of the question, so the cashier politely stood as well. "The smarter ones wait out the back for the last guy to leave, but we're careful about that, too. We don't open that door unless we got a clear view of the back parking, and if the camera's dark then we call the . . . you guys."

"Smart," Riley said. "Can you tell us if Marlon Toner filled his scripts here?"

The guy wore a sympathetic expression. "Can't tell you that, man. HIPAA laws. I wish I could—we're here to serve this neighborhood, take care of the folk who can't go far for what they need. I got no reason to protect the junkies, they're the ones who rob us. But you know . . ."

"HIPAA." The Health Insurance Portability and Ac-countability Act.

"Yep."

"But it all goes into a database, right?"

"Yeah, so the state can monitor frequent fliers who are getting way more scripts than they should need, or doctors who write too many. But that searches automatically when I put a new script in. I can't just go in there and browse around whenever I feel like it. I mean, can't you guys get a warrant or something and get the info from the state board? Something like that?"

"We probably could," Jack said. "But it would take time, and we've got a murdered woman right now."

"What about a doctor?" Riley asked.

"I can't tell you what scripts they write without accessing patient info, and that can't be done, like I said."

"But you said you verify the doctor's address, make sure he's legit. Can you give us the address of a particular doctor?"

The man seemed perplexed. "Can't you, like, Google it or something?"

"Tried that."

"Huh."

"All we need is an address. A legitimate doctor shouldn't have a problem with that."

"Huh. Yeah, I guess so." He reached over to the other side of the desk and retrieved a clipboard.

"Do you have a database or something—"

"Nah, we go old school with this. We get a list from the state, keep it updated." He showed it to them, a thick sheaf of paper precariously pinned to the board, with names and locations in alphabetical order. Many had been crossed out and corrections written in with different inks and hands. "Reason they're so big on addresses is all those pill mills and the docs who file fake Medicare claims were using PO boxes. So now they require a street address, and now the docs use empty storefronts—big help. Who you looking for?"

"Phillip Castleman."

The man flipped to the C's, perused, then said, "Yeah, right here. 1500 East 14th, Suite 214. Need the zip code?"

"No, thanks," Riley said with a satisfied grunt. "Thanks. Thanks a lot."

"Who's dead?"

"What?"

"You said there was a dead woman. Who's dead?"

"Sorry." Riley flipped his notebook shut, stowed it in a pocket, and didn't look too terribly sorry. "We can't comment on an open investigation."

They were guided back through the tight squeeze of the storage room and, after a careful check of the outer lobby using a monitor screen held to the wall with duct tape, released back into the wild. The young mother had been replaced by an older man who sniffled and coughed while the other staff member typed at a keyboard, speaking into the phone tucked under one ear.

The outdoors hadn't warmed up any and they hustled into the car.

Riley said, "Well, we found the mysterious Dr. Castleman. He does exist. Now, provided he's actually at his last known address, we can find out if he knew Jennifer Toner, check his shoes for drops of blood, and have this wrapped up before lunch."

Jack didn't bother to answer to this wildly optimistic scenario. He felt certain they would find only more questions.

The cashier at Herron's watched the cops leave, and then, while his coworker gave the sniffling man his antibiotics, retreated back to the tiny office, and shut the door. He called his boss.

"Yeah, wanted to let you know, there were cops here. Asking about that same doctor, Castleman . . . told them I couldn't tell them anything, rules wouldn't let me . . . then they wanted his address . . . it's just an address! . . . I *had* to, they know that ain't covered under the rules . . . but I had to! They was *cops*, not some crazy bitch yellin' about her brother! . . . yeah, they wrote it down and everything . . . I don't know . . . they said some woman's *dead*, what—well, I'm *sorry* . . . yeah, okay . . . I will."

He hung up, shaking his head. He had no idea who this doctor was, who the brother was, if the woman yesterday might or might not be the now-dead woman, or why his boss cared about any of it.

But he sure as hell wasn't going to ask.

Chapter 18

"Are you sure this is it?" Riley asked, peering through the windshield and the falling snow at the nondescript building tucked into an unpicturesque corner formed by the elevated innerbelt and East 14th.

"No. But it's what the GPS says."

"This is Eighteenth."

"Apparently, it's also Fourteenth."

"It can't be two different streets."

"Apparently it can, and is."

"All right," Riley huffed as if he'd reached a decision, switched off the ignition, and visibly steeled himself to emerge into the biting wind. "If we can finally run down this Castleman character, it will be worth it." He continued to grumble over the sounds of the cars along the freeway and their feet squeaking against the inches of snow coating the parking lot. "Though I don't know what we're going to ask him. Did you turn your patient Marlon Toner into a drug addict? Did you give his ID to another drug addict? Did an irate sister come looking for you because you turned Marlon Toner into a drug addict? Did you then track her down and leave her to bleed out on her living room floor? Gee, let me think: HIPAA law, HIPAA law, no, and no." He jerked open the door to the lobby and stamped the snow off his feet onto the already-sodden doormat.

Jack didn't try to reassure him that they were on the right track, because he had no faith that they were. He didn't offer any suggestions for an interrogation, either, because of course Riley spoke the truth and even if they did find this doctor, he wouldn't be able to tell them anything about a patient. But Castleman remained the only lead they had.

A floor directory had been mounted on the wall, but the glass had been broken and the letters rearranged to spell nasty words. The elevator call button produced a grinding, groaning sound and Jack looked around for the stairs. After a shuddering crunch echoed down the shaft, Riley apparently decided a bit of exercise wouldn't kill him and followed Jack to the stairwell.

The second floor appeared no more welcoming than the first, with worn carpeting and walls that hadn't been repainted for several decades. At least most of the closed doors were labeled: a dentist, a massage therapist, a CPA, a Dr. Sidney Jeffers, and one that used crayons on white copy paper to spell out "Kayla's Day Care" in curling letters meant to be whimsical. Business seemed to be booming, to judge from the soup of shouts, crying, and whines boiling behind the door.

Kayla's Day Care also seemed to be Suite 214. They couldn't be sure since the crayoned paper had been affixed with enough tape to endure gale-force winds, but it sat between 215 and 2-space-3, and so seemed a good guess. The two men sighed in unison, glanced at each other with identical looks of resigned unhappiness, and then Jack knocked on the door.

The cacophony inside did not shift. Jack knocked again.

No change in the noise level, but the knob slowly turned

and the door inched inward, revealing a small boy with dark skin, huge eyes, and a Hot Wheels car clutched in one hand. He stared at the two cops.

"Hello," Riley said. "Umm—can we speak to—"

A grown-up hand appeared around the boy's wrist and gently pulled it from the inner knob, then a tall woman with brown hair to her waist opened it the rest of the way. "Jamie, we let Teacher open the door, right?"

Jamie didn't agree, but he didn't argue, either.

The two detectives hastily explained their search for Dr. Phillip Castleman in Suite 214.

The woman's figure could be described as Junoesque, though the expression on her face suggested they should keep any such descriptions to themselves. The playroom inside had chipped paint and no décor other than a mountain of mismatched toys, but could easily have once been a waiting room. Two openings at either end led to hallways with a half wall in the center, behind which supplies were stacked on a desk or table. Preschool-age children roamed everywhere, clutching toys, arguing, chasing, laughing, sniffling, and coughing—at least until they caught sight of the detectives. Then they crowded toward the doorway like teen girls at a pop band concert, forcing the woman to exercise crowd control with both hands and one leg.

As she used this impressive balance to keep her charges from escaping, she told them in no uncertain terms that yes, this was Suite 214 but no doctor worked there or even visited the premises, and she had rented the unit for the past two years.

"Sorry to keep you from your work." Riley swished his body backward a few inches when a little girl aimed a particularly wet cough toward him. "Is there any way we could— could you tell us where the super or the landlord's offices are?"

"Basement," she said, and having reached the limit of her ability to stand on one leg, shut the door. They heard the knob click and the dead bolt, mounted six feet above the floor, give a *snick*. That would keep Jamie from letting in any Tom, Dick, or non-custodial parent who knocked.

"What were you going to ask?" Jack wondered aloud, ears adjusting to the relative quiet of the hallway.

"If we could look around. Running a pill mill out of a day care would be friggin' genius. Our Dr. Castleman could have an office in the back, be passing out scripts to customers who pretend to be picking up their kid. But I wasn't quite willing to risk infection with cold or flu or whooping cough or whatever else those mini-incubators are carrying around."

"I'm pretty sure she would have refused anyway." They moved toward the stairwell.

"Take it from me, a kid's great the first couple years, and then they start school. Once they do, anything some other kid in the class has, they have. And then you have." Riley paused outside 211, the suite belonging to Dr. Sidney Jeffers. "Think we should try this guy? A doctor, on the same floor. They might have been at least acquainted."

"Why not?"

Business also boomed at Dr. Sidney Jeffers's office. At least ten patients lined the walls, one coughing, one with rheumy eyes, one with a cast on his ankle, a tired woman with a squirming toddler on her lap. Their chairs all faced a small television on a rickety end table, away from the receptionist behind an opened, frosted window. It reminded Jack of about every doctor's waiting room he'd ever been in, the same general miasma of worry and discomfort. No one went to the doctor because things were perfect.

Only a few of the patients even glanced up as they entered.

The receptionist, a young man with his hair cut so short he may as well have shaved it, gave them a polite look but waited for them to speak. The office didn't stand on pomposity—files sat around in haphazard heaps, at least three used coffee cups had been scattered at irregular intervals, a (hopefully clean) pint milk carton had been cut off to make a pen holder, and a small animal sat in a cage to the receptionist's left, close enough for patients to get a look at the thing but too far for them to stick germy fingers through the wires for it to nibble on. A questionable precaution since the cage door sat open and the thing toddled out and climbed up the receptionist's arm to curl up on his shoulder. Jack had never seen a doctor's office with a resident pet. It looked like a cross between a rat and a squirrel to him, with short gray fur patterned with dark brown and white in spots, twitching ears, creepy pink feet, and eyes so oversized that it resembled an anime character. A tag on the cage read SUGAR GLIDER. Cute enough that the sight of it must lower a patient's blood pressure a couple millimeters of mercury . . . but it made Jack think of hantavirus.

Riley asked if there were a Dr. Castleman working in that office. No, the guy said, only Dr. Jeffers. Or perhaps on the same floor? The guy said he didn't recognize the name, and waited for the next question. How long had Dr. Jeffers's office been at this location? The guy—his name badge read WAYNE—had only been working there for about a year and a half. Could they talk to Dr. Jeffers? He was with a patient. They understood that. They'd wait.

Wayne said he'd let the doc know. True to his word he stood up and grabbed a crutch from the wall at his side, tucking it under his right arm and limping away, toward a door at the back. Perhaps not only an employee, but a patient as well.

Jack quietly turned one of the chairs so that he could sit with his back against the wall, able to see the TV, the door, and the receptionist window. Riley did the same. After a series of wary glances, the other patients uniformly ignored them, no doubt wondering if these interlopers might cut in line. Few things were more cutthroat than the waiting order at a doctor's office.

As it turned out, they were right to worry. Wayne reappeared shortly and asked the detectives to follow him. The door to the waiting room locked automatically behind them.

The examination rooms they passed didn't seem any more luxurious than the waiting room, but floors were clean and the counters uncluttered. Dr. Sidney Jeffers turned out to be a fortyish man with already-thinning brown hair, an already-paunching midsection, a stethoscope around his neck, and a few stains on his lab coat that hadn't quite washed out. "What can I do for you gentlemen? Is something wrong?"

Jack said, "We're trying to locate a doctor who is supposed to be at this address. A Dr. Castleman." He didn't add that by *address,* he meant the building and not the suite.

To his surprise, Jeffers said, "Yes, but he's not here anymore. He actually had the room across the hall, though we had a joint practice. He left—oh, I don't know, at least two years ago."

"But he was here?"

"Oh yeah. Phil was my partner."

"Where is he now?" Riley sounded buoyed by this bread crumb of progress.

"Ooo, I don't know. We haven't spoken since—well, since he left. Not that we had a falling-out or anything. Only a difference in views."

"Can you explain that?"

The man paused, leaning against the exam table. It formed the only seating in the room, and if he had an office, he didn't ask them to it. He had patients to get to, after all. "We met each other in med school, ran into each other after residencies . . . we both felt it important not to become another cog in the big healthcare chains, forced to put profit over patients. I didn't want to get sucked into that insurance payment morass. So we hung out our shingle, but, eventually, Phil needed a *little* bit of profit. I get it—he had a wife, kids, a mortgage. We parted ways."

"When was that?"

"Like I said, about two years ago . . . I think."

Riley said, "Are you aware that he's still writing prescriptions using this address?"

The doctor's eyebrows tilted upward. "Uh, no, I was not. He could be using old pads . . . but the thing is, I don't think he's even in Cleveland anymore. When he left our practice he said he'd accepted a position with Columbia in New Mexico."

"Did you have a problem with him overprescribing meds?"

"Antibiotics. He handed those out like aspirin—hardly unusual, that's why we're seeing so many antibiotic-resistant strains of—"

"Do you know where he is now? Where he lives? Phone number?"

"Um . . . no." He pulled out his cell phone. "Number, let's see. Yes, still got him in Contacts—" He read off a series of digits, which Riley wrote down. "But that's our area code, so he's probably changed it by now. He used to live somewhere in Lakewood. I was only there once, for a barbecue or something."

"He didn't leave a forwarding?"

"Oh, honestly . . . he probably did. I think I sent his mail on for the first month or two, but I'm sure I've lost any address he gave me by now." He glanced around as if the worn surroundings would bear him out. "I'm not very good at staying in touch. This place keeps me in a constant state of 'slightly overwhelmed.' "

Jack asked, "Are there any professional organizations that would have his current status on record?"

Dr. Jeffers screwed up his face in contemplation. "Probably the New Mexico state licensing board."

Jack thought of something. "Maybe the scripts aren't coming from him. Is it possible a patient or employee might have stolen his old prescription pads?"

More thought. "Sure, I guess so. I try to keep mine in my pocket, not lying out in the open, but I don't know how strictly Phil ran things."

Or Phil could have found another way to pay the mortgage, Jack thought, one that didn't require a move to New Mexico. He held out the photo of Marlon Toner. "Do you know this man?"

The doctor gave the photo his full attention. "I don't believe so."

"What about this one?" He showed him the mug shot of Raymond Winchester—the other "Marlon Toner."

"Nope."

"Do you have a patient by the name of Marlon Toner?"

"Ah, sorry. I can't discuss patients. You know—"

"Yes, we know that. But we mention it because he's the suspect in a murder. So if he does show up here, you might want to give us a call. For your own safety, and that of your patients."

Jeffers appeared somber. A professional dilemma—call the cops and violate patient confidentiality, or don't call them and risk Toner harming someone else.

But he would have to work that one out for himself, should the situation arise. The hobbling Wayne showed them out. The patients in the waiting room bothered to turn this time, most of them, so their faces could express the deep disdain they felt for those who jumped the line. Jack and Riley slunk out the door with hasty feet and didn't even consider the elevator this time.

Descending the stairwell, Riley said, "At least we know our Dr. Castleman isn't a complete fiction."

"A real person, who may or may not be in New Mexico."

"And if he is, who's using his name?"

In the lobby Jack zipped up his coat before exiting. The snowfall hadn't abated during their time indoors, and a half-inch already covered the windshield of their car. He didn't see the attraction of snow, never had. He didn't ski, and hadn't done a lot of sledding as a child in a city where the average winter temperatures never dipped below forty. But he did appreciate the quiet, the way the snow muffled sound in the early morning hours, made the whole world feel blanketed and waiting, its voice temporarily lowered. A man could think in that quiet.

Now he said, "There's one person who might know."

Riley zipped his parka up to the nose. "Marlon Toner."

Chapter 19

Sunday passed without progress on any front. Maggie mailed the Christmas gifts to her brother's family from the automated machines in an empty post office lobby, and fretted. Either Rick was in another state investigating Jack's past and didn't answer his phone because he didn't want anyone to talk him out of his mission—or because he had forgotten to charge it, something he often did—*or* he had, for some inexplicable reason, murdered Jennifer Toner and was now on the run from his former colleagues, including her.

She didn't know which scenario worried her more.

She tried to walk off her frustration, having bundled up for the trip. The icy blast from the river swept through her parka as soon as she left the protection of her apartment building, muffler and gloves and boots in place until only her eyes were visible—and, after a block or two she wondered if she should invest in ski goggles as frostbite nipped at her eyeballs. She thought of window-shopping—the store windows of the Higbee's and May Company used to be famous for their Christmastime displays. Those stores' traditions were now lost to time and she didn't think anything the casino might do would have the same joyous vibe. The city did its best to compensate, turning Public Square into a winter wonderland of lights and music, complete with an ice-skating rink.

Instead, she found herself back in front of the Justice Center, which had no music and very little joy. She could go inside to her office, try to find something useful to do, but knew there was nothing she *could* do, and that was the worst to bear. What the hell was Rick up to? Was he in Chicago, finding out stuff about Jack that she didn't want to know? Did he kill Jennifer Toner in a botched attempt to frame Jack for it?

Did Jack kill Jennifer Toner in a successful attempt to frame Rick for it? That seemed even crazier—how would he get Rick's fingerprint, unless Rick was dead, and if Rick was dead then what was the point of framing him for a murder? That made no sense at all. But if Rick wasn't dead, where was he?

And round and round.

She didn't push through the glass doors, knowing that she had gravitated there because she had no place else to go and to give in to that seemed too depressing to contemplate. She turned away, determined to go to the Chocolate Bar and have a hot chocolate martini instead.

But she didn't. She just went home.

And fretted.

Shanaya Thomas went to work with dark circles under her eyes and continued to convince unsuspecting citizens that she worked for the IRS—phones never slept and no one wanted to risk arrest with the holiday looming around the corner—while her gaze constantly swept her surroundings to see if The Guy might be coming for her. Or possibly her boss.

She didn't know which possibility scared her more.

*   *   *

Jack and Riley monitored the BOLOs for Marlon Toner, Philip Castleman, and Detective Richard Gardiner, but all three continued to exist only as whispers on the arctic wind. Riley spent the afternoon at his daughters' school's Christmas pageant, and Jack at least attended the autopsy of Jennifer Toner. It did not reveal anything particularly helpful: she had been killed by a single stab wound that penetrated the heart and nicked her aorta. The weapon was sharp and thin and round and at least eight inches long, approximately, and yes, once the pathologist reviewed the other pathologist's notes from the previous autopsy, did seem quite similar to whatever instrument had killed Evan Harding.

One of the ME specialists taped the clothing for him. Technically Rick was now a suspect, so technically Maggie should not interact with any of the case evidence. This strict adherence to conflict of interest protocol would eventually fall apart, however, since Maggie was the only hair and fiber expert in the city. But he could cross that unstable, shuddering bridge when he got to it. Much better, anyway, that he investigate Rick for the murder of Jennifer Toner than Rick investigating him for any number of events in other cities. That part of current events had righted for him, once again.

Jack then went home and drank coffee with Greta curled on his lap. He knew she sat there more for the source of warmth than any great affection—he and his cat did not see eye to eye on proper thermostat settings—but appreciated the company all the same. He told himself he was recharging, but knew the reality: he was stuck.

Then Monday came.

Monday, 8:36 a.m.

Denny greeted her with "Any news?" He knew better than to waste time in small talk. It would neither distract nor comfort her.

"No. No one can get hold of him, no one's seen his car, and they can't find the victim's brother either."

"And he hasn't called you?"

"Of course not!"

"Sorry," he said, divesting himself of coat and gloves and not quite meeting her gaze. "It's . . . I mean, he's your ex-husband. No one would expect you to . . ."

"I wouldn't protect him." But she couldn't be entirely sure of that. She *had* been married to him. She was sure as hell protecting Jack, and decided not to examine that fact right then. "I would *help* him, I mean . . . encourage him to come in and explain, but I don't believe he needs protection, not from us. I don't for a minute believe that he killed Jennifer Toner."

But she couldn't be entirely sure of *that*, either.

Carol entered, and Maggie caught her up with current events. The older woman drank two cups of coffee in rapid succession, such was her agitation as she expressed shock, amazement, confusion, and abject fury that Maggie hadn't called her to share this emotional turmoil. Maggie protested that she had not been particularly turmoiled in her emotions, but knew she had and knew that Carol knew. After Maggie promised upon her lifeblood to keep Carol apprised of any and all updates to future developments in this and any other drama that affected Maggie, Carol trundled off to her DNA analysis room, still shaking her head.

Maggie texted Jack: **Anything**?

A text returned with reasonable promptness. **No.**

Time to get to work, to make sure she crossed every *t* and dotted every *i* on all the other tasks, which the taxpayers of Cleveland routinely paid her to complete. Rick would be all right. He would surface, having been deep in pursuit of Jennifer Toner's killer, and for once he could be the hero of his own story, the toast of the department for at least a week or two. It would distract him from the pursuit of Jack's past, thus doing her a favor as well.

In any event, there was nothing for her to do right then, provided Jack had told her the truth.

She *definitely* couldn't be sure of that.

In exactly ninety minutes, Carol returned with a look on her face Maggie had never seen, and said she had something to tell her.

Monday, 9:10 a.m.

The guys in Vice hadn't been personally acquainted with Marlon Toner, but could offer some general suggestions on where to start looking. They also suggested the homeless shelters—if he were out of doors, this bitter cold would force him to seek shelter no matter how much he wanted to avoid the authorities.

"I'm not so sure," Riley said. He sat at his desk across from Jack's, warming his hands on a cup of coffee. He wore a Christmas-themed tie that must have been a gift from one of his daughters because Jack could see no reason other than sentiment to hang such a bright conglomeration of elves, three-dimensional reindeer horns, and gold lamé accents around one's neck. He kept this thought to himself.

"His sister said that he said he didn't need money," Riley went on. "So he may have a place to stay."

"She also said he hadn't showered in a couple days, so that could have been his pride talking."

"It's six degrees outside. I doubt he'd sleep on a grate purely to keep from having to tell his sister he was broke."

"True, but we don't have a lot of options. We can start at the hangouts first, try the shelters second."

Riley massaged the dip where his nose met his skull. "I'm going to need more coffee."

But then another detective walked in and told them they had a visitor. "Some little chick says she's here about somebody named Harding. Your guy in the cemetery, right?"

Riley got up with something like enthusiasm. A visitor, after all, put off the moment when they would have to plunge into the aforementioned six degrees.

Shanaya Thomas stood in what passed for a lobby for their floor, dressed in a parka she kept zipped to her chin. "I came to get Evani's stuff," she said without preamble.

"Let's find a place where we can sit down," Riley said.

"I don't have much time. I have to get to work."

"I understand," he assured her, which assured her of absolutely nothing because her getting to work on time was not their priority. Wringing more information about Evan Harding out of her, that was their priority.

They ushered her into an interview room, a much softer name than interrogation room, with only slightly softer decor. It held nothing save one simple table and three chairs. Two for them, one for her, but the disproportion didn't appear to bother the girl.

Jack thought she had changed in the past two days. The sweet, grieving and completely innocent persona had been set aside as unhelpful; she had decided on her goals and narrowed her focus to a laser point. This didn't make her cold or aggressive, only determined. He had to use that determination to get what he needed from her.

Problem was, he didn't know what he needed from her. She might have no more clue who had murdered her boyfriend than Jack had.

"Have you been able to locate any relatives of Evan's? Other friends?" Riley began.

"No."

"Where did he live before?"

"Before when?"

"Before your current apartment."

She considered. "He was sleeping at a Holiday Inn Express with some other guys when I met him."

"What other guys?"

"I don't know. They weren't great friends, just needed a place to split costs."

The detectives kept asking questions in an attempt to find any sort of hard fact, but according to Shanaya she didn't know where Evan had been born, where he'd gone to school, any former address, any doctor, dentist, or prison he might have visited, or a single name of a blood relative. "He didn't talk about anything before we met. I got the impression his life had not been a happy one. I don't think his parents were very kind."

When they began to ask the same details about her own life, she noticed the time growing late. She needed to go and didn't care to talk about herself anyway. Her past hadn't always been pleasant either. So could she have Evan's belongings now, please? She would feel so much closer to him if she could have his ring.

"Well, that's the problem," Riley said, dragging out the words in a way Jack knew would irritate her. He could feel the slight vibration in the table from the way her foot drummed on the floor beneath it. "We can't release the victim's property, except to his next of kin."

Jack saw an expression flare behind the girl's eyes. Not anger . . . more like despair. A soul-crushing, final-straw overwhelming of hopelessness, quickly shoved out of the way by a wave of fresh resolve. "I am his next of kin."

"Not according to the law. We need a relative, and you two weren't married. You aren't even on the lease."

"He didn't have anyone else."

"Forgive me for saying so, but we have only your word for that. I've never had a victim with less of a—well, *presence*. We can't find any sort of record, not school, residence, nothing in his name. The social security number he gave his employer was bogus. You two faked your enrollment to get the apartment so the college doesn't have anything for us. So unless you can flesh out Evan's life for us, we may have to keep his personal property . . . forever."

A full second of stunned silence. "You can't do that."

"We don't have a choice, Ms. Thomas. There are laws that govern this sort of thing."

Jack watched, waiting for her to break, waiting for her to figure out that the only way she could get that stuff was to level with them.

Provided she hadn't killed him, of course.

She hesitated so long that he began to think he'd been wrong. Perhaps she did only want the boy's ring as a memento, some small comfort to the deep grief she couldn't express because an unhappy life had taught her to keep her thoughts hidden. The guy might have kept the key taped to his ankle to hide it from her, and she truly didn't know of its existence.

Then she straightened and stood up. She said she understood and would try to find out from what few friends they had if Evan had mentioned relatives. Jack took this to mean she had not given up, not by a long shot—only that she would regroup and come back to them again.

He didn't want to wait. "Evan had a key."

A startled, wary look.

"A small, plain one. Do you know what it unlocks?"

Hesitation. Then: "No."

"You never saw a key, he didn't mention it?"

"No."

She held his gaze.

"All right, then," he said. "This way—we'll show you out. Incidentally, we're getting Evan's cell phone records from his carrier. It requires a subpoena, but we got one."

Perhaps the disappointment over the key had worn her

down, because she did an uncharacteristically bad job of hiding her worry over this. "Oh."

"We should get the full record in a day or two. With luck that will give us a direction to look in, to find out who might have wanted to harm Evan."

"Oh," she said again. "I hope so." And she left.

"No, she doesn't," Riley said as soon as she had disappeared into the elevator. "Why did you mention the key? You think it's got something to do with his death?"

"It's the only unexplained thing about the victim."

"You kidding? *Everything* about this victim is unexplained."

"Yeah," Jack admitted. "But we're not getting anywhere and she's stonewalling her black little heart out. She wants that damn key, which makes it the only leverage we have."

Riley cocked an eyebrow. "Yet it still didn't budge *that* boulder."

Chapter 20

"What is it?" Maggie asked Carol, a maelstrom of foreboding welling up in her heart. The fact that Carol sat down as well, as if this would be a long conversation, did nothing to calm it.

"I tested the blood from the scene, the spot where you say Rick's fingerprint was—"

"The victim's blood."

"Not the victim's." The older woman took a deep breath. "It's Rick's."

Maggie heard the words. She waited for them to rearrange themselves in some order that would make sense. "Rick's."

Carol carefully enunciated each word. "Yes. The blood on those swabs belongs to Rick."

Maggie gave herself a minute to think over the scene, visualize each relevant factor in her mind. Jennifer Toner had no blood on her hands, so she had not drawn any from Rick if they had, for whatever unknown reason, struggled. Unless she had struck him with some object, which he then took away with him. But most likely—"It's what I've been saying. He interrupted her murder, and the killer attacked him."

"Sure," Carol said. "But then, where is he now?"

The foreboding turned to dread, and panic threaded through her veins in a warm rush. "I don't know, but wherever he is, he's bleeding."

"Not much," Carol comforted with determinedly cool reason. "You only found that one smear."

"We have to tell Denny, and he has to tell Jack and his chief," Maggie said, getting to her feet. It seemed to require more effort than it should. "Wait . . . Carol . . . how did you have Rick's DNA profile in the first place?"

"The positive controls."

"Ah."

All scientific assays, especially biological tests, were run with both positive and negative controls. A negative control would be a sterile, unused swab of the same type so that if there were some contaminant or material in the fresh-from-the-factory item, it would show up in the results. A known sample, something that was definitely blood or definitely semen, would be used to make sure the test and its reagents were working properly. If the results showed no DNA present on the crime scene sample but the expected profile from the control, they would know the test had worked properly and there was, indeed, no DNA at the scene. For most labs, a secure, known, consistent, unlimited and best of all *free* source of positive control material came from their own staff. Employees could spill their blood, swab their mouths, and daub their nether regions without even waiting for a purchase order. When they had still been married, Maggie had contributed "mixed" samples of semen and epithelial cells, and so Rick's profile remained on file. Rick had been caught between feeling proud of his prowess and slightly skeeved at the whole idea, but more than willing to do his part for the cause of forensic science.

Maybe, she thought, it would end up saving his life.

She hoped so, with a fervor that caught her by surprise

and turned her voice harsh as she marched into Denny's office and demanded to return to the crime scene. "Tell the chief we have to go there *now*."

Denny gaped. His mouth opened and closed, but he began dialing the phone before he could even form words. Technically he did not have the authority to tell the homicide unit to do anything, but this revelation involved injury to one of their own and the man would hardly object.

"What do you expect to find?" he asked Maggie while the phone rang on the other end.

"I don't know. But it's where I have to start."

"Where we have to start," Denny said.

Twenty minutes later Maggie and Denny stepped out of the city station wagon and stared up at the second floor of the small building. Weekday mode on the street, with the tea shop brewing up a menu of smells, the hair salon busy coloring and pinning. Three men worked on the roof, which seemed like a dangerous place to be this time of year when ice coated everything and a biting wind gusted off the lake. The roof barely peaked, but still, any incline could be treacherous.

Denny's gaze followed hers. "That's got to be a damned miserable job."

"They probably say the same about ours," she said, trying hard—and failing—to act as if this were just another crime scene.

He held the door for her. "Not today, I'll bet they don't."

That remained to be seen.

They toted all the equipment they could carry in two hands each, a phenolphthalein kit, an alternate light source, a jug of water and the mix to make Bluestar, a reagent that would make blood glow, and Amido Black, a dye stain that turned even the faintest of blood prints to a deep purply black.

The second-floor hallway seemed as innocuous as ever, tidy, all the doors shut except for one at the far end where a woman of some advanced age watched them. Her apartment faced the road and she had probably seen them pull up. Maggie gave her a little wave, which garnered no response whatsoever, and made a mental note to tell—*suggest*—to the homicide cops that they interview the woman to see if she saw anything. Even though that had most likely been done the same night they found Jennifer Toner.

They reached the victim's doorway and stopped. No keys, of course, and no one from homicide had arrived yet. As Denny piled their equipment along the wall Maggie examined the hallway for signs of blood, a struggle, a weapon, anything. She had only been there in the dark, and even with all the lights turned on that was never the same as seeing a place in daylight . . . especially today's daylight, blessed with a rare spot of winter sunshine that reflected off the snow-covered surfaces and poured through the windows at each end of the hall with the brilliance of a nuclear blast. She couldn't wait to see the apartment under these circumstances, but contented herself with the hallway before it became overstuffed with cops.

The carpeting had been there for a while, thin indoor-outdoor stuff that had worn its floral pattern nearly bare in spots. It had plenty of stains, most unnoticeable and lost in the color scheme until she really looked, but nothing appeared to be recent blood. No fresh rips. No new-looking scuff marks along the walls.

She traced the path from Jennifer's apartment to the stairwell, and then from the apartment to the elevator. No blood, at least none she could see. Depending on what she found inside, they might have to spray the Bluestar up the hallway, and blocking out the light from those two windows would not be a picnic. Her mind raced, bouncing from possibility to possibility like a top bouncing off random barriers without losing speed. They might wait until nighttime for that. And it would probably annoy, greatly, the woman at the end of the hall.

There were a few dark stains that *could* be blood, though she doubted it. After all her years in forensics Maggie still couldn't identify a car or a gun or a shoe brand with one look, but she could tell blood from tomato sauce or paint or rust or cough syrup under nearly any circumstance.

Still, a phenolphthalein test couldn't hurt and would give her something to do until the cops showed up. She un-snapped her kit, but then the stairwell door opened and the cops showed up.

Jack, followed by Riley, followed by Will, followed by two other patrol officers Maggie knew by sight only. The area instantly became very crowded. Jack, to her surprise, approached her immediately. "You all right?"

"Of course," she said. There was nothing the matter with *her*. But he was trying to be empathetic to her conflicted emotions, and she briefly touched his arm before elbowing her way to the front of the line as Riley unlocked the door. No one would go inside until she had photographed the area. Yes, she had already photographed the area, but cir-cumstances had changed. She would approach this crime scene as if she had never been there . . . even if that didn't make a lot of sense.

She felt Jack's hand on her shoulder. "No. Her brother is the main suspect, and he could easily have a key to the place. You have to let us clear it."

She opened her mouth to protest, then shut it. He was right. She shouldn't even be standing there—Marlon Toner would hear the commotion in the hallway and, if armed, could shoot through the door. She stood aside, moved to a spot well behind the officers. Denny did the same.

The cops formed a phalanx outside the apartment door, the patrol officers in the front.

A sudden *thump* made Maggie start, until she realized it came from above them all. The roofers, moving over the planks or tar paper or whatever covered the building. She hoped they wouldn't fall through a weak spot and collapse it into her crime scene.

Jennifer Toner's apartment, however, remained exactly as she'd left it on Friday. The items she and the detectives had moved in their search were where they'd placed them, the deep bloodstains on the floor having hardened and filled the air with the faint but unpleasant smell of rotting garbage. No one hid in the closets or under the bed or behind the shower curtain, to the disappointment of the two patrol officers who had entered with guns drawn and a wild excitement in their eyes. They now withdrew to the hallway to stand a sort of loose guard, await further requests from the detectives, and decide where to eat lunch.

Maggie made a beeline for the credenza, this time determined to cut a chunk from it if not seize the entire item. The bright illumination streaming through Jennifer's filmy window treatments lit its surface with much more clarity. After close exam she realized, with both relief and disappointment, that she hadn't missed anything on Friday night. That one blood smear with the fingerprint truly was all there was to see. Ditto for the floor, the doorway, the rest of the apartment. She could find no additional clues to say that Rick had ever been there, what had happened to him, or where he might be now.

Well, perhaps one. Under the credenza, near the end by the bloodstain, she saw a scrap no more than half an inch long and a few millimeters wide. She pulled it out, found it to be rubber-band flexible—it seemed to be a scrap of latex, a little dusty but otherwise unstained. A piece of glove, or unused condom? It could even be something she'd left herself, except she didn't recall ripping any gloves on Friday night and her department didn't stock ones that color of aqua. The cops, she knew, used black ones. She had seen purple and a sky blue on the ME staff, nothing quite like this. It could easily have been there on Friday and she'd missed it in the dim lighting. She dropped it into an envelope but planned to check Jennifer's cabinets, expecting to find a match to the victim's cleaning supplies.

Then she saw what else she had missed on Friday night.

The area rug in the living room left about three feet of hardwood floor showing all the way around between this rug and the walls. A more functional welcome mat took up the space inside the doorway to catch the melted slush of winter shoes, and a second mat behind the door gave those shoes a place to stay. From where she knelt in front of the credenza, Maggie saw a long, straight disturbance in the fibers of the doorway mat like the furrow of a tire through fresh grass. It had been broken up and loosened by their trampling but retained enough shape to seem recent. Maggie tried to think if she and Denny had brought in any piece of equipment large enough to have a roller on the bottom, but they hadn't. Nor had she brought anything of that sort on Friday night. The body snatchers had left the gurney in the hallway instead of making the tight turn into the apartment, so they hadn't left the tracks. Jennifer Toner might use a roller case or briefcase for work or have one of those fold-up canvas shopping bags with two wheels. She might have dragged a can out to the garbage, who knew.

But Maggie followed it.

Tracks like that were all about angle and light. Tire tracks through a field might be invisible when viewed from the south but clear as a typewritten word from the west, and so on. She knelt by the door and ducked her head so her view could skim the surface, looking something like a jaguar scouting a tapir through the reeds. The two patrol officers must be staring down at her as if she'd lost her mind, their conversation awkwardly truncated. She saw nothing. But when she reversed the viewpoint, from the spot where Jennifer had been to the door, she could see the mark. It began near the credenza's end.

From a child's pose in the doorway she gazed up and down the hallway. The peculiar mark ran definite and straight to the left of the apartment door. Now there seemed to be two of them, roughly parallel.

It's probably a vacuum cleaner, she thought, and I'm wasting time with it. But since she had no better ideas, she kept wasting. She moved up the hallway and crouched again, thinking that if it had been a vacuum cleaner, she wished it had done a better job, because getting her face close to the average apartment building's public hallway carpeting was not how she preferred to spend her days.

A wheeled case, someone dragging something—they should head toward the stairwell, right? Apparently not interested in the elevator, which sat at the opposite end of the hallway, to the right from the doorway and down by the nosy neighbor. But the tracks didn't veer toward the stairwell door, only continued straight past it.

The boots overhead had been stomping back and forth as if the cold and unhappy workers outside wanted to make sure everyone knew of and felt guilt over their presence. But she heard one set come to an abrupt halt at the edge, nearly over Maggie's head.

A shout erupted as one called to the other; even though the words were unintelligible, it had a sense of urgency that made the hairs on her arms quiver. The men had been shouting to each other all morning, but suddenly the tone became very different.

And suddenly she knew, with absolute certainty, what had caused the marks on the rugs.

From her spot on the floor she looked up at the window, bare and blazing with light. Then without thinking she stood, moved to it, and undid the latch. She touched only the edge of the slide and pulled the handle up with two fingers, a decade in crime scene work keeping her hands from any surface large and smooth enough to retain prints. It slid upward easily and had no screen.

An icy blast pushed in as if it had been waiting for this chance, and cut through the fibers of her uniform shirt. She barely noticed. She braced her hands against the wall on either side to avoid touching the sill, and leaned far out, knowing what she would see.

The dumpster below had been positioned to catch the rotten shingles and wooden slats of the old roof, but either the workers or some tenants found it a handy catchall since plastic bags, some articles of clothing, and an old bicycle tire had also found their way inside. A thin layer of snow had partially obscured these, but she could make out their outlines interspersed with bare spots of color, fabric, even . . . skin.

And there, where the flakes had not perfectly covered him, lay the body of her ex-husband.

Chapter 21

She had screamed, though she could not recall it later on, and did not recognize Riley's gentle description of the sound she had made as "scaring the shit" out of every man there. Jack had been at her side in an instant, defying physical laws, but she had asked—demanded, actually—that Denny guard the window and keep anyone else from so much as breathing too close to it.

Then she had been down the stairs at a pace tailor-made to break ankles, and out the side entrance door to size up the dumpster and how to get inside it, moving around to survey the area for a ladder, a discarded chair, even milk crates, anything to—

"*Maggie,*" Jack said, catching her by the shoulders. "Stop. We'll get him out."

"No." He thought she wasn't thinking clearly, but she was. *Too* clearly. The killer had obviously pitched him out the second-floor window. Rick was a fully grown man with more than a few extra pounds, so that would have been much less work, not to mention faster and less exposed, than trying to lug him down a flight of steps and out to a vehicle or, worse, getting caught inside the elevator with a dead body. But once in the dumpster the killer might have climbed inside as well to try to cover the body, hide it from the roofers and the second-floor residents who found the dumpster placement such a handy setup for trash removal. So there could be fingerprints, trace evidence, left on the edges of the container, on items inside, though how to distinguish something left by the killer from something tossed in by a tenant or customer . . . and how to remove Rick's body and any evidence left with him when he lay on a shifting, unsteady medium of trash and old shingles. . . .

Something pricked her skin and she glanced down, only to realize it was the cold, frostbite searching for a toehold on her bare forearms.

"Maggie," Jack said again.

She turned to him, well aware that she had to be looking at the primary suspect in the murder of her ex. But that didn't explain Jennifer, and so she rejected the idea. Despite this faith in him, she could hear that the timbre of her voice had fallen a few degrees below the outside temps and didn't care. "Find me a ladder."

Denny got her to come back inside by assigning her the window to process. She could not oversee the examination of the dumpster and the body, he said. She was personally involved, giving any defense attorney a wedge with which to rip the investigation to shreds. She accepted this reasoning, because, of course, she was being utterly reasonable.

The two men working on the roof were only too happy to provide ladders, and offered ropes, winches or scaffolds as well. It gave them a reason to come inside, take a break, and drink hot beverages in the tea shop. They had the mistaken impression that the cops would want to search the roof area in case "the dead guy" had fallen from there, but neither Maggie nor the detectives believed the killer dragged Rick's body up a flight of steps to stage a fall when the hallway window seemed so much more convenient. Besides, the door to the roof had been locked by the landlord after the workers knocked off early on Friday, and now showed no signs of tampering. But the roofers were happy to loan their ladder and stay inside to drink hot caffeine all the same.

Maggie used every forensic trick she had in her kit to process the hallway window, oblique light, alternate light, black powder, magnetic powder, Amido Black. A child or two had squished tiny palms all over the pane, and either a child or an adult had pressed their nose to the glass a number of times, but the killer had not left her a usable print. Nor did she find any hairs or fibers caught on the frame, the wood worn too smooth for that.

Before all of that, though, she had noticed a spray of powder on the sill, too uniformly white for dust, too fine for about anything else. It might be some kind of cleanser . . . maybe building staff used scouring powder on the glass at some point. Or some mom had backed into the window with her diaper bag, producing a puff of baby powder onto the surface. Or their killer overdid the talcum . . . did people even use talcum powder anymore? Could one even purchase it? Since she thought it extremely unlikely the killer had cleaned the window, diapered a baby, or retained extremely old-fashioned habits of personal hygiene, she didn't expect it to be a helpful clue. But she lifted the powder with a piece of tape, folded the tape back on itself, and stored it in an envelope.

Because she was being thorough, logical, and completely reasonable. Under control, professional, and calm. She thought of nothing but preserving the scene, finding the evidence, collecting the evidence, and following where it might lead. Only that.

Even though everyone kept looking at her as if she had

two heads, both of which might burst into peals of hysteria at any moment.

What *was* one supposed to feel at the death of an ex-spouse? Surely not abject grief—after all, you divorced them because you *didn't* love them. If the breakup had been outrageously painful or involved actions too extreme to ever be forgiven, she might feel elation, or triumph, or simply relief. But sorrow, sadness, just as you would for any other acquaintance—she couldn't honestly use the word *friend*, because even if they had never married they wouldn't have been friends, not with so many areas of conflicting attitudes and beliefs—whose life had been cut short unexpectedly.

But what about *relief*? A touch of that would be understandable, she thought, for any divorced person. Now the spouse would never demand entry back into one's life, now children or other family or even mutual friends would no longer be caught in between the two of them, now those awkward encounters in hallways or offices or grocery stores would no longer occur. A simple fact: there were definite advantages to the death of an ex-spouse. A fact that no one, anywhere, would ever say out loud.

Someone up the hallway opened their door, then shut it again. It penetrated her senses that the same thing had happened about ten minutes earlier. It further penetrated that tenants had probably begun to wonder why icy drafts flowed under their inner doors, and that she could shut the window now, instead of staring down at Rick's unseeing face and the nearly comic efforts of the detectives to securely place a ladder so Denny could get inside the dumpster without either falling or disturbing any possible evidence on the edge of same.

She might not feel grief at Rick's death, but she still felt obligation. She had still been married to him once, no matter how it had ended. His life, health, and happiness had for a while been her responsibility. He not found a replacement for her since then, so. . . .

Okay, perhaps she was not being 100 percent logical.

But human beings cherish loyalty, perhaps above all else. Nothing could be as important as our connections to each other; without it, why bother being human? Rick was here, he was dead, and he had no one else. Therefore, like it or not, she must step in to protect his interests.

And he would definitely have been interested in finding out who killed him.

It hit her now that her determination to help would be expected. He had been more than her ex-husband. He had been a *cop*. His death in the line of duty could make national news. The force would be galvanized, all other crimes in the city immediately went to the back seat. Memorials would be established, ceremonies would be held. She would be expected to be front and center, somber and angry. The slightest show of disinterest in Rick's murder and she would feel the disapproval of every man in blue like a wave of prickly heat, pervasive and inescapable.

So it was okay that she couldn't make herself turn away from his body, even as it slowly disassembled, moving farther and farther from this earthly realm. She would not abandon him. Even if they'd barely been on civil terms. Even if, were the situation reversed, he might not feel any particular obligation to guide her to her own funeral. Even if he would have found some reason to believe that any demise of hers would be due, somehow, in some way, to her own doing. But she was made of different stuff, and she would not abandon him.

Denny found a place to enter the dumpster and climbed up the ladder with his camera in one hand. Riley kept one hand on the ladder. Rick's partner, Will, arrived, his skin under a stocking cap more pale than the temperature warranted. The two patrol officers strung up crime scene tape, maybe more to keep the inevitable media presence at a distance than to secure the scene, seeing as the dumpster below *was* the entire scene. Jack stood to one side, chin tilted upward, watching her in the open window as if he could guess her thoughts, every single conflicted one of them.

Or he might be wondering why she had stood there until her teeth chattered.

She needed to close the window.

She needed to close a lot of things.

Monday, 11:30 a.m.

Well, Jack thought, he no longer had to fear Rick Gardiner. Now he only needed to very much fear his ex-wife.

Maggie was in turmoil. She might not be shouting or physically bouncing off the walls, but all the same he knew he had never seen her this completely freaked out since he had shot the man who had been trying to rape her.

He had suggested she go back to the lab; that suggestion, unsurprisingly, didn't even warrant a reply. It might not have been an improvement anyway—without the distraction of a crime scene and the constant murmur of the cops assuming they knew exactly who had done this, Maggie might begin to think things through. And those thoughts would quickly lead her to the conclusion that the one person with the motive, ability, and opportunity galore to murder her ex-husband was, of course, Jack. The rest of the police force might now be mobilizing to locate, arrest, and maybe shoot on sight one Marlon Toner, but Maggie would make different assumptions.

She would assume that Jack had much more to fear from Rick's investigations than Jack had let on, which was true. Rick may have told Jack of his plan to re-interview Jennifer Toner here, with the first floor empty and dark after business hours and traffic on the streets minimal on a frigid evening. Jack could have offered to come along since Will had already left for the weekend. Jack might have seen an opportunity to remove the last challenge to his identity in the city of Cleveland—excepting Maggie herself—and taken it.

She might reason exactly that way.

He consoled himself that she would then have to come up against one question: If Jack killed Rick with malice aforethought and for purely practical reasons, then why was *Jennifer* dead?

Maggie had to know that even if he could get himself to murder a fellow police officer, someone whose worst crime might be a slack work ethic tinged with misogyny, Jack couldn't possibly slaughter an innocent, caring woman like Jennifer Toner. If Rick posed that serious of a threat, Jack could simply leave town, disappear, and slip into a new identity somewhere else, what he'd been promising to do for months.

And yet you're still here, a voice in his head pointed out.

Yes, Maggie would have to come up against that wall in her theory of Jack as Rick's killer. If she didn't, he wouldn't hesitate to bring it up . . . as soon as they had a private moment, which had not yet occurred.

He looked up again. At least she had closed the damn window.

Jack watched Denny climb back down from the dumpster, pull off his latex gloves, and trade them for leather ones to warm up his fingers for a few minutes. The captain, the head of homicide arrived, ineffectual as ever, as well as the *real* head of homicide, detective Patty Wildwind with her talent for organizing, coordinating, and inspiring. The cops grouped at the interior end of the scene, as far from the street, the media, and the public as they could get. The chief of police would be showing up shortly and the Channel 15 van had already secured a good spot along the road, sending their camera up a short crane to get a view of the entire lot.

But next to the dumpster, Denny spoke to Jack, explaining things Jack didn't need to know, almost certainly because he believed Jack and Maggie were an item and thus he got special treatment. Unnecessary, of course, but Jack appreciated the thought. "Footing is less than secure in there, as you can imagine. The shingles are nice and heavy, solid, unlike garbage bags, but they can slide around. Normally I wouldn't even think to process the edge of the bin, since it's filthy, snow-covered, and there's no reason to think the killer ever touched it. But since it's a cop—"

"Yes," Jack said. "Since it's a cop." All sorts of things would be different about this investigation because of that.

"Not to mention Maggie's . . . you'll keep an eye on her," he said to Jack, halfway between a question and a statement. "Right? She'll . . . um . . . need you."

"Yes," Jack said again, because he didn't know what else to say. Because the last thing Maggie Gardiner needed, had ever needed, was Jack.

He felt Denny watching him. But then the forensics supervisor went back to the crime scene, not bothering to keep the sigh out of his voice when he said, "We'll have to empty the whole thing, after we remove the bo—him. It's supposed to be there for the roofers to use but there's a few garbage bags in there as well. We'll have to open them."

"Sure," Jack said, forcing himself to be amiable, to be—human. "In case the killer cleaned up after himself."

"Yes. And we'll have to pull out each and every shingle down to the bottom, in case the killer dropped something when he threw the bo—him—out of the window. An ID card would be nice. Dog tags. Driver's license. Isn't there a way to open these things from the side?"

"That latch," Jack pointed out, and they continued to discuss the most effective way to open and empty a dumpster of its heavy, bulky, dirty contents, while the CPD chief arrived and made a statement to the media. Denny pondered aloud whether to retrieve Rick's body by lifting him over the edge or to open the side and begin removing contents until the body lowered by default. Which would cause more disruption to the crime scene, meaning not only the body but its immediate surroundings? Though the final decision would be up to the Medical Examiner's office—it was, Jack saw, quite a knotty problem. The dead could cause problems for the living in an infinite number of ways.

"They'll probably want to take him over the edge," Maggie said, nearly causing Jack to give an unmanly start at her materialization between them. He had no idea how long she might have been there, as silent as the snow. "Excavation would take too long and risk him slipping off the pile or something."

Denny agreed in a somber tone. "They're on their way. I tried SPR along the top edges, but no prints. Other than that, there's nothing we can do until we get him out of there. And the powers that be want him transported as soon as possible."

"Transported," Jack thought, sounded so much more positive than "removed."And they wanted it ASAP because no one wants the bodies of dead cops lingering on the television screen. That would only fan the inevitable firestorm of comments on social media, on the street, in print, comments of horror, glee, condemnation, celebration and from every corner, outrage. The last thing the city, the entire planet, needed was yet more outrage.

Riley approached, after giving Maggie a sweeping, searching glance of assessment; Jack knew this came from a place of kindness, but it still came off as if he had judged her degree of radioactivity and how close he could safely get without risking a burn. Then he followed this up with a look for Jack, one Jack might as well get used to because he'd no doubt see it often in the coming days: that look of *you're the man in her life*—do *something*!

So Jack put his arm around her shoulders, temporarily bewildering her and failing to visibly satisfy Riley, who sniffed and said, "I don't know how he did it, but the chief—*the* chief, not our chief—got them to agree to turn the cameras off when we remove . . . him. Whether we can trust them or not, that remains to be seen."

"I have to tell his parents," Maggie said, her voice turning scratchy with panic as this thought occurred to her. "Right now. They can't see this on the news. I should go there, tell them in person."

"Already done," Jack told her. "The Dayton police were dispatched to make notification." Meaning the cops would go to the house to tell Rick's mother and father that their child had been murdered. They would bring a Victim's Advocate with them, a kindly, sympathetic person who would help them through the first few hours of questions, arrangements, and contacting other family members and friends.

"Strangers? They can't be told this by strangers, someone they don't know." Maggie obviously pictured her former in-laws receiving the news, and quivered under Jack's arm as if her knees might give out. He tightened his grip and told her quietly that it was better they heard it in person, from people trained to deal with such situations and who knew all the avenues of help available, even if they weren't personally acquainted.

"It's a three-hour drive at least," Denny added. "More in this weather. You couldn't make it there before they heard it through other channels."

She accepted this but didn't appear satisfied. She would not be satisfied by anyone's performance in this situation, Jack knew. Not the detectives', not his, and definitely not her own.

The Medical Examiner's investigator arrived, followed by the "ambulance crew." The investigator agreed with Denny's evaluation and they climbed back into the steel box, out of sight to everyone except birds and the second-floor window, where a young mother and her two children were watching the activity with wide eyes. Why the woman thought staring at a dead body might be an educational opportunity for her toddler and the toddler's older brother . . . Jack hoped she got fingerprint powder all over her clothes.

Everything took longer when a police officer had died. Not because there was more to do than any other homicide, but because no one wanted to make a mistake or be seen to give less than 200 percent. The ME investigator took copious pictures and whispered a tome's worth of notes into an app on his phone—so much easier than trying to write with freezing ink and freezing fingers and in the snow, which had once again begun to fall.

But nature provided a limit to how many *i*'s and *t*'s they could dot and cross. Lingering became impossible when the temperature hovered below five. Maggie shivered no matter how close Jack held her, and he thought his fingers might fall off later along with both ears and the tip of his nose. The investigator wrapped up his investigations much more quickly than anyone expected, including the body snatchers who had been staying warm inside their van. They wasted no time in climbing up and inside the bin, carting a body bag with loops of mesh straps at intervals all around, so that it could be carried between several people, as pallbearers carry a coffin. The two men, with Denny and the investigator, managed to hoist the corpse over the side without actually falling out themselves. Jack had no idea how they did it.

Cops stood ready on the ground to bear the weight the rest of the way. Jack found himself in a paroxysm of indecision. Should he show solidarity with his fellow officers and shoulder some of the burden? Would that be considered insincere since he hadn't even liked the guy and now dated—they thought—his ex? Would staying by Maggie's side be the higher duty? For once he truly needed the advice of his *de facto* life coach: Riley.

He turned to his partner, who said, "Let's go."

Jack let his arm fall from Maggie's shoulders, and walked with Riley to the group of officers. They all reached upward, palms open and flat, as the men inside the box lowered the bag as best they could. Body bags were always transported flat, to maintain the corpse as close to their original position as possible. But since the men inside the dumpster couldn't walk on air, the bag had to be held at its ends like a hammock. Jack grabbed a strap, held it up until the other ones were grasped so they could lower the whole bag at the same time. It wasn't only to preserve evidence. It was to preserve dignity.

Truthfully, they tried hard to preserve that for each and every victim, but today they would be especially cognizant.

Once on the ground, with the dumpster on one side and a phalanx of cops forming a protective barrier from the media and other prying eyes on the other three, the investigator zipped the bag open. Cameras clicked, the investigator's and Denny's.

Rick wore the same clothes she'd seen him in on Friday, black denim pants, scuffed brown leather athletic shoes, and a lightweight maroon parka zipped to the collarbones. Only a tiny red stain on the parka, middle front, gave any indication of how he died.

"What killed him?" someone in the group asked.

Denny stated the obvious: "There's no signs of a struggle. No injuries to the hands or face."

"Clothing intact," the ME investigator added.

Someone crouched next to the body reached out a latexed hand and pushed at the parka's cuff. "His watch and ring are still here." Jack realized it was Maggie, examining her ex-husband's murdered corpse. Her arm was steady but her voice trembled ever so slightly.

The investigator must have decided that decorum might

be all well and good but they had neither the time nor the climate for it, and began to unzip the parka.

"Wait," Maggie said. Everyone froze. She said, "Wait, wait, wait," and bustled off, the men behind her parting instantly to create a path. No one else moved. They waited.

She returned with clear tape to press on Rick's maroon parka, at his left shoulder. She muttered something about powder.

Denny peered. "Are you sure that's not snow?"

"Too fine."

She folded the tape in on itself, then dropped it into an envelope. The investigator finished unzipping Rick's parka.

Underneath his coat Rick wore a long-sleeve polo shirt with a T-shirt showing beneath it. More pictures, this time of the clear wound to Rick's center mass.

"Shot," someone behind Jack said. Will stood by Rick's head, one hand at his mouth, and said nothing.

"Bullet wound?" Maggie asked.

The investigator pulled Rick's shirt and T-shirt out of his belt to reveal the pale, rounded belly. "It's a circular hole. Smallish caliber."

Maggie folded the parka back and together they found the corresponding hole in it. Without the small bloodstain it would be easily lost in the puffy folds of the coat, the slight protrusion of fiberfill stuffing hidden by the dusting of snow.

Maggie said, "So he still had his coat on. Badge and gun right here on his belt."

"He didn't see it coming," the investigator said.

Denny, also crouching, mused aloud: "He didn't have a clue. For whatever reason, he did not feel threatened."

"Neither did Jennifer Toner," Maggie pointed out.

"Who leaves a gun?" one of the cops mused aloud.

"Too risky to be caught with a cop's gun," theorized another.

"How come nobody in this building heard a gunshot?"

"How come nobody noticed a body getting thrown out a window?"

Someone else found this wording a little cold and hissed *Dude!* at the speaker. Rick Gardiner was not, would never be, "a body." He was a *cop*. He would not be put in the same category as all the other homicide victims they investigated.

The man from the ME's tried to heft Rick onto one side—not an easy task, so Maggie and Denny helped. Jack wondered what it must feel like to hold on to your ex-spouse's hip so an investigator can check their back for an exit wound. The guy had to be as cold as a Popsicle. Nearly forty-eight hours . . . he must have been frozen solid, or rigor mortis had been slowed by the low temperatures. He'd have to ask—

Maggie stood up, nearly knocking into the men crowding behind her. Jack followed her gaze.

The tenants had indeed taken advantage of the dumpster's presence and two strands of sauce-covered spaghetti had adhered to the back of Rick's head, frozen to his short hair, one end curled over his ear. This final indignity broke the back of Maggie's resolve. A strangled sob escaped her lips, both a cry and a whisper.

"That's it," Denny said, with enough resolve for the two of them. He turned to Jack. "Get her out of here."

Jack put one arm around her shoulders and pulled her from the scene. She let him.

Chapter 22

Monday, 12:10 p.m.

She had thought the ride would be silent, but they hadn't even reached the Lorain-Carnegie bridge before Jack said, "How are you feeling?"

A curious question, she thought. She answered honestly: "I don't know. I don't know what I'm supposed to feel, what I'm supposed to do, how I'm supposed to act. But really, none of that is important." She lapsed back into silence, tapping the envelope on her lap. When the nerves in her fingers thawed enough to allow sensation, she realized she still carried it. The smear of lighter color on Rick's jacket had looked like powder; it might be the same powder as on the windowsill. She didn't have the instrumentation to analyze any old substance . . . it had to be something the machinery had already been programmed to recognize, such as DNA, adhesives, or nylon fibers. The mass spectrometer might be able to tell her something. If it were an illegal drug, cocaine or fentanyl, the toxicology department could identify it as easily as she could flick a light switch. A powerful drug might explain why two people who had been searching for an addicted man were now dead. . . .

Jack switched off the car and turned to her. "Maggie—"

She hadn't noticed, but they had entered the police department parking garage and now sat tucked in a dark corner space.

He actually took one of her hands, and said her name again, as if he had to speak and yet didn't want to. Jack was rarely uncertain about anything, and right now he seemed as uncertain as she'd ever seen him.

The words came out in a rush. "I didn't do it."

She blinked.

He clarified. "I didn't kill him."

He meant Rick.

After a pause she found her voice: "Do you really think I'd be sitting here in a car with you if I thought you *did*?"

Surprise erased the lines on his face, then a puffed breath of relief. "I hope not."

It wasn't as if the idea hadn't occurred to her. Of course it had.

Jack had feared what Rick might find in Chicago and Minneapolis, no matter what he'd told her. Rick had been the only person in Cleveland who suspected Jack had something to do with the vigilante killings. Rick had motivation to pursue his suspicions, and enough bloody-mindedness to keep pursuing. Jack was the only person she could think of who had any motive to kill Rick at all. He could have known of Rick's plan to re-interview Jennifer Toner, could have suggested it in the first place. Jack had no hobbies, no weekend activities, no one at home to whom he had explain an absence on Friday afternoon. Neither Jennifer nor Rick would have been on guard against another police officer. Jennifer would have let him in, Rick wouldn't have felt the need to keep his gun in hand. And if anyone on the planet knew how to kill without leaving any clue behind, it was Jack.

And yet she felt calmly positive that he had not.

Was it because she had bought in so deeply to his world

that she could no longer reason freely? Had she become so lost in the woods he created that she would never find her way back to the path?

No. It was because—

"I could be wrong. I won't know until—"

Jack, still leaning toward her in the front seat of the car, seemed to be breathing in her air, drawing the thoughts out of her. "Wrong about what?"

"I don't think Rick was shot. A hot bullet at that range should have melted some of the synthetic fibers around the entrance on the parka, just has it would have to Jennifer's sweater. I think he was probably stabbed, exactly as Jennifer Toner was stabbed."

"Okay . . . that would make sense. No loud noise to attract attention, giving him time to get the bo—body up the hallway to the window."

"And I'm betting he was stabbed with something long and thin, like Jennifer. And just like," she added, "Evan Harding."

Jack escorted Maggie back to her lab, guiltily relieved to leave her there. He sucked at the whole emotion thing—and, truth be told, Maggie wasn't terribly expressive herself—and thus didn't feel he could help her navigate the potential minefield of mood in the wake of the death of an ex-spouse. Plus, he could see the lab served as her refuge, not merely her workspace, and more comfortable for her than probably any other place on earth. Her coworkers knew her and would know better than to assume she grieved deeply. Indeed, as he left, he heard Carol say, "Well, this has to be a weird feeling."

By the time he returned to the two-story building on West 29th, the emphasis and the atmosphere had shifted. The body was gone, Denny now packed up his equipment and the cops had formed a huddle, for warmth more than for privacy. The chief of police barked out orders; the captain of homicide hovered at his elbow with a stern expression and kept his mouth shut. Shock had passed; now an abiding anger, colder than the thermometer could measure, took its place. One of their own had fallen. His killer would be pursued with a dedication and vigor that bordered on caricature, so deeply was it felt.

Jack joined the circle, mercifully unnoticed for a few minutes, and withstood the tiny shiver of awkwardness that traveled like electricity as soon as he was. He wasn't everybody's favorite guy to begin with, too unboisterous for that and a transplant to the area, and he was now dating Rick's ex. Even though Rick had *definitely* not been everybody's favorite guy, now he was dead, leaving the group to wonder exactly where their loyalties should lie. But Jack didn't expect this undercurrent to rise to the level of a real problem. It would pulse way down low, then disappear entirely in a month or two.

A rough plan emerged. Rick had been interviewing Jennifer Toner in relation to a drug death, so drugs were likely to be the base of these crimes. The narcotics division would rattle every box of syringes, canvas every treatment center—diplomatically—and grill every Confidential Informant they could. The homicide guys would then follow up their best suspects. The rank and file would comb the city to find Marlon Toner, who had just become Cleveland's number-one most wanted. "Now," the chief said, "let's get the hell out of here before we all get frostbite."

A rookie had been tasked to circle the lot, taking down the crime scene tape. This freed the pretty Channel 15 anchor as well as a couple other news people to fast-walk up to the group and probe for quotes. Jack helped Denny pack the alternate light source in the city station wagon, they exchanged vague statements of concern for Maggie's emotional well-being, and the forensic supervisor drove away. Riley found Jack, they exchanged more vague statements about Maggie, and Riley told his partner that he and Will and

Denny had personally removed and examined every garbage bag, crumpled rag, and weathered asphalt shingle in the entire dumpster. They had found very little. Not even blood since Rick had landed on his back—his heart must have stopped pumping very quickly.

Jack said, "Like Jennifer Toner and Evan Harding."

"You think Harding's connected?"

"I can't for the life of me see how. But it's a damn weird coincidence if they were all killed by the same type of weapon."

Riley considered this. "I guess we'll see after the autopsy. We did find a pair of glasses. Denny got all excited about that. He thinks the guy tossed out the body, leaned out to see his handiwork, and the glasses slipped off his face, and maybe we can trace the prescription. The garbage bags all seemed to be regular household garbage, no bloody rags, mail belonging to people who live here. Nothing belonging to Jennifer. We also found a small stack of empty snack containers, gum, chips, and a few scraps of paper, somebody's phone number, somebody else's grocery list. Oh, and a USB drive."

"Seriously?"

"Oh yeah. We all got *real* excited about that. Let's say our killer had it in his shirt pocket and it fell out. Maybe it's got his whole life on it. Maybe it's got the landlord's porn collection, too, but I like to think positive."

Jack gazed up at the building, feeling the cold work its way into his jaw and make it sluggish. "If the tenants were using it as a receptacle, how did they not notice—?"

"The snow. We figure this happened right around quitting time Friday afternoon. The roofers had knocked off early— Friday, you know—and well before most of the tenants got home from work. It snowed most of the day Friday, melted a little bit Saturday and Sunday but not all, and then started again today. You can't see inside the dumpster from the second floor unless you actually open the window and stick your head out, which of course no one is going to do in this weather, except to pitch out their own stuff, and then they'd do it quickly and probably after dark. No lights this side of the building . . . so they never saw him. And get this—the bin is scheduled to be picked up every Tuesday. A little more snow, and he might never have been found. We'd have thought Gardiner went on vacation and never came back."

"Maggie knew," Jack said. "She knew there was something wrong."

"Dude," said a voice behind them. "What's going on?"

Jack half turned. A man stood there, a heavy stadium coat covering him up to his ears and a knit cap pulled down until it had to impede his vision. His smell placed him somewhere on the homeless spectrum.

"There was a death here," Jack told him.

Whatever influence the man had fallen under turned him both hyper and mellow, though the bouncing and bobbing could have been him trying to keep his blood from freezing in its veins. "Aw, man. That's too—who was it?"

"It was a police officer."

The nearly-hidden eyes grew wide. "True? Wow, that's— wow. I gotta get in there. I can go in the building, right?"

Riley said yes, he could. "Do you live here?"

"No, I'm just visiting my sister."

Certainty poked Jack's heart with one quick icy thrust. "What's your name?"

"Me?"

"Yes, you."

The man calmly replied, "I'm Marlon Toner."

Chapter 23

Jack and his partner, in unison, looked at each other, at the group of cops at the end of the lot, at the Channel 15 van with its mounted camera, back at Marlon Toner, and made an instant, unspoken decision.

"Mr. Toner," Jack said, "you're going to want to come with us."

The man didn't feel *that* mellow. "Wha? No, I don't got to—"

Jack stepped in closer, speaking quietly, hoping he could penetrate the drug-induced fog. "You see that group of cops over there? They are ninety-five percent certain that you are the one who killed their fellow cop. Come with us right now and we'll get quietly into our vehicle and drive downtown and we can talk there. Because if you stay here, we cannot guarantee your safety. Do you understand me?"

Marlon Toner didn't; that was clear. He seemed about as perplexed as a man could get and still be upright. But despite the confusion, the abruptness, the fog, Jack's tone spoke to something primal in him, some survival instinct that helped him recognize true danger. A few officers turned to see what Jack and Riley were doing, frowned as if trying to read an unfamiliar code, and Marlon Toner's face paled from more than the cold.

"Okay," he said.

All three men pivoted and, Toner between the two detectives, strode toward the unmarked cars parked along the curb. They walked slowly, calmly, purposely keeping every step unhurried and casual. Jack guided Toner into the back seat, shut the door on his most cooperative arrestee ever, and heard a voice shout, "Hey!"

Riley had the driver's door open, slipped inside. Jack turned, waved at the two cops now moving toward them, dropped into the passenger seat, and shut the door with a shuddering *thump*. "Go."

They pulled away, leaving the cops staring after them. Riley drove slowly, casually.

Behind him, Marlon Toner let out a sigh of deep relief he probably didn't understand, and neither did Jack. Wasn't driving into the Justice Center, if one feared violence against the suspected cop-killer, like jumping from the frying pan into the fire?

And did he truly think his fellow officers would have lynched the man right there, or arrange to have him mysteriously hang himself in his prison cell? No, Jack didn't *really* believe that would happen. But . . . neither did he want to take the chance.

He also wanted to talk to Marlon Toner before the circus of outraged cops and posturing higher-ups could get their parade organized.

"What is going on?" Toner demanded.

"That," Riley said, "is what we hope you can tell us."

Monday, 12:55 p.m.

They put him in an interrogation room and with a guy Riley trusted on the surveillance camera who could make sure it would not be turned off under any circumstances. Again, Jack didn't really think his fellow officers would burst in and beat Toner to death right then and there, but violent scenes from too many movies and black and white newsreels haunted the edges of his mind.

He had his doubts about Toner's guilt, but if the man *had* killed his own sister and their own cop, then the case would have to be airtight. There could be no areas of the investigation for a decent attorney to negate. Marlon Toner must be treated with kid gloves, afforded every right and privilege, and each minute in their presence recorded, documented and utterly transparent. The other officers knew that, but it only took one or two cowboys to undermine a by-the-book investigation.

Except for legal representation—at least for now, Jack and Riley concluded. If they questioned him while he was under the influence, his statements could be thrown out. If they got him a lawyer, the first thing any attorney who had been awake through at least a few of his classes would be to postpone all questioning until the client's sobriety could be established, and they didn't want to wait. They wanted to get at least a few questions answered before the cops from the scene returned and asked who the hell it was they had in the interrogation room.

Toner didn't have any obvious outward signs; he wasn't slurring, staggering, or speaking nonsensically. His eyes were bloodshot but not jumping . . . at least not too badly. The two detectives figured it was worth trying. If he turned out to be higher than they thought, then they'd have to stop the interview and get him some representation.

The next hurdle: getting him to agree to talk without a lawyer. Surely a truly sober Marlon Toner would not, but according to his sister he had been a productive, law-abiding citizen until only recently. He didn't think of himself as a criminal or he would never have approached them in that parking lot, whether under the influence or not.

They avoided most obvious problems by not arresting him. They had enough probable cause to arrest him for the murder of his sister, if not Rick; but they didn't have a warrant, so they could honestly tell Marlon Toner, on video, that he was not under arrest and could leave at any time.

But the creepy scene at his sister's apartment had spooked the man and besides, the police department had a good heating system. Jack got him a glass of water and a cup of coffee and a heaping plate of cookies from the break room. Police departments were full of food during the Christmas season, gifts from well-meaning citizens and civic groups and grade schools.

So it was on.

The temperature in the interrogation room felt a little too warm after the frigid outdoors and all three men quickly shed their coats. Jennifer Toner had said her brother smelled as if he hadn't showered in a few days; Jack guessed that had spread to a week. He tried to breathe through his mouth without making it too obvious.

Cooperative didn't mean clueless. Toner refused to tell them where he had been and what he had been doing unless they told him why they asked—and why the Cleveland police department thought he had killed one of their cops.

"It's turning out to be a long story," Riley said, briskly but not aggressively. "It goes back to last week. A man died of an overdose at the West Side Market and had your ID on him."

"What, like my driver's license? I got that, I just showed it to you."

"Right. His driver's license had his picture, but your name and your sister's address. The man's name was Raymond Winchester. Was he a friend of yours?"

"Never heard of him."

They showed him a photo. Still nothing.

From this somewhat benign starting point, he took them through his activities since that time. Unfortunately, those were all amorphous and indistinct, with lots of "walking around" and "hanging out," eating fast food and sleeping at St. Malachi's or inexpensive motels.

"So you didn't visit your sister on Friday afternoon, or evening?"

"No, man. I ain't been there in a couple of weeks."

"You're sure?"

"*Yes.* Why don't you ask her? She'll tell you."

They circled back a few more times, but the answer didn't change: he had not been to his sister's apartment building in two or three weeks. He spoke to her on the phone, but hadn't gone there.

"Do you have your phone with you now?" Jack asked.

"Yeah."

"Could I see it?"

All the cookies in the world couldn't sweeten that deal. "No."

"I just want—"

"No."

Riley said, "We only ask because your sister told us you've been having some issues with medication."

The man rolled his eyes. "She exaggerates. She's like our mom, a bit of a nag. Thinks it's her job to tell me what to do."

"Sisters can be like that," Riley agreed. "She seemed especially concerned about a Dr. Castleman."

A wary look came over the man. He said nothing.

"Who is Dr. Castleman?"

"He's my doctor. That's what I keep telling her. I take those pills because they're prescribed to me." He enunciated each word with careful clarity.

"Where can we find him?"

"You can't talk to him about me. That's violating patient confidentiality."

"We understand that. We only want to talk to him."

Toner crossed his arms. "Not my problem."

"We'd like to know where he is."

"Try the phone book."

"He isn't in it. That seems very strange for a doctor, doesn't it?"

He shrugged. "Not my problem."

"Did Jennifer speak with Dr. Castleman?"

"No." But he seemed uncertain.

"Did you tell her where to find him?"

"No!"

"Are you sure? I was on your same medication once, Percodan," Riley said, and Jack assumed he lied—about taking it, not about the drug. Jennifer Toner had told them what the label on her brother's bottle had read. The drug combined aspirin and OxyContin. "After I fell out of a window chasing a suspect, landed right on my knee. I know it made me feel light-headed, a little confused. Even a big guy can get loopy on that stuff."

Toner said nothing, arms still crossed.

"Perhaps part of last week gets a little mixed up in your mind. Because of the medication."

"No."

"Maybe you went to Jennifer's and then forgot about it."

"No."

Riley backed off. "Okay. So what *did* you do on Friday?"

"I told you." Another litany of walking around and hanging out.

Riley leaned back in. "Jennifer told us how concerned she felt about Dr. Castleman and his treatment of you. She tried very hard to locate him so she could talk to him personally. Did she tell you about that?"

The sugar boost of the cookies provided an energy boost, and Toner fidgeted in his chair. "No. Why don't you just *ask* her?"

"You're positive she never confronted the doctor?"

"No, man! He would have told me, or she would, or something."

"You're sure?"

"Yes! Why're you asking all about Jenny and my doctor? They don't even know each other. What's any of that got to do with anything?"

"Quite a bit, Mr. Toner," Riley said. "Because your doctor is the only other person who might possibly have a motive to kill Jennifer. Besides you."

No reaction. Fingers gripped the coffee cup and his other hand stilled over the cookie plate and his. Jack pulled the cup from his hand before he could break the Styrofoam shape into pieces. The expression on Marlon Toner's face turned from intense bafflement to a ghastly knowing.

"She's *dead*?"

Monday, 1:45 p.m.

The interview went downhill after that, Jack reported to Maggie. The man had burst into wails of grief so profound that they lost twenty minutes trying to calm him down enough to speak with any sort of coherence at all.

She and Jack sat in the lab, surrounded by the comfortingly familiar sounds of lab work being done—Denny in the wet lab spraying Ninhydrin on what looked like fake currency, Maggie's computer humming as the program did a search through its fingerprint database, Carol bustling about in the DNA lab, and the boxy mass spec moving sample vials around on a carousel. At least Jack hoped Maggie found it comforting. It did nothing for him.

Josh and Amy were at the police impound garage processing Rick's assigned city vehicle, which had been located in Euclid at nearly the same moment that Maggie first saw his body—a complete coincidence. The vehicle had been sitting in a Park and Ride lot for who knew how long until a bored transit cop out having a smoke happened to run the plate. The killer might have dumped the car and gotten on a bus, or might have been picked up by a cohort, or might have walked home for all they knew. Video cameras only covered the bus loading area; they could start canvassing commuters, but with no idea when the car had been dropped that seemed like a desperately hopeless task.

"You don't think he did it," Maggie instantly guessed.

"Not quite yet, I don't. We could not shake his timeline—he hadn't been to his sister's apartment in two or three weeks. I said, maybe he dropped in to borrow a few bucks, but he insists he has plenty of money, as Jennifer had said. But if he has plenty of money, then why isn't he spending it on a place with good running water? But maybe he is but isn't bothering with the water because he's too busy shooting up. He's not starving, either. A little hungry this morning, but not starving. Of course he could have had money all weekend because he got it from Jennifer before he killed her. Who knows? Riley and I went round and round."

"So he didn't kill Rick, either," Maggie said. "If he's telling the truth."

"Maybe not. Maybe he crushed up a boatload of Oxy, went there and killed them both, and now honestly has no recollection of even being in the area. He seemed really devastated about his sister, but it's hard to tell. We'll wait until the stuff clears his system, and then see what kind of answers we get."

"Where is he now?"

"We transferred him to the special detox cells, private room, suicide watch, lots of eyes on him. He went voluntarily—safer for him and strict adherence to protocol for us."

"What about Rick's autopsy?"

"They were going to do it immediately. Unless they had to wait for, um—"

"For the body to thaw," Maggie said. She spoke matter-of-factly, Jack saw, because her ex-husband's half-frozen corpse was, at heart, a practical problem with a practical solution. Sometimes Jack thought she was more like him than she would ever admit. That could be why their weird partnership hadn't imploded . . . yet.

"Yes."

"Who's going?"

"Johnson and Padlecki. The chief wouldn't let Will go."

"I should think not." She seemed aghast at the idea, more solicitous of her ex-husband's workplace partner than—"We need to know, ASAP, whether he was shot or stabbed. And if stabbed—"

"Was it the same weapon that killed Jennifer, which would make sense, as well as the same weapon that killed Evan Harding?"

"Which wouldn't."

"No," Jack said. "Not at all."

His phone rang.

Riley said, "You're not going to believe this."

"*Don't* tell me we have another body."

"No, not that. It's Harding's little girlfriend. She got mugged on her way to work."

Chapter 24

The attack had been witnessed by two of Shanaya's coworkers, who had also been arriving for an afternoon shift at the building on East Ninth. The patrol officer who had taken all the reports provided Jack and Riley with this concise summary: Shanaya had been walking up Bolivar, a busy street in broad daylight, with the two witnesses approaching from the opposite direction on the other side of Ninth, coming from the Rapid Transit stop at Tower City. Though they were approximately 350 feet away, across a busy road, they clearly saw the man stop the young woman. It seemed that a short conversation ensued and then the man pulled her into an alley, where she clearly did not want to go. The two young women instantly dashed against traffic, across East Ninth and sped to the alley, where they found the man punching Shanaya in the midriff. One of the witnesses called 911 while the other leapt onto the man's back, doing her best to choke him. The first gave police their location, then hit the man across the knees with a piece of rebar she found on the ground. After that he put up his hands and told her to stop and that he would cooperate fully provided she didn't hit him again. The second witness slid off his back. He made no attempt to leave the scene and even thanked the first witness for calling the cops.

Shanaya, however, ran farther up the alley until one of the witnesses called her name. The patrol officer guessed she'd been about to run out on the whole drama until she realized that they knew her.

"Unless it was just nerves," the officer told them, confiding his take on her behavior. "Totally panicked and all. *And* this alley's a dead end, so she had nowhere to go. I ran all their names and she came up in relation to a homicide of yours. I told Dispatch to inform you and here you are." He seemed pleased to think he could get back into his car and roll on to the next incident. Not all patrol officers want to make detective or sergeant. Many are perfectly happy where they are, addicted to the constantly changing landscape of law and order in a large city.

"What's the guy's story?" Riley asked.

"Once he heard me say there were detectives coming, he declined to give one. His name is Eric Hayes, and he lives on Franklin. He's a construction worker, commercial jobs. I asked him why he assaulted the young lady, and he said, and I quote, 'That punch I threw is nothing compared to what she deserves.' I asked for clarification, and he said he'd wait for you. The two witnesses gave me their info so I let them go."

A note of caution had entered his voice, and he paused.

"What?" Jack asked.

His word flow, strong until that point, seemed to ebb and falter. "The two witnesses were, well, totally typical. Adrenaline high, both talking at once, jumping all over the place in their story, yak, yak, yak. Since they said they knew the victim because they worked with her, which is where all three were heading, I asked where they work. Dead stop. They said, practically in unison, we work in customer service.

Dead stop again. I got them to give me the name and address . . . it's in that building on the corner, right on—"

Riley said, "Yeah, we've been there."

"Really? Huh." The officer waited a split second to see if more explanation would be forthcoming, saw that it wouldn't, and went on. "I got curious, pressed a bit, but they kept saying either technical support or customer service like they were friggin' yoga mantras or something, and after that they weren't so excited and talkative, like the adrenaline had drained right out of them both at the same time. It was kinda weird. Then *that* one"—he jerked a chin toward Shanaya, huddled in an alcove within the alley—"has been trying every which way to wriggle out of here. When I put the guy in my car, she tried to take off but turned around when I started to chase her. I'm not only standing in this alley because it blocks the wind. I figured if I didn't keep her cornered, she'd try again."

Riley jotted a few notes before giving up. Trying to write on a tiny pad with thick gloves didn't work well.

"What do you guys want to do with these two?" the patrol officer asked. "Want them in your car?" When they hesitated, he added: "I only ask because it's colder than a well-digger's ass out here, wind block or no wind block."

"You book him in," Riley said. "We'll take her."

"Keep a firm grip," the officer warned, and left the alley.

Shanaya Thomas flat-out *begged* not to be taken to the station. She couldn't miss work. She was already late and that was bad enough, but to miss part of the day would probably get her fired—which added insult to injury since she was the *victim* here. So why did she have to suffer? She had already told them everything: the guy came up, said some nasty things to her, then dragged her into the alley and hit her. Then the other girls showed up.

"What nasty things?" Riley asked, raising his voice slightly. The city-issued Ford had seen better days and the heater made a droning whine, especially when turned up full blast, and Riley had it turned up full blast. He and Jack faced the young woman in the back seat. She wore knit pants tucked into boots, oversized nylon gloves, and a parka, that didn't seem to have quite enough padding for the weather. Her black hair hung in silky tufts around her face. No puffs of warm air had reached her yet and she had her knees drawn up to her chin, held in place by both arms. And still she shivered.

"That I was asking for it, walking along the street by myself—strutting, I think he said, strutting. I figured, okay, some random nut, but it's the middle of the morning, right? Daylight. I told him to leave me alone and went to walk around him, and that's when he grabbed me."

"Then what?"

Jack let Riley handle the questions; he was much better at expressing sympathy in his tone and expression, whether he felt it or not.

"He pulled me into the alley and told me to give him all my money. I still didn't believe anything that bad could happen. It was the middle of the *day*."

Her voice trembled at points, but she seemed much more angry than upset . . . as well as perplexed. Jack could not decide if she honestly didn't know why the man had targeted her or if she honestly didn't know what to do about it. As usual, there seemed one thing she still didn't want to do under any circumstances: tell them anything that would help.

No, she didn't know Eric Hayes, had never heard his name or seen his face, and had no idea why he would decide to mug her.

"Really?" Jack said, letting his voice get as harsh as it

wanted. "Excuse us if we don't buy that, since you have lied to us about every single thing from the get-go."

"I have not!"

"Evan's workplace, your location, why you abandoned your apartment—" He didn't mention her quest to get Evan's personal property, including that little key . . . no reason to alert her of his interest in it.

Their anger didn't register or didn't affect her. She stonewalled, being very good at that, with the bald-faced declaration that she had never lied to them about anything. And that she really, really needed to get to work.

"We'll call your boss for you," Riley promised, and pulled away from the curb. Shanaya Thomas muttered something under her breath and slumped back in the seat, pouting like a toddler who'd been denied ice cream.

She continued to protest, trying a new angle every couple of blocks. She'd already told them everything she knew. She was the victim, and it wasn't fair for her to lose her job because of some crazy guy. As they rolled into the Justice Center she pointed out that since she wasn't under arrest, she could leave if she wished. And she *definitely* wished.

Inconvenient as it may be, Jack told her, she was the material witness to a crime as well as the victim, and if she tried to leave, they would then arrest her for hindering prosecution.

Riley promised to call her boss and insist that Shanaya could not possibly help being late to work. This did not thaw her, any more than the car's heating system could. Shanaya had great worries in her life, and they were not one of them. She did not *fear* the police or the police station, as many people did. She just really, really wanted to be elsewhere.

So they let her cool her heels while they interviewed Eric Hayes.

Chapter 25

He had been placed in an interrogation room, officially under arrest but not "booked" yet. Jack wanted to hold out the carrot of dismissing the charge before it became official, should Hayes provide a good enough explanation—though he doubted that could be done, particularly now that he got a look at the guy. Eric Hayes stood a couple of inches over six feet and carried at least two hundred and fifty pounds of weight, most of it muscle. If he could produce an acceptable reason to intercept and then strike a young woman easily half his weight, Jack would be very surprised. Hayes sat at a table, wrists recuffed in front to make him more comfortable and therefore more likely to talk. Or so the thinking went.

He wore jeans, a Cavs sweatshirt over a white T-shirt, fairly new athletic shoes, and an olive green parka, which the officer had slung over the back of the chair. His mustache and short beard were trimmed and he regarded them with clear, wry blue eyes.

"Seriously?" he asked, holding up his wrists. "Is this necessary?"

Jack said, "You attacked a very small woman for no apparent reason. So yes, it is necessary."

"Oh, I have a reason. I have an excellent reason."

The detectives sat down, formally introduced themselves, and asked to hear it. They did not say they were from homicide. It would only confuse matters, and matters seemed confusing enough already.

They went over Hayes's Miranda rights and his vital statistics. The man had recently turned twenty-seven, had a wife and a toddler, lived on the west side of Cleveland "almost to Lakewood" and had been employed by Turner Construction for five years. Other than a few speeding tickets and a juvenile charge for possession, he had no record. They knew this last part to be true because they'd already checked.

He spoke forcefully but easily, eager to explain, so Riley stayed friendly in return. "Tell us how we got to be here today."

"Okay," Hayes said with increased enthusiasm. "It was about two months ago, the last home game of the World Series. I'm at home, watching it on TV. The wife took our kid out to the library and park 'cause she knows how I get during a game, and we don't curse around my kid. Third inning, Atlanta was up two, we had two outs. Right?" He gazed at the two detectives, waiting for a sign that they remembered the ball game as clearly as he did. Riley hesitated. Jack had no idea what he was talking about. Hayes gave a disgusted snort and continued. "Lindor hit a single, they cut to a commercial, I got another beer, and my phone rang. I answer it, and it's a recording telling me that the IRS is auditing me and I need to call this number to avoid prosecution."

Jack felt his eyebrows raise.

"Yes, yes, don't look at me like I'm a moron. I *know* I'm a moron. But I'm watching the game, I'm sitting there by the phone anyway, and I figured it had to be a mistake, right? But who wants to take chances with the IRS? I'll call them back, have it all straightened out before they're even done with the eight thousand commercials they show every break, right? I call the number, this chick answers. She's got no idea who I am, but it's the IRS. There's got to be tons of people in the country being audited on any given day, right? I'm not paying enough attention 'cause I'm watching a funny commercial, even they don't make as much of a fuss over the World Series commercials like they do the Super Bowl . . . the Super Bowl commercials are such a big freakin' deal. Football gets all the love in this country."

"And the money," Riley said.

Under the table, Jack tapped his foot.

"So she's asking all these questions and I'm rattling off my info, address, birthdate, Social Security number, because it's the IRS, right? No harm in telling them; they already have it in a database somewhere. First she tells me me I owe a forty-dollar fee because I underpaid the Medicare tax. I didn't see how that was possible since work takes it out automatically but hey, the game's back on, I can afford forty bucks if it gets the IRS off my back. So I get out my credit card, pay it. Done, right? She put me on hold, we got another hit, Lindor's now on third, the hitter's on second. Cut for a commercial."

"Mr. Hayes—" Jack began.

Hayes ignored him, as did Riley. "Then this chick on the phone says that was only *one* of the fees. There's a much bigger penalty due for underpaying on the actual income tax. She says I owe seven thousand dollars. Okay! *That* got my mind off the game. I can afford forty bucks—but thousands? I'm a construction worker! I can't pull that out of my butt and not miss it. I protest, she ignores me like I'm not even speaking. She says I have to go to the bank *right now* and get the money or she'll have no choice but to have the arrest

warrant issued. I tell her *I simply cannot do that.* I don't
have seven thousand dollars that I can hand over."

Jack said, "I'm guessing the chick is Shanaya Thomas?"

Hayes's heavy hands, moving in time with his words despite the handcuffs, froze. "Who?"

"The woman you attacked."

"Oh yeah. Yes, I mean. To answer your question."

"How did you find her?"

"I'm getting to it. She's on the phone, right? She does *not*
care that I don't have seven thousand dollars to spare. So I'm
protesting, the bank's about to close, I won't get there in
time, and even if I do, what am I supposed to do with this
wad of cash? Walk around town with that much money in
my pocket? Do I take it to the federal building here? *No*, she
says. I am not supposed to take it anywhere, I can change it
into a number and give it to her over the phone. Meanwhile
Lindor tries to steal home, so I get distracted by that; I
missed exactly what she said next but when I listen, she's
saying something about iTunes cards."

Jack felt himself frown. "What?"

Hayes waved his hands toward them. "Yes! Doubleyou
tee eff, exactly! I said, *What?* This chick says that once I got
the cash, I should immediately go to a CVS or Walgreens
and put it all on an iTunes card and give her the number.
That would take care of the issue and the IRS would no
longer have a reason to arrest me or seize my assets. I stood
there in my living room, with the phone pressed to my ear,
staring at the game on the screen. And before I can say, 'Either you are out of your mind or I'm being punked,' Rodriguez hits a home run. Lindor comes in, the guy on second
comes in, Rodriguez dances around the bases. I'm torn between doing a flamenco over the floorboards and figuring
out where the hell I'm going to get seven thousand dollars.
But I've got the sound up a little, right?"

Jack ached to hurry him up but swallowed his frustration. Physically.

"The crowd screeches like raccoons caught in a trap, this deafening wave of sound, must have blown out the eardrums of everyone at the stadium. Then it falls until the next guy reaches home, goes crazy, then waits to see if Rodriguez is going to make it or if Atlanta is going to get the ball back into the infield and beat him to home. As I'm sure you both know—"

No, I don't, Jack thought, grinding a few molars.

"—he makes it. Noise is like, that first colossal sonic boom raised to the tenth. And it went on and on." Hayes paused to sip his coffee which he had, miraculously, not spilled in the midst of his gestures, and finally got to the point. "Here's the thing. On the phone, I hear the crowd. The exact rise and fall of the roaring, in unison, with what I'm hearing and seeing on the TV."

"So they were watching the game," Riley guessed, but his voice seemed uncertain.

"That's where my brain went at first, even though way back in my mind I'm thinking, the Nationals aren't even in the series—I mean, as *if*, right? And they've got a TV on? IRS agents are staring at the tube while they're threatening citizens with arrest? Talk about our tax dollars at work. But that wasn't it. Suddenly I *knew* everything she'd said was total BS." Hayes gesticulated with his hands, straining against the cuffs. He would probably have bruises on his wrists in another ten minutes. "I said, 'Where are you?' She said D.C., but there was a hesitation, you know? She could tell from my voice that the tide had turned. I started shouting. I called her a liar, she wasn't the IRS, told her to give me my forty bucks back. She tried to give me the same lines, shouting back about warrants and arrests, but she didn't last long. I was out of my mind, you know? I called her everything but, well, human."

"And?" Riley leaned over the table.

"*Click,*" Hayes said.

"Click?"

"Click. Bitch hung up. Figured she wasn't going to see a penny of that seven thousand dollars so she gave up. I'm standing in my living room listening to a dial tone. The crowd on the screen is still going wild, and all I can think about is *I gave that chick my credit card number!*"

"Okay," Jack said. "What happened then?"

"Garcia came up to bat—"

"I meant with the woman on the phone. I assume you think she was Shanaya Thomas."

"I'm *getting* to that. So Garcia comes up to bat and hits a pop fly, so okay, I watched that for a couple more minutes but that was *all*, and then I got the eight-hundred number off the back of the card and called them to say I was scammed out of forty bucks. Of course I had to go through the whole menu system because you can't get a friggin' person on the line anymore and you have to listen to all the options and I got the wrong department and they had to transfer me and then they friggin' cut me off and I had to call *back*. But finally I get Fraud and I tell *that* chick the story and she keeps telling me to calm down and I'm saying stop the card, just stop the card, don't let anyone charge anything to it. But she's gotta check this and that and then recent transactions and—it's too late. Forty bucks, it was supposed to be? Four thousand. This chick charged four *thousand*. So I ask what she bought and the chick on the phone—the *new* chick on the phone—says 'financial services.' I'm like, what the crap are financial services? Did this chick—the first chick—pay for her accountant with my card or something like that? I mean sure, she could probably use an accountant, but—"

"She bought a money order," Jack guessed.

Hayes blinked, surprised and encouraged by the detective's ability to track. "Yes! No—not a money order, but a gift card. In the couple of seconds after she hung up on me, she used the number online to add funds to a reloadable gift card."

"Wait," Riley said. "She used your credit card to buy a gift card?"

"Yep. That's what the credit card company told me after the chick filled out a report, sent me some 'we're working on it' follow-up letters, and finally said it had gone to a gift card."

"Whose gift card?"

"No idea. I don't know if they really can't track it, don't have the legal ability to do that, or if they figure four thousand dollars isn't worth their time. They're a credit card company, so it probably isn't. They take the loss and raise my interest a couple percent." He seemed to run out of breath, exhausted by this recitation. "Eventually, they cancelled the charge."

Riley said, "But how does this get around to—?"

Instant reenergizing. "I started to think, this chick wasn't in India or Pakistan and she sure as hell wasn't in D.C. She was *here*, someplace close enough to the ballpark to hear the crowd, maybe even through closed windows. I mean *really* hear them. A pretty narrow area, when it comes down to it. And winter comes, work slows up, I got a lot of time on my hands, right?"

"You came downtown and looked for her," Jack said.

"Damn skippy. I started at the ball field and circled outward. I went up and down every floor of every building, popped into every waiting room, put my ear to the door if the places weren't open. When she was talking to me I could hear a ton of people in the room with her, all yakkin' away doing the same shit she was. It was *loud*."

"So you walked around town trying to find a noisy office. No one called the cops on you?"

He seemed surprised. "No. Why would they? They're offices, open to the public. I wasn't doing anything wrong. I'd walk in, say sorry, wrong place, and leave. No one cared."

"But you came to the building at East Ninth and Bolivar."

"Yep. No nameplates, no signs. I rang that little bell in the air lock there and said I was trying to find a place called Beaver Industries—"

"Beaver?" Jack asked.

"Yeah, uh, my little joke. Some guy said I had the wrong address. I tried saying I was looking for work, what did they do there—nothing. Just repeated that I had the wrong place, and then stopped saying anything at all, let me stand there in the air lock pushing the button and talking to myself. So I put my ear to the door—you can't see through the door, they have them painted on the inside—"

"We know."

"And I heard it. That buzz like when you have a beehive in your wall, right? I knew I had it. That was the place that had called me. I'd found it." His face glowed with triumph. "That was about three weeks ago. I started doing surveillance."

"Surveillance?" Jack pictured Hayes dressed in black, with camo makeup on his face, lurking behind the benches outside the stadium entrance.

"From the Thirsty Parrot, if you look over the cars in that parking lot, you can see the front door. I downed a lot of chicken wings and brewskis hanging out there, until they got tired of me bolting out the door whenever I saw a group going in or coming out. I'd always go back and pay for my stuff, but finally they told me I wasn't welcome. I borrowed my cousin's camera with a big telephoto lens and I guess that made them nervous . . . anyway, I had to do something. Intercom guy wouldn't tell me anything, I Googled the address, and the rental agency wouldn't tell me anything. That left the employees. I still can't figure out what kind of hours they work. They seem to switch off in groups of seven or ten but at random times during the day. Other than that, let me tell you, no one goes in and no one comes out."

"And you saw Shanaya Thomas?"

"Probably, but I didn't know what she looked like, of course. I only knew she was a chick, and most of the people there are guys. I counted maybe ten different women. I couldn't make it over there from the Thirsty Parrot before they scattered, so a few times I had to hang out by the ballpark and wait. Got friggin' cold, too. I'd go up to the people leaving, say I'm looking for work, what do they do, are there any openings? They'd look at me like they're Amish and I'm a biker with chains hanging off me and a bourbon in one hand and a porn tape in the other. Like they were afraid of *me*. It was weird, man. So finally I would follow the women until I could hear them talk. Easy, if I could get behind them and especially if there were two of them, because then they'd chitchat and I could hear their voices."

"Ah," Jack said. Eric Hayes had taken a logical, methodical approach to his task: collect possibles, then eliminate until you identify your target. "So today you found Shanaya Thomas."

"That bitch, yeah. I had seen her before, knew she usually approached from east on Bolivar. I had gone to the Subway on East Eighteenth to get something to eat and I saw her cross the street. I caught up, asked her if she knew where a gas station was. Yeah, don't ask me why a gas station, it was the first thing that popped into my head. She said no, but I couldn't tell from that, I needed her to talk more. So I asked if she worked in the building. No answer. So I figured the hell with it. I got in front of her and told her I knew what they were doing, it was illegal, and she was going to be arrested instead of me. *That* got her to say more than two words! What was I talking about, leave her alone or she'd call the cops, she didn't know what I was going on about.

Then I knew. It was her voice. Especially the way she said that I would be arrested and not her. She's got a funny way of saying it, like *ah*-rest instead of uh-*rest*."

Jack skipped ahead. "And then you punched her."

"No! I mean, well, yes, but that—I wanted her to admit it. I wanted her to admit she's a thief, I wanted her to tell me who she worked for and what they were doing with all this money, and what she did with my four thousand dollars. But she kept up the innocent act and tried to dodge around me until I grabbed her arm. She wasn't going to listen unless I made her, obviously."

"And you pulled her into the alley because—"

"She kept saying she's gonna be late, I'm gonna get her fired. I know her office or whatever you'd call it is right there on the corner so I thought if we hid so she couldn't be seen from a window or something, she'd be more likely to talk. But then those two other girls saw us."

"And," Jack added, "you punched her because—"

"She kept trying to run away! I had spent two months looking for her! I wasn't about to let her weasel out of it. I was going to keep her there until she either told me the truth or you guys got there. I was doing your job for you, actually."

He sat back, arms crossed—as well as he could with the wrists still cuffed—and fixed them with a look both accusatory and slightly disappointed. And, Jack had to admit (only to himself), not completely unjustified.

But Hayes's cool demeanor had a short shelf life. "Then those other two chicks showed up and waylaid me with the stick—that one's got an arm, let me tell you. I'll bet she plays hockey. But I'll take a broken shin before letting that bitch get away. Only then, she's trapped in the alley, right? You should have seen her trying to tell her little friends not to call the cops. She said it's no big deal, then she says it's a misunderstanding, finally she's flat-out shrieking at them to hang up the phone. And they look at her like she's nuts, like why *wouldn't* you call the cops, this guy's attacking women, yada, yada. And the one with the stick, man, she's *hot*, she's ready to take me out herself if you guys are a little busy or something. So my girl was screwed. Screwed, screwed, screwed."

A grin split his face. He had won. He had a bruised shin and cuffs on his hands, but his target now rested in the custody of the police.

"Okay," Riley said. "So you admit approaching and working to restrain Ms. Thomas?"

"Hell yeah, I admit it. As long as I can add *why*."

"You can. Did she answer any of your questions? Anything about the money or her job?"

The grin faded somewhat. "Not a word. What was I talking about, she had to get to work, leave her alone. Nothing else."

Jack said, "One thing, Mr. Hayes. You got your money back."

"Yep. Took a while."

"So you're not really out anything, except the time you spent—"

"Doing surveillance."

"To find the woman you think called you."

Hayes nodded happily.

"Why?"

Hayes blinked. "Why? You're asking me *why*?"

"It seems like an awful lot of time and effort, when you're not even out the money."

The scruffy man's mouth fell open briefly. "*Why*? Because it needed to be done, that's why! This chick and whoever she works for are parasites, feeding off the rest of us. Earlier this year, back before Easter I think, someone took my mother for two hundred bucks! Told her her computer was sending out error messages, that stupid crap, but my mom's not a technical wizard. She still thinks e-mail is amazing futuristic shit. So this turd calls on the phone and she buys it! She—well, she does the same thing I did; she hands over her credit card number. I guess we're lucky they only took two hundred instead of two thousand. And she's only got a little pension from my dad! So why did I punch this bitch? Because she freakin' deserved to be punched! She's lucky I didn't kill her." He sat back, glanced up at the bubble camera, thought better of his last remark, and waved his fingers dismissively. "In a theoretical sense, I mean."

"Got it," Jack said. "Theoretical."

Riley said, "You don't think she works for the same people who scammed your mom."

"Nah. But that's not the point! They're all people who would take a naïve old lady's rent money! What kind of complete scumbags would do that?" Hayes crossed the arms, jerking the cuffs, and gave his parting shot. "And *you* guys aren't doing much, that's for sure."

Jack said, "I'm not going to argue with you there."

Chapter 26

Not even being booked on an assault charge could dim Hayes's elation at having finally found and confronted Shanaya Thomas. Jack and Riley turned him over to his attorney, who planned to get him released that same afternoon with minor bail. All Hayes wanted to know was if they were going to arrest Shanaya as well.

"Her interrogation is next on our list," Jack promised, purposely using the harsher word. Hayes smiled, satisfied, no doubt imagining a much more unpleasant future for her than Jack or Riley could most likely provide.

They took a break at their desks to regroup and rest their eardrums. Rick's autopsy had been completed and had provided no more information than they'd already surmised. Rick had no injuries other than a fatal stab wound, made by something long, relatively thin and pointed and yes, extremely similar to the weapon used on Jennifer Toner and Evan Harding. An unusual weapon, the pathologist had told the attending officers. Nearly every stabbing he'd ever seen had been with a knife. He'd seen a few accomplished with screwdrivers or even a piece of rebar, and he couldn't be 100 percent sure this could not be one of those, but it resembled an ice pick . . . a tool from a bygone age that shouldn't even exist anymore.

Shanaya Thomas paced in an interview room, having nagged the officer assigned to watch her every five minutes to be allowed to leave. He told her that she could but would then most likely be arrested. He plied her with coffee, snacks, the Wi-Fi password, anything to keep her happy—with obviously limited success to judge from the pleading look on his face when Riley and Jack snuck by.

Rick's murder case had been officially assigned to the unit's star detectives, Patty Wildwood and her partner, Tim. Technically it should have been Jack and Riley since they had already been working a related case, but no doubt the higher-ups felt that since Jack reportedly dated the victim's ex-wife, well, the appearance of bias in any direction could be a problem. This was fine with Jack.

He fought the urge to check in with Maggie. She would only ask questions he couldn't answer, and he could do nothing to help her through her current tangle of emotions. Denny and Carol would look out for her. Still, he could drop by the lab for a minute or two, maybe ask about that powder—

Riley said, "The connection between Rick and Jennifer is obvious. Same place, same time, so the killer had to take them both out."

Jack said, "But which one had the killer gone there for?"

"Had to be Jennifer. If he'd wanted to kill Rick for some reason, he would have done it on the street or in his car, anyplace but an occupied building."

"True."

"But where does Evan Harding fit in? He had no connection to either, other than a brief conversation with Jennifer Toner."

"We need to go back to that."

"What?"

Jack tried to organize his thoughts. "We have to assume all three were killed by the same person. Jennifer wanted to track down the people responsible for supplying her brother with opioids. We've found nothing to suggest that Evan Harding had anything to do with the drug trade."

"Although it would be easy," Riley said, and it became Jack's turn to ask what he meant. "A check cashing store would be a great cover. They're passing small items over the counter, lots of cash changing hands, security cameras, great protection from rip-offs."

"Huh. I didn't get any hint of that—"

"Me neither. Not from our buddy Ralph. But Harding could have been a different story."

Jack said, "True. Either way, as far as we know there is no connection between Evan Harding and Jennifer Toner, except for her visit to the check cashing place."

Riley pondered this and came to the same conclusion Jack had. "We need to go back there. We need to look at more tapes, see if Marlon Toner had been a frequent visitor, or if Jennifer had shown up more than once."

"And what Evan Harding had to do with her brother."

"If the stuff ever gets out of his system, maybe he'll tell us himself." Riley rubbed his face, premature wrinkles more prominent around his eyes than they had been only a few days before. "There is one person still alive who could probably tell us something. And won't. And we can't even punch her in the stomach."

Jack said, "Maybe instead of a stick, we need a more persuasive carrot."

Monday, 3:00 p.m.

She began speaking as soon as they opened the door. "If you're going to arrest me, do it. But you can't keep me here. I know my—"

"Sorry for the wait," Riley said. "We were retrieving Evan's property for you."

She stopped midsentence, gazing at the clear, labeled bag he held as if it were Medusa's head. A diamond-encrusted Medusa's head.

"Please sit down," Riley said.

She did.

Jack went right into it. "We think you know more—perhaps everything—about Evan's activities. We'll make you a deal. Tell us about the call center and the check cashing store, and we'll give you the key."

She didn't even pretend it wasn't the key she wanted, and took her time to consider this offer. Jack pictured her mind moving like mercury, pulsing forward, around, probing for hidden traps or gaps or vulnerabilities, debating possible outcomes.

"Okay," she said.

"What do you do at the call center?"

She took them through it. An automated system dialed numbers and played a recorded message about lowered credit card rates or pain medication by mail, and if the person first answered and then pressed the number 1 or whatever, then the switchboard at the center routed it to a free headset. A red light appeared on her headset's base, and she had to push the button to connect to the call. The base had four different red lights with masking tape labels corresponding to each narrative—interest rates, free medical equipment, IRS, whatever. They changed from time to time depending on what they were having success with and what had burnt out. When the light lit up, she had two seconds to connect the call . . . more than five and she'd hear it from the pit boss.

The IRS narrative she'd been working recently had one extra step somewhere along the line because the first call was made and then the people—

"Victims," Jack couldn't resist clarifying.

—would call back. But it remained the same process from her point on. When the red light lit up, she had to take the call, the point always being to get the card numbers. Credit card numbers, gift cards, iTunes cards, anything that had funds attached to it. When she got the number, any relevant info, the expiration date, the three-digit security code, address, zip code out, she put them on hold and called the 800 number for the credit card company to find out the available credit. "If they have a seven-thousand-dollar limit but they've already charged six thousand eight hundred, it's hardly worth it," Shanaya explained wearily.

"Of course," Riley deadpanned.

This confirmed the card as valid. A good number of people tried to recite their card number from memory or elderly people had a hard time reading the embossed numbers and transposed digits, and Shanaya would get back on the line and tell them it didn't work. But if they had a decent amount of available credit—in practice, if they had any at all—Shanaya would type it into her monitor and dispatch it to her boss—not the pit boss, whose entire job it was to pace up and down the aisles, and make sure each employee gave 150 percent effort—but the floor supervisor, who worked in an office on the second floor and did nothing but transfer funds. Then Shanaya would repeat the process with any other credit cards on which the person wanted lower interest rates. Once possibilities were exhausted, she thanked them for their time, told them they would see the new interest rate reflected on their next statement or their application for the equipment or the pain meds would be in the mail or the IRS would cancel the warrant for their arrest. Then she would hang up and wait for the red light to beam again. They didn't leave their desks or take a break without signaling the pit boss. Ignoring the red light or waiting too long to answer would get them fired. "It's pretty grueling," she finished.

Jack held himself back from saying *A real job can be pretty grueling, too.* But with difficulty.

Riley said, "So when the floor boss gets the credit card or gift card numbers, what does he do with them?"

She seemed surprised by the question. "I don't know."

"What I mean is, how do those numbers translate into money for your boss?"

"I don't know. That part of it, they handle. Once the call ends, I'm done." Then she added, "But I get a percent. Of whatever they make, I mean. We're all paid on commission only, there's no actual salary or hourly wage."

"There's a work incentive for you," Riley said. "What happens on the screen when you add in the victim's information?"

"Nothing. When I have the numbers and amounts verified I click on 'Dispatch' at the bottom and it goes."

He asked a few more questions about the name of the program itself, the browser, the brand of computers and headsets even, anything at all. But she had not paid much attention to that, or said she hadn't. "There's nothing else on the computers except the program. Internet access has to be granted by the floor boss and he can see everything you're looking at." There would be no surfing the web, checking your Facebook status or playing Candy Crush at work, she explained. One girl sent a quick e-mail to her kids' day care center and a couple minutes later the pit boss came down, ripped off her headset, and escorted her off the property by dragging her to the door by one arm. Same went for any personal work on your own smartphones. A quick text before the red light came on again could be done, but once you had a person on the line you kept your full attention on the job.

Okay, Jack thought, maybe a *little* grueling.

"I had a bit of Internet access with the IRS narrative because I needed to search the people to make them believe I had all their information—like where they lived, worked, where their kids go to school."

"Seriously?" Riley breathed.

"It was *not* easy," she told them, mistaking the disgust in his voice for interest.

"The man who attacked you said his credit card charge ended up on a gift card. Is that what your bosses do?"

"Could be. I told you, that part of it isn't my job."

Riley said, "Just for the record, you *are* aware that this is grand larceny, and a crime?"

She didn't answer, her gaze flicking to the camera in the corner of the ceiling.

"Shanaya?" he pressed.

She wouldn't admit it, not on record. "I had to have a job."

Jack asked, "What did Evan have to do with the call center?"

Her head jerked up. "Nothing."

"Nothing?"

"No. I worked there, he didn't."

"Did he visit you there?"

An unladylike snort. "No. Staff didn't have *visitors*. Even the kids in the day care—if you checked them in, they had to stay the whole shift and leave with you. Nobody could have, like, the dads come get them when they got off work. *No one ever in the building except us.* I was amazed he let *you* in."

"Mr. Hawking? He's the floor supervisor?"

"No, he's *the* boss. There's a couple of floor bosses. I don't know their names—I never see them."

"Evan was murdered," Jack reminded her, his voice firm. "If it had nothing to do with your illegal business, then why?"

"I don't know," she said, apparently miserable.

"What was he doing?"

"Evan? Nothing."

"What was he doing at the check cashing place?"

"Nothing. It was a legitimate job," she said in defense of her dead boyfriend. "I mean, he did whatever his job was, I guess."

She looked up through her eyelashes, gauging their reactions. Apparently the look on Jack's face told her she might want to do better than that.

"It wasn't his fault," she said at last. "He figured they were bogus, but what could he do about it?"

"What was bogus?" Riley asked.

She told them, "Every day a few guys would come in and cash checks for medical payments, usually checks, Medicare, private insurance. The guys would have the correct ID, claim numbers on the memo lines; the checks looked legit, so he'd cash them."

"But the checks were faked?" Riley guessed.

"No, the checks were from the government. They were perfectly good."

"So what was the problem?"

"Twenty-, thirty-, fifty-thousand-dollar checks," she added. "Every day or two. The same maybe ten different guys cashing them."

"That's a lot of cash," Jack said.

"No, it wasn't, because the guys would take only part of it in cash. They'd put the rest on a money order, and then wire the money order to a bank account."

"Wait," Riley said. "They'd get the cash, and then get rid of the cash?"

She ignored this interruption. "Evani did the math—the amount that the guys took out in cash of each check always equalled five percent."

"Their fee," Jack breathed.

Black hair fell over one eye and she batted it away. "He couldn't tell what kind of medical condition they were supposed to have, or whether they really had it, of course. The checks only had claim numbers on them."

"No doctor's name?"

"No. But the funds all got transferred to the same bank

account—something Therapeutics. That's what made him realize it had to be some sort of scam."

"Therapeutics?"

"Or pharmaceuticals, something like that. He said he tried to look it up once, but nothing came up."

Riley said, "So a man comes in with a thirty-thousand-dollar check. What's to keep him from cashing it and skedaddling?"

She hesitated, and Jack thought she might ask him to define *skedaddling*. "I don't know."

Jack said, "Because they'd never get another. They had to look at this as a job and play it straight or else their revenue stream would dry up."

"Drugs," Shanaya muttered. "A lot of people go in and out of that store. Evani said he could tell whether it was meth or painkillers or booze or only pot just by looking at someone. He thought painkillers most of the time."

Riley said okay, but wouldn't all these guys have to be over sixty-five to be eligible for Medicare? Maybe they really did have some heavy-duty medical conditions?

Shanaya tapped her foot, not particularly interested in the details.

Jack said, "You can also get it if you have a long-standing disability, like kidney failure. Same with Medicaid, especially for those with minimal income, children and single mothers. So, what did Evan do with this information?"

"Nothing," Shanaya said, as if that should be obvious.

"He didn't tell anyone, call the police, alert the feds?"

She laughed without humor. "No! He had no proof. It wasn't up to him to decide that Mr. Smith didn't really have diabetes. The checks were legitimate. He mentioned it to his boss one time and was told to mind his own business. As long as the store didn't lose any money, it wasn't a problem."

"Then why is he dead?"

"I don't know," she said. "Maybe you should ask Ralph."

Chapter 27

They had her write a statement, then insisted she do it over after she noted only that Evan Harding had concerns about certain money exchanges and his workplace and left out every other detail of her testimony.

In the meantime, they needed some expert advice. And, for once, not from Maggie.

After asking around, Jack and Riley were directed to Manuel Rodriguez in the white-collar unit. The detective did, indeed, have a white collar, set off by a navy silk tie and what appeared to be "skinny" jeans. Or perhaps they only seemed that way because Manuel Rodriguez reached six feet three without topping two hundred pounds.

He tapped at a keyboard, absorbed in his screen, apparently unaware of their approach until they pulled up a pair of his coworkers' vacated chairs. Then he stopped typing, glanced at them, and waited.

Riley explained that they needed some advice about a call center. Rodriguez forgot his screen, pushed his keyboard aside, and rested his elbows on his desk. "A call center here? Local? Totally cool. Most are overseas."

"Right here. Problem is, we have no proof. This girl isn't giving anything up. Like, nothing. We think it may be involved with a couple homicides but can't begin to guess how. Our question is—"

"What's the scam?"

"She claims to be an IRS agent—"

"Ah, yes." Rodriguez grinned, his head bobbing up and down so fast it made his black hair splay over his eyes. "I love getting those. They want you to call back so they use the same number for twenty-four hours—usually the scammers spoof a new number with every call so caller ID doesn't do you any good. But those, I spend the rest of the day dialing it to tell them their mothers were whores—" He clapped a hand over his mouth, wide eyes scanning the area for any females within earshot. "Probably shouldn't say that. But they tick me off. And I figure if they have any sort of a conscience at all, they'll burn out after a couple of weeks. If I can guilt one scammer into quitting, then I've done my daily good deed."

"But how does it work?" Riley asked.

Long fingers sketched the air as he talked. "These groups—usually overseas, but not necessarily—steal people's IDs, then use them to fill out a generic gift card, held by a physical person here. No money has gone anywhere yet. Then, when the call center gets some dumb schlub like me to give up his credit card number, they use it to load funds on the gift card that's ready and waiting. The runner—the physical person with the gift card—takes it to one of the money stores or goes online and buys a money order with it. The money order is deposited in an account. Offshore, of course. It seems weird, like these numbers are going back and forth over the ocean, but that way the connection between me and my credit card and them and their bank account is completely severed."

"It's worth it? That many people believe the IRS is calling them?"

"Never underestimate Americans' fear of the IRS. And if it doesn't work, then maybe your grandson calls and says he's been arrested and needs bail money. Or there's a new government plan for health insurance, or medical equipment, or, my personal favorite, pain meds. Or they want to lower your credit card interest rates—I still get that one twice a day."

Riley said, "How come—"

"The government can't stop it? I get asked that at least three times a day, five if I do any socializing outside video games. Because a phone call is a pretty ephemeral thing. Do Not Call lists don't work because fraudsters spoof the number. Phone services like RoboKiller can cut it down but can't catch everyone. We're starting to see text scams—I'm sure those will be all the rage in another year, if not in another month. Like any business, they adapt to changing conditions. Having a Junk folder decimated the Nigerian prince e-mail scams—so now they seem to come from Amazon and Apple thanking you for your purchase of something bizarre that you know you wouldn't buy, so you click on that handy link to dispute the charge. Your bank wants you to confirm your account. Your credit has been frozen due to some problem, click on the link to fix it. Don't ever," he warned them, his face momentarily as grave and solemn as a tangible eulogy, "click on the link."

Jack spoke quickly. "Can we get a search warrant for the call center? Based only on this one guy's testimony?"

Full stop. Rodriguez straightened up as if someone had pushed his elbows off the desk. "Thaaaaat . . . might be difficult, a raid on a place like that, if they say they're customer service or tech support . . . then there's the practical difficulties. You've got a room full of phone routers and computers, right? You'd have to collect all of it, the router, the server, the computers, the files. We'd leave them with some empty cubicles, that's all. Depending on the intranet setup, we might only need the servers and not each individual PC, but even if so, then the desktops are probably useless on their own. Either way, you're gutting their business for an indefinite period. How big of a place are we talking?"

"We saw at least twenty, and there's a second floor, so over forty," Riley said.

"He said he had fifty employees," Jack said.

"So, conservative estimate, forty terminals. If our tech guys know exactly what to look for, they might be able to do a few per day, if they push all their other cases aside. If you want *everything* on every computer, that will take longer still. We've probably told you how much we hate it when you detectives say you want everything, because you don't mean everything. Then we hand you twelve Blu-Ray disks full of e-mails and photos and programs and you say, well, I didn't mean *everything*. I meant only e-mails and photos. You know what we say then?"

Jack did know. "No."

"That's right, we say no. Not our job to sift through your evidence for you. I admit, we get a little testy about that. Anyway, my point is you'll be shutting this company down for a long time. *Months*, realistically. You think a judge will give you a warrant based on one guy's story?"

Again, Jack knew. "No."

"Probably not, dude," Rodriguez said. "You asked me for my opinion, and that's it. But hey, you still got this girl."

"Do we?" Jack asked aloud.

This took up an hour while the police chief got Marlon Toner an attorney and assigned detectives to canvas all of West 29th in order to place him near his sister's apartment on Friday afternoon. With luck he would erupt in an airtight confession and corroborating evidence would not be needed, but better to check every box. Besides, it gave the cops something to do other than stew. The obvious killer had been apprehended without argument and no urgency existed, yet the boys in blue felt the very normal need to *do* something after such an upset, and merely sitting around waiting for Toner to sober up only made it worse.

In this general upheaval Jack managed to borrow a few guys from another department.

By this time Shanaya Thomas had finished her statement. Jack handed her the plastic bag with Evan Harding's property. She took it, signed the form, turned on her heel and left, without a good-bye or a backward glance.

Riley stood at his elbow, and watched the woman walk away. "We're never going to be counted among her favorite people, you think?"

"She definitely isn't one of mine. I'm still not sure she's told us a single true thing."

"At least she stopped bitching about being late for work."

Jack said, "That one makes me think she's either resigned herself to losing the day's pay, or she's decided on a career change."

"The two undercovers in place?"

"I sure hope so."

"This might get really interesting." Riley spoke with relish, then added: "Patty wants me in the room with her to question Toner. She figures since we rescued him from what could have turned into an angry mob, he'll look at me as some sort of protector. Then she can be Bad Cop. If you and Tim are in there, too—"

"He'll feel like he's in front of a firing squad and shut down entirely. That's fine with me. I'll stick with our girl."

"You're going to have the better time, I think. Have you checked on Maggie?"

"Why? Something else happen?"

Riley rotated the coffee cup on his blotter, as he often did when approaching a delicate topic. "No, but"—he checked his watch—"her husband's on a steel table getting his chest cavity excavated."

"*Ex*-husband," Jack said, more stridently than he had planned to. "Ex."

Ex or no, Maggie Gardiner was right then observing Rick Gardiner's clothing. Denny had brought it back from the autopsy. He spread each item out, noting its description, size, condition, location of any defects left by weapons, taking photos both overall and close-up—exactly as they did for any homicide victim. Maggie stood, listening, watching, remaining a resolute four feet from the exam table. She did not want to contaminate any evidence with her conflict-of-interest status, but in no way would she be shut out and Denny knew better than to try.

He talked to her as he worked, spreading out the T-shirt with its small hole inside a patch of blood about five inches in diameter. "No surprises at the post, as I said. Zero injuries other than the fatal wound, no bruises, not even a scratch."

"No struggle."

"The organs were normal. A little hardening of the arteries, but who hasn't got that?"

"Maybe people who don't eat fried food at least once a day," Maggie guessed aloud.

"The weapon went up under the rib cage and directly into the heart. He died almost instantly." He glanced at her, making sure she heard what would surely be a comfort to any victim's family: Rick hadn't suffered.

"Uh," she said. "Yes."

Denny took a closer shot of the hole in the chest area of the shirt, then one with a disposable paper ruler under the defect. He measured the distance between the left shoulder and the hole, the left side seam of the shirt and the hole, and wrote these numbers in his bench notes. "The heart stopped pumping, this shirt soaked up most of what did bleed out, then the polo shirt soaked up a little, and the inside of the parka a bit more. So we saw that minuscule amount on the outside of the parka and that was it." He flipped the shirt over and photographed the back. "Whoever moved the body probably didn't get a drop on himself. Certainly not enough to attract any attention."

"He'd have to be pretty strong," Maggie noted. "Rick wasn't a small guy."

Denny put the T-shirt back into its brown paper bag, and pulled out the parka.

Maggie opened her mouth to say, "We need to tape that," and then shut it again. Denny knew they needed to tape it. Telling her boss how to do his job did not seem like a great idea under any circumstances, as well as unnecessary.

Ideally it would have been taped at the scene, but with the dusting of snow the tape would only pick up water, if anything at all. Adhesive also lost its sticky quality at such low temperatures—which was why, when they received crumpled-up duct tape as evidence, they would put it in the freezer until it could be unraveled without too much stretching and distortion.

On top of that the contamination from all the other items in the dumpster might render examination of trace evidence pointless, since anything they found might have already been inside the open, publicly-accessible space.

But the victim was a cop, so—dot all *i*'s, cross all *t*'s.

Normally, taping wouldn't come into play with a gunshot, as the cause of death had first appeared. But since the killer had to transport the body up a short hallway and then wrestle it out a window, the trace evidence had been on Maggie's mind from the first.

Denny pressed the clear tape all over the garment, then flipped it over and did the back. Then he emptied the pockets. A pair of gloves—so Rick had at least taken those off, probably when he entered the building—and a wad of napkins from Subway.

"He always had terrible sinuses," Maggie said, as explanation.

Two wrapped mints, a quarter and a dime, and a crumpled sticky note with a case number written on it. Maggie recognized it as belonging to the deceased man found behind the West Side Market, the one originally identified as Marlon Toner.

Denny flipped the side of the coat open to see the inner surfaces. A smaller area of bloodstain around the hole left by the weapon, but still much larger than the few drops that made it through the padding to appear on the outside of the jacket. No inside pockets.

"No keys," Denny mused aloud.

"The killer took them to move Rick's car."

"That's right. He would have had us looking in Euclid for Rick, if we'd only found the car sooner."

This meant Josh and Amy had the best chance of finding helpful evidence, Maggie thought. They would swab and tape and fingerprint Rick's car. The killer most likely stabbed Rick and disposed of his body in less time than a commercial break. But then he drove Rick's car out to Euclid and dropped it in a public parking lot, where a snow-covered vehicle wouldn't be noticed for quite some time. That would take at least twenty minutes. He had to drop a hair or maybe pulled off a glove and then forgot himself, adjusted the radio or the mirror. Josh or Amy needed to bring back DNA and fingerprints and maybe a lost driver's license, something, anything, to make this task easier.

Or Marlon Toner needed to confess. That would make everyone relax. They'd still have to do the same amount of work—Maggie had seen too many confessees change their minds and their stories by the time the trial rolled around in a year or two or three—but they could work at a more leisurely pace.

"No phone, either," Denny said.

"Our killer likes phones. He took Jennifer's, too."

"But not the wallet—Rick's wallet. It was in his pants."

He waved at another of the paper bags. "Left the cash, the credit cards."

"Maybe after seeing the badge on his belt he wanted to get out of there as quickly as possible. Or didn't want to add enough felonies to make a death penalty case. Or," she added, "he didn't need the money."

"But took the cell phone."

"Not to sell, I bet. He took it to see if Rick had texted or called anyone about being at Jennifer's. He wanted to know if more cops were on their way."

Denny said, "The detective at the autopsy said that Will said that Rick had planned to stop by Jennifer Toner's apartment to have her look at a six-pack of mugs of known pill mill hustlers, see if she recognized any. It should have taken five minutes."

He always said he had lousy luck, Maggie thought. "What happened to the six-pack?"

"Don't know. The killer must have taken that, too."

"I knew he hadn't killed her."

"You can say 'I told you so.' It's okay."

Maggie said, "I told you so."

She wanted to repeat it a few more times, but not to Denny. Denny had been smart enough not to suggest it in the first place.

Her boss continued to describe articles of clothing, photograph them, and then package each item back in its individual paper bag. He handed the tapings from the coat to Maggie. "There you go," he said weakly, straining to find a comforting way to say that since she was their only hair and fiber expert, she would have to do the analysis, conflict of interest or no . . . but also that she should go home if she really needed to. Either was fine as long as she went away and stopped watching him work over his shoulder.

She took the tapings, dredged up a smile for him, and went back to her bench.

Chapter 28

Monday, 3:45 p.m.

Jack did run by the forensics unit before he left, an idea forming in his mind. There, he asked Maggie if she could leave to accompany him on a stakeout.

"A *what*?"

"Bring your print kit."

"Silly boy," Carol said from behind her computer monitor. "She doesn't go to the grocery store without her print kit."

"I do, too," Maggie protested, but mildly.

"Is this legal?" she asked ten minutes later.

"Parking in the alley? We've got this." He pulled a rigid plastic placard from beneath the driver's seat. It bore the official department seal and read CLEVELAND POLICE—OFFICIAL BUSINESS. "That should keep us from getting towed for at least ten minutes. After that, it gets risky."

"I meant following Shanaya Thomas."

"For that," he said, "I've got this." He patted the search warrant in his coat pocket, and they reluctantly left the shelter of the vehicle. The wind howled and Maggie could feel it pushing at her, threading its way through her parka, but that proved only the merest hint of chill compared to stepping out of the alley and onto the city sidewalk. East Ninth Street ran north to south and created the perfect wind tunnel for the howling gusts off the lake. She buried her mouth and nose in the fake fur edging the parka's collar and hustled along toward the bank's entrance, focused on the primitive need for safe shelter above all.

Jack checked the lobby through the large glass windows, then opened a brass-edged glass door and ushered her in. On a soaked indoor-outdoor mat she stamped her boots out of habit even though the wind had been moving too quickly to let snow settle.

The vast lobby of the old Huntington Bank building spread out and demanded attention, driving everything else from her mind until she had seen and acknowledged its majesty. Pillars, topped by huge and elaborate carvings, lined each side and stretched up through three stories and ending at a curved glass atrium ceiling. Champagne-colored marble covered the walls, the columns, the floor. A child's shout bounced off the stone, as did several conversations of office workers and bank tellers. The pillars were—

Jack pulled on her left wrist, gently but firmly. "Come on. Stop staring."

"How can I help it?"

He moved them toward the third bench from the front. Benches sat back to back, lined up the center of the lobby to neatly bisect the area. A man sat at one, apparently playing a game on his smartphone. He wore a parka something like Maggie's but not laundered nearly as often, a stocking cap, untied boots, and dirty jeans.

Jack sat at the other end of the bench from him and Maggie tucked herself in between Jack and the armrest.

The man pretended to make a call. "She went down with one of the managers about three minutes ago. The security guard confirmed that that's where the safe deposit boxes are.

I asked him if it is 'safe deposit' or 'safety deposit,' 'cause that's always bothered me. He said he didn't really know. I couldn't believe it—how can he work in a bank every day and not know if it's safe deposit or safety deposit? We always said safety deposit in my family, but that doesn't seem to make sense if I think about it."

Whether a passionate interest in language usage or simple boredom prompted this discourse, Jack remained on target. "I only have a warrant to 'examine and possibly collect any personal contents stored at this facility,' so she will have plenty of legroom to protest if she wants. And knowing her, she'll want. I don't have time to waste arguing with the bank, so I'm hoping they won't ask us to leave if we're quiet." He turned to Maggie to say he might need her to fingerprint the contents of Shanaya and Evan's safe deposit box.

"You're assuming they have one because of the key."

"Yes, the key. She'd been trying to get it from us for days, but without admitting that she wanted it. Why? Because it holds her proceeds from scamming money out of innocent people on the phone, and maybe whatever Harding could embezzle, skim, or extort from the Medicare or -caid recipients. She bailed out of their apartment and I think she's given up on the job. Once she gets what's in that box, she's going to disappear."

"That's a somewhat large assumption."

"It is. But Evan Harding kept that key taped to his ankle to keep it from someone—why not his girlfriend? Otherwise he'd have left it in their apartment. If that box is full of cash then who else, besides her, had a motive to kill Harding?"

"Maybe whoever the cash belonged to."

"And there's no way to determine that without her cooperation," Jack pointed out. "Nothing else has gotten her to talk. Maybe seizing whatever she's got in that deposit box will. You find anything interesting on your end?"

The change in cases discussed did not throw her off; she'd

long become accustomed to the scattershot approach of most detectives. "Amy and Josh aren't back yet, so I don't know what they found in the car. Rick's jacket—who knows. It's outerwear, and we all probably carry around traces of the entire city with us. He had natural and synthetic fibers in nearly every color, plenty of his own hairs, two blond ones."

Jack cleared his throat. "Did he have a girlfriend? Currently?"

"Rick always has a girlfriend," she told him. "Of sorts. But I don't know who, so someone will have to ask Will. He'd probably get all embarrassed about telling me." Ridiculous, of course, but Will had always been the complete opposite of his partner. Will thought about people's feelings more than he really needed to. "I found seven animal hairs, some kind of weird thing."

"He didn't have a pet?"

"No—he likes animals as well as the next guy, I guess, but I can't see him actually getting one without me there to clean its cage. But that's not what's weird. The roots . . . I'm sure it's not a dog or a cat. Other than that, all I can guess is that it's some kind of mammal. I was working on it when you came in. There were also some wool fibers, don't know what . . . Rick didn't like wool, so I doubt it's from his clothes. They could belong to Jennifer Toner's carpeting, if Rick stayed there long enough to fall to the ground after he had been stabbed. I'd been figuring the killer stabbed him, then grabbed him and hauled him out immediately. It would be quite a struggle to get him off the ground once he was there, and I bet his clothing would have been more disarrayed. That's more or less a guess, though."

She noticed Jack watching her. Perhaps he wondered what kind of person could sit and so dispassionately picture the ice-cold killing of a man she'd not only slept with but once loved enough to marry.

She wondered, too. But all that passion had been another

time, another life, and both had ended long ago. Now she felt only professional responsibility. And sadness that things had not turned out well for Rick. Right now it seemed things had not turned out very rosy for either of them.

But all Jack said was, "Unless there were two of them."

Maybe they were both ice-cold, she thought. Maybe they were just sensible. "That would always make things easier, checking the hallway for witnesses, getting the body out the window, moving the car to Euclid without having to leave your own car behind."

"That leaves our girl here out," Jack said, "if we could ever have considered her in the first place. As far as I know she had never heard of Rick or either of the Toners and couldn't have hefted a sack of kitty litter out a second-floor window."

"There she is," the undercover officer said.

Maggie followed his line of sight to a very young woman with jet-black hair and a gray Columbia jacket. She exited the main part of the bank and entered the lobby carrying a small purse in one hand and a backpack strapped to her shoulders.

Jack strode parallel to the woman, staying to the side of the lobby. The undercover promptly took off in the opposite direction. Maggie stayed put.

Shanaya Thomas strode toward the main doors, her gaze sweeping the area from side to side, even up and down, as if snipers might be positioned on the upper landings. It took her only ten steps to spot Jack. Of course, he hadn't made much effort to stay hidden and Shanaya knew, only too well by now, what he looked like.

She froze in the exact middle of the vast lobby, indecision on her face. Now Maggie could see the oversized backpack she carried. It spread from the back of her skull to below her hips.

It took Shanaya only a split-second to make her choice.

She whirled and ran, arms pumping, boots squeaking against the marble floor, legs churning with visible effort under the heavy backpack. She might be young and strong and gripped with adrenaline, but the laws of physics still reigned.

That, and the undercover officer positioned in front of the other exit, who now flashed a badge and told her to stop. He didn't shout, Maggie noted. No reason to alarm the bank patrons.

Maggie watched all this; she did not consider trying to head the woman off should she change direction yet again. Body-blocking fleeing suspects was not her job and even more, not her jurisdiction. She had no legal authority to restrain or restrict anyone.

Besides, Jack had somehow closed the gap between them and now materialized behind the woman as she spun again, searching for any avenue of escape. He clamped a hand on her elbow and her face fell from fear into shock, hopelessness visibly piercing her heart as a spike had pierced Evan Harding's.

Possibly wielded by this same woman, but that couldn't temper Maggie's empathy right then. She watched Shanaya Thomas stop, close her eyes, and stare at the floor in either shame or utter exhaustion. No matter what she had done, she remained a very young woman in clear agony.

Maggie moved over to them, catching up as Jack said: "Shanaya Thomas, we have a search warrant for all items currently in your possession, as said items are presumed to be material to the murder of Evan Harding."

"Why?" the woman cried. "Why are you doing this to me?" Her voice bounced off the stone walls, thin and weak and despairing.

Jack answered, "Because we're trying to find out who killed your boyfriend. Don't you want to as well?"

"That has nothing to do with this! This is my stuff. You can't take it!"

"Maybe. Maybe not. But this warrant says I have the right to look at it. And if it is obviously the proceeds of illegal activity, then we may retain it until a warrant can be obtained for seizure."

"You can't do that! It's mine!" Tears squeezed out of her eyes and she brushed them away with the back of a hand. "It doesn't have anything to do with Evan!"

"Maybe," Jack said, "Maybe not."

Chapter 29

The bank gave them a small conference room to use, happy to get them out of the lobby and the public eye. There were probably, Maggie thought, several reasons for examining and processing the contents there instead of back at the station. For one thing, Jack had a warrant for those contents but no warrant to arrest Shanaya, and his statement indicated a right to examine the contents but not necessarily seize them, unless they indicated criminal activity. If Shanaya carried nothing more in the oversized backpack than her birth certificate and a family photo album, then he could let it and her go without further custody or paperwork. Maggie doubted that would prove the case, from the *thud* the bag produced when Jack dropped it on the conference table. Besides, the homicide unit and the entire department still churned with the agitation of a police officer's murder, the pervasive disquiet of a large and disturbed organization, so the bank conference room provided a quiet space in which to focus their attention on Shanaya Thomas.

Maggie was officially present to photograph and fingerprint any items of interest, to see if Evan Harding's prints turned up, but she wondered if she might be moral support. Perhaps having another female in the room—along with the intimidating Jack Renner and the stocky undercover guy who sat near the corner and did nothing but stare coldly— might help the young woman relax and speak more freely. Perhaps she could be a silent "good cop" to Jack's bad . . . though Maggie didn't want to dwell on how accurate that title may or may not be when applied to Jack. Besides, Shanaya Thomas didn't seem to need or want the support, company or sympathetic glances of her own gender or any other. She didn't so much as glance at Maggie, only occasionally at the undercover officer, and at the bag on the table. The rest of the time she stared at Jack as if trying to bore through his skull with her gaze. She didn't seem scared. Upset, worried, a touch despairing here and there, but for the most part *angry*. Really, really angry.

"You have no right to seize my property," she stated, enunciating every word.

Jack read her the rights printed on the Miranda warning card, even though she wasn't technically under arrest, then reminded her that she had told them how she spent her days committing fraud. Any reasonable officer of the court would assume that this bag of money had resulted from those fraudulent actions. Surely she didn't expect to keep the money.

"My *employer* is fraudulent. He has all the money I obtained for him. That's got nothing to do with what's in that bag."

"That should be easy enough to establish, then," Jack said. He asked Maggie to proceed.

She took a picture of the unopened bag. Sturdy and new, it had been constructed of black canvas with straps and mesh areas most likely designed to carry pup tents and bedrolls. It had three large outside pockets, two of which were empty. The third was not.

With latex-gloved hands, Maggie carefully—the possibility of needle sticks or potential weapons ever kept in mind—removed the contents. She spread them out and took a picture of the whole group, then the individual items.

There were seven different drivers' licenses, four for Shanaya, three for Evan. Seven different names, seven different addresses, and three different states. Also copies of fourteen birth certificates, five Social Security cards—some of these matched the birth certificates—and eight miscellaneous identifications such as medical insurance cards, student IDs to colleges in Pennsylvania and Indiana, and a commercial truck driver's license with Evan Harding's picture in the name of Chad Kaiser.

Even Jack seemed a bit taken aback by this find. How did these pieces fit into a puzzle that would show who murdered three people, and why? "Do you want to explain these to us?"

Shanaya Thomas, or whatever her real name might be, answered with a defiant stare and without a single word.

Maggie unzipped the center section. Photograph, spread the opening wider, photograph again.

The stacks of money inside shouldn't have come as a surprise, but seeing a four-foot-by-two-foot bag nearly full with tidy bundles of currency—well, that one usually saw only on television.

Jack said, "I assume all this stuff had been in a safe deposit box? Which you opened with the key your boyfriend kept taped to his ankle?"

One eyebrow twitched when he said this, as if she had been wondering what Evan Harding had done with that key, but she said nothing.

"The safe deposit box you just vacated? We spoke to the bank manager. He confirmed that you were the owner of the box, along with Evan—"

"Exactly. It's my property."

"—and today you had decided to close it, along with the account you two had here together. He couldn't give me any details, of course, but he could tell me that you were a valued customer." He indicated the stack of money. "I didn't know they made deposit boxes that big."

Maggie, meanwhile, had begun stacking the bundles into piles of five, photographing as she went. There seemed no need to categorize the bundles—all of them had fifty-dollar bills in bundles of fifty. A brown-edged band let her know a bundle contained one-hundred bills so that her little stacks of five totaled $25,000 each.

Jack pointed at the stacks accumulating on the table, Maggie pulling ever more from the backpack as if they were loaves and fishes.

"This is why you killed him," he said to Shanaya Thomas.

For a second, pure shock wiped the sullenness off her face. "*What*? I didn't kill him! How can you say that?"

"Who else, then? No other person appeared to ask us for this safe deposit key. No one else had a motive."

"I didn't have a reason to—"

"*This* isn't a reason? He taped the key to his ankle to hide it from you, but both your names were on the account. Now that he's dead, the whole shebang is yours and yours alone."

She said, "He kept the key on him because he was always afraid that someone would burglarize our room and find it. Student housing, security's pretty basic and there's always kids around—I know it was stupid, paranoid, but that's how he was. He kept it anywhere but on a key chain, not even on a chain around his neck, in case the store got robbed or he got mugged by one of their low-life clients when he closed up at night."

"Look at this from our point of view," Jack said, calmly but not casually. "Only you and he had access to this money. His body's barely cold, and you're heading out the door with—this."

"We did all this together . . . I didn't kill him, I *needed* him. I loved him," she added.

This last should have been heart-rending, yet it seemed more like an observation absently made. Evan Harding had been her partner first, her lover an off-in-the-distance second.

"Shanaya," Jack said, "where did this money come from?"

She continued to speak with exaggerated clarity: "It's our savings. We've been saving everything we could for years—you saw where we lived, no car, cheap phones, hardly any clothes. We wanted a nest egg so we could get married and move. We worked hard for that money, and it's *mine*, and you have no right to steal it."

Jack didn't show even a flicker of anger at this accusation. "It will be inventoried and counted and you will get a receipt for every penny. But we will have to establish where it came from."

"I told you."

"You said Evan was your partner. You meant that literally, right?"

She stopped speaking. Maggie continued to stack bundles of bills. The undercover guy in the corner had his chin propped on one hand, its elbow cupped with the other hand, as if waiting for the next twist in a stage play.

Jack said, "He skimmed from Ralph. Then he brought the cash here and deposited it in your account through, what, the night depository? That's why he wasn't found on a direct route home, because he came here first. Then what, every so often you withdraw from the account, bring the cash down here, and put it in your box? Transactions under ten thousand don't have to be reported anywhere, and a simple account withdrawal wouldn't leave much of a paper trail."

If he had gotten any of that wrong, she didn't correct him.

"So here's the thing, Shanaya. Who did he skim from? Those bogus medical checks? How did he do it without Ralph finding out?"

"I don't know."

"You just said you were partners."

"I don't have to prove anything to you. You have no right—"

He pointed out, with surprising patience: "I've been to the check cashing place. I know what Evan made per hour. You, on the other hand, admit that your take-home pay was commission on a first-degree felony."

"My boss was fraudulent. He got all the money, I didn't. I only made an hourly wage—"

Maggie had emptied the bag and now tallied the contents, doing the math three times to make sure she got it right. She had thirty-eight stacks of five, nine-hundred and fifty thousand, plus three extra stacks so—

Jack turned to her.

She said, "Nine-hundred and sixty-five thousand dollars."

He didn't bat an eye. Neither did Shanaya, but the undercover guy in the corner sat up a little straighter.

"And what was your hourly wage?" Jack asked the girl.

Shanaya seemed to be desperately calculating in her head to come up with some amount that explained how she or Evan or both of them could legally have made nearly a million dollars over the course of a few years.

Maggie, meanwhile, tried out mental arguments for *not* processing each of the nineteen thousand, three hundred bills, which would be largely pointless—the money had obviously been bundled by the bank employees. She could process the two outer surfaces of the two outer bills and the band of each bundle, only what Shanaya or Evan would touch when moving them from a teller window to a safe deposit box. That made sense.

Shanaya continued to work on an innocent explanation.

Maggie double-checked the oversized backpack. Other than the cash, the main compartment held only a worn metal box with a wire handle and a simple clasp, the kind a social organization might use for petty cash. She pulled it out, holding it carefully by the edges. It had a duck sticker and a piece of masking tape that had once been some sort of label on the top.

"Don't touch that," Shanaya said.

Maggie stopped; the woman had not said a word to her while the bills stacked up, so perhaps this box—

"That's personal. It's none of your business."

"Unfortunately, Shanaya," Jack said, with the most painstaking show of patience that Maggie had ever seen from him, "everything about you is now our business."

Maggie decided to fingerprint it, now that she'd finally discovered a decent surface for prints. Superglue fuming would be better, but the box had already been jostled around inside a canvas bag and she didn't think further transport would help matters. But how to use black powder inside the bank's conference room without creating a mess for the cleaning staff or, heaven forbid, leaving a dark sheen that might rub off on an executive's expensive suit?

Shanaya said, "You can't prove anything about that money."

"Maybe not," Jack said, "but neither can you."

"I don't have to. I'm innocent until proven—"

"Except you're not. We've already established that you're part of a criminal enterprise aimed at defrauding innocent citizens. You don't get to benefit from crime. It's as simple as that."

Maggie found a roll of paper towels tucked in a single, sparsely populated cabinet in one corner of the room. She spread that over the table and placed the box on top of it, then applied powder with a light brush, keeping her strokes short and concentrated. No sense throwing the fine dust off in every direction or the bankers would be collecting dark smears on their file folders, fingers, and clothes for weeks to come. Shanaya watched this inexorable process with dread.

Maggie found three prints that might be of value for comparison, spread clear tape over the dark lines, then transferred the tape to white glossy cards. They were distinct with strong lines, fresh. Most likely Shanaya had placed them there ten minutes earlier, but nothing could be done about that.

"You have no right to go through my stuff," the woman continued to argue, aiming this fury at Jack.

"I do, actually. That's what a warrant means."

Maggie opened the box, gingerly; she couldn't help but expect live snakes or a small explosion after that vehement objection. But the box held only loose papers and a few keepsakes: a scratched gold band, a worn gold necklace with a light blue stone, a picture that must have been Shanaya as a toddler with an older couple—her parents?—and a brown and white feather about five inches long. Maggie spread it out and photographed, while feeling the woman's eyes burn into her scalp.

"That's just—stuff," Shanaya said, her voice small and weak.

"I see that." Maggie tried to sound soothing. She would have liked to assure the woman that she could have it back, but that would be up to detectives and attorneys. These apparent family keepsakes couldn't be considered relevant evidence. The stack of fake IDs, however . . .

"I'm not a criminal," Shanaya told Jack. "It's not my fault my boss is defrauding people. Did you make the staff at Enron give their paychecks back because it turned out to be one big pyramid scheme?"

Maggie detected surprise in the brief tilt of Jack's eyebrows before he spoke. "That's a good argument—except you've already admitted that you knew it was fraud."

"I didn't know—"

"So you really believed that you were an IRS agent, sending deputies out to arrest delinquent taxpayers?"

That stopped her. The "I didn't know" defense wasn't going to fly. She tried another. "You can't prove I did that."

"We have a witness in custody who is *begging* to identify you on the stand."

"He can't identify a voice. That's not *proof.*"

"Maybe. Maybe not. We'll see what the jury thinks."

She sat back, appraising him coldly. Blanket denial had gone nowhere. Next approach: "You want your cut? How much is it going to take?"

The undercover guy stirred again, either wondering what *his* percent might be or wondering if that had been Jack's goal all along. After all, he didn't know Jack, who might be the kind of cop who assumed every working stiff could use a little extra folding money.

Maggie knew better. Jack had many faults—to put it gently—but avarice was not one of them.

"No one is taking a cut. As I said, this will be inventoried and you'll get a receipt. If it cannot be established that these are criminal proceeds, it will be returned to you. If they are criminal proceeds but the original owners cannot be located, part or all of it may be returned to you. I truly cannot say. That depends on what else we discover in this investigation and what the state attorney wants to charge you with, and whether you cooperate."

She looked up, seeing the glint of a life raft bobbing atop a crashing wave. "Cooperate?"

"You're a businesswoman," he said. "Maybe we can make a deal. You're on the inside of a large criminal enterprise. Maybe, *if* you help us take them down, *if* we don't find proof that you had a much bigger role in that enterprise than you are letting on—"

"I didn't."

"*If* they did not keep records of who was defrauded and how much of that money went to you—"

She snorted.

"Yeah, I can't see why they'd helpfully maintain all the evidence that we could use to hang them, either. So *if* no victims can be identified, *then* there's a chance that some or all of this money could be returned to you."

"Seriously?" She didn't sound convinced. It didn't sound very likely to Maggie, either.

He said, "If we can't prove that the money is stolen, we have to return it to you. But, full disclosure, our goal will be to prove where the money came from."

"Not much incentive for me, then, is there?"

"That's up to you," he said, his tone brisk, matter-of-fact. "Here's the situation: I'm walking out that door with your almost-a-million dollars. You can run, or you can come with me and try to work out a deal with the state attorney. I have no idea if a deal will be doable. I have no idea whether you will or will not eventually be arrested and serve time in jail. I make no guarantees. I hope I have made that sufficiently clear."

"Crystal," the girl snapped.

But she didn't run.

Maggie had been packing the money back into the oversized backpack. Shanaya Thomas watched every movement, her gaze following the tidy stacks of bills as one by one they disappeared inside the black canvas. Maggie could only guess at the mental calculations she must be making. Take the loss and move on? She was young and healthy and most importantly, not in jail. But she had also spent a long time accumulating this cash. Plus Jack now had all her alternate identities, leaving her no funds to buy a new one. She would truly have to start from a zero sum. A year or three formed only a blink on the timeline at her age, but it probably didn't feel that way. It probably felt like it had taken forever to accumulate that fortune—and she might never see another.

Shanaya Thomas said, "Okay."

Chapter 30

"Let me get this straight," Patty Wildwind said to Jack. "We have a murdered detective and you want to do an undercover sting op to catch a phone scam ring?"

"Yes."

She looked tired, Maggie thought, and not remotely triumphant, not the way she should look with a cop-killer in custody and tied up with a bow for the prosecution. Not at all. Neither did Riley, who stood next to her in the hallway outside the homicide unit.

Then Maggie thought, I probably don't look so daisy-fresh myself—not much sleep the past couple nights, haven't eaten since breakfast, black powder on my nose . . .

Riley said, "Crazy as it sounds, the phone scam girl's boyfriend died from exactly the same kind of wound as Rick and Jennifer Toner. There's got to be a connection, though I'll be damned if I know what it is."

Jack said, "And you have a suspect in custody for Gardiner."

Patty flicked him a glance that said he wasn't fooling her.

No one standing on that worn linoleum thought Marlon Toner had killed his sister and Rick, but not one of them wanted to say so, either. "A suspect who's a long way from convicted."

Riley said, "He won't admit it, but also won't give an alibi for Friday. He can't stop crying about his sister but won't give up his drug connection, Castleman. Won't tell us where his office is, when he last saw him, whether the guy knew Jennifer existed. Marlon's all pathetically devastated until we start asking about the good doc. Then he gets this cagey look in his eyes and shuts the hell up."

"Addict," Patty added, as if that explained everything. And it did. Marlon Toner felt an overwhelming body blow at the death of his sister, but he needed his pills—now, he would tell himself, more than ever.

"So what are you going to do with him?" Jack asked.

"Let him stew for a while, hope his public defender can talk some sense into him," Patty said.

Riley held up a plastic bag labeled INMATE PROPERTY. "We have his most current prescription from good old Dr. Castleman right here. He's already burned through half of the bottle."

Jack glanced at the other items in the bag, besides the orange pill bottle. "What's that?"

Riley said, "That is the stub for a reimbursement check that our Marlon cashed this morning, to the tune of thirty-five thousand dollars."

Maggie said, "Sheesh, what'd he supposed to have had done? A heart replacement?"

"Doesn't say. Even more interesting is what's behind the stub—three receipts for money orders, sent out for deposit in the amount of nine thousand dollars each."

"Staying under the federal reporting rules," Maggie noted.

"Care to guess where he purchased these orders?"

"A to Z Check Cashing?"

"*Bing*! The lady wins a prize."

Jack said, "Time to have another chat with Ralph. You should come," he added to Maggie. "He likes you."

"Oh hell," she said.

Monday, 4:47 p.m.

And Ralph was, indeed, happy to see her. The two cops, not so much. After presenting themselves inside the front lobby and then walking around to the entry door on the other street, he made them wait on his step until Maggie's teeth threatened to chatter.

When he finally opened the door he greeted them with: "What you want? I already told you, I don't know who killed Evan. It's worst for me, I am making myself sick here trying to fill in for missing employee myself. I keep interviewing, no one seems right. Everyone who comes is either stupid or shifty. I can't let anyone shifty in here, no matter how much I watch them." He threw a dark look at the opening to the counter area, where a boy with shaggy blond hair had draped his entire upper torso along its surface while he texted.

"Tell us about this," Riley said, holding up the money order receipt.

Ralph recoiled as if Riley had swung a mace, but then recovered. He spared one quick glance for the slip of paper in its clear folder. "It's a receipt. So what?"

"From this morning."

Ralph leaned in, peered more sharply. "Yes. So what?"

Riley ticked off his points with erect fingers. "One, we'd like to have Maggie here download the video from this exchange. Two, we'd like to know where this money went. Three, we'd like to see the check he cashed to get it."

Ralph blinked, and began to shake his head *no.*

"Let's start with the video," Riley said, his tone kindly. "That will help jog your memory about this interaction."

"Not me. Let me see the time—eight-thirty, no, you need to talk to Curtis—"

"No, man." The kid, obviously sharper than he appeared, spoke without even turning to look at them. "I clocked in at nine. I always clock in at nine."

Three sets of eyes swiveled back to Ralph. "Uh, yes . . . okay. Our video system . . ." His voice trailed off as he wandered toward his desk, no doubt remembering that they were already familiar with his video system. Once again he ushered Maggie into his chair and hovered while she searched the stored video to locate Marlon Toner entering the A to Z Check Cashing store. No one else had been in the lobby. They watched Ralph take a check that Toner slid under the plexiglass barrier. The two men clearly spoke, but the conversation appeared desultory to Maggie. Neither man seemed agitated or conflicted. Marlon Toner waited patiently, signed the papers Ralph handed him, and left as soon as he had secured his thirty-five hundred dollars. Maggie guessed he had done that before, more than once, and had no more questions about the process.

"Okay," Riley concluded as Maggie saved the video to her USB drive. "So he cashed a check."

"That's what we do here." Ralph couldn't keep the sarcasm out of his voice.

"He's a regular customer of yours?"

Ralph shrugged. "Probably. I have a lot of repeat customers."

"Looked like he knew exactly what to do."

Ralph didn't bother to respond.

"Let's see the check he cashed."

Real worry sprang into the older man's face. "Why? No. I don't think I can show you that. It's confidential financial information." Whenever agitated, his slight accent grew stronger, which Jack had never been able to place. Middle

Eastern? South American? Atlantic Islands? Who knew, and right now Jack certainly didn't care.

"We already have the stub. We want to see its other half."

That argument made no sense at all, but Ralph began to sway. Maggie figured he had to be weighing how much of a fuss he should make. The cops *should* have a warrant, right? Wouldn't a cashed check be the same as someone's bank account or medical file?

"My clients expect security here—"

"And money orders are capped at one thousand dollars."

"It's not a money order. It's a wire transfer. Not capped."

"True. But if it's over ten thousand, you have to fill out a currency transaction report. Breaking them into nine thousand apiece doesn't change that. So why are you bending the rules for a homeless addict?"

This argument had more validity. Check cashing places were meant to provide convenient services to people looking to cash their paychecks or send money back to friends or families, amounts usually written with three digits, sometimes four. But in unscrupulous hands the stores could be easily converted to money laundries, and across the country arrests had been made. Obviously that was what went on here, though even Ralph didn't know from whom and to whom the money got laundered.

Sweat pricked out of the pores covering the man's nose, and Curtis peeked at them from the front desk, finally finding the cops' visit more interesting than his apps.

Ralph said, "The funds came from a government check, so, secured. It's not my business who gave who what money. You can't just look at my books—"

"You're right. We'll need a warrant."

A silence fell, during which Maggie watched Ralph weigh his options. He could capitulate and risk the ire of clients who cashed five-figure checks. He could demand a warrant, but that might easily wind up exposing other frequent customers. He could demand a warrant and then torch any documents necessary before they returned with it, but would almost certainly land him in front of a jury, charged with obstruction and money laundering.

"You need to see his check?" Ralph reiterated.

"Sure," Riley said, ignoring his earlier inquiry about the wire transfer deposits. One step at a time.

"What has all this got to do with Evan getting killed?" Ralph demanded.

"We're hoping this information will help us with that."

"It won't."

"Really? How do you know?" Riley asked, and a guilty look crossed the man's face.

Then Ralph noticed Maggie watching from the desk, straightened, and said: "Well, if it will help you catch who killed that poor boy, then okay." He even put his hand over his heart, and seemed a little disappointed when the two detectives didn't respond with murmurs of great empathy and human feeling. They only waited.

He went over to an unlabeled cardboard box, fished around, pulled out a simple blue-colored check and handed it to Riley, who asked if the cardboard box represented the extent of Ralph's filing system.

"Checks gotta be sent back to the issuing institution. I let them pile up and then take care of that at the end of the day. There may be more than one going to the same place."

Maggie got up and joined their huddle. Indeed, a simple check, issued by the United States Social Security department of Medicare, made out to Marlon Toner in the amount of thirty-five thousand and some odd dollars, dated the previous week. About the only interesting item on the piece of paper was a long number written on the memo line.

"See?" Ralph said, his tone a bit petulant. "I told you. A

check. Perfectly good. Why would I cash bad checks? I'd be the one who loses."

"I never said it was bad," Riley said. "Do you know what this reimbursement was for?"

"No! Of course not."

Jack thought aloud, "Toner's only about thirty-five. How is he getting Medicare?"

Maggie said, "He could be on disability."

Riley said, "Nah. Unless he was diabetic, he'd have to be on disability for two years before being eligible for Medicare, and his sister said his plunge down the rabbit hole only began four months ago or so. What? So I look ahead . . . I'm not going to be a bug on the windshield of my future."

"Quite admirable," Jack said. "Did he mention diabetes during his interview?"

"Not a word. I think we have to assume these hefty checks are all a scheme cooked up between him and Dr. Castleman."

Maggie heard a tiny but sharp intake of breath, and Ralph's fingers tapped a staccato beat on one meaty thigh. "You know Dr. Castleman?" she demanded.

"What? No. Uh-uh." His face had smoothed. Sweat glistened over his upper lip and nose, but then he did keep the office heated to near-saunalike temps.

Riley had Maggie take a picture of the check and then handed it back to Ralph with sweet thank-yous before he moved on. "Now, the transfers Mr. Toner sent—"

"You can't get it back. That money's gone."

"We don't want it back. We want to know where it went."

"I can't tell you that. It's a security thing," Ralph added, as unconvincing as a toddler found in possession of his sister's toy.

"Yeah, that doesn't make any sense," Riley said. "But that's okay, we don't need you to tell us, because we've got these." He pulled out the receipts for the money orders. "Toner came in here with thirty-five thousand dollars and left with thirty-five hundred. Mr. Bank Deposit got twenty-seven thousand. Forty-five hundred never left this place—I'm guessing that was your cut."

Jack said, "You know what that's called? That's called money laundering."

"No," Ralph said firmly. "That's transaction fee. Is standard."

Riley went on as if he hadn't spoken. "No, we don't need access to Mr. Bank Deposit's account or account numbers or anything. We only need to know his name."

"You sent this money order."

"Is not money order!" Ralph exploded, exasperated with this inaccuracy. "It's a wire transfer. It's different."

"Right, no pesky cap. So where did this transfer go?"

"I don't know."

"Let's start with something easier, then. Where is this bank? Is it local? If it is, we can go bother them."

"I don't know—there's only the account—"

"Panama," Maggie said.

All three men stared at her.

"The bank's in Panama. See?" She pointed to the eight characters written on the line next to the words *Swift Code.* "The first four letters are the bank, the second two are the country. 'PA.' Remember, that's where our mortgage broker hid all her money a few months ago."

"No," Riley said, "but I'll take your word for it. So, not local. Then let's at least have the name. It will be in the record of your transaction."

"I don't think I—"

"We've got a murdered cop in this city," Riley pointed out, leaning harder than Maggie had ever seen him lean, and without even raising his voice. "I think you can."

"Cop? What cop? Evan no cop." Panic suffused his face. "Was he?"

"Account name."

Ralph twisted his lips, darted his gaze around the shop in a futile search for rescue, and sweated. Finally he said, "Let me check."

"Great idea!"

Riley's bonhomie seemed to frighten the shop owner more than Jack's glowering bulk. For the rest of the visit he ignored Jack, but kept Riley in sight as if he were an unexploded bomb. Ralph returned to his desk, took the laptop from its surface, placed it on his lap, and pointedly pivoted so that they could not see the screen. He tapped keys. He tapped more keys.

"Not that it will matter much," Jack muttered to Riley. "It will be some shell company that one guy traveled to Panama to create with invented names and structure. As soon as the cash transfers to it, it will be shifted right out again to other shell companies with other invented names and no one in Panama or Cyprus or Lichtenstein or wherever will 'violate client confidentiality' to tell us who's behind it."

"The banks won't even know themselves," Riley agreed.

Maggie shifted her weight on tired feet, torn between anticipation that this money trail might finally unlock this inexplicable group of deaths, and doubt that some international kingpin's laundered money would have anything to do with Rick's murder. She itched to get back to the lab and identify those animal hairs. She was sure she'd seen the distinctive roots before, in one of her texts. . . .

Ralph's shoulders loosened, and some of the wrinkles flattened out. Before he even opened his mouth, she predicted that he honestly couldn't find what they needed, or he could and for some reason didn't mind telling them.

"Wayne Hawk Therapeutics."

Apparently, the latter.

Jack and Riley both stirred at this. They turned to each other and then back to the little man in the desk chair.

"Hawk?" Riley said.

"Wayne?" Jack said.

Ralph appeared considerably less happy at having told them something actually useful, and Maggie felt a quick thrill. This meant something.

"There's the connection," Riley muttered.

"We need to revisit that office."

"Both of them. You think it's—"

"Possibly any one of them. Maggie," Jack said suddenly. "Those animal hairs. On Rick's coat?"

"Um . . . yeah?"

"Could they be from a sugar glider?"

She turned to Ralph but he couldn't help, as confused by this change in topics as she. "What the hell is a sugar glider?"

"I think it's a kind of flying squirrel."

"Squirrel . . . oh yes, that could . . . the scale pattern . . . I'll need to find the reference sample in my cabinet. . . ."

"Let's go," Jack said to Riley.

Chapter 31

Her cop babysitter had fitted Shanaya with a wire—as in, an actual *wire* that ran from a two-inch square digital recorder and battery clipped to her underwear up to a fake gold pin that looked like a sunflower weighing down the edge of her collar. The stupid thing only recorded, didn't transmit, so no one at the police department would be listening in real time. They didn't have the manpower for that, thanks a lot. They gave her a phone to use for emergencies, while the recording would be made for future prosecutions. No one was supposed to notice that the patterned center of the sunflower was actually the sieve covering a microphone. Or that a woman her age, with her style, would ever wear anything as old-lady as a tacky pin.

Not to mention if the pit boss felt her up again, something he'd been doing with increasing regularity, he'd rub on that wire and she'd be dead before she ever got the chance to call her cop babysitter. No matter where he stationed himself along East Ninth Street, she would be inside a locked building with one exit, surrounded by men ruthless enough to steal little old grannies' life savings. They wouldn't hesitate

to choke the life out of one girl with a headset and dump her
body in the same alley where Eric Hayes had attacked her.
And since that idiot had been released on his own recog-
nizance, he would make the perfect fall guy.   .
She stepped into the foyer and rang the buzzer.
But if the pit bull kept his hands to himself, she could still
pull this out. She'd let the wire record what it could. She
would write down every coworker's name and their position
in the hierarchy, as best she could. She'd keep a record of
names, credit card numbers, phone numbers, how much
money each lost. And she'd try to snap as many pictures
with the new phone they'd given her—yeah, like *that*
wouldn't attract attention, and they hadn't even given her a
decent phone to do it with. But she'd do it.
Then, she might, just might, get to keep some or all the
money she and Evani had worked so hard to accumulate if
she made the cops too grateful to ask where it came from.
For that, she'd walk into the mouth of hell itself. The door
lock buzzed and she pulled it open.
And this place was pretty close.

Monday, 5:15 p.m.

"Wayne Hawk," Riley mused as he drove, dodging another
car, all four tires sliding on the slush-covered pavement.
"Wayne, our little receptionist, or Hawk as in Hawking Industries and Mark Hawking?"
Maggie tensed as they approached a red light. The vehicle
slid to a stop by some margin not visible from the back seat.
"Good question," Jack said. "We could have walked there
faster than this."
Indeed, the distance from A to Z to Dr. Sidney Jeffers's office building might have been one and a half city blocks,
tops. But—"You want to walk in this? Your shoes would be
soaked through before they tapped 14th."

"I guess not."

"What makes you so sure this doctor's office has something to do with it?" Maggie asked. They hadn't wanted to take the time to drop her back at the station, and she sure as hell wasn't going to hang out with Ralph until someone could send a ride.

"I don't even have a guess," Jack said. "Somehow they've got to be part of the same concern. We have the same killer in all three cases, but no connection between Evan Harding and Jennifer Toner except for Marlon. Castleman is providing Marlon with pills, maybe through Jeffers, or Wayne, because Wayne's pet's fur winds up on Rick."

"Maybe," Maggie corrected, ever the scientist. She hadn't even seen Jeffers's office pet yet, much less examined its fur.

"Marlon is laundering money in exchange for the pills, through Ralph. Ralph nearly has a heart attack when he hears us discussing Castleman."

Riley said, "Yet he gives up 'Wayne Hawk' without hesitation . . . or without *much* hesitation. Because he didn't recognize the name? Assumed it was fake and couldn't be traced back to anyone?"

"Or because he's willing to sacrifice them?"

Maggie said, "And this Dr. Castleman is in hiding?"

"Apparently," Jack said. "Because he's sure impossible to find."

"But he's a legitimate doctor?"

"Sure. But in the pill mill craze most pushers were actual doctors, too, though not always in the specialties they were supposed to be."

"So why is Castleman in hiding?"

"Because he's a pill pusher," Jack said. "Why are you turning?"

Riley said, "You can't get there from here. Not with that weird fork at 18th."

"But a legitimate one," Maggie persisted. She knew something about the pill mills that had swept the country only a few short years before. One of the most frustrating things about them proved to be their brazen operations, with billboards and large parking lots, lobbies that didn't try to hide the quick in-and-out of patient visits where physical exams were reduced to a few questions on a form. Granted, new laws had been put in place specifically to combat such mills, so perhaps that had forced such doctors underground. "If you can't find him, how do his patients?"

"Same way they find the drug dealers, I guess. Word of mouth."

Maggie said, "Maybe Castleman started taking his own product and lost his license. Fell on hard times, started selling pills. I can't see any other reason for him to stay out of sight if he's legit. Do you know if his license is still in good standing?"

Jack said he had no idea. Riley didn't answer, waiting for a break in the next lane. A large pile of snow outside a parking lot had collapsed into the street and then frozen again, hard as a glacier. It blocked the far right lane.

"Did you call the A.M.A.?"

Silence. Which meant they had not, and neither of them wanted to admit it.

"I have a friend who's the national secretary. I could—"

Yes, the detectives said in unison. Call her.

While Riley negotiated their way through three lanes of traffic where snow obscured the lines on the asphalt, Maggie Googled the number for the A.M.A. She listened through two sets of phone menu instructions, then connected with the main office and asked for Tanya Schroeder. They had met at college, played in the band together, and still exchanged birthday cards.

"Tanya! I got your Christmas card. First one of the season, as always."

"Gotta send 'em out the day after Thanksgiving. My mom's training."

"Isn't that kind of cheating? You should at least have to wait until December."

"It is not," Tanya assured her firmly. "Check Emily Post."

Maggie explained why she called, that they needed to ask the mysterious Dr. Phillip Castleman some questions regarding a murder. Actually, several murders.

Mentioning murder did not open any floodgates when it came to Tanya Schroeder. Any woman who would not violate Emily Post would also not violate even an unimportant regulation of the American Medical Association. "I can't tell you anything about his record, or any personal information—"

"No, no. All I want is the most impersonal information possible. His office address. That's it."

"That's all you want?"

"Yep."

A pause. "Have you tried the phone book? Or, today's version of the phone book, Google?"

"Yep."

Another pause. "Okay, let me see what we've got. Hey, how's your brother doing?"

In their dorm days Tanya had invariably shown up to "help" Maggie move in or out when Alex was there as well. "Today? Playing a gig in Hilton Head, the lucky stiff, then they're off to a ski resort. And yes," Maggie told Tanya before she could ask, because she always asked, "he's still married."

"Damn."

"Tanya, so are you."

"Don't bother me with trifles." Keys clacked in the background.

"Would a woman who sends out her Christmas cards on a

strict schedule really be happy living and raising kids in constant motion from town to town, gig to gig?"

"Maybe I yearn to leave schedules behind."

Maggie doubted it but didn't argue.

"Okay. Dr. Phillip Castleman, licensed in Ohio. What a
name. Sounds like something out of a romance novel."

"It does."

"His license is in good standing."

Maybe not for much longer, Maggie thought.

"But currently on hold for renewal."

"What does that mean?"

"There's a number of reasons . . . I probably can't tell you,
you know, but . . . it's not . . . oh. That's cool."

"Cool? What's cool?"

Riley had maneuvered the car into the lot and plunged
into a spot at the edge. If there were any lines to indicate
separate parking spaces, they had been lost under six inches
of snow, but that hardly mattered since only a few vehicles
dotted the lot. He and Jack made no move to get out, waiting
for her to finish her call but, mercifully, left the engine running along with what heating element it had.

"I see why you're having trouble finding the dashing
Dr. Phillip Castleman. In light of this info, I might throw
Alex over for him on the spot."

"Tanya—"

"He's in North Kivu."

Maggie waited.

"In the DRC. Democratic Republic of Congo."

"Congo?" Jack and Riley had both turned in the front
seat, watching her with a uniform, unsettling intensity. "As
in African Congo?"

"You know another? Your very good doctor is currently
attached to Doctors Without Borders, working in a war
zone with the worst Ebola outbreak—Ebola. I may still

throw Alex over for him but not until Phillip is out of quarantine. That stuff is nasty."

"How long has he been there?"

"Aboouuuttt . . . a year and a half."

"Huh. Could someone be here still prescribing meds under his license number?"

"They *shouldn't* be."

"Yes, I assume that. But if they were—"

"They'd probably get away with it for a while." Tanya sounded as if she were musing this over. "Nobody's going to check the license number every week, and even if they did, it's still good. Until the handsome Dr. Castleman returns from serving as the salvation of millions."

"How do you know he's handsome?"

"Did you miss the part about him taking care of Ebola patients in the Congo? How much more beautiful can a soul get? Besides," she added before ringing off, "he has a cool name."

Maggie put her phone away. "Get this."

From their expressions, the two detectives were more than ready to get it.

"So Dr. Castleman's identity was stolen," Riley said, when she had finished.

"More like borrowed. And who better to borrow it than ex-partner Sidney?" Jack said. "He turns addicts into high-cost patients with fictitious diabetes or whatever. They deposit the government funds into his account and he pays them with pills and a little cash. If anyone comes around asking questions, he shifts the blame to the ghostly Dr. Castleman."

"But whose account is it? Jeffers? Nurse Wayne? Or Mark Hawking of our illegal call center?"

"Which we just sent Shanaya Thomas back to."

Riley said, "I wouldn't worry about her. That girl can take care of herself."

Chapter 32

That girl, at the moment, would have agreed, since she had already withstood a solid ten minutes of the pit boss ripping her a new one over the *entire day* lost to her tardiness, her lack of a work ethic, and overblown estimates of how much money she had forfeited by refusing to do the job she had so generously been granted, as well as his grave pity for any children she might bear in the future since they would not make it past their fifth birthday under the care of such a thoughtless and uncaring mother.

Nine hundred and sixty-five thousand dollars, she reminded herself. Nine hundred and—

He finally accepted that he would never wrench a properly remorseful apology from her and snapped, "Get to your phones."

She went to her desk and slid into her chair. The legs creaked and a piece of duct tape covering a tear in the seat padding tried to stick to her pants instead of the upholstery, but right then it felt as familiar as a mother's comforting arms.

With the pit bull's gaze burning a hole between her shoulder blades, she picked up the call as soon as her red button lit up and played the enthusiastic employee until he wandered away. Then her words became lackluster and she mumbled the script by rote, barely aware of what she said. She'd get that nine hundred thousand plus. She'd gather all the evidence they wanted, absorb all the names and faces and numbers, all those details she'd largely ignored, until now.

And the cops would get none of it until they coughed up her money. She'd hold the information hostage, keep those notes and the tiny recorder to herself and say, you want this juicy, high-profile conviction? Then we're going to make a deal. They couldn't arrest her—it wouldn't do their case much good to have a convict as their star witness. They'd have to deal.

But she hadn't gotten off to a stellar start. The guy on the phone had begun to squawk, saying he was an unemployed student and not required to file an income tax return at all, much less pay any tax, and then she felt a hand on her shoulder and the acrid aftershave. Her heart went into triple time. Could he feel the wire? No, it snaked around her waist, not near the shoulder—

The pit boss leaned down, and she waited for a combination come-on and threat, something along the lines of how she needed to show her gratitude to him for not firing her.

What he actually said was much, much worse.

"Mr. Hawking would like a word."

Monday, 5:25 p.m.

If the building had a cleaning staff, Maggie could see no sign of it, either in the hallway or inside the office of Dr. Sidney Jeffers. The nurse at the desk, "Wayne" according to his name tag, told them that they were about to close and the doctor had already left for the day. He had been doing a little cleaning himself, wiping the counter around what must be the sugar glider's cage with a wet-wipe and latex gloves. Then he noticed Maggie, his gaze traveling over her from curls to boots and back again, lingering as if she had appeared before him in a bikini instead of three layers of cold-weather clothing. He didn't even protest as they walked through the door he had propped open and into his workspace.

Jack said, "Actually we're here about your pet."

That got his attention off her, Maggie saw. A frown creased the guy's brow. "Rambo? What's the matter with him?"

"It's his fur."

"What about it? You allergic?"

"We need a sample of it."

Wayne, Maggie surmised, was no slouch. He knew right away there could be no explanation for this request that would not be disastrous. He made up his mind about that immediately. The decision regarding what to do about it took a bit longer, calculating the odds of two armed cops and an unknown woman against one guy on crutches. Cooperate until a better solution appeared. Stay calm and reasonable and innocent.

Calmly and reasonably, Wayne asked, "Why?"

"Exotic pet fur has turned up at a crime scene."

Calmly, reasonably: "So . . . you're inspecting every pet in the city?"

"No," Jack said. "There's also this."

He held up the deposit receipt, which looked quite official in the plastic folder sealed with red evidence tape.

"Are you Wayne King?" Riley asked.

"Uh, no. Hamilton, Wayne Hamilton. Why?"

"You're not associated with Hawking Enterprises?"

"No. I'm not."

Oh yes, he was. That could be seen in living Technicolor from the widening of the eyes, the way the foot—the injured foot—began to tap. But Maggie left him to the cops and crossed over to the pet cage. The cute bundle of black and gray and white, had curled into a ball in the shavings, its tiny sides rising and falling with each quick breath. Wayne demanded to know what she planned to do.

"Oh, I'm not going to hurt him. I'm only going to use a piece of tape to pick up his loose fur." She spoke as soothingly as if Wayne were the animal, but couldn't stop from asking if Rambo tended to bite.

Still frowning, Wayne said, "No, he's super easygoing. Spends most of the day riding around on my shoulders. The kids love him."

"Where's Dr. Jeffers?" Jack asked.

"Told you. He's already gone home."

"What about this guy?" Maggie glanced behind her. Jack held up a picture of Marlon Toner and asked, "He a patient of yours?"

Maggie considered her task. She planned to slap—gently—a piece of tape on the small creature and when she removed it or Rambo wriggled away, whichever happened more quickly, she would have a sample of his fur. She had also planned to collect some from the bottom of its cage or ideally a brush or some sort of grooming tool his owner might have, but doubted that had ever been thought necessary, as short as the fur seemed. Her main goal remained thus: Don't get bit. She suspected anything in the squirrel family would have sharp teeth and might not like waking up to a strange hand in its personal space.

"You know I can't tell you anything about our patients."

She pulled out her own leather gloves. They weren't terribly thick, but still better protection than latex. Then she borrowed a pair of examination gloves from a box on the counter, conveniently sized Large, and pulled them on over the leather. Aqua colored, they slid on easily. Next she ripped off a piece of clear fingerprint tape, heavier than household transparent tape, about two inches long.

"You don't have to tell us what's in his medical file. We know it's all fake, anyway. You do have to answer a direct, non-medical question—have you seen this man in this office?"

"No," Wayne said.

"Are you sure that's what you want to answer? Dr. Jeffers has been dealing pills out of this office, using his ex-partner's name. There's no way you could be his right-hand man here and not know that. So you can cooperate and make some points with the state's attorney, or you can go down with him."

Maggie angled her arm so that it could reach to the other end of the cage and still allow her some range of motion, moving slowly and quietly. Then she lay the tape, ever so lightly, across the animal's back and haunch.

Riley said, "Or maybe it was you. Who else would be able to find his ex-partner's medical license number and have access to the prescription pads? Who else but the admin assistant would know all the codes and forms needed to file fictitious claims for fictitious conditions?"

So far so good. Maggie laid her fingers on the small, warm body, petting but also making sure the tape made good contact and would pull away plenty of loose hairs when she removed it. It wouldn't hurt any more than brushing him would, but still she half expected it to wake, turn, and bite in a flash so rapid that she wouldn't have time to react, and then she'd have to explain to Denny how she not only bled all over the evidence but needed to file a worker's comp claim as well.

"It would be a lot easier for your customers to make contact with you. They could walk through that door, come up to the counter, exchange money, receipts, bottles, and no one would bat an eye."

Maggie needn't have worried. Rambo's eyes opened as she pulled the tape off, but remained unconcerned. He even gave a tiny yawn, exposing the razor teeth he hadn't, to her relief, used.

"I don't know what you're talking about. I'm a nurse. I prep the rooms and do the patient billing. That's it!"

"Fine, kid," Riley said. "Good luck with that defense."

She folded the tape back on itself and dropped it into an envelope. Then, staying at the unoccupied end of the cage, brushed aside the shavings and used a second piece of tape on the cage bottom. She hoped it would have more dander, both the distinct guard hairs to the fine, nearly invisible undercoat. These two samples should give her enough to compare to the fur she found on Rick's parka.

The animal rose and tottered over to the cage door, grasping it with tiny claws and peering out at the visitors. The door had been open when she arrived, so Maggie left it for Wayne to manage.

In the doorway, Jack stiffened. "Is there a rear entrance to these offices?"

Wayne said no.

Jack walked out of sight, and Maggie heard him open a door.

"Hey!" Wayne said. "You can't wander around in here."

Riley said, "We're just going to make sure we're alone, kid. Relax." And he followed his partner. Maggie heard another door open, elsewhere in the offices.

Abruptly eager to get out of there, Maggie packed her samples into her kit and turned around, peeling off the latex gloves. Wayne stood by the doorway, torn between wanting to stop Jack and Riley from looking around, and knowing he couldn't.

Maggie looked at her hands. The leather now appeared dusty and ancient, with white caked into the seams. She could see why the latex had slid so easily over the heavy gloves—Dr. Jeffers's office still used the type with a dusting of powder inside each glove. They slid onto hands every time, unlike the non-powder type that could stick and grab. But only in removal did one discover the disadvantage.

She remembered the thin slice of aqua rubber under Jennifer's credenza. And that spray of powder along her dead ex-husband's shoulder.

Suddenly, she stared at Wayne Hamilton.

"It's you. You killed him."

It made no sense—yet she knew, *knew* to her core, that it was true. And if she had any doubt, the look on the nurse's face erased them completely.

Wayne Hamilton recovered first.

He dropped his crutch and came at her, one hand upraised. "Just shut up until—"

She never discovered what he had intended to do once he got there—probably keep her from screaming until he could get to the outer door, perhaps use her as a hostage. But before he had a chance, she swung the sugar glider's cage at Wayne's head with every tendon in her upper body, spraying the small office with wood chips and food pellets. The lightweight item couldn't do much more than scratch him, but it broke up his stride and let her see what he had in his fingers.

Wayne hadn't dropped his crutch, he'd pulled it apart. He now grasped the bottom part of the tubular crutch, the round rubber foot on one end, and at the other, a long, pointed dagger. The crutch wasn't a crutch at all but a very large, and innocent-looking, sheath.

This weapon had killed Evan Harding, Jennifer Toner, and Rick.

All he had to do was bring it down, or thrust it up, getting behind the rib cage and directly into her heart. No ambulance would be able to arrive in time to save her; she'd be dying as she hit the ground.

Blood dripping from cuts on his cheek, hatred flaring from his gaze, his arm sliced downward through the air.

One relevant point regarding an ice pick-type weapon, Maggie thought: while the tip was sharp, the sides were not. And she was wearing leather gloves.

She grabbed the shaft, willing all the strength in her body to move to her fingers.

It didn't work. She felt the tip enter her flesh, piercing her skin and her muscle.

And there it stopped. Wayne's face flashed his fury and he said nothing, only intensified the force. She could feel the ice pick in her body as she tried to move down, back, away from the pain but she already arced over the counter's edge, which left her nowhere to go. She didn't speak, didn't shout. All her focus remained on that shiny metal pick.

The sugar glider, safe on the counter, protested the theft of its cage with a raspy trill, like a cross between a cicada and a parrot. Wayne's gaze flickered to his pet, and that was all she needed.

She pulled up one thigh and slammed the sole of her right foot into Wayne's right knee.

He screamed.

Maggie took a step forward but didn't let go of the crutch-dagger.

Then Jack was there and leapt on the younger man, punched him hard so that his head rebounded against the linoleum twice and Maggie heard the crack of bone. Jack drew back his fist to hit him again but Maggie grabbed his arm, feeling the muscles quiver like molten steel under his skin.

"Jack," she said, "we need him alive."

Chapter 33

Monday, 5:35 p.m.

Shanaya kept her hands plunged into her hoodie pockets, not feigning the chill she felt. The temperature on the floor stayed only warm enough to keep the workers from wanting to leave. With her thumb she flipped open the phone they had given her. She'd originally greeted the phone with derision, a cheap thing with ancient technology, actual buttons instead of a flat screen, but now she saw the benefit of something that could be dialed by touch alone.

But did she want to? Pull the plug before she'd gathered enough information to ransom her money back from the cops?

The pit boss led the way up the stairs; some other goon, a guy she'd never seen before, walked behind her.

She and her escorts made an ominous little parade and some of her coworkers noticed, watching them go with worried expressions. Not concern for her—they were too busy wondering what had happened and how they could avoid it to spare a thought for the condemned. But she understood. They were afraid, walking a tightrope between the threats outside the building and the ones inside. Even the pit boss seemed afraid, his shoulders twitching, and as they approached the office door, he waved her on ahead, trying for a stern look but unable to hide his bafflement. He did not know what was going on and was just smart enough to not want to.

As she passed the second-floor cubicles, the noise level changed in her wake. The normal constant, deafening buzz turned to an agitated rolling murmur of voices raised in question, arguing, then muffled sounds of chairs rolling back and groaning under various weights. Her heart leapt in a brief instant of hope—maybe it wasn't only her, maybe a bunch of people were being called in for some sort of shakeup or housecleaning or—award for high productivity? Maybe she had misread the whole situation—

No. From the perplexed, annoyed, slightly stunned expressions of her coworkers, the truth would not be so benign. Call-takers were rising, getting their coats and purses, hissing quick questions at the man making the rounds to inform them and not liking the answers or lack of same. Most appeared irritated, some curious, some simply relieved to have an excuse to end the day early.

They were leaving.

She passed the day care center, where the harried teacher seemed to be passing out coats to several toddlers. The kids cooperated for a change, jumping at this chance to go home early.

The big boss had decided to clear the entire building. He meant to forgo any income the rest of the evening would have brought in—it was still light out on the West Coast. This had never happened before.

He didn't want any witnesses to Shanaya's fate.

Run. *Run*. Turn and run right now, squeeze between the exiting workers and don't stop—

Without conscious thought her body had slowed, pivoted . . . and the goon behind her grabbed her elbow with enough force to stop the blood flow to her fingers.

The running option had expired. In the last few steps before the office, she fought to still her mind and proceed carefully. Phone numbers would be set in the standard grid, three across, four down. Nine would be three across, three down. One, easy, upper left. Press, press, press. Do nothing. If the 911 operator answered and asked after her emergency, the voice would be lost in the cacophony of the call room. The goon and the pit boss would never hear it, muffled in the depths of her pocket. She strolled as slowly as she could, planning to flip the thing shut again before entering the boss's presumably quieter inner space. The cops would have to figure it out. Supposedly the phone only dialed one number, that of the detectives who assigned her this little task, but surely it would call the main emergency line, too. Right?

And flipping it shut would end the call. It wouldn't keep yakking while she marched up to Mr. Hawking, would it?

Either way, nothing she could do about it now. Brazen it out. She'd done it before.

They reached the boss's door.

Shanaya had not been inside the inner office since the day she'd been hired. It had not changed since—three cluttered shelves on the wall, forcing anyone who walked around that side of the desk to lean away from them; the other side of the desk against the wall, bisecting the room. It stank of cigarettes, though none burned in the ashtray.

She did not know the man seated behind the desk, though she had seen him there on occasion. Mark Hawking stood beside him, wedged into a corner between the desk and the shelves, looking uncomfortable from either the position or the prospect of what they might be about to do to her.

She willed her face to stay calm, and stepped up to the

desk. The goon stayed at her right shoulder. She could feel his body heat even through her hoodie.

The man behind the desk took her in. She ignored him, couldn't find the man behind the desk remotely as terrifying as the object placed on the desk, resting in the exact center of the calendar blotter.

A cell phone.

Evani's cell phone. A silver-colored model that he'd taken a red Sharpie to during one particularly boring shift.

They had Evani's phone. Someone in that office had killed Evani.

But that wasn't what worried her.

"Clever," the man behind the desk said. "You two were clever. Any cash business is prone to skimming—numbers, prostitution, drugs—because the guy at the top, like me, can never be sure how much comes in at the entry points, or persons like you."

She could barely hear him over the blood pounding in her ears, but she tried. There had to be an opening. There had to be a crack she could use—

"This is a cash business without the cash. Data entered on a screen. All digital, ones and zeros and routed to a central server. One person couldn't do it. But two, working together—"

She gripped the back of the chair in front of her. "Mr.—"

He didn't supply his name. "You'd get the mark's card number, security code, type it into your screen exactly as we instructed you. The good little employee, except before you'd hit *enter*, you'd—well, I bet you'd look around to make sure that idiot out there wasn't paying attention, then pop out your phone, take a picture of the screen, and text it to your little friend Evan."

She hadn't thought she could feel worse, but now . . . that near-million was gone. If the cops didn't take it all, these guys would. They had figured it out. She thought she might be sick, and felt almost glad of it. Puke all over Mr. Hawking's desk. At least leave them a bad smell to remember her by.

"He'd buy money orders on the cards. Charge as much as he could. You'd send the card information on to the central unit, but by that time there would be a lot less available credit. We didn't know, how could we? So the cardholder had a high balance, so what? Everybody abuses their credit, that's why there's a debt crisis in this country. Meanwhile your little friend cashes out the money order he bought— easy enough, he's sitting inside a place that does exactly that. And you pick up another phone call. Never leave your desk, never shove anything into your pocket, never open an account. No trace. I never would have been the wiser."

Admit nothing, she told herself.

"But then your little friend got greedy. Decided to skim off a few other concerns as well. Problem is, that concern also belonged to me."

The checks, Shanaya knew instantly. Those huge medical reimbursement checks. A percent to the runner who brought it in, the rest deposited in some offshore account. Evani took out more than was requested, gave a fake receipt to the runner for the right cut, kept the difference, and deposited the bulk. It was *so much money*, these huge amounts coming in every day. Surely whoever owned those offshore funds couldn't be checking each and every deposit, right?

It wasn't fair. That two businesses would launder funds through the same money store did not surprise her. That they were both owned by the same man was karma, biting her in the ass.

Damn Evani. The one time he broke from his cautious, paranoid, too-careful persona, and it had exactly the result he had feared. She'd told him not to do it . . . but yes, not too strenuously. The faster they built up their own account the faster they could blow town. Then it wouldn't matter who noticed what.

The classic embezzler's downfall. They'd waited too long to get out.

The man said, "I knew it wasn't Ralph, since he's the one who alerted me to his own cashier consistently cashing money orders. Took him a damn long time since it didn't leave *him* out any money. When he finally got curious, thought the kid was pickpocketing, stealing card numbers. Ralph wanted to be cut in, that's all. Only your bad luck that he mentioned it to me before he talked to Evan. Once we looked at the card numbers we knew where they came from. Wayne figured your system out almost instantly. Wayne's a millennial, like you. I guess you brats think alike."

She didn't know what to say to that, had no idea who Wayne might be.

"So I sent him out to take care of Evan, but even with a spike halfway to his heart, he didn't give you up. That probably makes you feel good."

Not especially, she thought. Poor Evani.

"We didn't find the money, didn't find an ID, home address, nothing. We found this"—he held up the phone again—"and I checked texts, voice mails, call history, got us nowhere. You had the sense not to answer, I'll give you that."

He waited for her response, but only the span of a breath. It didn't really matter what she said now.

"I checked the photos. Well, singular: photo. But I'm old. Without my reading glasses it looked like a blank page, a picture of the floor or ceiling. I do that all the time. My toddlers can use my phone better than I can. Plus I've been distracted with other things this week. But when I looked again—" He thumbed to the image, turned the phone around so she could see the screen. She didn't want to look, knowing what she'd see. A photo of the monitor at her work station. Evani had always been careful to delete each one once he'd gotten the numbers, and she would delete them from her own phone on every trip to the ladies' room. Apparently he'd gotten careless or distracted with this last one. She couldn't read the details on the tiny screen, the name or the numbers, but she could pick out what had betrayed her: the sticker with the cherries on the lower right-hand corner of the monitor frame.

All he'd had to do was walk through the cubicles until they found the right monitor.

"I don't know what you're talking about," she said instantly, surprised at how strong her voice sounded. "That's the computer at my workstation, but I'm not the only one who uses it. There's the other shift. And the pit bull—boss, he sits down at it sometimes when I'm on break." She couldn't stand the guy anyway. If she needed to sacrifice a goat in her place, it might as well be a nasty, horny one.

"We've already eliminated them," Mr. Hawking said, garnering a quick glare from the man behind the desk. In front of that man, she realized, Hawking became another flunky, no better than her.

"I want the money back," said the man behind the desk. "Now."

"I don't have any money. I've been working so hard here trying to—"

"I want every penny you and Evan stole from me. Hand it over and I might let you live." He held up his hands in a show of expansiveness. "A simple trade."

"I don't have it." This was, of course, the truth. It rang out into the room with the peal of a silver bell and convinced the man. She could see it. He didn't want to, but he believed her.

Which in no way meant he would give up. "I've already killed—well, had Wayne kill for me—three people in the past week. Making it four would take no skin off anybody's nose, except for, well, *yours*. So you'd better have something more to say than that."

A silence ensued while she contemplated her next move. Despite the frantic pounding of blood in her ears, the sweat pricking out of every pore, she thought she saw a glimmer of light in the black hole of her future.

She said: "The cops have it. And I'm the only one who can get it back for you."

No reaction at first. But then the boss pinched the bridge of his nose, rubbed the deep vertical line between his eyebrows. The other two men in the room did not move, did not seem to breathe. Neither did Shanaya.

"Okay," he said at last. "I'm listening."

Chapter 34

If Wayne had been faking his knee injury in order to keep his crutch-weapon close to him, he no longer needed to. He clutched his knee and groaned about the now-torn ligament, the lumps on his head, and the cuts on his checks and mouth. He sat on the floor of the reception desk area, its harsh fluorescent lights illuminating every grimace—not that the others spared any sympathy. Riley had called for an ambulance, but no one told Wayne that.

Maggie, meanwhile, helped herself to medical supplies from one of the exam rooms and taped a large gauze pad to the small wound next to her breastbone. It hurt, but when she steeled herself to look at it, she could see how shallow the track went. "Just a flesh wound," she told her reflection in the mirror over the exam room sink, then repeated it more forcefully when she saw a sneaky tear well up in each eye. Death had been, quite literally, only an inch away. She pulled her stained shirt back down and opened the door, not about to give herself time to think how an adhesive bandage couldn't fix all that had gone wrong. If she did, she would be there all night.

Jack had cleared all the rooms of the office and lights blazed from each. She passed a door, saw movement, and found Jack combing the good doctor's office, a tiny space with framed diplomas and swag from pharmaceutical companies and not much else. Jack rummaged through the drawers of an old metal desk but stopped when she appeared. "You okay?"

She drew a shaky breath, feeling the tiny ache where the wound gaped. "Yeah."

As if she had said *no* he crossed the room in two steps and grasped her shoulders. "Is it still bleeding? Do you need stitches? Can you breathe okay?"

He started to pull her shirt up and she slapped his hand, so hard and so instinctively that it gave her the giggles. The idea of maintaining her modesty under these circumstances suddenly seemed friggin' hysterical, and she clapped one hand over her mouth to stifle it. He dropped his arm and stood back, awkwardly hovering.

She insisted through a giggle, "I'm fine. It's nothing. Did you find anything?"

"These." He waved his hand at the desk, where four prescription pads with *Phillip J. Castleman* preprinted at the top. "A fairly perfect setup. Should we come looking for Phillip J., he gives us the innocent routine—*ex-partner, don't know where he is, sorry.* If we thought about asking his customers to put a face to the name, none of them would want to give up their pill supply to help us out."

"What was he planning to do when the real Castleman comes back from the Congo?"

"He probably hoped he wouldn't. It's a dangerous place. Found this, too," he added, holding out a paper. It was a bill for rental of a business space, but not the space they stood in.

"What is it?"

"It's the link."

They burst back into the reception desk area, where Wayne sat and moaned and Riley searched drawers while pointing out how he, Wayne, had killed a cop so whether he, Riley, turned him over to an angry mob of homicide detectives or the state with its new and improved method of lethal injection, Wayne's future appeared less than rosy. If he cooperated now, he might spare himself a bit of mistreatment—as in, death—down the road.

Wayne wasn't buying it. Or he writhed with too much pain to buy it. Maggie had probably dislocated his knee, about which she felt not a twinge of guilt. She felt worse for the sugar glider. She straightened up his cage, refilled his food and water, and scooped him back inside.

Jack waved the invoice in the guy's face. "Who rents this place? You or Jeffers?"

Wayne glanced at the paper, puffed short breaths in and out, and said, "That's got nothing to do with me."

"Then what is it? Why is Jeffers renting it?"

"I just work here."

"You killed three people for this guy. And you can't tell us what's in this building?"

Wayne looked up at Jack with the ghost of his old insouciance. "I didn't kill nobody. And you can't prove I did."

Jack straightened. "Fine. We'll go there and see for ourselves, then."

"*No.*" The word seemed to burst from Wayne before he could stop it, and they watched his face as he tried to think of something clever. "I'll . . . I've got information. . . . I can tell you about the pills—"

"Wayne, Wayne, Wayne," Riley said, clucking regretfully. "Too little, too late, dude. Our next step is plain, and I'm kinda feeling like we don't need you anymore."

And on that note the backup officers and the paramedics arrived, ready to take over, and Riley and Jack left them to it. Maggie heard the nurse/killer continue to protest as they slipped out the door.

Chapter 35

Maggie had thought the cold air might make her wound feel better, like putting ice on a sprain, but of course this nonsensical piece of wishful thinking did not come to pass and the frigid air gave her only a small but sharp headache instead of functioning as a balm to her sore chest. At least it kept her alert.

The sky had turned to pitch black without even a moon to brighten the clouds. Heavy, wet snow fell, threatening to turn to ice if the temperature fell even a single digit, which of course it would do as the nighttime arrived in earnest. Riley drove past the cemetery where they'd found Evan, the tires straining for traction every time he turned a corner or changed lanes. The ballpark loomed to the left, a barren, ominous shape in the dark. Even wedged between the two men, Maggie shivered; the heater hadn't even begun to make a difference in the temperature during the very short trip. "Where are we going and why, again?"

Riley said, "This place Shanaya works is a call center—"

Jack said, "Hospital."

Riley stopped talking.

Maggie said, "Which is it? A call center or a hospital?"

Jack said, "No, we're taking you to a hospital, and then we'll go to the call center."

Maggie protested that she didn't need it. Jack said she'd been stabbed. She swore that she was not being funny or quoting a movie and it really *was* just a flesh wound. There was nothing the hospital could do that she hadn't already.

Jack said the hospital sat only a block away and they had time and wasn't that fresh blood peeking through her shirt after her hospital-quality bandaging?

Riley, for once, said nothing.

Jack peered down at her. She noted his expression—dying to get to the next scene, but genuinely worried about her, and suddenly she didn't feel cold. However, she still didn't need—

Riley spoke, or rather murmured: "Uh—"

In the street ahead, at the intersection of East Ninth and Bolivar, a man hustled across the pavement, his right hand lifting up the bottom of a stadium coat to reach the gun in his holster. He headed for a two-story building, dark with only a single light burning somewhere on the second floor.

Riley said, "Isn't that—"

"Stop," Jack said. To Maggie he said, "Stay here."

"What's hap—"

"That's Shanaya's babysitter" was all the explanation he had time to give before Riley slid to a shuddering halt, rim scraping the curb, and they bailed out. Two thumps of the doors and she was alone, watching them intercept the other police officer and hold a quick conference. Then all three turned toward the building.

They disappeared into the foyer.

She sat. She waited. She hated it like hell, left to stay safe like some helpless female. But Maggie had tried all her life to *not* be stupid, and barging in like the standard character in some late-night movie would be stupid. She *was* helpless, more or less, and being female had nothing to do with it. She was not armed, not trained, didn't know karate, didn't even have a flashlight. She should no more try to participate in a police raid than she should try to perform an emergency appendectomy on her neighbor's child.

Then a loud sound and a blast of light flashed from the dark foyer, and her determination to be sensible went out the door along with her body. She promptly slid on the ice and went to her knees, banging one knee good and hard but catching herself with her gloved hands. Then she was up and running, managing to stay upright long enough to reach the glassed-in cubicle where she knew she would find Jack shot to death, bleeding out too quickly for any help to—

She hit the glass door before even registering what lay beyond it.

At first, nothing made sense. Jack did not lie there in a pool of blood; no one did, not him, not Riley, not the other police officer. The foyer stood vacant, a black hole of nothing, with only a glimmer of less dark black at the center.

She stepped forward and reached out blindly, made brave by the leather gloves, that layer of protection between her skin and whatever she might touch. And when contact occurred, the glimmer wavered.

Her eyes adjusted. The inner doors of the air lock had been painted over, presenting a blank slate. The inner door must have been locked and one of the cops had shot the lock, producing the sounds and muzzle flash she saw. She pushed through it to enter a large and dark—office. A desk, then a large room of cubicles, all dark, all empty. The cops were nowhere in sight.

Well, she thought. What would be the not-stupid, sensible thing to do now? As far as she could tell, no one needed her to call an ambulance, and she remained untrained and unarmed.

She couldn't hear the cops barking orders to suspects or

moving through the place searching room to room. Three grown men shouldn't be that quiet, right?

So she stood still, and listened.

Then someone grabbed her arm.

Jack shot the lock to gain entry. He remembered the door only too well and knew no amount of human-battering-ram action would break it. If this turned out to be another of Shanaya's games and he had to pay for damage to commercial property, so be it.

The dim interior appeared vacant, the noisy, crowded cubicles now empty and dark. From the girl's description it sounded as if the place went full blast all day, but perhaps they closed up once people in the farthest time zone stopped answering their phones.

"Take this floor," he said in a quiet voice to West, the cop assigned to watch Shanaya Thomas.

"Everyone poured out of this place like ants from a smashed mound about fifteen minutes ago, right after your girl called nine-one-one with a hang-up. It took Dispatch that long to associate the number and get hold of me."

"She didn't come out with the crowd?"

"I didn't see her. It's possible I missed her, but I don't think so. There weren't that many women. And the GPS in the phone says it's still here."

"Got it."

Jack hoped Jeffers would be in the boss's office on the second floor, where he and Riley had been. He and his partner climbed the steps, guns drawn. Whoever was there must have heard their less-than-subtle entry but knew better than to come running. Jack heard no whispers, footsteps, grinding clicks of magazines as they were jammed into pistols. What he did hear sounded strangely like a child's laugh.

At the top of the stairs they turned up the corridor, finding one lit doorway. With Riley behind him, Jack approached along the wall, then hazarded a glance through the glass in the upper door frame.

The day care room, with two children in it. A boy of about five, with a mop of unruly hair, building a cityscape out of square wooden blocks and apparently explaining every detail of the construction to another child of perhaps three, who rocked on the floor with a battered stuffed dog and did not appear to be listening. No one else in sight.

The hell, Jack thought. He peered around to the corners of the room, as much as he could. The solid metal door had only one square window at his eye level, perhaps ten inches square. No adult in sight. He debated—call Dispatch and tell them to send a child's advocate over to possibly take custody, or wait to see what the situation turned in to. Again, this could still be some feint of Shanaya's, and he and Riley would find nothing more on the premises than a lonely bookkeeper working late. And Jack would have to pay for a door lock. But if the situation turned much more ominous then he didn't want to have children present.

He turned to Riley, already texting Dispatch to have a child's advocate on standby. They moved silently past the door. The children took no notice.

The second floor appeared like the first—empty, dark, and silent, the row of inner offices unlit except for the one at the very end, where Jack and Riley had interviewed Mark Hawking.

If this *wasn't* some feint of Shanaya's—

Jack gestured around the room at large. Riley nodded and slunk off to the outer wall, examining the perimeter while Jack moved directly to the open office door. The cubicles appeared empty, surfaces gleaming slightly in the small amount of ambient light and what penetrated from the streetlights outside, but there were many barriers and desks and if he were the bad guys, he would have scattered into their depths when they heard the door downstairs splinter open.

He continued along the inner wall, ambush-ready dark cubicles to his right, ambush-ready dark offices to his left. At the doorway there remained nothing to do but show himself. He couldn't see inside and calling out would simply forewarn them. The chances were good that he would accomplish nothing other than getting himself shot and really wished he had stopped to put on a vest first, but either way, better him than Riley.

Or he could peek around the corner like a girl in kindergarten, quickly enough to keep whoever waited inside from sighting and firing in time, and then at least he'd know what or who awaited him. Not dignified, but perhaps wise.

He peeked like a girl in kindergarten.

Only two people present, standing behind the desk: Shanaya Thomas, and Dr. Sidney Jeffers, currently holding a gun to Shanaya Thomas's head.

"Come on in, Detective," the doctor called.

Chapter 36

Jack stepped into the opening, watching Jeffers's gun hand carefully. If it so much as twitched in his direction, he must step back. Returning fire would not be an option with Shanaya used as a human shield.

It didn't twitch. The barrel remained firmly in place at the girl's right temple. Her eyes were huge and terrified, and she barely seemed to breathe.

The doctor said, "Tell your partner to stop where he is, because there's two of my men out there with him."

Jack called, "Riley! You're not alone."

No response, but that made sense. Riley wouldn't want to make it easy for the hired goons to find him. Those goons would stand down, waiting for orders, as Riley cooperated with a temporary cease-fire—or so Jack hoped. The longer they could put off a firefight, the better, but Jack didn't see how one could be avoided altogether. Jeffers had no options. The office had only one door and Jack stood in it. Pointing a gun at Shanaya seemed almost an empty threat; if he killed her, he'd still have nowhere to go but jail. All Jack would have to do is wait.

He hated waiting.

He said, "Dr. Jeffers. I would say Dr. Castleman, but—what did you plan to do when he came back from the Congo?"

"*If* he comes back from that hellhole. I'd have done what I'm going to do to now—close up shop and move on. This kind of work always has an expiration date. Linger too long, and the cement hardens around your feet. Classic mistake."

"You won't believe me," Jack said, "but I know exactly what you mean."

The man studied him, as if wondering. Shanaya breathed in with one short gasp, every atom of it audible in this tight space.

Jack pointed out, "But you're a doctor. Med school, board exams, license. You're going to walk away from all that?"

"Why would I have to? Nothing can connect me to this little enterprise, and *I* didn't give opioids to patients who didn't need them, or bill for procedures never done or durable medical equipment never purchased. The bad Dr. Castleman did. I'm kindly Dr. Jeffers, ministering to those who can't afford care because other doctors only care about paying the insurance on their Lotus or keeping up with the country club fees."

"Except you can't get out of this building."

"Without going through you, you mean?" Jeffers asked. "Good point."

And he moved the gun from Shanaya's temple and fired it at Jack.

The guy was quick—surgeon's hands, Jack supposed. He jerked backward around the corner and felt the bullet graze his coat, the hot metal jerking the cloth with such speed that he had dropped to the ground and scuttled several feet away before he even smelled the fabric. One more shot blew through the office wall, showering Jack with tiny tufts of insulation. Feathers.

How to keep himself and Riley alive; and Shanaya as well,

when she stayed stuck in a hole with a man more than willing to kill any inconvenient person he saw. He had to get out of it but couldn't leave the room without his shadows making the movement obvious.

His two gunmen, however—

Off to his right he heard Riley say, "Jack?"

"Here."

The light in the office went out. So much for shadows.

Jeffers would leave the room with Shanaya in front of him, an impossible target, while Jack sat there in the open. Not good. He straightened enough to walk in a sloping crouch and hustled toward the far corridor and the stairwell.

A shot flared but missed him in the dark. He picked up his pace as another shot answered.

"One down," Riley called, his voice pinpointing his location. Another shot rang out, then landed with the *thump* of a soft target rather than the *thwack* of a floor or wall. Jack's adrenaline spiked. Had Riley been hit?

Jack had nearly reached the end when a divot exploded from the wall in front of him, showering his face with tiny specks of paint and brick. He broke to the left, away from the corridor and stairwell, dropped to his knees, and hazarded a glance behind him.

His eyes had adjusted somewhat and he could see the edges of the cubicles, the interior doors, and Jeffers approaching with Shanaya plastered to his chest. She had both hands on his arm as if trying to pull it away, but the gun at her face kept her from struggling too much.

At the same time Jack heard a chair skitter away and a soft footfall. He hoped to hell it was his partner and not the guy who might have just killed him.

He had left the stairwell open for Jeffers, to at least keep him moving in a straight line. Otherwise they'd wind up at the same impasse as in the office. Officer West had remained downstairs. Surely he would have heard the commotion and gotten into position. Besides, Jack hardly wanted gunfire right outside the day care center, though its door looked bullet-proof.

"What's your plan, Jeffers?" Jack called. "You going to take out the entire Cleveland police force? Right now you only have fraud and unlawful imprisonment of that young lady. We know Wayne actually killed Evan Harding." While, of course, acting on instructions from Jeffers, and he had left out Rick and Jennifer Toner. Jeffers didn't need to know that they had connected the murders. It hardly boosted the incentive to put down the gun and make a deal.

Jack heard the brush of shoes on carpet at the outer wall and decided not to be a sitting duck for two different gunmen. He duck-walked over to the center aisle, took a peek, saw no one. Unfortunately the cubicles had been arranged in two solid rows. If he wanted to go up the center, cross to the interior wall, and come up behind Jeffers, he'd have to move all the way to the other end of the floor and then the full distance back to reach him.

He hadn't bluffed about backup units responding. He and West had to keep Jeffers in place until they arrived, keep him from leaving the building with Shanaya, or she was as good as dead. It would be helpful, however, if Jack could get them all in a better position—take out that second guy, find Riley, and get Jeffers into a corner where he could see no other option but to surrender.

In other words, Jack needed to do the one thing he'd never been particularly good at—talking someone down. He needed Riley for that. He needed Maggie.

While he debated, he heard Jeffers shuffle around the corner and a sudden uptick in noise from the day care room. Jack hazarded a glance. In the vague blue light from outside Jack saw him pause outside the door, peering through the glass. Then he said, "Be right back, kids," and Jack realized what the children had been shouting.

"Daddy!"

Then Jeffers took the gun from Shanaya's head and fired at Jack, pulling her backward toward the steps as he did. Jack heard the pings of shots hitting the outer wall, the inner wall, the pipes snaking down the corner near the exposed wall. Then a hiss and a *boom*.

The room exploded with a blast that rocked his head back against the cubicle partition.

All of Jack's senses failed at once. The light blinded him, the shock stunned him, and the shuddering noise deafened his ears. The ball of fire sucked all the oxygen from the room, and when he could breathe again he stumbled to his feet.

One of Jeffers's shots had hit the gas pipe. Why that had caused an instant inferno, Jack couldn't guess.

He turned to see Jeffers disappearing down the stairwell with Shanaya.

A scream, a primal, animal wail, cut through the choking air. A man, a figure cloaked in flames, came flailing through the smoke. Something—perhaps wishful thinking, perhaps the build or the cut of the fitted Columbia jacket—made Jack certain that this man on fire was not his partner.

Jack raised his gun but it would not be necessary—the guy sped past him without pausing, running senselessly to find some relief for the pain. The sight of his flesh burning was enough for Jack.

He ran toward the flames.

One floor below, Maggie nearly screamed when the officer grabbed her arm.

"What are you doing here? You're the forensics tech, right?"

She shook her head in assent, momentarily speechless.

"Go back outside and get away from the entrance. Units are on their way."

A shot rang out from the upper floor. Maggie abruptly understood the cliché about jumping out of one's skin.

Jack.

She moved toward the staircase without thinking, confused when the officer grabbed her arm again, more forcefully than before.

"*Now!*" he hissed.

She hesitated. But this was their world, not hers. She needed to trust the officers to do what they did. She had to trust Jack. "Okay. Anything I should tell them when they get here?"

"Get across the street and out of sight. But if you can safely approach officers, tell them unknown number of suspects, unknown weaponry, unknown if possible hostage situation."

That sounded less than helpful, but she turned to go. Then the explosion happened and the ground quavered underneath her feet.

The officer moved toward the stairwell, Maggie behind him. But when she realized what she was doing, she stopped again. She should not be here. She would only get in the way of the officers doing their jobs if they had to protect her as well as themselves, and Shanaya, and anyone else who might be in the place. But—Jack—

Two people came into sight. A man she did not recognize, with his arm around Shanaya's neck and a gun in his hand, which he used to fire at the officer in front of her.

He missed, and the officer retreated, leaping to the left behind the curved reception desk instead of diving to the right into the sea of cubicles with their thin walls. Maggie imitated him. She would not make it across the open area to the door. And she didn't really want to.

Though she really wished she had a gun.

Chapter 37

Whatever had been used to carpet and upholster the main room on the upper floor, it did not seem to be particularly fire-resistant. The feathers combusted at will and the gaping, open wall had instantly become a sheet of flame, licking out from its hole with darting tongues of fire. The speeding tendrils followed their own unpredictable trails. Jack went up the far aisle, next to the outside wall, where the smoke and flames were the thickest. The fire danced along the floor, shadowed by patches on the ceiling, and leapt through areas of the wall where some past residues fed its needs. He bulldozed into this miasma toward the limp form lying underneath one of the windows.

The smoke grew thick. Visibility became a problem, but moving past one smoldering piece of carpeting, his foot landed on something soft. He crouched to feel rather than see a hand, attached to an arm. An arm wet with blood.

His hands moved farther, to a chest clothed in a sweatshirt and bits of blood and gore from the hole in it. Not Riley, then, who had been in his usual shirt and tie. Jack felt a wave of relief he wouldn't have expected.

He felt the neck for a pulse, found none, and abandoned the man, moving toward another figure on the floor. That had to be Riley, alive or dead—unless another unknown remained in play. Which, given the events to date, would not surprise him in the slightest.

Then he heard Maggie call his name.

Shanaya also wished she had a gun. Or a knife, or even a ballpoint pen that she might be able to pull out and stab this asshole in the thigh to get him to let go of her as soon as he moved the gun from her face to shoot someone else. But she had nothing. Except—

The boss—she still didn't even know what his name was—pivoted her toward the receptionist desk, keeping her between himself and the cop. The light drifting down the stairwell from the day care room gave a dim illumination to the foyer, enough that she could see the two people now half-cowering behind the marble desk. The cop emerged, slowly. That forensic chick who had counted all Shanaya's money peeked over the heavy marble counter, staying safe, the lucky bitch. She looked at Shanaya and not the man with the gun.

"Let's take a second here," the officer began.

"We don't have a second," the man said. "In case you haven't noticed, the building's on fire. So I'm going to get out of here, and if you try to stop me, I'll—"

The gun that had been grinding into the skin of her right temple slid toward her eye, hovering in front of her brow as the guy couldn't decide whether to aim it at her or at the cop.

She had had just about enough of this shit.

"You're not going to get out of here," she told him. "You might as well let me go and give up."

"Shut up."

"They're cops. There are more of them than there are of you."

In response, he moved his arm from where it choked her to curl one hand over her mouth, squeezing her face and smashing her skull into his collarbone so hard it hurt.

The cop kept talking, trying to offer the guy some way to let her go that would sound acceptable, trying to couch "give up and go to jail for, like, ever" in appealing terms.

This guy had no intention of giving up or going to jail or doing anything other than killing everyone who got in his way. And that would be her as soon as he no longer needed her.

Shanaya opened her jaw, struggling against his hand, and one of his fingers slipped inside. Then she bit. She clamped down as hard as she could.

He yelped, and she jerked down on his gun hand. It went off but didn't hit her.

She couldn't see a lot of options here. He was stronger than her, and even with taking the flesh of his fingers down to the bone didn't get him to let go of the gun. Even if he let go of *her*, she'd never make it to the door before he shot her. Bullets remained the biggest threat, so that's what she dealt with.

Keeping his finger grinding between her teeth, she grasped his other hand with both of hers, snaked her digits around his and pulled. The gun fired and fired again; she kept her elbows locked and didn't care so long as the bullets didn't go into any part of her own anatomy. She heard more screams—whether they came from the guy or the cop or the woman, she didn't know, but hoped to hell she hadn't hit either of them or the cop might start shooting back while she still provided a warm flack jacket for her captor.

Finally the gun only gave empty clicks and the slide locked back.

Her cue to run. Her jaw released his bloody finger and she spit, the taste making her want to puke even with so much else for her body to think about. With his bleeding hand free he instinctively pulled away from her and she didn't hesitate, bolting for the door. She felt him snatch at her shirt, but gave up or changed his mind or couldn't grasp it with his injured hand because she made it to the glass doors and kept going. Hit the second set and found herself on the sidewalk.

The cold bit into her with sharp pricks before she even realized she had made it. Surely the cop back there would grab the guy . . . but to be sure she ducked around the corner. He had no motive to attack her now except for revenge.

One lone car moved slowly up East Ninth, but she heard sirens getting close.

She had made it, once again. Survived. She could melt back into the landscape and by the time the cops got done with that guy in there, they would have forgotten all about Shanaya.

Except that the cops still had her money. Maybe, maybe she could get some or all of it back. They had to return it if they couldn't prove she had committed fraud, and again, if that guy in there died or the building burned down, *especially* if the building burned down, they wouldn't be able to prove it.

The first two cop cars appeared, moving as fast as the roads would allow. As they slid to a shuddering halt in front of the building, she ran to the edge of the sidewalk, waving her arms.

She started to scream the second their doors opened. "Help! Help! There's a guy in there killing cops! He kidnapped me! He held me at gun—"

The door to her left slammed open, and the man stood there with his bleeding hand, taking in the array of red and blue lights brightening the street.

"*Him!*" Shanaya pointed.

Chapter 38

Maggie would admit later that she had yelped and hid behind the police officer when the gun began to fire, bullets wildly *thunking* into the walls and steps and two into the officer. He fell backward into her arms and knocked them both to the floor, which may have saved her life as more shots riddled the reception desk until she felt marble shards rain down on her shoulders. She felt wetness against her skin but it was only her wound, wrenched into oozing again underneath its saturated bandage.

When she looked up, the barrel of the gun formed a straight line between the man holding it and her forehead. She saw the fingers around it clench.

It gave an empty *click*.

Even in the dim light she saw the shock on the man's face. Then Shanaya pulled away from him and ran for the door.

The man bent over his injured hand, coughing as the first wisps of smoke drifted down the steps.

The cop partially on top of her groaned and rolled to one side, sucking in air. Chest wound, she thought, penetrated the lungs which are now filling with blood—

Then, with her hands on his chest and back, she felt the body armor underneath his uniform shirt and realized the bulletproof vest had stopped the projectiles; he gasped because the force had knocked the wind out of him. He pushed himself to his knees before she even let go of him.

He reached for his gun. It had slipped from his hand and lay on the floor to his right.

The man saw this, looked from the cop to the door and back again, and in an instant Maggie saw his reasoning. He could follow Shanaya and run for the door, at which point the cop would probably shoot at him. Or he could get the still-loaded gun from the weakened cop who even now shrank into a rasping cough as his emptied lungs tried to re-fill with smoky, gaseous air.

He lunged for the officer.

Maggie stepped into his path, plowing into him with all the force her small body could muster. It knocked her to the ground, nearly on top of the officer's gun, but forced the man to stagger back as well. Only a step or two, but long enough for the cop to get his fingers on his weapon.

Change of plan. The man pivoted and ran for the door. He disappeared through the set of inner doors as the cop fired and a bullet plunked into its frame. Maggie rolled to her feet but did not pursue him, finding she didn't care much whether he got away or not. She cared only that the building was on fire, and Jack remained upstairs.

She moved to help the officer up, but he had already regained his footing. He shouted at her to get out of the building and then followed the man . . . a mixed message, since he hardly wanted to send her out to the street where a violent criminal had just gone, yet she clearly shouldn't remain inside where the smoke now thickened to block one's sight.

No matter. She had no intention of leaving anyway.

She left him to find and arrest the man who had shot at them, and fled up the stairs. On the landing she promptly stumbled over a body, clad in still-smoking clothing that hurt her hands when she shoved him onto his back. Even with the dim light and the soot on his face she saw no one she recognized, and with a quick check she learned his carotid did not pulse with even the hint of a heartbeat. She left him there.

The air on the second floor, she immediately found, made the first floor seem like a meadow on a bright spring day. Wafting columns of black smoke swirled in front of her, ghostly visions of the Grim Reaper backlit by a yellow flickering glow of multiple flames. She called Jack's name, listened for a response. Then she moved forward but more slowly, the heat and her own fear pushing her back.

She heard a cry that ran as a vein of ice up her spine and through her bones, not thawing even in the face of the blasting heat from the inferno ahead. Jack—

It wasn't Jack, she realized as a lighted window appeared on her left. It came from someone much smaller.

Through the small window at the top of the door she saw two small children—*children*? What appeared to be a boy and maybe a girl, preschool ages. The older child cried and banged on the door, pausing only when he caught sight of her through the glass. Hope lifted his features. The other child sat on the floor a few feet away, rubbing the copious tears away with tiny fists.

Maggie put her hand on the knob, remembering too late the warning about fires and metal doorknobs, but though it warmed it did not burn. But it also did not turn. The door was locked.

She put her face to the glass, also uncomfortably warm. The boy worked the knob, his little hands twisting one way and then the other, as the sound of the blast and the smell of the smoke drifting under the door spoke to the inborn, animal instinct to run from danger.

"It needs a key," Maggie called to him. "A key." She held

up one hand as if holding a key, and made a twisting motion with it. Surely an adult had been in there with them? Maybe left the key on her desk or in her purse, somewhere this small boy had seen it and could find it?

But he only stared at her, blank and uncomprehending.

"Maggie!"

She turned, relief washing over her like a warm surf, happy and joyful to know he lived, her world righted before she even saw him. She let out the breath she'd been half holding, but choked on its replacement.

He staggered out of the swirling mass, a double shadow. He held Riley's arm around his own neck to support some of his weight. Blood covered half of Riley's face.

"Help him out," Jack said. "I'll get the kids."

"The door's locked," she said, positioning herself under Riley's other arm.

"I'm okay," Riley protested. "I can make it."

She thought, *Really? because it looks like you were shot in the head*, but couldn't speak through the coughing. Blood flowed freely from a gash along his left temple. In the light from the door's window she could see the graze . . . but that could cause swelling on the brain—possibly why he now had trouble walking. He needed medical attention *now*.

"Break the glass," she told Jack, but even as she said it she could see the difficulty. The window sat five, five and a half feet off the ground, too high to reach the inside knob from outside and too high for the kids to climb out through. Also too small for a man Jack's size to crawl through to get them. It was a sturdy, metal door made for an industrial setting, unlikely to be forced open by anything less than a battering ram.

"I know where the keys are," he said, and began to turn away.

"*Jack!*" The name ripped from her throat without conscious thought. She didn't want him to stay. She wanted him to leave the building with her, right *now*.

But she didn't want two children to burn to death either. The fingers of one hand brushed her cheek. "I'll be all right. Get him out of here." Then he went back toward the main room, the vortex of heat and flame and smoke.

"I can make it," Riley said again, but his weight leaned on her until her knees threatened to buckle.

Hanging on to the arm around her neck with her left hand and stretching her right arm around his waist, she pulled him toward the steps. He grabbed the banister and the extra bit of stability helped as they made a lumbering but hasty progress down the steps. Riley said nothing and neither did she. They barely had time since each breath produced at least a small cough and sometimes a hacking, stop-and-bend rasp.

They made it to the bottom, Maggie listening more for Jack's feet on the steps behind them than for any activity outside. She did not hesitate at the doors to the sidewalk. She had heard the sirens and figured there would be plenty of cop cars, firetrucks, and ambulances out there on the street, and the bad guy had either been cuffed and guided into a back seat behind a cage, or he had fled. Either way, she and Riley had no choice. They had to breathe or they were going to die.

The outside air hit her with a cold slap and she sucked it in with appreciation. Then she coughed it out with much less appreciation and repeated same.

As expected, they walked into a sea of red and blue and white lights. Officers with guns dropped them when they recognized Riley and herself. Strong hands hustled them over to the ambulance as EMTs emerged from its cab. The firemen snaked hoses around all of them and began to break the upstairs windows with concentrated beams of water. She could hear the glass tinkle across the sidewalk and the fire howl as it received a boost of oxygen.

"Is the building clear?" someone asked her.

"No! Jack's in there. And two kids!"

"Suspects?"

"I don't know." On the other side of one of the cop cars, she saw a uniformed officer guiding the man who had shot at her into the back of a car. From his position she guessed the man had his hands cuffed behind his back. Good for him.

Shanaya stood nearby, getting a blanket draped around her shoulders by another officer.

"One down on the second floor," Riley told them. "The kids are in a room on the second—"

Then the EMT pulled him onto a gurney and his weight fell from Maggie's shoulders. She turned without a good-bye or a kind word and headed straight back to the foyer entrance.

She didn't make it. As her toe touched the sidewalk's edge she found herself encircled and lifted and pulled away. At first she thought the building had exploded again, but the force turned out to be a fireman who had to stand six-five in his stocking feet.

"Jack's in there!" she screamed at him.

"I know."

"You have to get him out!"

"You can't go in," he said, which did not address her statement. "Leave this to us."

But "us" now stood around outside in the mist from the hoses.

She said, "There are two children locked in a room on the second floor. Top of the stairs on the left."

A trump card. A grown man didn't push the hero button like vulnerable children did. And that's where Jack would be, she told herself. If he collapsed from the smoke, she would not be able to move him, even drag him out, and then they would both perish. But a team of firemen could get him *and* the children.

"Stay behind the trucks," he told her, and went back to

work, as if the idea that she might ignore any command of his could never enter his mind.

He still blocked the entrance, so she returned to Riley's side behind the ambulance. At least she had a clear view to the sidewalk—though "clear" view could not be considered accurate with the smoke and the wall of water from the hoses. The EMTs were cleaning and examining the detective's head wound, asking him questions, and prodding his limbs to check for other injuries. They didn't notice the blood on her shirt underneath her jacket, which she kept zipped up lest they strapped her to a gurney as well.

"I don't know why the place went up like that. It was like the walls were flammable." He had to raise his speaking voice to not quite shouting to be heard over the engines and the clatter.

"Feathers. You said they insulated with them."

"Feathers are flammable?"

"Extremely." She took his hand, more to calm her own pounding heart than to comfort him, since he seemed more annoyed than distressed.

"Just put a bandage on it! It doesn't even hurt that much. Can't I get *up*?"

The EMT told him no, and that he'd have to be transported for X-rays and a possible CT scan.

"No way," he said. "I don't need that—"

"Yes," Maggie told him firmly. "You do. A blow like that could cause a subdural hematoma."

"What's that?" In his haste it came out "wuzzat."

"Bleeding on the brain. You don't want that."

He tried to sit up. "Jeffers—"

"Neither do Hannah and Natalie," she added.

He lay back down.

Kids. The best motivation in the world.

"Was Jeffers the guy with the gun? If so, they've got him

cuffed. Don't worry about it." She squeezed his hand and told him she'd keep him posted, a weak promise that things would be all right. She didn't even know where they were taking him; she felt about ready to collapse herself, and not even the burning building could keep the cold from worming its frigid tendrils into her flesh. The spray from the hoses had coated her with water, now turning to an icy rime on her clothes.

But as the EMTs moved to knock out the legs of Riley's gurney and load him up, he gave Maggie's fingers a jerk. "Make sure they bring him out of there."

"Count on it," she told him, and went to do exactly that.

Chapter 39

She could no longer see the building's entrance through the smoke. The hoses did their best to trip her but she snaked her way forward until she stood next to two men struggling to keep a stream of water aimed at an upper window.

"Everybody out?" one asked, and the other said something unintelligible.

"What do you mean?" she shouted. "Where is Jack? Where are the kids?"

The fireman could only spare her a glance without losing control of the water. "We can't go in. It's too hot and there's industrial contaminants—*hey*!"

She made it five feet before someone grabbed her, for about the fourth time that day, and that became four times too many. She whirled and hit him in the chest, punching a second time with her other fist for good measure.

This accomplished nothing. Layers of fireproof garb protected him and hurt her hands. It didn't stop her. She kicked, shoved, punched, screamed as the firemen held on tight enough to dislocate an arm bone or two. But she did not give up.

A window broke overhead, showering them with glass.

The fireman reacted, his grip loosening by a millimeter. That was all she needed.

Two steps into her mad dash to the double glass doors, a figure emerged from the smoke.

Jack couldn't see the exit doors, had no idea where he might be, but the steps had ended so he must be in the reception area. Red and blue and white lights strobed through the enveloping smoke; he followed the wisps of their beams, hoping like hell they would lead him to the door and not misdirect him to a window farther inside the building. Not until he plowed facefirst into the painted glass doors and felt the patches of ice-cold air through the smoke and flames did he believe he had actually gotten out.

The kids, one under each arm, were squirming and crying and coughing, but that meant they were alive. He focused on staying on his feet long enough for one fireman and one cop to emerge from the chaos to grab them before he let them slip. As they rushed the kids off, relief flooded through Jack, threatening to drop him to his knees right then and there.

Then a figure ran into him.

Actually it ran *onto* him. Maggie leapt into his arms, throwing her own about his neck—a bit unwisely, because he tottered and struggled to keep his balance, his body exhausted by lack of oxygen and the hazards of moving people and vehicles and hoses and damn cold air. But it was all right. He didn't mind the strain in his calves, the ache in the arms that held her, the discomfort of his seared lungs, because he was still alive and so was she.

For a moment the world was perfectly all right.

Then it got a bit confusing.

Maggie was kissing him. Hands on his face, her lips moving over his, insistent and pulsing and only the tip of the iceberg as her whole body hummed and quivered and pulled him in with a power he had not known she possessed . . . or had not been allowed to see.

Worse, he was kissing her back, one hand supporting her bottom and pushing it into his hips and the other entwined in her hair, holding it too tightly and even in the fetid air he could smell her skin and—

Oh *hell*.

Chapter 40

Jack stared at his bedroom ceiling, the air finally warm enough to satisfy even Greta, curled against one knee. He went over the whole case in his head, from beginning to end. Evan and Shanaya had been skimming from the phone scams, with Evan turning the stolen numbers into cash at his workplace. Meanwhile, Evan recognized the Medicare scam between Jeffers and Marlon Toner for what it was and figured he could trim a bit off for himself from the funds Toner duly deposited in the offshore bank account. Ralph never noticed because it didn't affect his coffers, until Jeffers checked the books and found that the numbers didn't add up. Toner had his receipts, so Jeffers knew it wasn't him. Ralph must have also sworn his innocence, and reviewed the tapes to figure out exactly which of his employees it had been. Then Jeffers sent his trusty lieutenant Wayne to find out where his money had gone.

With luck Wayne would eventually talk and tell them exactly what had transpired when he confronted Evan. Evan must have left the store with its inconvenient cameras and walked toward the bank to make his nightly deposit of the stolen money. Wayne approaches, Evan runs away, jumping the fence into the cemetery. He must have looked at that crutch and figured Wayne could not follow him—not knowing that crutch served only as a prop. And a sheath. Simple, low-tech, effective, and completely innocuous-looking.

Whether Evan had told him anything before he died, Jack couldn't guess, but he hadn't given up Shanaya. She continued to go to work as usual and probably hadn't needed to abandon the apartment. Neither she nor Evan could have guessed that the boss she stole from and the doctor he stole from were one and the same. But Wayne took Evan's cell phone, and soon their boss realized exactly that.

Shanaya had told them as much, standing outside the cop car, coughing on smoke, shivering in the cold while the EMT trying to put an oxygen mask over Jack's face told him that Riley would be fine. All neurological signs indicated he hadn't even gotten a concussion and had been transported only as a precaution.

Jack had ordered a protective custody warrant for Shanaya, to give her a place to stay while they could get her statement nailed down. This would afford her some protection, should Jeffers have any other employees as dedicated as Wayne running around. It also meant they'd have an eye on her if she decided to bolt rather than answer questions about how many people she had defrauded. But Jack didn't believe she had any intention of running. Shanaya was being very, very cooperative, totally focused on getting her money back. The odds that she might seemed better than even. Jack wondered how he felt about that, and decided it sucked.

Nothing, of course, sucked as badly as Jennifer Toner making a fuss over Jeffers's pill mill activities right when he already faced a hemorrhage in his offshore account. He had had the sense to use his employee's names and not his own, but that wouldn't keep the cops away for long if Jennifer got the authorities to look into the absent Dr. Castleman. They might subpoena all the reimbursements coming from Medicare and Medicaid and track the funds to the account. They might track down the real Dr. Castleman in Africa so that he could make a really good guess as to who had appropriated his name and license number. His whole very lucrative world might cave in too quickly to be able to salvage any part of it, including his freedom. Jennifer Toner had to be stopped. Not a tough choice for Jeffers, a man so depraved he abandoned his own children to a blazing inferno.

Jack suspected that Jennifer had gone looking for Castleman at his last known address, as he and Riley had. Then Ralph had no doubt reported to Jeffers about the confrontation between a woman of that description and Evan on Evan's last night at work. When Jeffers realized she had also been at A to Z, Jennifer became enough of a threat to be dealt with. But unlike Evan, they didn't want information. They just wanted her to go away.

Unless Wayne confessed to the murder of a police officer—unlikely—they would never know exactly what had happened at Jennifer Toner's apartment. Jack guessed that Wayne had knocked, said he had something to tell Jennifer about her brother, and walked in to find Rick there as well. Jennifer might have immediately pointed him out as Jeffers's nurse, sealing Rick's doom. Wayne stabbed him—Rick would have no reason to be on guard against a nurse on crutches, especially one who had knocked on the door so politely that it didn't even disturb the neighbors—and then stabbed Jennifer before she had a chance to react. Because if he had already killed Jennifer before Rick came to the door, Wayne could have simply not answered. They both had to be in the apartment already.

Then Wayne dumped Rick's body, and probably decided not to take the outrageous chance a second time to dump Jennifer's. Besides, Jennifer's murder had a built-in fall guy: her addict brother.

Terrible luck for Rick.

Good luck for Jack? He could see no remaining threats to his life in Cleveland. If Rick had voiced his suspicions to Will, Will seemed to have chalked them up to the usual dislike a man had for an ex's new beau. Jack was safe. He could stay there as long as he liked.

Maggie herself no longer seemed to be a problem, though even if she didn't threaten to expose his past, she greatly threatened to expose his future. Living alone, keeping himself strictly separate from other humans, compartmentalizing his actions, had allowed him to continue his work. Meeting Maggie Gardiner had thrown all that into chaos.

Not to mention what it had done to *her*.

His actions, his pride, had dragged her into his world, and her one rash decision had imprisoned her there. A sense of responsibility had then isolated her from her family, her friends, the core of her own personality until she must have felt she had no one she could confide in, no one she could really talk to, except him. She must have convinced herself that the cause of all her problems had become her only refuge from them, that she and Jack were somehow twined together in ways that could not be undone. The proximity had driven her.

That's all it was, proximity. It couldn't be more than that. It couldn't become more than that.

"This can't happen again," he declared aloud. Greta meowed her disdain for people who spoke while she was trying to sleep.

Then Maggie rolled over and stretched one languid arm across his chest. Pressing her face into his neck, she set him straight: "Oh, this is *definitely* happening again."

Acknowledgments

As always, I have to thank my fabulous agent, Vicky Bijur, and her agency's brilliant team, as well as my fantastic editor, Michaela Hamilton, and the rest of the dedicated staff at Kensington.

I also received help from Nicole Navas at the U.S. Department of Justice, Cape Coral Police Department detective Josh Silko, and Andrea Jacobson of the Alaska State Troopers.

As always, I made great use of my family and friends. My husband, Russ, told me that feathers were flammable, Dr. Ted Druhot explained medical licenses, my sisters Mary and Susan read the rough drafts, and approximately 2500 overseas scam artists gave me both the impetus and the background to write this book by calling each day to explain how they could lower my credit-card interest rates.